MAKING A KILLING IN ARAMEZZO

MURDER IN AN ITALIAN VILLAGE · BOOK 4

MICHELLE DAMIANI

RIALTO
PRESS

MAKING A KILLING IN ARAMEZZO

MURDER IN AN ITALIAN VILLAGE · BOOK 4

RIALTO PRESS
P.O. Box 1472
Charlottesville, VA 22902
michelledamiani.com

For Angelo,

My teacher in all things.

CAST OF CHARACTERS

CASALE MAZZOLI

Stella	*ex-chef who runs her ancestral home as a bed-and-breakfast*
James and Cindy Copeland	*guests*

JOBS IN AND AROUND ARAMEZZO

Domenica	*local bookshop owner*
Matteo	*streetsweeper*
Marta	*sheep farmer, mother of Ascanio*
Leonardo (Leo)	*ex-racecar driver who now operates the family porchetta van*
Cosimo	*antiquarian and expert on local lore*
Don Arrigo	*village priest*
Marcello	*mayor*
Romina and Roberto	*couple that owns Bar Cappellina*
Adele and Vincenzo	*couple that owns Trattoria Cavour*
Orietta	*pharmacist*
Flavia	*owner of flower shop*
Cristiana	*owner of Aramezzo's grocery shop*
Rocco	*mechanic*

VILLAGERS

Veronica	*the mayor's wife*
Luisella	*Stella's neighbor*
Mimmo	*hunter and former caretaker of Casale Mazzoli*
Giancarlo	*Matteo's childhood friend, visiting*

THE POLICE

Luca	*police officer*
Salvo	*Luca's partner*
Captain Tribuzio	*local police captain*

Stella forced her footsteps up the cobblestone streets.

She'd figured yesterday's gossip about today's heat wave was just that—gossip. As casually debated over coffee at Bar Cappellina as whether the Americans would sell their villa (they didn't, despite loud insistence that they refused to live in a crime scene). Running her hand through a vine sprouting through the rock wall, her fingers snagged in a tendril. How was it not a shriveled nest of twigs and leaves?

Stella wondered if it had ever been cool, or if the memory of fresh breezes was some kind of fever dream.

In front of Bar Cappellina, Stella braced herself. A counter with an espresso machine constantly pumping out coffee—the interior had to be bruising.

She stepped through the door and stopped.

Not cool exactly, but the thick medieval stones held the memory of cool. Why didn't her house feel this comfortable? She'd turned like a rotisserie chicken all night. In an instant, Stella remembered Cosimo's last visit, when the octogenarian chided her for keeping her shutters open during the day. At his lofted eyebrow, she'd breezily shrugged. "I like a view."

Now she understood—her American ways, burning her again.

Inhaling the scent of coffee, she smiled as if greeting an old friend.

Even though her mother had cut off all ties with Italy, she had never abandoned her morning espresso. Long before thimblefuls became a Starbucks standard, Stella associated the chocolatey scent—warmth and shadow intertwined—with a morning's clean slate. Clean that was, until her mother ridiculed Stella for wearing two different socks or for the blotches of toothpaste that inevitably found their way to her shirt.

"Enjoying your aneurysm?" Her friend Matteo's chuckle broke through her reverie.

She joined him at the bar. "Having a moment."

"And why not?" He gestured magnanimously, indicating wide acceptance. "Signor Ford left this morning?"

"An hour ago." Stella glanced around, casually. "A cappuccino, Romina, when you have a moment." She tried to remember when Giancarlo said he'd be home, but the memory of their last walk in the groves muddled her thoughts, distracting her with the image of moonlight drifting through the olive trees to filagree his face. He'd stopped, and touched her chin before leaning forward—

"You should really get that checked out," Matteo said, draining the last of his espresso before setting it onto the saucer with a clink. "You miss him already, don't you?"

"Signor Ford?" Stella asked, innocently. "Guests don't usually leave that kind of lasting impression."

Romina, her white hair held in its usual loose bun, smiled to herself, pretending she hadn't eavesdropped as she set down Stella's coffee.

"Nice try," Matteo said with a grin. "Ah, those early relationship days, when every moment apart seems an eternity."

Stella stirred sugar into her coffee. "You speak with some authority. Anything you want to tell me? Is there finally a man in your life?"

He let out a low chuckle. "I wish. Anything you want to tell *me*?"

She shrugged. "We've only had a few dates."

"At least twenty!"

"More like ten." She sipped her coffee and added, "And as Giancarlo's best friend, you know how much time he's spent in London with his coach."

"Manager," Matteo corrected with a shake of his head. "You're hopeless with professional soccer."

"I know the goal is to get the ball down the field."

Matteo leaned forward, waggling his eyebrows. "And is Giancarlo succeeding? Getting the ball down the field?"

"I will not dignify that with a response."

"Pretty sure that counts as a response," he shot back with a smile.

Stella thought of Giancarlo's eyes trained on her as he leaned down. She smiled in what she hoped was a vague way.

Giancarlo had been respectful of her need to take it slow. Or maybe it was just that her guests and his physical therapy hadn't left them with enough time together to let this frisson of attraction turn into . . . more.

Romina asked Matteo, "How did his evaluation go?"

Matteo drummed his fingers on the marble counter. "It was a big surgery, but you know Giancarlo, always pushing himself. He's coming along well."

"Thank the Madonna," Romina breathed. Her husband Roberto must have caught the conversation because his eyes flicked to the Inter Milan poster hanging above the Aperol, taken before Giancarlo had transferred to the Premier League. Roberto touched the image of Giancarlo lightly before he placed the milk back into the low refrigerator.

Few villages had a hometown hero like Giancarlo, so of course everyone followed his recovery closely. Even if that recovery meant losing him to England again.

The bell over the door tinkled as the mayor and his wife strode in. Veronica held leads attached to bejeweled collars of her two russet-colored, long-haired Dachshunds. One of the dogs startled at the sight of Stella, nails skittering on the tile. The dog must associate her with her one-eared cat Barbanera, who swiped at canines whenever possible. She'd left the silver-spotted tabby snoozing on the pile of laundry she needed to fold before new guests arrived.

The mayor's eyes slid past Stella. "Giancarlo not back yet?" he asked Matteo, his voice expressionless.

Stella noted Matteo's cheek muscle ticking. The mayor usually spoke to her friend as if he were still in short pants, unless Matteo had Giancarlo at his side, when the mayor suddenly oozed charm. "Not yet."

The mayor narrowed his eyes.

Matteo cleared his throat and added, "He'll land soon. Then he has physical therapy before he drives home."

The mayor nodded. "Tell him to watch his speed. The *autovelox* is back on line."

Stella caught on the word. "*Autovelox?*"

The mayor rolled his eyes. "You're really not from around here, are you?"

Roberto leaned against the counter. "They don't have them in America?"

Matteo said, "Remember that box on the side of the road on the way to Assisi? You thought it was a mailbox. When it's working, it takes photos of speeding cars."

The mayor broke in, "Your job was to pass the message onto Giancarlo, not hold a press conference."

Stella watched Matteo's ebullience melt away like fresh butter in a too-hot pan. As Matteo drew out his phone to text Giancarlo, she stirred her coffee with a series of clinks against the cup.

The mayor watched her with thinly veiled disgust. "The sooner Giancarlo gets back on the pitch the better."

Just as Romina began asking Stella if she'd used different chocolate in her latest *crescionda*—the *amaretti* and chocolate torte that Romina adored—Marcello raised his voice. "Veronica, wasn't Giancarlo telling you last week how impatient he is to rejoin his team?"

Matteo's eyebrows flew upward like cricket legs.

Stella rolled her eyes. On another day, she might have a cutting rejoinder. But today was too hot. She marveled at her growing ability to hold her tongue.

Veronica smirked. "What an amazing memory you have, my love. Giancarlo, oh, the boy looked close to tears, such is his longing to return to England." Matteo turned his face from the couple and mouthed, "Longing?" Stella snickered as Veronica went on, "How he must miss being off on his conquests—soccer and ... otherwise."

Stella ran her finger around the rim of her cup.

Veronica snapped her fingers to get Roberto's attention. "Cappuccino, Roberto, if you will. More milk than coffee. I need to settle my nerves." She collapsed onto a stool. "What an ordeal. Darling, we need an *autovelox* right here in Aramezzo!"

The mayor put his arm around his wife, who curled into his shoulder before peeking out to count the eyes on her.

Stella's cooling coffee demanded her attention and she took another sip.

Matteo examined his hands stretched on the bar.

Stella heard Romina over the sound of the steaming milk. "What happened, Veronica?"

"Oh, you wouldn't believe it!" wailed Veronica. One of her dogs leapt into a cowering position. "Luisella! That woman is a menace!"

The words had a worn-in quality. How many times had Veronica told this story?

Veronica's voice heightened. "She practically ran my dogs down in the street yesterday! Just because she's jealous of me is no excuse for reckless behavior. Right, Marcello?"

"Exactly so, my treasure," the mayor cooed.

Roberto, drying a coffee cup with a snowy white towel, paused. "Luisella got her car up the tunnel?"

Stella looked up with a start. Indeed, how would Luisella have mown down the dogs? Aramezzo was built like a wedding cake, with tunnels connecting the ring roads. Tunnels too narrow to fit most vehicles, which made emergencies requiring ambulances a challenge, as Stella had learned during her three seasons in Aramezzo. Her pulse ticked audibly in her ears.

Veronica lifted her chin imperiously. "Of course not. We were in the main road."

Stella's back stiffened, and she set her cup down. "In the road? Where cars drive? Not on the side of the road?"

Veronica gasped, clutching a necklace that was not there. "The side of the road? With the damp and dirt? Stella, surely even you know that's impossible."

Stella ignored the pressure of Matteo leaning against her hip. "You're saying you were in a road known for its blind curves. And you think this near-tragedy is Luisella's fault?" Luisella was an odd sort, sipping coffee alone in her impeccable suits. But Stella had grown fond of her neighbor, who had finally started responding to Stella's pleasantries. Mostly with grunts and nods, but still.

The pressure on her hip increased and she glanced at Matteo. He mouthed, "Stop."

Stella frowned at the milk bubbles collapsing against the side of her cup.

Maybe she hadn't learned to hold her tongue, after all.

The tension of the room shattered at the sound of the bell tinkling over the door.

Stella exhaled in relief until she clocked the man's police uniform. Luca glanced from Matteo to Stella to the mayor to his wife. He seemed about to turn on his polished heel and stride back out. Romina hailed him with a smile. "Luca! The usual?"

He nodded, keeping his eyes trained straight ahead. "Grazie, Romina."

Gathering a breath, Stella said, "*Buongiorno*, Luca."

Turning his head slowly toward her he said stiffly, "Oh. Hello, Stella. I didn't see you there."

Had he really not noticed her? He'd been so strained with her since she and Giancarlo had started dating. She flashed a grin too wide, the kind that belonged in a yearbook photo. "Yes, I wore my marble shirt today to camouflage with the bar." She winced.

Luca's jaw worked and he said nothing.

Stella opened her mouth to cover up her gaffe, but before she could, Romina handed Luca a cup of espresso and said, "How's your mother?"

He shot one last glance at Stella before saying to Romina, his voice even, "Just about recovered from the flu. I'm sure she'll be in later."

Romina chuckled. "She was in yesterday."

Luca's eyes widened. "Then why did you ask—"

"She had been complaining about Lilliana leaving."

"Oh. That." Luca's eyes slid to Stella who rubbed at a non-existent spot on the counter. Her hand froze, fingers splayed, as though pinning herself in place.

The mayor settled on a stool beside his wife. Stella considered asking if they wanted popcorn to go with their show, but at a quick glance from Matteo she pressed her lips together.

Romina threw her white towel over her shoulder. "Don't blame your mother for venturing out so soon. She's been indoors for a week."

"It's not that," Luca looked on the verge of saying more but instead plucked a sugar packet from the container and shook it noisily.

"Ah," said Romina, her voice warm. "You don't want her talking about your girlfriend."

"Understandable," Roberto said, his head bobbing in agreement.

Romina said, "You know your mother has been wanting you to find somebody for years . . ." Her eyes flicked toward Stella, and her voice trailed off.

Stella stared at her coffee, heat rising to her cheeks. She had no right to feel anything. Still, the sting was sharp as lemon on a cut.

Luca fumbled as he put the cup back on the saucer.

Did everyone know Luca had once asked her out? Domenica's hints suggested she understood more than she let on—that Stella's feelings for Luca had been there from the start, buried perhaps, but not evaporated.

And now there was Lilliana. Elegant, polished, perfectly matched to Luca's strong jaw and broad shoulders. They looked like they stepped off a magazine cover. Without quite realizing it, Stella's hand was in her hair, tugging at her curls in a futile attempt to smooth them, only making the frizz more unhinged.

Stella forced her hand to the marble counter. Matteo placed his on top, his warm eyes searching hers. Maybe Matteo also knew. Maybe he felt for her. Even though he repeatedly insisted that Giancarlo and Stella make loads of babies they named versions of Matteo and Matteandra.

Romina said, "Stella, love. Have you eaten? I have your favorite pine nut cookies." Roberto put one on a plate before Stella could answer.

Luca cleared his throat. "By the way, Roberto, I asked Lilliana's father for that list of contractors."

The mayor frowned. "You asked Gino for contractor recommendations?"

Veronica said, "You should have asked Marcello! He knows all the quality people."

"I don't remember seeing a permit request come through my office," the mayor said in a sing-song voice.

Roberto held up his hands. "It's not a renovation. I could probably do it myself, but when I told Luca we need to shore up the wall in our cantina, he said he'd ask Gino."

Veronica twitched irritably. "What wall? I don't know anything about a wall."

Romina smiled brightly. "Sure you've heard me complain about this over the years. That earthquake in '97? The crumbling has worsened."

Stella looked down at the tile floor, as if she could see through to the dirt-floored cantina below. She loved how Italians called basements "cantinas." Much more lyrical.

Luca said, "Gino said it's good to get a professional to look at it. Most people on this middle level of town sustained damage to their cantinas and don't even know it."

"Cosimo's shop is only a few doors down," Stella's voice rose. The shop had a tipsy quality to it. She always assumed it was because of all the chandeliers and mirrors, but maybe the floor was sinking. She pictured the old man shuffling about his shop, ignorant of the fractured foundation beneath his feet.

Luca's hand shifted toward her, then stilled. He shoved his hands into his pockets.

Roberto nodded. "Cosimo checked his foundations a few years ago, after Antonio found cracks in the walls of the bakery's cantina."

Romina added, "He bought a round of coffee to celebrate his good fortune."

Stella touched the pendant hanging from her neck, a gift from Cosimo. Matteo followed the gesture and they both grinned. She was growing as superstitious as her neighbors.

Marcello scowled. "That kind of work requires expertise. You need to use one of my—"

Once again, the bell signaled the arrival of more patrons. Who now?

Veronica and the mayor straightened to take in the new actor in the unfolding play. Mimmo, the ex-caretaker of her bed-and-breakfast, tracking in mud and crowing about his recent hunt? Maybe the Americans, returning out of season?

At the mayor's widening eyes, Stella turned to face the door.

Strangers.

Strangers in suits.

Strangers in suits who withdrew from their pockets shiny badges that made Stella think of the Wild West. Why was she thinking about saloons and swinging doors now?

Her spoon slipped against the saucer, the clatter explosive in the hush.

One man pulled handcuffs from his pocket. "Roberto Giordano. Romina Bianchi. You need to come with us."

The officers, for that must be what they were, droned a string of words. The Italian version of Miranda rights? Stella's knowledge of police procedurals from reading *gialli*—Italian mysteries known for their yellow spines—failed her, before the rising bedlam recalled her to the present.

Matteo shouting.

Luca leaping backwards, knocking over his coffee.

The cup, crashing to the floor.

Stella couldn't catch her breath as she watched men handcuff Roberto and Romina. At the click of the clasps closing around Romina's shaking wrists, Roberto's face seemed to cave in, settling into lines and gaps.

Words left unformed in the chaos suddenly snapped into place and Stella said, "Is that necessary? You can see they won't run away!"

The men ignored her.

She whirled to face the mayor, frozen on his stool. "Do something!"

Veronica stood, and for a moment Stella thought she might intervene. Instead, Veronica bristled, "You can't speak to your mayor this way!"

The mayor himself sat silent, his eyes wide.

Forcing down a silent scream, Stella ran to Romina, calling behind her, "Luca! Why are they taking them?"

"I don't know!" Luca was at her side, had been, the whole time.

As the men shoved Roberto and Romina to the door, Roberto stumbled, the snowy cloth falling off his shoulder. One of the men stepped on the fabric as he pushed Roberto forward.

Stella stared at the footprint on the white cloth. She blinked, uncomprehending. Hearing her name from what seemed a divide away, she looked up.

"Stella!" Romina called, her hair loose from its bun. "Stella! Help us!"

Veronica shot a look at her husband, still sitting mute. She swallowed, rose, and shouted, "What did you do, Romina? You must tell us. Only then can Marcello help you."

"Nothing!" Romina cried out, her chin trembling. "Stella! I don't know what this is . . ."

Stella rushed forward to touch Romina's arm, to offer even this modicum of support. The man bodied her out of the way. Fighting the urge to punch him, Stella held out her hand to Romina. "We'll figure this out. It will be okay."

"Promise me, Stella!" Romina lost her footing, stumbling against one of the men. He yanked her up and out the door.

"I promise! Romina? Do you hear me? I promise!"

Romina gave no sign of having heard Stella as the men jostled the couple into Aramezzo's clear morning air. A cloud of crows billowed in the distance. The cacophony thrummed as Roberto and Romina turned the corner, out of sight.

Stella remembered the first time she walked into Bar Cappellina, unsure how she'd be received in her mother's birthplace. But Romina . . . Romina. Her voice warm, her eyes knowing. She'd offered Stella a coffee as if nothing in the world could be more natural than to have Stella at her marble counter. How many times had Roberto, sensing her fatigue, slid food onto a plate, handing it to her without explanation?

The memories continued to swell—the expression of baffled joy when Stella had pushed a pot of sausage sauce across the counter after their grandson's motorcycle accident. Before that day, the couple had felt like kindergarten teachers, placidly helping Stella find her way. But after the sauce, their embrace of her had become more intimate, familiar.

Kin.

Stella, who felt the deprivation of family deeply since a twist of fate had taken her father and sister, leaving her with a cold and removed mother and no extended family, warmed to the home Roberto and Romina offered. Why else would she come for coffee every morning, when she could make it at home?

Matteo, his breathing ragged, said, "Who were those guys?"

Stella shook her head. "They didn't smell like they were from around here."

Did she mistake the half-smile that flashed across Luca's face?

The door swung open and Leo hurried in, his eyes fixed on the street behind him, his handsome face pale. "Who are those men with Roberto and Romina?" He scanned the bar, back and forth, waiting for someone to answer. Stella could only shake her head. As if watching her body rather than being in it, she noticed Matteo putting an arm around her. Through clenched teeth, Leo said, "Somebody say something!"

Veronica nudged her husband, but it was Luca who spoke. "We don't know, Leo. Those men took them."

"Men? Like . . . *kidnappers*?"

Luca shook his head. "Officers of some kind."

Matteo said, "I didn't catch what they said when they flashed their badges." His brow furrowed over his large eyes. "Did anyone see what kind of badge?"

Quietly, Luca said, "It happened so fast." A spasm of pain contorted his face.

Stella knew that pain—powerlessness, loss, a feeling that perhaps if one had acted sooner, faster, better . . . things would be different.

Luca blinked and turned to the mayor. "You're quiet."

The mayor gagged briefly. "Me? What do you mean?" All eyes turned to him.

Luca's lips straightened into a line. "A person can't patch a wall around here without your consent. You must know something."

Stella watched the mayor as his mouth opened and closed uselessly. Finally, he said, "I'm not at liberty to disclose official business."

Veronica said, "We won't stand here to be scolded." With a huff she turned to her husband. "Come, Marcello. I'm needed at the regional Cultural Society." She scooped up her dogs and lifted her chin like exiting royalty.

Stella said, "You aren't paying for your coffee?"

Veronica stopped short. The mayor slammed into her.

Veronica stumbled only briefly before turning to Stella. "Who should I pay, child? Perhaps you've yet to notice the proprietors have left."

Stella affected an air of innocent bewilderment. "The register is right there. Not paying for their goods and services is stealing. Right, Luca?"

Luca ducked his head, and Stella caught his smile flickering. He looked up with all seriousness. "I'm afraid I can't stand by and watch a robbery in progress."

The mayor and his wife exchanged glances. Marcello shoved his hand in his pocket, and pulled out a fistful of coins, sending a few wadded up tissues to the ground. He selected a few coins and smacked them on the black-veined counter. Grabbing his wife by the elbow, they strode from the bar, the bell tinkling a goodbye.

Matteo sagged against the bar and Stella dropped her head onto her hands, folded on the counter. Luca took out his phone and started tapping. Leo looked around. "So the men, they just arrested Roberto and Romina?"

Stella raised her head. "This has to be a nightmare."

Matteo turned to Luca, "Can you ask at the precinct if anyone had advance warning?"

Luca kept his gaze fixed on his phone, his thumbs moving across the screen. "On it," he muttered.

Stella drew in a steadying breath. "It's all a mistake."

"It has to be," Matteo agreed. "No way Roberto and Romina did anything wrong."

"Come on," frowned Leo. "Everyone has a backstory."

Luca slipped his phone back in his pocket.

Leo went on. "Look, one thing I learned in racing is that you have to evaluate the course without prejudice. Otherwise, you're dead in the water."

Stella shivered.

Luca's phone buzzed and he scrutinized the screen.

Softly, Stella said, "Anything?"

Luca shook his head. "Not unless you consider my mother asking me to pick up bread a news flash." He thought for a moment. "Much as I hate to admit it, Leo has a point. Those officers didn't storm the bar for no reason."

Stella protested, "You know they would never hurt anyone—"

Waving his hand, Luca said, "I'm not suggesting they're accused of a violent crime. Could be tax evasion, or something like that."

As Luca spoke, a memory bloomed in Stella's mind. "Or something altogether different." She snapped her fingers. "Oh! In the States, restaurant owners get fined for selling liquor without a license."

Matteo said, "Fined. Not arrested."

Stella shrugged. "Maybe it's different here? Or it's a more severe version, like falsifying a liquor license? Or maybe health code violations?"

Luca shook his head, "Possible, though not probable. Nothing has changed in this bar for decades. Everything from the coffee supplier to the grappa they get from that producer in Montefalco, it's all unchanged."

His voice heavy with thought, Matteo said, "Except the briefcase."

All eyes turned to him. He gestured to the counter. "The briefcase by the bar. One of the guys took it."

Stella whispered, "How did I miss that?"

Matteo took her hand. "All you could see was a guy yanking Romina."

Leo said, "Did they open it? The briefcase. Before taking it?"

"I . . . I don't know. I couldn't tell," Matteo stammered.

Luca said, "Where was the briefcase? Exactly?"

Matteo walked around the bar to where it opened into the customers' space. "Right here, on the floor beside the counter. Brown, I think. Dark brown. Maybe black."

Luca nodded and drew out his notepad. "Any marks on it? Anything to help us identify it?"

Matteo shook his head. "I figured it was Roberto and Romina's."

Stella said softly to herself, "But why would they keep a briefcase of theirs here? They live upstairs." She walked behind the bar and around it, looking for anything out of place. Luca joined her behind the bar as she rooted in the trash, empty except crumpled milk containers.

As Leo scanned the window ledge, Stella straightened, remembering. When the mayor threw change onto the counter, something had fallen from his pants. Her eyes scanned the recessed area between the counter and the floor. Bingo. A few wads of Kleenex and a slip of paper. Stella jammed the ball of papers into her pocket before picking up Luca's cup, which had fallen to the floor when the officers came in.

She placed the cup gently on the bar with a small clink.

From behind her, she heard Luca mutter, "A briefcase doesn't fit with tax evasion, that's for sure."

Stella searched her memory of mystery novels. "Smuggling, maybe?"

Matteo tried to smile. "No chance. What would they smuggle? Coffee grounds?"

Stella's heart fell. "Coffee grounds . . . isn't there some kind of drug that's smuggled in coffee grounds?"

"Cocaine," Luca said sharply.

"Cocaine," Stella agreed. They looked at each other briefly before Stella's eyes slid away. She stammered, "The smell of the beans confuses drug-sniffing dogs."

Matteo shook his head, "I don't know what you guys are on about. Roberto and Romina would no more smuggle cocaine then they would mug someone on the street."

Stella said, "Mistaken identity?"

"Well, we're not figuring out anything sitting here." Leo sighed. "I'm out. I want to be the one who tells Marta…" His voice trailed off and he gazed into the corner of the bar.

Stella stared at him. "What is it?"

"Marta…I remembered something she told me." Leo shook his head. "It feels wrong, like telling tales. What if it's not true?"

Luca clicked his pen. "The more information the better."

Leo hedged, "Keep in mind, it's speculation. But Marta confessed she thought Roberto and Romina were struggling. Financially."

"Impossible," Stella protested, "the bar is always packed."

Shrugging, Leo said, "Sure. But most people spend a euro on espresso if they spend anything at all. It's plenty busy, but costs have gone up, the economy and all."

Luca said, "What did Marta say, exactly?"

Leo shook his head. "I shouldn't have said anything. Please, don't ask her about this. It was an offhand comment that they'd bought some of her wool and put off paying. She didn't care about the money. But it seemed out of character."

The bell over the door chimed and Stella startled.

The baker stood in the middle of the bar, the light glinting off of his magnificent rust-colored mustache. "What's going on? Where are Roberto and Romina?"

Luca glanced at Stella, "Can you…"

"Of course," she said, ducking behind the bar to where Romina kept a drawer of paper and pens for kids to doodle. More than once Stella had noticed Roberto rummaging around in the drawer before taping a "back in five" sign to the door. She had always figured he'd dashed out to

Cristiana's shop to grab a container of milk. Where had he gone?

As Stella pulled the tape out of the drawer, she noticed a photograph among the pens, matchbooks, and rubber bands. It was creased and faded, as if it had been kept in a wallet for years. A younger, sunburned Roberto, beside Romina, her face smooth and laughing, their arms around a boy no older than eight. The child beamed into the camera, one missing tooth and an explosion of dark curls. Stella ran her finger over Roberto and Romina's faces. Roberto's smile—quiet, protective, proud. It was how Roberto smiled at her when he brought her a cornetto she didn't ask for but needed all the same.

Tears pricked her eyes.

She turned the photo over and saw written in thick black ink, "Yared, 8." Must have been a family vacation or something. Or maybe not a "family" vacation as the child's dark complexion didn't square him with the family Stella had met. But how like Roberto and Romina to befriend children wherever they went.

As she put the photo back, she noticed a figure in its background. A nun in a blue habit, mid-step, looking over her shoulder as if calling to someone just out of frame.

"Stella?" Luca's voice recalled her to her task.

"Right, right, sorry." She scrawled "*Oggi chiuso*," closed today, across the paper.

Antonio stared at one of them after another. "Anybody want to tell me what's going on? I need to get back to the bakery; I can't leave my new apprentice for too long."

Stella remembered. "Their family! We need to contact them!"

Antonio's eyes narrowed. "Roberto and Romina's family? They're on vacation. In Slovenia."

The room went quiet.

Leo shook his head. "Well, I'm out. I gotta tell Marta before she hears it from a neighbor."

Antonio's eyes widened. "Hears what?" he asked, as the door closed behind Leo. Antonio glanced around the bar. When no one moved to answer him, Antonio turned and hurried after Leo.

As Stella hung the sign, Luca said, "I'll head to work and see what I can find out."

Stella bit her lip as she smoothed the tape, over and over.

"I can't believe I have to go to work," Matteo said to Stella as they walked down the street. "It feels like there's been a natural disaster. And yet there are cigarette butts in need of sweeping." He glared at an offensive remnant of somebody's nicotine addiction.

She hardly noticed the temperature, which had risen in the time she'd been in Bar Cappellina.

"You going to Domenica's?" Matteo asked, into the heavy silence.

"I should tell her. But how can I sit still at a time like this?" She thought for a moment. "Can I come with you? To work?"

"You want to collect trash? I didn't think I was selling it particularly well."

She drew the ball of papers from her napkin. "I've already started. Marcello dropped this when he paid."

"Garbage is historically my job."

"Why should you get all the perks?" Stella asked, her voice toneless. Walking to a trash can, she placed the ball on it and started pulling it apart. A lipstick-stained napkin, something that looked like it had been used to blow a nose. And a slip of paper.

"What is it?" Matteo asked.

"I don't know. A receipt, I guess. But I can't tell for what. This might be a bank routing number?"

"Domenica will know," Matteo said, nodding.

She started to toss the napkins in the trash and then stopped. "How do you take the top of this canister off?"

"What are you doing?"

"Don't you see? If the mayor can leave something behind on the table, maybe somebody put something in the trash. Something important—"

Matteo pulled off the top of the can to show her the inside. "Empty, Stella. I emptied it this morning. Just like every morning that's ever been or ever was."

Her face lit up. "Wait, where do Roberto and Romina put their trash?"

"At the corner of the piazza—"

Stella was already moving. She raced across the piazza, where it met the alley that ran behind the bar. She strode to the pile, tossing aside empty boxes from San Carlo, the potato chip distributor, and what looked like an empty box of cleaning supplies. She stopped at the final box and held it up.

"Is this weird? It's weird, right?"

"What?"

"Look," Stella held out the box. "Stickers on the box say it holds wine, but the original shipping label was ripped off and the address is written in Sharpie."

"So?"

"So wineries or wine distributors are far more modern than that. A printed label at least, more often with a barcode." She turned the box to show Matteo.

"In the States, maybe, but I'd hardly call Umbria modern."

Stella didn't answer, her attention on a piece of bubble wrap falling from the box. "Bubble wrap? To protect wine?"

Matteo gently took the box from Stella. "A small producer, who can say? Besides, maybe it fell out of another box." He placed his hands on her shoulders. "Stella, I'll go through the trash. It's why I get paid the big bucks. You tell Domenica what happened and see if she can figure out if it means anything."

She nodded dumbly.

"Give Domenica my love." Matteo leaned forward and pressed his cool cheek against hers.

Her eyes followed him as he took his cart and set off.

She sighed and rehearsed how to tell Domenica about the arrest quickly so they could get to work.

She needn't have bothered, as Domenica met her at the door saying, "Any leads?"

"You know already? Do you have some sort of emergency alert notification on your phone?"

"Leonardo."

With a weak smile, Stella said, "That guy sure gets the word out fast."

Holding the door for Stella to enter, Domenica said, "I was unlocking the door when he passed."

Stella climbed the few steps into the shop, as cool as Bar Cappellina. Domenica's shutters were all closed, save one with the slats open for light, which fell across the sun-warmed brocade of Stella's favorite chair, currently occupied by Ravioli, her favorite of Domenica's cats. The patchwork calico squeaked in protest when Stella lifted her, but settled quickly onto her lap without complaint. Maybe that's why she enjoyed Ravioli so much. Her own cat seemed to delight in doing the opposite of what Stella wanted, surprising her by leaping out of the pantry as she reached in for a box of pasta or jumping onto her lap soaking wet, which forced Stella to spend the evening drying her enormous cat with a towel, his nails working faintly as he fought the urge to make pizza on her lap.

She inhaled the scent of burbling coffee as her friend bustled around the hot plate. Closing her eyes, Stella tried to gather her thoughts, letting the theories from the bar settle and form into leads.

Domenica prompted, "Tell me what happened."

"Didn't Leo tell you?"

"He told me what you all told him. I want it straight from the book."

Stroking Ravioli's patchwork fur, Stella walked Domenica through the morning.

"A briefcase?" Domenica frowned. "Of what?"

"If we knew, we might be able to figure out who took them and why," Stella said. "But since we don't, I figure we need to check out a few possibilities. One, bar-related trouble—health department, liquor license." Stella started numbering on her fingers. "Two, are there civil filings against them? Debt collection, maybe? And three, financial trouble that might explain smuggling." Out of breath now, Stella inhaled.

"Are you done?" Domenica asked.

"I think so," Stella said.

Domenica said nothing but began shuffling around her desk, removing scarves and sweaters from atop her computer. She switched it on, and as the hum grew louder, Stella felt her shoulders unclench. Matteo was right; they needed Domenica on this.

Muttering to herself, Domenica began typing madly. Stella caught a glimpse of different color boxes flying on and off the page. Finally, Domenica turned around. "No dice on your first two theories."

"Are you sure?"

Domenica gestured to the computer. "Any sort of legal filing like the liquor license or a health department violation is public record. Luca probably already rejected those as possibilities. Whether or not Roberto and Romina are being sued is slightly harder to find, but still in the public domain. Nothing there."

"So that leaves us with the briefcase."

Pushing her glasses onto her nose, Domenica agreed, "Someone was dropping something off or picking something up."

"Something illicit or illegal in some way, hence the army of guys with badges storming the bar." Stella closed her eyes to ward off the memory.

"Certainly it sounds like they found what they were looking for."

"Maybe it was cash. Or maybe illicit goods of some kind," Stella said softly. "But what?"

"To know that, we'd have to know why they were arrested."

Nodding, Stella said. "But you can find out pretty easily if they needed money, right? If their account was steady, no big payouts or deposits, it argues against smuggling."

"The fact that they're innocent argues against their smuggling." Domenica turned back to the computer, her fingers running over the keys without pressing them, as if willing her hands to start typing the magic answer on their own.

"You know what I mean." Stella sighed. Her thoughts turned to the cocaine in coffee grounds. She shook her head. "We need to know what would make them suspicious enough to get nabbed by officers. So can you check their bank account?"

Domenica spun around. "Most definitely not."

Ravioli flew off Stella's lap. "Sorry, I assumed you knew how to do that—"

"I do know how to do that. "

"Maybe that would help. They did ask—"

Domenica shook her head. "She didn't ask us to pry into their personal life."

Stella patted her leg to call Ravioli back, and her hand brushed her pocket. "Oh! I almost forgot." She pulled the slip of paper from her jeans and placed it on the desk. "What do you make of this?"

Domenica pushed her glasses higher onto her nose. "What is it?"

"The mayor dropped it at the bar."

Domenica's eyes ran over the numbers quickly and then slowly. "It's a receipt."

"That much I got. But for what? I don't see any items listed."

"There are no items. It's for wiring money."

Cocking her head to the side, Stella said, "The mayor is wiring money? How much?"

"Ten thousand euros."

Stella whistled. "To whom?"

"Wire transfers are to banks, so there's just a routing number." Domenica tapped the slip of paper.

"I guess the real question is . . . why?"

Domenica's eyes widened. "You think the mayor might have something to do with Roberto and Romina being taken?"

With a shrug, Stella said, "He certainly didn't seem bothered by it."

Domenica reached for the slip, pulling it closer. "Oh, wait. This is a deposit into the mayor's account. Which makes sense. They probably got the insurance payment for her stolen ring."

"What stolen ring?"

Domenica frowned briefly at the receipt before tossing it onto her desk with a sigh. "Never mind. It's definitely a transfer out of their account, not into it."

"Domenica, what stolen ring?"

Domenica rearranged the scarves around her neck. How could the woman wear scarves in summer? "Didn't you hear? It happened back when Marcello and Veronica were at the sea. Oh, wait, you had that family from Florida staying with you."

"The ones with two kids that demanded chicken nuggets."

"I still think you could market those. Far better than the packaged variety."

"A low bar," Stella said.

Domenica got up and poured a cup of coffee.

Stella said, "Tell me about the robbery."

"You think it's related?"

"It could be, if there were jewels in the briefcase."

Domenica considered. "I see that. But better to ask Cosimo. I heard about the robbery from him."

"He always takes the loss of heirlooms hard."

"He does, though I don't know if Veronica's ring from her starlet days counts as a family heirloom," Domenica said, a slight smile playing about her lips.

Stella stared at her. "What are you sitting on?"

"Oh, nothing. Cosimo's interests are so varied, aren't they? You actually can't ever predict what hare he'll chase next." Domenica's cheeks turned shell pink.

Realization dawned on Stella. "Do you mean . . . *you*? Are you the next hare?"

Domenica gasped. "What? No! We've just been talking more since he dropped in a few weeks ago, looking for a book about chandeliers, which I didn't have."

"I'm shocked. This shop feels like Mary Poppins's bag. You can always find anything in it, and it holds more than it should."

"I'm unclear on the Mary Poppins reference, but I appreciate what must be a compliment."

"You are not unclear on anything, but get back to the point. The robbery."

Domenica took a noisy sip of her coffee. "Well, Cosimo and I were having coffee and he asked me if Giancarlo had given you any sort of ring."

"We've hardly started dating! I don't even know if I like him!"

"Stella, there is no need to strain my credulity. I know you like him. You know you like him. The cats know you like him."

Stella said nothing.

"It's not an insult, *cara*. Nothing wrong with wearing your heart on your sleeve."

She didn't want to talk about this anymore. Not when Roberto and Romina were gone. She prompted, "So you told him that there is no ring with Giancarlo and he told you about Veronica's?"

Domenica nodded and rolled backward to her desk. "Right. Well, I told him he was speed reading your relationship and then I told him about my own engagement ring, from Ahmed. Then he told me about Veronica's ring."

Frowning, Stella said, "Ahmed."

"I'm sure I told you about him. Ahmed. Remember? Family roots mingled with Ottoman royals, which really just meant he shared rights to a grand house on the Turkish Riviera. For the heirloom aspect alone, my friends said I was nuts giving Ahmed back that ring."

Domenica often wisecracked and she frequently quipped, but Stella had never seen that tender look on her friend's face. Softly, Stella said, "Why did you return it? The ring, I mean."

"It's a chapter for another day."

"You miss him," Stella realized, patting Ravioli's head as he put a tentative paw on her leg.

Domenica looked away. "He made me laugh like nobody else and could talk about anything under the sun. Plus, that body. It wouldn't quit."

"Why must you always turn these stories into a joke?"

Domenica pushed her overlarge glasses higher onto her nose. "I didn't think I was."

Stella gazed levelly at Domenica.

Who gazed levelly back before saying, "The man was seriously ripped."

Chuckling, Stella said, "What happened to him?"

"Probably married a princess of Lichtenstein. I know his family was not fond of his attachment to a confirmed commoner like myself. No trace of my lineage is gilded." Domenica paused. "Speaking of gilded. Veronica's ring. I just realized something strange. After I told Cosimo about Ahmed's ring and he told me about Veronica's, he added something curious. He said Veronica's ring was enough to buy a bar."

"He said a bar, specifically a bar?" Stella furrowed her brows.

"What an odd thing to say."

Domenica nodded. "It didn't register as strange at the time, because we were at Bar Cappellina. He made a gesture to encompass all we saw around us. But now, looking back…"

Stella frowned. "Did Roberto or Romina have a reaction to it?"

"No. I don't think they heard." Domenica thought for a moment. "And then we stopped talking about it because Leonardo asked if the ring was from Veronica's Cinecittà days."

"Cinecittà?" Stella asked, confused.

"Italy's version of Hollywood. Founded in Rome during the Fascist era to fuel the Italian film industry. Where Luisella and Veronica got their starts."

Stella considered Cosimo's comment. Could Roberto and Romina not own the bar? She remembered something Luca had said. "Taxes. Maybe they owe back taxes, and the government put a lien on the bar. And somehow Cosimo knows?"

Domenica hunched over the keyboard and started typing. "The man loves his gossip."

"And that's just what this is. Gossip. I can't believe I'm trafficking in gossip. Like some village nonna hanging laundry."

"You're not doing it for sport, *cara*," Domenica said, without turning. "We're looking for light in the dark."

"I hate being in the weeds," Stella muttered, remembering the frantic pace of her restaurant days. "So if you aren't looking up their financial situation, what are you looking for?"

Distractedly, Domenica spoke as she typed, "Agenzia delle Entrate. Let's begin with seeing if the government is moving on them for anything tax related."

Stella sat tense for a few moments. So tense, she didn't notice Ravioli's return to her lap. Tax evasion couldn't be good, but they could start a Go Fund Me or pass a plate at church or something, couldn't they? Surely, once they paid it off, Roberto and Romina would be released. Stella wondered how much was in her bank account now. It might be enough to pay down a chunk of the taxes. Sure, it would mean not being able to leave Aramezzo as soon as she hoped, but maybe that wasn't so bad—

Domenica smacked the keyboard. Ravioli looked up.

After a beat, Stella said, "Domenica?"

Domenica shook her head and began typing again. "It's not taxes. They are paid up. But maybe it's something related. I'll see if they own the bar outright."

"That's not prying?" Stella ventured.

Domenica muttered, "It's in the public record. The history of the bar's ownership could give us a clue as to why they might have been taken."

After a few more moments, Domenica whirled to face Stella. "Okay, finally. We're on to something."

Just then, the door swung open.

Domenica sprang to her feet, covering the computer with scarves. Stella peered at the figure in the doorway, silhouetted by light.

"Hope I'm not interrupting anything?" Luca said.

"Of course not!" Domenica said, flapping about. "Pull up a seat. I don't have any new books though, unfortunately. I mean," she laughed uncomfortably, "I have new books, but no romances. Or historical romances."

Lingering in the doorway, Luca said, "Actually, I need to talk to Stella. Figured I might find her here."

"Me?" Stella rose, Ravioli falling from her lap. "Why?"

"Go outside and talk to the man, Stella!" Domenica ordered her, falling back onto the chair with a loud exhale.

Stella said nothing, but stepped outside as Luca held open the door. Once in the street, she staggered backward at the wall of heat.

She blinked frantically for a moment. "What is it?" Just as Luca asked, "How are you?" His eyes searched hers and she tried to quell her stomach's slide to her knees.

"I'm fine," she squeaked out. "Or, you know. Not fine. But . . . fine." She laughed uncomfortably.

Luca said nothing, still studying her.

Stella affected an air of casual disinterest. "So, have you learned anything?"

With frustration, Luca shook his head. "I quickly ruled out what we came up with this morning—no legal suits against them for the bar or in civil court. But you must know that already."

Stella adopted an air of innocence. "Oh, well, that's something right?"

He frowned. "Not enough. I can't figure out why nothing comes up when I search their names. If I hadn't seen the badges, I would have started wondering if Leo was right and our friends were kidnapped from under our noses."

Stella frowned. "Can badges be counterfeited?"

Luca shook his head. "I'm not ruling it out, but it's not likely."

Biting her lip, she ventured, "Do you think that briefcase is relevant?"

"Are you asking if I think our friends were smuggling something illegal, or selling something they shouldn't?"

Stella shrugged.

"I think that's all we're left with." With a sigh, Luca said, "I'm hoping you've had better luck."

"What do you mean?"

He hesitated. "I put in a request to see if they've paid their taxes, but it's going to take days to get that answered. Do you know?"

"How would I know?" Stella widened her eyes.

He gestured toward Domenica's shop. "You're going to beat us to the punch again aren't you?"

"Me?" Stella asked innocently. "I would never dream of stepping on official toes."

Luca chuckled. "It's not my toes I'm worried about." The smile dropped from his face and he looked away. Finally, he made his voice firm and said, "Stella. We don't have time. You and I both know that Domenica has a kind of . . . access . . . that we mere mortals lack. Whatever you learn, you have to tell me. I can't get them out if I don't know where they are."

Stella paused. She wasn't sure she trusted Luca anymore than she trusted improperly whipped egg whites to lift a soufflé. But even if she trusted Luca, Domenica insisted on keeping up the facade of a slightly-addled bookshop owner with no idea what an app was, let alone with the capacity to build one in an hour.

At her silence, Luca's jaw worked. Finally, he said, "Let me guess, too busy texting your new boy toy to think about your friends Roberto and Romina?"

Her eyes widened. "Boy toy?"

He shrugged. "What else should I call him? After you were insistent that a date with me would be untenable given your plans to escape this hell hole as soon as—"

"What are these words you're putting in my mouth?"

"And then two seconds later you're swooning over a soccer star like some teenage girl."

"I do not swoon." Did she swoon? Probably not. She hoped not. "And did it ever occur to you that there may have been another reason I turned you down?" Her heartbeat quickened. Now. Now was the time to tell him how many times she'd kicked herself for refusing him. She might regret it, but she had to say it.

Luca held up his hand. "Ah. Okay. I get it. Say no more."

Stella blinked, confused. "What—"

"I told you. I get it," Luca said. "You didn't turn me down because you're leaving. You turned me down because I'm not good enough for you."

Stella stared at him. "You got all that from my silence? Talk about a radical interpretation of the text." But she'd given him no information since then, why wouldn't he leap to this conclusion? She constantly cycled between blurting impulsively and avoiding conversational precipices—both got her into trouble.

Luca examined her face, seeming to follow the shifting emotions. Finally, he said, "You're right. That's not fair. Apparently I completely misread the connection. And that's on me, not on you."

"But Luca—"

A voice from behind them made Stella jump. "Back off, Luca."

Giancarlo.

Stella looked from one to the other.

Through gritted teeth, Luca said, "This isn't your concern, Giancarlo."

"Isn't it?" Giancarlo put his arm around Stella.

Who slid away and said, "Okay, let's all take a breath."

The men glared at each other.

"Apologize to the lady," Giancarlo said, his eyes narrowing.

"What?" Stella gasped. "Giancarlo, really. I don't know what you heard, but—"

"It's okay, Stella. I've got this." Giancarlo growled, his eyes fixed on Luca.

"How ridiculous," she said, rolling her eyes. "Don't we all have bigger fish to fry?"

Luca kept his eyes on Stella. "I don't need this. Have a good day."

As he turned to go, Giancarlo reached for his shoulder to pull him back. Luca said softly, "Careful, Giancarlo. Not everyone lets themselves get shoved around for free."

"I wouldn't push into my half unless you're ready to play." Giancarlo set his jaw.

Stella's legs gave out. Finding herself on the ground, she drew her knees up to meet her forehead, saying, "Can't you both just stop with the testosterone show? It's so stupid and I can't, I just can't right now." She hated the tears streaking her cheeks.

Giancarlo crouched beside her, shooting a look of thunder at Luca. But his voice was soft as he said, "Hey, hey. It's okay. It's over now." He rubbed her back in gentle circles. "Right, Luca?"

Luca watched them for a moment before turning on his heel and striding away.

She watched him go, her eyes hazy with tears.

Murmuring with a warmth she had never before heard from Giancarlo, he said, "Matteo called me. I'm so sorry, Stella."

"It was awful."

Giancarlo pulled her against his chest and stroked her curls, winding his fingers in the coils. "I'm here now. We'll figure this out."

Stella stumbled to get her feet under her again. "I don't know how I wound up here."

"Who does?" He said with a wry grin. Even as he helped her up, his eyes stayed trained on hers, as if she were the only thing in the universe.

Stella wiped the seat of her jeans. "I'm fine. Sorry about all that."

He clucked and said nothing.

Wiping her cheeks, Stella said, "How was London?"

His eyes seemed briefly hooded. "Too far away. I missed you."

She bit her lip. His gaze dipped to take in the gesture. He moved closer.

Putting a hand on his chest, she said, "The doctor. Didn't you have an appointment today?"

He shook his head as he cupped her elbows and leaned his forehead against hers. "I drove here as soon as I landed. The appointment can wait. Until then . . . I'm yours." He leaned down and brushed his lips against hers.

A clattering crash.

"What the—" Stella said, jumping backward while holding her heart.

Giancarlo pointed at the shards of a coffee cup shattered across the cobblestones. Following Giancarlo's gaze, Stella looked up to a second floor window and caught the flash of a housecoat ducking down under the sill as a curler bounced off the ledge to land beside the broken coffee cup.

He called out, "*Buongiorno*, Signora Crespi. How is Luigi?"

A woman rose from below the sill and patted her curlers. "Luigi? He's fine. Just fine. Napping, you know." Stella, who considered herself quite the expert on blushing, gave Signora Crespi's five out of five stars.

"Luigi?" Stella whispered. "Her son?"

"Her cat," he said from the side of his mouth.

Giancarlo saluted Signora Crespi before putting his arm around Stella and leading her down the street. She started to protest, Domenica waited for her, but her mind was too tousled to think of a credible reason to go back.

She cast one last look over her shoulder, hoping to make eye contact with Domenica through the door, to communicate that she'd be back as soon as she could. But Domenica was in full batty shopkeeper mode, dusting the coffee pot before tripping over a cat.

Giancarlo pulled her down the road and Stella felt the woman with one less espresso cup watch them until they rounded the corner.

"This town . . ." she began.

He grinned. "This town is okay." He tucked a loose curl behind Stella's ear and leaned close again.

Summoning more power than she knew she had, and also wondering how her body could react so strongly to Giancarlo's touch when she'd ached at Luca's gaze on her only a little while ago, she backed up. She gestured to where they'd just been standing. "What happened back there—"

"A kiss, Stella," Giancarlo's grin lightened the green in his eyes, making them more seawater than moss. "I should think you wouldn't need that explained."

She shook her head, frustrated. "No. With Luca."

"Oh, that?" His eyes widened. "It was nothing. Sometimes you just have to remind guys like that to stay in their zone of defense."

The words tumbled out before he could cut her off again. "I didn't like it. Unnecessary. I had it under control. And it made me feel like a thing."

He nodded. "I see what you're saying, but you don't understand the history here. Luca and I, we were in the same classroom, the same playgrounds. He knows I'm competitive. I couldn't be where I am if I weren't. I'm not going to allow another man to chase my girl."

"Your girl?" Stella said, her eyes wide. No one had ever called her his girl. She shifted her weight.

He grinned and kissed her forehead. "I'm falling for you, Stella. How can that be a surprise? Now, Matteo had no updates since Roberto and Romina got taken from the bar. Have you learned anything?"

She couldn't help but say, "Well, I was trying to talk to Luca about it, but—"

He waved his hand. "Some men enjoy pretending they know more than they do. I made some calls."

"You did? You have government contacts?"

He laughed. "Stella, when that government wants you to play on the National team for the next European Championship, they tend to bend over backwards to be helpful."

Stella stopped in the street. Was he joking?

But he looked down at his feet and shuffled, as if ashamed of the admission.

"Are you serious?"

He shrugged. "I'm not saying it's right or good that I have perks. But it's the way life works. We might as well use it to our advantage."

She linked her arm through his, feeling his body warm against hers as they continued walking.

"So did you learn anything? From your phone calls?"

"A bit," he hesitated. "But I don't want to say anything. Until I'm sure."

"What do you mean?" Stella asked, her heart in her throat.

"Just . . . prepare yourself, Stella. There may be a reason this didn't look like a typical arrest."

"You have to tell me if—"

Giancarlo held up his hands as if convincing a referee he didn't foul anyone. "I can't, Stella. Let me wait to be sure."

She scowled as she fanned herself. Not even midday and the heat already felt brutal. "I hate waiting."

He chuckled. "I've noticed."

Stella stole a glance at him, wondering how he meant the comment. She felt the words rising up, *what's that supposed to mean*, but remembering her earlier realization with Luca, decided maybe she could aim for something midway between avoidance and ire. She shook her head regretfully, "I am impatient. It's true."

"It's adorable. Don't change a thing."

They continued walking in silence, Stella wondering if she could convince, entreat, or wheedle Giancarlo's information out of him. She needed something to bring to Domenica. Unless . . . maybe Domenica already knew?

She tried to read Giancarlo's silence. A small smile playing about his lips as she darted sidelong looks at him suggested he wasn't thinking about much of anything, not even the heat.

Stella envied him.

Within a few moments, they approached Stella's house.

Luisella stepped outside and winced at the sudden sunshine. She gave Stella a curt nod before descending onto the street, her elegant suit just so, her pink quilted purse on her arm. She clipped away from them with quick steps. Stella remembered Veronica's story of Luisella on the road and hoped the dogs were squirreled away.

Giancarlo watched Luisella in her pink dress recede around the corner. "Friendly one, isn't she?"

"Luisella?"

"No '*buongiorno*'? No 'how do you do'?"

"Are you kidding? It took me months to get the nod."

He said, "I saw one of her movies at a festival."

"How was it?"

He cocked his head to the side, considering. "Pretty good, actually. Her role was small, but moving."

"Are you saying you felt an emotion?" She nudged Giancarlo with her hip.

He chuckled, sweeping his hair off his forehead in a boyish gesture. "Got pretty close there for a moment."

A church bell clanged the half hour, startling a pigeon from the eaves above.

Stella wondered, "I wonder why she stopped. Acting, I mean. And how she wound up here." She shook her head. "How can I be having these stupid thoughts when Roberto and Romina just got hauled away?"

"Hey. Even detectives go grocery shopping."

She shook her head, not understanding.

He stopped in front of her house and faced her, his hands on her shoulders. "Regular thoughts, regular needs. They will intrude, even when you're down two-nil with stoppage ticking. Cut yourself some slack. It doesn't mean you aren't worried, and it doesn't mean you don't love them." He checked his phone and said before she could ask, "Still nothing."

Nodding slowly, Stella said, "Regular thoughts. Regular needs. Thank you, that's helpful."

Giancarlo grinned. "Anytime. Anyway, what makes you good at this sleuthing thing is that you are curious, right? How can you turn off that curiosity? You can't."

After a moment, Stella said, "That's something my dad might have said." His eyes narrowed. "I'm not saying you're like my father or anything, just that, you know . . . you give solid dad advice."

He smiled and Stella felt relieved. She asked, "Do you want kids someday, or does that not fit into the life of a soccer player?"

Shrugging, he said, "A few of my teammates have kids. They come to the games, it's pretty cute."

Stella's eye caught on her cat, appearing on the steps beside her. "Barbanera . . . how did you get out?"

The cat regarded her evenly, flicking the end of his tail. He cast his gaze away to the other end of the road, where Stella noticed a silhouette clattering down the cobblestones. Matteo. He arrived out of breath. "There you are! Giancarlo . . . heard anything yet?"

Giancarlo once again checked his phone. "No. Not yet."

Stella's heart sank. "Did you want to call again? Maybe whoever is on it forgot. I mean, we can't expect strangers to care like we do. Maybe—"

Giancarlo reached for her hand and lifted it for a kiss. "Nobody has forgotten. Don't worry."

Matteo sighed. "If you two could wrap this up sometime soon, we have friends to save."

Giancarlo lowered Stella's hand but kept it in his own. "Getting ahold of people in government takes time."

"Time we don't have," muttered Stella. She widened her eyes at Matteo. With studied casualness, Stella said, "Well, I better check in with Domenica."

Giancarlo's brow creased. "Weren't you just there?"

The sound of something wet hitting hot oil drifted from a nearby window followed by the smell of browning onions.

"I was, that's true, I was," Stella nodded, her mind like a lobster trying to escape its pot. "Umm, Matteo?"

"Right," Matteo said, watching her. "But you only popped in to let Domenica know Roberto and Romina had been taken away. You wanted to wait for me so we could tell her together."

"Right! Those details. Weird how fuzzy they get. The whole thing…intense."

Matteo nodded.

Giancarlo's brow furrowed. "Why don't I come? That way I hear the details too."

"Well," Stella glanced at Matteo. They didn't need Giancarlo tagging along.

"That would be great," Matteo started, then hesitated. "But…we promised Domenica help with shelving this morning."

"Shelving!" Stella blurted, smooth in a voice of mock neutrality. "Pretty boring work. Not recommended."

"And Giancarlo," Matteo added, "don't you need to see your grandmother? If she hears you skipped…"

Stella spotted Barbanera blinking at her from the stoop. Pretending resignation, she said, "Grandparents, right? Okay. I'll let you go. I need to feed Barbanera. Matteo, meet me at Domenica's in fifteen?"

Matteo nodded. "I'll drop the cart off and meet you there."

Giancarlo looked from one to the other again, saying nothing.

On impulse, Stella leaned in and kissed his cheek. "But I'll see you later?"

He pressed her hand. "Dinner? A…walk?" He regarded her knowingly. A walk. That meant seclusion, which meant…her stomach swooped.

"Why not both!" Matteo piped up, merrily. "After all, you gotta get in all the together time before Giancarlo has to…you know."

Stella turned her head away. Giancarlo leaving was always on the menu. It was just a question of which course it would follow. She couldn't think about that now. Giancarlo seemed to have the same thought as he leaned forward to brush his lips across her other cheek. "We have time."

With a nod, Stella said, "All right, Barbanera. Ready for lunch?"

The cat regarded her for a moment and then stood slowly, as if doing her a favor.

Stella waved to the men at the base of the stairs. "See you!"

"Dinner at Trattoria Cavour. Be there before the clock strikes," Giancarlo grinned.

She grinned back, remembering how last time they accidentally timed their clinking glasses with the church bells.

Giancarlo jogged down the street as Stella turned into the house. Barbanera strolled to his plate and sat, waiting, his one ear flicking back and forth.

Stella pulled out the food she'd made over the weekend, scooping it into a chipped saucer rimmed with wild strawberries. "It's liver. You love liver."

He looked up at her and sat down, wrapping his tail around himself until the tip flicked the ground at his front feet.

"Okay, yes, you love beef liver and this is chicken, but you remember what the vet said." As if in answer to his retort, she added, "I'm not body shaming. All that rich food I gave you after the accident may have been great for our bonding and excellent for your shiny coat, but a streamlined cat is a healthy cat and a healthy cat lives longer."

Barbanera seemed to sigh before lowering his black chin.

Stella washed the spoon and the remnants of dishes she'd left when her guests had taken off that morning. Drying her hands on a towel, she asked Barbanera, "Want to come with me?"

There was no way he could know she was going to Domenica's, which he refused to enter, and yet there seemed a grim determination in the way he crouched lower over his saucer of food. Though he'd grown civilized with her, he still did not play well with others—which explained the total lack of feline visitors to her property. Canine either, when it came to it.

She patted his head. He pretended disdain but she noted the slight lean into her hand.

By the time she got to Domenica's, she found Matteo settled in the armchair. "You took my seat," she said, her nose wrinkling.

Domenica waved at the folding chair. "A little hardship never hurt anyone."

"A hard seat has, though. I'm fairly certain," Stella said, falling into the seat with a thud. Her thoughts flicked to Roberto and Romina. Her throat tightened. Were they even together? She shook her head. *Get in the game, Stella.*

"I've filled Domenica in on what Giancarlo told us," Matteo said.

"Or didn't tell us," Stella muttered.

Violetta draped across Matteo's lap like a damp towel.

Catching her gaze, Matteo rolled his eyes. "Barbanera would never stoop to such undignified behavior."

"Barbanera would take a swipe at you for lumping him in with other cats."

"If you two could pay attention for five seconds," Domenica said.

They dipped their chins like chastised children. "Sorry, Domenica," they said in unison.

She gestured to an imaginary audience. "Really. The Twitter generation. Can't stay focused for the length of a paragraph."

"Hey!" Stella protested.

"Did Luca have any information?" Domenica continued.

"Nothing. Do you think he overheard us? Or noticed you drinking in your computer screen?"

"Too dramatic by half, Stella," Domenica admonished, still typing. "I covered the computer in time."

Stella said, "Did you already tell Matteo what you found?"

"I was waiting for you," Domenica said grimly. "Bar Cappellina. When Romina's father died, ownership of the bar went to Romina's little sister, Lavinia."

"Her little sister? That *is* odd." Stella squinted, trying to remember if she'd heard anything about Romina having a sister.

"Why is it odd?" Matteo said, turning to Stella, confusion in his wide eyes.

Domenica offered, "For Stella, Roberto and Romina are as much a part of Bar Cappellina as their De'Longhi espresso machine."

Matteo stroked Violetta. "Lavinia. I'd forgotten about her. Little sister is right, did she ever get above five feet? I remember as a kid wondering why they let a child run the bar." He chuckled. "I figured it out pretty quick, though. She was so…so…what's that word, like a strict teacher."

"Severe," Domenica supplied.

Snapping his fingers, Matteo said, "Severe! Yes. But it was an act, wasn't it? The way she'd sprinkle cocoa powder on my steamed milk when my mom wasn't looking."

Stella pressed her hand to her forehead. "Wait. Too much. A sister I never heard of?" She turned to Matteo, "And why did your mom object to cocoa powder on your milk?"

Domenica grumbled, "As if that's the plot we need to follow when we still don't even know why Roberto and Romina were arrested."

Matteo held up his hand, sending a flurry of cat fur into the air. "She's more focused if we satisfy her insatiable need to know." To Stella, he said, "Before I hit adolescence, I got pretty bulky. Fat, really. My mom tried to limit my calories, scared of my staying big. Didn't know I'd use that bulk to shoot up like a pole bean."

Domenica sighed. "As I was saying. Lavinia."

Stella turned to her. "Lavinia was the *little* sister? Why didn't their parents leave the bar to the older sibling?"

Matteo shrugged. "Before my time. I just wanted that cocoa powder."

Domenica smiled. "Stella, you're imagining the way it went down as if Romina is who she is now, keeper of the keys to Bar Cappellina. But when she was younger, Romina had no interest in the bar. And from the old gossip, I always got the sense that there was some unspoken reason Romina stayed away for years."

Stella shook her head. "So Lavinia handed off the bar to Romina?"

Matteo nodded, "She got sick and couldn't run it. I guess that's why Romina came back."

"Actually, there's more to it," Domenica said looking toward her computer, shrouded in sweaters and scarves. She turned back to face Stella. "Prepare yourself."

The sound of Stella scooting her chair back sent a squeak into the waiting silence. "What? Why? What did I do?"

Domenica and Matteo exchanged glances. Finally, Domenica said gently, "One of these days you'll stop assuming you are always in trouble." She took a breath. "Once Lavinia died, ownership of the bar transferred to Anna Maria Mazzoli."

"Anna Maria? My *aunt*?"

Domenica nodded.

"Are you sure?"

Domenica stared at Stella and said nothing.

"Of course you're sure. I don't know why I asked."

Shrugging, Domenica said, "You're surprised."

"Gobsmacked is more like it," Stella muttered in English. "Why would Romina's sister leave the bar to my aunt instead of Romina?"

"Property records only show ownership, not motivation."

"You knew all the players. Speculate," Stella demanded.

Matteo chimed in, "Well, if Romina wasn't around, maybe Lavinia assumed she wouldn't be interested in the bar. And somebody needed to run it."

"Maybe," Domenica thought. "Romina's sister was fading by the time I got here. I barely knew her before she became confined to her bed."

"And my aunt Anna Maria? What do you know about her?"

"Like I said," Matteo shrugged. "Before my time. Or I guess not, she only died a few years ago."

Domenica leaned forward. "*Cara*, I can't tell you any more than the last twenty times you asked about your family—Anna Maria kept to herself. She didn't invite intimacy."

"Yes, yes, I remember," Stella said, waving her hand. "But surely you must have a sense of her. Or her connection to Romina's family. Is she related? Which I guess would mean that I'm related to Romina?"

"I don't know how she would be. Your family has been here so long the village is built on the roots of your family tree. Romina's parents moved here after the war and converted the decommissioned church into a bar." Domenica shook her head. "All I know about your aunt is that she was reserved, but charitable. No matter how little she had, she'd always give a coin to a wandering beggar. And you know about her volunteer work making meals for the school."

"That I remember!" Matteo said with such vigor, the grey tabby flew from his lap.

"You would," Stella said fondly.

Domenica went on as if she hadn't been interrupted. "Anna Maria never talked about her service, but her giving nature was as much a part of her as the clothes she made."

"She made clothes?" Stella said. "You never told me that!"

"I figured you knew," Domenica said, her eyes widening. "Didn't you once tell me she sent you clothes when you were young?"

"I assumed she bought them from a store!"

"Not surprising," Domenica said. "She had a gift. Everyone figured she'd move to Rome to sew for a great fashion house. In fact, Orietta told me that the wife of a bigwig at Gucci rented a house outside Assisi for a summer in the sixties and heard about Anna Maria. The woman commissioned your aunt to make a dress for a party to open the season and was so pleased with it, she convinced her husband to offer Anna Maria a position. Your aunt refused."

"What! Why? It could have been her ticket out of here!"

Domenica smiled sadly. "Not everyone is anxious to leave Aramezzo, *cara*."

Stella paled. "I didn't mean it that way. I meant my mother was so desperate to leave, I assumed her sister would have been, too."

Shaking her head, Domenica said, "I told you. Anna Maria felt her ties to the community."

Stella mused, "Those boxes of clothes in the closet. I need to go through them."

"You haven't?" Domenica asked. "I thought for sure you would have inspected each one three times."

"If you haven't noticed, I'm not much of a clotheshorse," Stella said, indicating her uniform of Doc Martens, jeans, and a faded t-shirt, this one emblazoned with the logo of her friend Lou's diner in the Lower East Side.

Domenica grinned. "It suits you. But when you and Cosimo tore through your house—"

"We were on the hunt for jewelry, in particular the medallion Cosimo remembered my grandmother having. Neither of us paid the slightest attention to the clothes." Shaking her head, she said, "We're getting off track again. Does Romina own the bar now?"

Domenica adjusted her glasses and peered at the screen. "A month after your aunt inherited the bar, she sold it to Romina for ten euros."

"What!"

"It makes sense, Anna Maria had her hands full with the bed-and-breakfast. Looks like right after that, Romina added Roberto to the ownership." Domenica drummed her fingers on the desk. "But this is the truly strange part. About four months ago, they must have mortgaged the bar because the bank now owns it."

"Four months ago. Soon after I got to town."

"I can't imagine that's connected."

"No, of course not. But I like context."

Domenica grinned. "Okay, context-girl. Try this on. Doesn't that timing line up with when their grandson got into the motorcycle accident?"

Matteo whistled under his breath. "I'd forgotten about that accident. Romina hates that he's riding again."

Stella wondered, "The medical bills . . . maybe that's why they mortgaged the bar?"

Chuckling, Domenica said, "Spoken like an American unused to socialized health care. No, those bills would have been paid by the state."

"What then? Maybe because he couldn't work? Or his parents couldn't, to take care of him?"

Domenica shrugged. "All we know for sure is that Cosimo, accidentally or on purpose, was on to something when he mentioned the bar as if it was for sale."

At a shrill peal from Matteo's pocket, Stella jumped.

"It's my phone, Stella, not a bomb," he said softly as he pulled the device from his pocket.

"I'm on edge," she muttered. "So sue me."

Matteo moved to turn off his ringer but then noticed the caller. He looked up. "It's Giancarlo."

Domenica frowned and opened her mouth to begin invoking the rules around devices during sleuthing meetings. Rules she devised and Stella and Matteo ignored. Stella waved her down.

Narrowing her eyes, Domenica closed her mouth and began adjusting her scarves as Matteo pressed his phone against his ear. "Giancarlo? What? You're breaking up."

He rose and hustled out of the shop to find reception, often spotty given Aramezzo's thick walls.

"I still can't believe that boy has access I can't get." Domenica mused. "And here I thought he was just another pretty face."

Stella said simply, "He has connections." Pride straightened her shoulders. Connections. Giancarlo was a man who commanded respect, who got things done. A man she could lean on.

Domenica and Stella turned their eyes to the doorway through which they watched Matteo gesturing as he spoke to Giancarlo. Matteo's hand pulled at his face.

"This can't be good," Stella breathed.

Violetta jogged to the doorway, her feet padding across the floor before she sat and watched Matteo.

He put his phone in his pocket but didn't come back in. In fact, he walked away. Stella rose to follow him. But she sat back when Matteo crossed the doorway again in the other direction.

He's pacing, Stella realized, each pass ratcheting her nerves tighter. She sat straight in her chair, as if waiting for a teacher to call on her.

Matteo faced the shop. He paused for a moment then opened the door, so slowly Stella wondered if the hinges had caught on something.

Matteo made his way to them in silence. Finally, he opened his mouth, but no sound came out.

"Matteo?" ventured Stella.

Matteo cleared his throat. "It's bad. Worse than we suspected."

"How—" Domenica started.

"Organized crime."

A flopping sound from the stacks indicated two cats tousling. A bird called in the distance.

"The *Mafia*?" Stella's voice cracked as it rose an octave, her nails digging into her palm.

Matteo closed his eyes. He opened them and said, "Roberto and

Romina have gotten mixed up in something awful."

Stella broke out laughing.

His eyes fixed on her, Matteo said to Domenica, "Has she gone insane?"

Stella tried to catch her breath, pinching her side. Then she said, "The Mafia! The *mob*!" and burst out laughing again.

Frowning, Matteo said, "Stella. It's not funny."

Stella gasped, trying to catch her breath. "Roberto and Romina? In the mob? This has to be a joke!"

Domenica regarded Matteo. "It does seem improbable, Matteo."

Matteo flung himself back into the armchair. "Don't you think I said that to Giancarlo?"

"And?" Domenica prompted, raising her voice over the sound of Stella's laughing which had quieted, but still bubbled out erratically. "What did he say?"

He sighed. "He told me that some small men make great goalkeepers."

Stella sat up straighter, her hand still pressing her side. "Is that code for something?"

Domenica nodded slowly. "You can't judge a book by its cover."

Stella scowled. "What are you two on about?"

Matteo took a breath. "I guess Giancarlo is saying that maybe Roberto and Romina's kindly shopkeeper act is just that—an act."

She frowned. "Or maybe they are in fact kindly shopkeepers and your facts are wrong."

"I know that would make you feel better—"

"It's not about me. It's Occam's razor—the simplest explanation is usually right."

"What?" Matteo blinked. He shook his head and held his hand up before she could explain. "It doesn't matter, Stella. It doesn't matter if they are actually affiliated with the Mafia—"

"Of course it matters!" she said hotly.

"It doesn't," Domenica said. "For our purposes here, now. It doesn't. Later we can debate whether Occam's razor holds or whether the very fact that we've had three murders in Aramezzo in the last year defies Occam's principle of parsimony. For now, the relevant information is that this explains why none of my hacking turned up where they are. Their Mafia connection—"

"Alleged Mafia connection," blurted Stella.

"Well done, Stella," Domenica grumbled as she rose to clear off the fabric clutter from the computer. "That will look far more judicious on the court transcript. In any case, now I know why I found nothing. The DIA has different firewalls; I should have guessed."

"DIA?" Stella said, suddenly serious.

"*Direzione Investigativa Antimafia*," Domenica muttered, the clatter of her typing filling the bookshop.

"Ah," Stella said. After a moment, she turned to Matteo, "What are they supposed to have done wrong?"

Matteo shrugged. "Giancarlo didn't know. Only that his source said the DIA is pressing charges. Which means whatever they are assumed to have done, it was as part of their involvement in the Mafia."

Domenica muttered to herself, the glow of the screen reflected in her glasses. When Stella couldn't make out the pages flying on and off the screen, she plucked Violetta from the ground and held her tightly.

The Mafia? *Impossible*!

But hadn't Domenica told her that there was a hole in Romina and Roberto's history, when Romina's sister ran the bar?

Stella's heart stopped. The Mafia. Maybe Romina's sister refused to leave Romina the bar for a reason. Matteo nudged Stella's leg. "You have thought face. What gives?" he whispered.

She shook her head, her eyes on Domenica, willing her to find something, anything that would suggest that these idle speculations were just that. Idle.

To herself, Domenica breathed, "Bingo." She spun in her chair to face them. "I can only access the arrest warrant. But … it's damning."

Stella's throat went dry.

"Go on," Matteo said, his wide eyes even wider.

Domenica took a breath. "Apparently, government officials have been monitoring Aramezzo for some time. From a tip they got a few months ago, they knew drugs were coming into Aramezzo, and money for those drugs was going back out. It took some time, but an officer infiltrated the operation and though no one revealed the accomplice's name, they managed to bug a bag of drugs."

"Bug a bag?" Matteo asked.

Domenica nodded. "Yes, put in a tracking device. Then, a shade over a week ago, it arrived at Bar Cappellina, where it was picked up by someone and tossed in the dumpster outside of town. Then it happened again."

"So," Stella said slowly, holding Violetta tighter against her chest. "They think that Roberto and Romina were using the bar to launder money?"

Glancing back at the screen, Domenica said, "That part is fuzzy. I think it's more likely that they presume Roberto and Romina transferred the drugs to runners for a cut of the profit. Though I suppose the theory goes that if they had this side hustle going, they would need to launder that money through the bar."

Matteo shook his head. "I can't see it. Maybe the Mafia was using the bar as a drop point without Roberto and Romina knowing."

Domenica paused to think. "How could Roberto and Romina not know? They know when a bottle of Aperol is out of place."

Stella remembered the briefcase. "But that bag was there the whole morning. None of us noticed. Is it impossible they didn't either?"

"Every time?" Domenica peered over her glasses at the screen. "Twice Roberto and Romina missed a bag sitting unattended in their bar?

Plus today?"

Stella said hopefully. "Maybe it wasn't unattended the other times. Maybe there was a quick handoff—somebody left the bag and the drug runner picked it up a few minutes later. But this time, the pick-up person was delayed. Or the Mafia arrived early."

Domenica shook her head. "Italians are never early."

Stella said, "I can't imagine normal rules apply to the Mafia. But sure, so the person picking up the drugs was delayed. And the bag sat." She had an idea. "Do the records indicate how long the bag was in Aramezzo each time?"

Whirling back to the computer, Domenica pushed her glasses higher on her nose to read the screen. She nodded and said, "You're on to something, Stella. Each of the other times, the bag arrived in Aramezzo and then left town in under a half hour. Given how long it takes to walk from the parking lot to the bar, it couldn't have sat in the bar for more than a few minutes."

Then Matteo shook his head. "Wait! You said the bag came from the mob, but then was picked up by somebody who took it away and dumped the bag, presumably keeping the drugs to pass along to smaller distributors. But Roberto and Romina, they never leave the bar! So it couldn't be them!"

Stella's heart sank. "They do though. Remember? Roberto leaves sometimes when Romina is away. He puts a sign that he's back in five. So in those moments neither of them is at the bar. I suppose someone could make the argument that the reason the bag sat this time was that the bar was full and they couldn't close it."

Domenica mused, "But they would really only need to take the drugs upstairs, right? They live right above the bar. It's hardly a long journey."

Stella shook her head irritably. "None of it makes sense. Maybe they were only middlemen, and someone else was picking it up. So they had to keep it there."

"Okay, if you have the Mafia on one side, who is on the other side, picking up the drugs?" Matteo trailed off and then said with a start, "Why is the government bothering with them anyway? DIA is shaking down the mob, why not find where the drugs started from and bust them? This part of the operation had to be small, right? Where the drugs came from … that's the place they should focus."

Domenica nodded. "They did. Apparently there were busts all up and down Italy today."

Matteo sagged back in his seat.

Domenica went on, "A coordinated effort so the higher ups didn't get wind and scatter. I suspect it's mass confusion, which is why no one is getting back to Luca. I can only imagine the amount of finger-pointing happening right now."

They sat in silence, processing.

"Aramezzo," Stella wondered aloud. "Why here?"

Domenica pressed her lips into a line. "Precisely because you ask the question. No better place to run drugs than in the last spot anyone would expect."

"Hidden in plain sight," Stella mumbled. If Aramezzo's innocence made it the perfect way-station, didn't that also mean that Roberto and Romina were the perfect runners? "They were framed," Stella said, sounding more convinced than she felt. "They had to be. Or it was a mistake. Maybe the real culprit got caught up in the bust elsewhere."

Domenica waved to the computer. "The thing is, the informant suspected Roberto and Romina even before they placed the bug."

"Why?" Stella asked.

"The arrest warrant doesn't say much, just that they knew it was a business in Aramezzo and then landed on the bar." Domenica ran her fingers over the keys, muttering, "I need to get deeper into the system."

Matteo said, "Maybe it's that money laundering thing you said, Stella."

Stella said, "But there are loads of businesses in Aramezzo. The *fruttivendolo*, the florist, the bakery, Cristiana's market." Awareness dawned. "Oh."

"What?" Domenica and Matteo said at the same time.

"All those are places frequented by locals. Some stranger coming in and dropping a bag, people would notice. But the bar, that's a place every visitor stops in. It's logical, really."

Matteo sputtered, "Trattoria Cavour! I see visitors there all the time! From Assisi, Foligno . . . even farther! I met someone there last week from Trieste!" His wild gesturing knocked a book off the end table. He picked it up, muttering.

"Trattoria Cavour only opens at night," Stella reminded him. "Anyway, since the drugs were actually found at Bar Cappellina, it doesn't seem like the informant was off base with that suspicion."

He bit off, "You want them to be guilty."

She lurched so hard, the cat sprung from her lap. She'd forgotten Violetta was there. "How can you say that? I'm not saying they did it, just that it makes sense that the runner used the bar."

"Oh," Matteo said, mollified. "Okay."

"Though," Stella said, "If they were laundering money, then that changes things. Do we know for sure that the site of the drop was the site of laundering?"

Domenica shook her head. "No, the informant didn't speculate."

Stella hesitated. "Are you still against checking Roberto and Romina's financials?"

"You do think they did it," Matteo said, softly.

"Of course not," Stella said. "But if their bank account shows a steady, expectable trickle of income, with no large deposits, well, then we'd be on a different path than if the opposite is true. We can help them better with more information."

Domenica shook her head. "I won't do it."

Stella crossed her arms over her chest.

"There are other ways." Domenica sighed, a sound Stella had rarely heard from her. "Stella don't you have guests coming tomorrow? Prepare for that, give yourself a break, we'll need you fresh and ready once we have new information on board. Matteo, get back to work before anyone notices you've ducked out yet again."

They started to argue, Stella pointing out that changing the sheets didn't take hours and Matteo reminding Domenica that he was off duty. Domenica held up a hand. "I need to get deeper into the system, which will be easier without you two looking over my shoulder." She smiled to soften the words. "Let me fly solo the rest of the day. See if I find anything. At least where they are being held."

Stella sighed. "We'll think through who could be running drugs through Aramezzo."

"It can't be Roberto and Romina." Matteo pulled his chin."But then who?"

Stella set her jaw. "That's what we need to find out."

Stella trudged home, feeling like she was tugging her body through warm molasses. How could she think when this crackling heat singed her thoughts?

Stella felt the need to keep moving at the best of times; about the only way she could force her body to settle was with one hand wound in Barbanera's fur and the other holding an Italian mystery novel. Did she have a *giallo* on deck? No, she'd finished a mystery last night and had meant to see if Domenica had any in this morning. The arrest had banished the internal reminder.

No matter. She didn't feel like reading anyway. Peering up at the sun, Stella realized it was already afternoon. The day had sped away without her. Or maybe the heat clogged her awareness.

This was why Italians paused after lunch. The heat, the light, all a body longed for was the still and cool of a stone house.

Lunch.

She realized she'd fed Barbanera but had neglected to feed herself. Her mind turned to the contents of her pantry…could she bake something? No, it was too hot. It occurred to her that she always baked her way toward clarity when things spun out of control. She longed for American air conditioning.

Yes, she nodded along when villagers mocked Americans' need to live in an icebox, but she secretly wished to feel the prick of cold cutting through the muggy heat.

Maybe this could all be sorted out without baking.

As she walked home, she ran through the leftovers in her refrigerator. She'd taken a plateful of the pasta with meat sauce that she'd served her guest last night and put it aside for herself, proud that she'd remembered, finally, to hold back a little for her own hungry moments.

She'd pan-fry the pasta in plenty of olive oil. Italians would tremble in horror at reheated pasta, but she loved how the oil caramelized the starch of the pasta, making delicious crispy bits. Maybe she'd toss in a handful of *caciotta* cheese. She wondered why *caciotta* wasn't available in the States. It melted as well as mozzarella, but with more nuanced flavor. She always considered mozzarella in a perpetual identity crisis.

Her mind turned back to the pasta she was already cooking in her head. A scatter of fresh basil would bring it home.

Within twenty minutes she was sitting at the table, slurping up the pasta, delighting in the shatter of burned edges. She had to remember to slow down. Soon enough she'd polished off the pasta, including every leaf of basil. Moderation—a skill Stella had yet to master.

Staring at the empty plate, the day forced itself back into her consciousness. Drumming her fingers on either side of her placemat, Stella's mind roiled. Could Roberto and Romina really be connected to the Mafia?

She shook her head.

Stella didn't know much about the Mafia, but she remembered, probably from books or movies, that people joined the mob for one of two reasons—power or money.

Power or money.

Stella pushed her plate away.

She thought of Roberto, proudly polishing the dented steel of their espresso machine. How Romina slid the clasp of her simple gold chain to its rightful place below her bun when it caught in the crucifix pendant she wore every day.

Roberto and Romina seemed to want what they had. Wasn't this the recipe for happiness?

No way they'd be lured by money.

But they mortgaged the bar. Why?

The fan ticked above her, lazily.

Maybe they didn't have everything they wanted if the bar was in jeopardy.

No, Stella thought. She couldn't wrap her mind around their getting drugs into addicts' hands. No matter what their financial woes might be.

But that meant someone else, maybe a neighbor, was working with the Mafia.

Stella picked up her dishes with a clatter. She yanked her apron over her head, releasing a cloud of flour. Washing the dishes, she wondered . . . who? Who would run drugs through Aramezzo?

Power or money.

Power. The mayor? She shook her head. He already had power—or what passes for power in a medieval village. Besides, as much as she despised the man, she didn't figure him for putting his constituents at risk. And even if his soul was as blackened as a well-used cast-iron pan, there was no way he had the mental acuity for this kind of sleight of hand.

She couldn't think of anyone interested in elevating their lot in life.

They all seemed satisfied, more than satisfied, with the small circles their life inscribed on the canvas of Aramezzo—work, battered pans to make an evening sauce, and stirring a little sugar into their coffee in the morning.

Maybe power wasn't the driver, but something akin to power.

Respect.

But respect, too, was so amorphous. Nobody stood out.

Money.

Money was tangible. Maybe someone had a debt. A debt they'd inadvertently hinted at. Or someone wanted something costly, more than their small circle in life entitled them to.

A click into place. Yes. In a town this small, she must have heard something about a villager needing or wanting more money. But who?

Her fingers itched.

She needed to cook.

Barbanera strolled in, sniffed at his empty saucer and sat in front of it as if asking when he could expect another serving.

Stella grinned. She flung open the refrigerator and pulled out the jug of milk. Did she have any cream? Yes, there, just enough, right behind the jar of *giardiniera*. Matteo had once impulsively tossed *giardiniera* onto pizza she fired in her wood-burning oven, and now neither of them could think of pizza without pickled vegetables.

Panna cotta. She needed only to warm the milk and stir in gelatin... Did she still have gelatin? She yanked open her drawer of baking spices and sighed in relief. Yes, plenty.

It would come together quickly, maybe too quickly for her to untangle who might be motivated enough to work with the mob, but maybe it would still her mind just enough that preparing for her next guests would seal the deal.

She added gelatin leaves to a bowl of water, wondering how to flavor her *panna cotta*. The creamy milk created a blank canvas, perfect for letting creativity fly. She thought for a moment. Something vanilla-ish, but not vanilla. Peppercorns! That would give the milk almost vanilla notes, but with a little kick. To complement the peppercorns…Closing her eyes, she imagined orange zest…and bay leaves. From her bay leaf bush, a never-tiring miracle.

As Stella zested the orange and rubbed it into the sugar, she considered: Had anybody in town mentioned having money trouble?

She poured milk into a saucepan and added a bay leaf and a fall of peppercorns. The woman who helped Stella with the *casale* had taken a hit when her husband fell off a ladder. For a while, money had been tight. But once he'd recovered, they'd both worked double-time to get back on top. Nothing that suggested drug-running for the mob.

Watching bubbles form on the side of the saucepan, she thought through the other townspeople she knew. She turned off the flame, allowing the flavorings to steep.

She couldn't think of anybody who struggled financially—which struck her as strange, until she remembered homes were passed down. Plus, citizens didn't have to worry about health care. Even food costs were low here. She regularly left Pia's *fruttivendolo*, where she bought all her fruits and vegetables unless Cristiana had a produce box beside the cash register—some local gardener always seemed to have extra *puntarelle* or fennel to sell—with two bags heaving with shining tomatoes from Puglia, thin-skinned eggplant from Sicily, and a new kind of local melon so sweet it took her breath away, all for ten euros.

Squeezing water from the gelatin leaves, Stella listened to the buzz of cicadas outside.

Minimal health care costs, inherited housing, and access to inexpensive food leveled the social playing field. No wonder she saw electrical engineers chatting with plumbers in the street; no wonder Matteo, who noted that newcomers to Aramezzo wanted to pretend he didn't exist as he swept the streets, was invited to birthday parties for stonemasons and doctors. Maybe it also had something to do with them all attending the same schools.

Adding the flavored sugar to the steaming milk, Stella realized that the exceptions to the egalitarian scene in Aramezzo were Luisella and the duo of Marcello and Veronica.

But did Luisella count? She held herself separate, certainly. But it didn't seem to come from a sense that the villagers of Aramezzo weren't good enough for her so much as she wielded privacy like a shield.

Still. Stella needed to think it through. Luisella…she dressed elegantly, but never showy. In fact, Stella always considered Luisella as having a kind of timeless elegance, like her clothes all came from Chanel, circa 1950. She had nothing new or noteworthy that would cast suspicion on her. Her car was old, but she never complained about wanting a new one.

Stella stirred the milk, listening to the whine of a Vespa in the distance.

The mayor and his wife had a new Mercedes. They crowed about it constantly. And wasn't Veronica always going on and on about exclusive parties in Rome that demanded yet another new gown?

Stella stopped stirring. That receipt, on the ground. Was it related after all? The deposit receipt. Maybe it wasn't insurance money. Stella thought of that slip of paper, lying innocently on the floor of Bar Capellina. Perhaps not so innocent after all.

At the thought of Bar Cappellina, Romina's face swam before her. Stella's stomach hitched and she focused again on stirring the milk. She inhaled, wondering if the peppercorns and bay leaves had steeped long enough. She closed her eyes and let the green and floral fruitiness drift over her like sunshine. Almost there. In the meantime, she readied old jelly and yogurt jars, washing them with plenty of soap and hot water before drying them with a clean towel. She inspected the hem of the linen—had her aunt made this one?

She shook her head. One mystery at a time…

Her mind returned to the bar, circling like a bird in a thermal draft.

Veronica…those gowns…they had to cost a pretty penny.

Stella tapped the spoon twice on the side of the pan.

There was no way Veronica would recycle an old dress the way Luisella did. The new car. Stella remembered with a start that when a rumor started floating around a few weeks ago that the Americans might sell Villa delle Acque, Veronica airily suggested that she and her husband were in the market for an upgrade. And then when no one said anything but continued sipping their coffee or pulling the end off a *cornetto* filled with apricot jam, Veronica delivered the news, again, only more loudly.

As it turned out, the Americans were not putting their house on the market. At least not now. Stella wondered if the rumor had been started by Veronica herself, just to be able to toss out that she had the means to buy a property with the leavings of an ancient aqueduct, which Cosimo believed meant the house sat on a Roman bath.

But how did Veronica have those means? A small-town mayor couldn't possibly earn a rich salary. Could the money come from her former film roles? Maybe she'd invested wisely.

Stella would have to ask Domenica tomorrow. If her friend refused to dig into her neighbors' bank accounts, maybe she could at least use her internet powers to estimate how much Veronica earned in her film days. And what had Marcello done before his career as Aramezzo's mayor?

If neither of them had the means to support all the designer dresses, expensive cars, and a fancy home, then it would make them suspects in a drug operation that accidentally caught Roberto and Romina in its web.

The spoon clattered to the floor. Until now she'd thought of it as a mistake—a bag left behind, bad luck, sloppy work. But what if it wasn't bad luck? What if someone wanted Roberto and Romina out of the way?

Could someone have purposefully left that bag of drugs in the bar uncollected in order to pin blame on the bar owners? Maybe that person even knew the drugs were being tracked…they could have seen something suspicious once while emptying the bag before tossing it into the dumpster. So they knew that the authorities were onto them. Then they made sure the blame was pinned on Roberto and Romina to get the focus off themselves.

Or maybe it was even more intentional. Maybe someone wanted Roberto and Romina out of the way.

But . . . who?

Roberto and Romina had no enemies.

Did they?

Nodding appreciatively at the waves of scent coming from the warm milk, Stella strained it into a large measuring cup before mixing in the gelatin sheets. Once the leaf faded into the milky liquid, Stella filled the jars and settled them into a roasting pan. Sliding the pan into the refrigerator, she calculated how long they'd take to set.

With a glance at the clock, she jumped. Where did the time go? Making *panna cotta* was the work of a quarter hour and it had been hours!

She darted into her room, tripping over Barbanera, stretched across the doorway.

What with all the stopping and thinking disguised as steeping and waiting, the minutes had evaporated like water in a hot pan.

Stella waved at Giancarlo, already seated outside Trattoria Cavour. Her steps slowed when she spied the white CLOSED sign on Bar Cappellina's door, glowing ghost-like in the darkness. Straightening her shoulders, she forced herself to keep walking.

"Sorry I'm late," she said, dropping into the seat.

Giancarlo shrugged with a small smile.

"Yes, yes, I'm always late. I'm always late. I wish I could give you credit for a groundbreaking observation, but it'll probably be emblazoned on my tombstone."

His small smile stretched to a grin, which lit his green eyes. "What I'm wondering is what you've been cooking that held you up?"

She looked down at her outfit. "How did you know I've been cooking?"

He leaned forward and brushed her cheek. She smelled the faint dust of flour more than she felt it on her face. "But I didn't even use—" she remembered. "Oh. It must have come off the apron when I pulled it on. Or off."

"That would do it."

"Well, Giancarlo," Stella said expansively, holding out her arms. "Now you know the wicked truth. I'm a mess. Pretty much full time. I can only manage punctuality by accident and I wear cooking products like make-up. And I should tell you now, in case it's escaped your notice, that I'm terrible about returning texts."

"Or phone calls."

She sighed. "You *have* noticed."

He chuckled and took her hand in his. How many of her previous relationships cracked when her boyfriend took her scattered approach to life personally? Maybe this was an advantage of dating someone so sure of himself.

Stella said, "Dating me is a nonstop thrill ride. Beware."

His eyes found hers and searched them for a moment. He switched to English to say, "I'll take that ride."

Stella hoped the gathering darkness cloaked the blush creeping up her cheeks. Instantly, she felt awash in shame. How could she be engaging in banter when her friends...her friends...she couldn't even finish the sentence.

"You okay, Stella?" Giancarlo leaned closer.

She bit her lip. "Fine. Just...you know."

"The heat," nodded Giancarlo.

"No. Roberta and Romina." Stella frowned.

"Of course," Giancarlo said easily.

"Did you need menus?" Adele asked, arriving at their table.

Stella said, "Better leave one. He hasn't memorized it like I have. Any specials?"

"Umbricelli with sausage and greens."

Stella loved umbricelli. The pasta's flour and water chew reminded her of ramen. "What kind of greens?"

Adele shrugged. "Whatever I found on the mountain."

Stella's eyes widened. This place never failed to surprise her. She wondered if she'd ever go back to fine dining with its tweezers and foams after this period of time feasting on sun-warmed greens pulled fresh from the earth in the morning and sautéed with oil from the olive trees stretching out around them.

Maybe this could be her restaurant hook. Elevated dining, but grounded in Umbrian sensibilities. She scanned through her old menus. Grilled lamb chop—yes. But with roasted garlic purée. Lighter, maybe. Rosemary? Too blunt. Rosemary flower. That worked. And those yellow potatoes, the nameless ones from some town nearby. Could she get them in New York when she didn't know what they were called?

She startled at his gaze. "Oh, um. Yes, that sounds perfect. I'll have that."

Giancarlo pushed the menu away. "I'll have the same. And a salad."

"To drink?" Adele asked, scribbling their orders in her mini-notebook.

Giancarlo seemed to read her mind. "Too hot for red. How about a bottle of white, Stella?"

"You pick." She pulled off the scarf wound around her head and used it to tie her hair into a loose ponytail.

Adele walked away and Giancarlo leaned forward again, this time to tuck a stray tendril of Stella's hair behind her ear. "I like your hair this way. It makes curls around your face."

Stella couldn't help but smile at his phrasing.

Then her face fell.

Giancarlo leaned close to her, his hand on her knee. "Detectives not only go shopping, they also eat dinner."

She blinked, confused, before remembering.

He went on, "You need to eat. You might as well enjoy it, fill your tank."

She nodded. "Domenica said something like that."

With a grin, he said in English, "Great minds."

Adele's husband Vincenzo arrived, plunking down the bottle before fishing around his apron for the corkscrew. As he ripped the foil from the neck of the bottle he gestured to Bar Cappellina, camouflaged in the darkness of the piazza. "Good riddance, am I right?"

Stella looked up. Of course. Vincenzo's old gripe: without the bar, *aperitivo* crowds would drift to Trattoria Cavour, to sip his wine, ordering a plate of the region's salami and *torta al testo*.

If Vincenzo begrudged the bar, Adele relished it—leaning across the marble counter with Romina, laughing until they wiped their eyes. The two even swapped spare keys to cover for each other during holidays.

Stella narrowed her eyes at Vincenzo as he poured the wine.

He went on, "It's about time somebody picked them up. I always thought it would be because of whatever they put in the coffee to keep people coming back day after day."

Stella's hand stalled in its arc to pick up her glass.

A shutter clacked open in the distance to catch and hold the evening breeze.

Vincenzo said, "But lately I realized something far worse. They use fake ice cubes! That's why they don't melt. Leeching microplastics into everyone's drinks." He chuckled to himself. "It's about time someone got wise to their scheme."

Oblivious of Stella and Giancarlo's stares, Vincenzo wandered back into the restaurant.

"That man," Stella grumbled. "I'm never unhappy to see him walking away."

Giancarlo shook his head. "Quite a chip on his shoulder."

"As if the world did him wrong," Stella nodded. "I wish he cooked instead of Adele so we'd have better table-side company."

Giancarlo paused and smiled before saying, "But if his cooking is like his personality..."

"Terrible!" Stella said with a smile.

Giancarlo poured the Grechetto. Stella lifted the glass and took an introductory sip. "I love this wine. I can't believe I never had it until I came here."

"I don't think I've met anyone in England who has heard of it." Giancarlo said. "Then again, I don't hang out with foodies and sommeliers. But don't chefs know about wine?"

"Not this chef," Stella said, settling back and trying to focus on enjoying her limited time with Giancarlo. Still, her thoughts flew to Adele's husband. He clearly wanted Roberto and Romina out of Aramezzo's culinary picture... could he have done something?

She corralled her thoughts. "Did you hear any more from your contacts? About Roberto and Romina?" She flinched at her abrupt segue.

He gestured to his phone on the table. "As soon as I do, you'll be the first to know."

She nodded and tried again. "So tell me, Giancarlo. How hard has it been for you, not playing soccer?"

"Oh, you know. You never like to be injured." He grinned and touched her hand lightly. "But somehow I'm keeping the ball rolling."

Stella took another sip, delighting in the flavor—almost like lychee, a South Asian fruit she hadn't had since moving to Italy. "But to go from whole days being built around training and pushing yourself physically... the loss of endorphins alone must be rough."

"I have plenty of endorphins," Giancarlo said softly with a knowing smile.

Adele arrived with their plates.

Giancarlo watched Stella breathe in the steam from her pasta before twirling strands around her fork and lifting them to her mouth. She had to stifle a sigh of pleasure—the vibrancy of the greens tamed by the earthiness of the sausage.

Giancarlo grinned at her delight. He took his own first bite. "Good." He nodded perfunctorily.

She put down her fork. "Good? That's it?" She could have written a sonnet to the slippery pasta, heady with flavor.

He frowned. "Isn't it good?"

She shook her head. The pasta probably had more sausage or less red pepper flakes than his mother's. "Did you get to your grandmother before she heard the news?"

He swallowed with a nod. "Just in time. Signora Crespi stopped by right after I got home."

"Signora Crespi?"

"You've met. This morning. The woman who made it rain coffee cups," he chuckled warmly at his joke.

"I can't believe the Aramezzo gossip train failed your grandmother so. That must have been hours after it happened."

He shrugged. "My mother tried to tell her earlier. She called from my brother's house in Foligno after she heard from Cristiana. But you know my grandmother loses track of her phone. So really she has only herself to blame for being behind."

"Brother? I didn't know you had a brother."

After a pause, Giancarlo said, "We're not close."

"Really? Why?" she blurted. Her thoughts darted to Signora Crespi, hiding at the window to glean information. Stella winced inwardly.

He shrugged.

Stella added softly, "I'm sorry about that. I loved feeling close to Grazie."

With a frown, he said, "If she didn't die, that would have changed. Siblings wind up with different lives."

Stella went quiet, her hands still in her lap. "No," she whispered. "Not me and Grazie."

He held her hand for a moment and poured her another glass of wine.

As her thoughts spun from one loss to another, she forced her mind home. She coughed.

Giancarlo leaned forward, concerned. "You okay? I hope you're not getting sick." At the thought, he scooted backward, his chair scraping against the stone.

"Something stuck in my throat."

She smiled at the look of relief that flooded Giancarlo's face. As someone who always seemed on top of the game, she found it rather charming to see him so disarmed by the thought of a virus.

At her smile he leaned forward. "I'm glad you're not sick." He scooted forward another few inches and placed his hand on her cheek. He leaned a little further to brush his lips against hers.

She kept her eyes closed long after he pulled away. When she opened them, she saw Adele's husband Vincenzo smirking.

Giancarlo asked for the check and Vincenzo pushed himself off the wall to drop the bill folder on the table saying, "In light of some changes around here, we're going to be open more of the day."

Stella stared at him. "Looks like you're finding the upside to not having the bar open."

Vincenzo shrugged. "You pick the figs before the birds do."

Stella watched him leave, her jaw tight.

"You keep slipping away," Giancarlo said with a frown.

She smiled. "Sorry. He's just…it's probably nothing."

She reached for her purse as Giancarlo said, "I've got this." He waved away her protestations that he paid for the last meal. And the one before. "Let me spoil you," he said, tucking a few bills in the folder. "You might like it." He took her hand, pulling her arm through his. "Fancy a moonlit walk?"

She looked back at the restaurant. Through the window she watched Adele toss pasta in sauce before plating it. "I'll be right back," she said, withdrawing her arm from Giancarlo's.

"Where—"

"Nature calls."

Once in the restaurant, she scanned for any signs of drug running. Little plastic envelopes?

Her eye caught on the overflowing trash.

Casting a glance over her shoulder to check that Adele had her hands full at the stove and Vincenzo still lurked outside, Stella pulled a collapsed shipping box from the can—hardly sinister. A wine spill obscured the sender's name. Beneath the box lay only crumpled paper towels. Was she desperate enough to dig through them?

At the sound of footsteps, Stella dropped the shipping box back into the can and pushed open the door of the ladies room. She waited, catching her breath.

She washed her hands, running the cool water over her wrists and her hand across the nape of her neck. Opening the door a crack, she peered out.

Strolling, she hoped casually, she met Giancarlo in the piazza.

He pulled her closer and put his forehead against her own. "So. About that walk."

She bit her lip. "I ... I can't. There's something I have to do."

His eyebrows lifted. "This late at night? Should I be worried?"

Her mind elsewhere, it took a moment to catch his meaning. She affected a laugh. "Not remotely. It's just…I just need…" Her eyes slid to the bar.

Giancarlo's face broke into a smile. "You're on to something!"

She shrugged. "Probably not. But that was weird, right…what Vincenzo said?'

"You'll have to narrow it down for me."

Stella chuckled. "All of it, I guess. I mean, doesn't he seem *too* happy to have the bar closed?"

"Not a surprise. He never liked them." He paused. "Are you thinking he had something to do with the arrest?"

"I mean, probably not, right?" Stella hedged. "Only that thing he said at the end about being open for more hours. It made me think…it's probably stupid."

"It's probably no such thing." Giancarlo tucked a curl behind her ear. "You want to do some sleuthing?"

She kept her gaze low until finally lifting it, caught by his steady waiting. "Yes."

He took her hand. "Where do we start?"

"You want to come with me? It's not very…romantic."

Giancarlo pulled her gently toward him and kissed one cheek and then the other. His face against hers, he inhaled deeply. "If you're with me, it's always romantic. Even garbage runs."

Her stomach once again swooped stupidly. Stammering, she said, "I scanned the inside of the restaurant, I didn't see anything."

Giancarlo said, "Though they'd have to be pretty stupid to keep something incriminating where anyone could find it."

The briefcase. Hidden in plain sight. Maybe that was the common theme here.

"Maybe in the trash?" How many times could she dumpster dive in one day before it was officially a problem?

Giancarlo gestured to the bins at the end of the piazza. "If you're okay with an audience."

"That's the trash?" Stella said. "I thought the bins would be in an alley."

Giancarlo nodded. "Usually, yes. But the villagers in the alley behind the restaurant petitioned to have the bins moved. I remember Vincenzo was bent out of shape about it."

Stella nodded slowly. Her hands itched to bake. Finally, she said, "Adele and Vincenzo live above the restaurant, don't they?"

"Yes. Why?"

"Where does their trash go? With the restaurant bins? Or in the alley?"

Stella watched Giancarlo thinking. His eyes widened. "Only one way to find out." He grabbed her hand and pulled her through the piazza, turning left onto the main road and then left again into the alley.

They stopped. "No bins," Stella said, disappointment heavy in her voice.

"I guess tomorrow isn't trash day." He laughed. "Were you so eager to go through garbage?"

She shifted uneasily. "Kind of? But ..." She stopped and lifted her nose.

"Stella? What is it?"

"Something burning. Or burned. But not that long ago." Breathless, she moved to the recess in the wall. The wood-burning oven, built into the wall, a leftover from days when most of the cooking in Aramezzo happened in the streets, neighbors rotating pizzas, shoving a chicken toward the ash. "Is this theirs, do you think? Adele and Vincenzo's?"

Giancarlo backed up to evaluate which door went with the oven. "I think so. That's their door."

"How do you know?"

He pointed at the aprons hanging from the window.

She put her hand close to the oven. "They burned something in here recently. Today."

Giancarlo's eyes widened as he replicated her movements, holding his hand close to the warm door of the oven. He took out his phone, flicked on the flashlight and nodded to Stella.

She nodded back and pulled open the metal door, wincing at the dramatic squeak, far louder than the fading cicadas. Giancarlo shone the light into the oven as she inhaled the scent of scorched paper. Her hand trembled as she reached in and pulled out a piece of cardboard.

"What is it?" whispered Giancarlo.

"I can't tell." Stella ran the light over the surface of the cardboard. "It looks like a box of espresso cups. Lavazza brand."

"Okay," said Giancarlo. "That's not weird, though, right? They serve espresso. I don't like it after dinner, but some people do."

"Technically they make espresso, though their machine is pretty weak." She closed her eyes. "And they use Segafredo beans, not Lavazza." Her eyes opened. "Roberto and Romina use Lavazza coffee, that's why they have Lavazza cups."

She heard Giancarlo take a sharp intake of breath. "Adele and Vincenzo must have raced out to buy a box of these cups to resemble the bar's."

Stella remembered the shipping box in the trash and almost dropped the charred cardboard in her rush to explain. "Bars and restaurants contract with coffee bean vendors. They don't buy the cups, they come with the contract. Which means Adela and Vincenzo switched their supplier to Lavazza. And they must have done that some time ago since they already have the cups."

His voice quickened in the darkness. "Like they knew they'd be getting the bar's business?"

"Let's find out," Stella marched out of the alley, into the piazza, and seeing Vincenzo talking to a customer, she walked into the restaurant and stood next to the kitchen door.

Adele glanced up at her. "I don't have time for recipe swapping now, Stella. We're slammed. Why a closed bar means a packed restaurant, I have no idea."

Stella held up the box fragment. "I found this outside, Adele," she said. "I wonder if it's yours?"

Wiping sweat from her brow, Adele narrowed her eyes. Her voice tight, she said, "Stella, I just told you I don't have time to talk. Especially about the trash." She blinked quickly and turned back to the oil hissing and spattering on the range.

Giancarlo pulled Stella outside. "You won't get anything from her."

"Did you see how she reacted when she saw the box? And she all but admitted it was theirs."

"She said it was trash, which it clearly is."

"But did you see all the blinking? I mean, that's a tell."

"I don't know. She was fighting to keep on top of a losing game. Weren't she and Romina close?"

Stella sighed. "I guess you're right. I probably over-interpreted her reaction." She looked up. "Vincenzo, though. He wanted the bar closed; maybe he's acting without Adele's knowledge?"

Giancarlo glanced at Vincenzo, now scrolling on his phone. "Let me handle it."

"What?"

"Vincenzo is the kind of guy a woman needs to flirt with to get anything out of him." She opened her mouth to protest and he held up a hand. "It's been a trying day. Watching you flirt would do me in."

She nodded, reluctantly. Then said, "Do you want this?" She held up the singed cardboard.

His eyes fixed on Vincenzo, Giancarlo said, "I think I need a different approach."

Stella watched him sidle up to Vincenzo. Within moments, they were guffawing. Vincenzo's fast shuffling feet suggested they were talking about a soccer game.

Giancarlo ducked his head and spoke seriously to Vincenzo. After a whispered conference, Giancarlo slapped him on the back and returned to Stella, "Let's go before he figures it out."

"Figures what out?"

"What he just told me."

"What did he just tell you?"

"Stella," he said and took her arm, ushering her out of the piazza. Once clear, he said, "I buttered him up, talking about how he always knows something is going down before it does. Like he can call a play before anyone knows we're on offense."

"What does it have to do with this?" She waved the cardboard.

"Nothing to do with the cardboard, the box just gave me the idea. Listen, it doesn't matter what I said, what matters is what he said."

"And?" Stella waited as Giancarlo took a breath. "*And?*"

"He said, 'Some people read the news, I read the signs.'"

Stella stopped walking. "He said that?"

"He did."

"That sounds incriminating, right?" Stella said, walking again. "You called it. He was powerless in the face of your fame."

Now, Giancarlo stopped walking and faced her. "You play it pretty cool. But does the fame do anything for you?"

She laughed. "Probably not as much as your ability to get Vincenzo to talk to you. That is impressive."

He moved closer, ducked his head against her ear. "Is it now?"

"Mm-hmm," she breathed, concentrating on not letting her knees give out as he ran his finger down her cheek, pausing at her lips.

"Stella?"

"Mmm," she murmured nestling a touch closer.

"Is it yet time for us to take this show from the road and into your house?"

Her body went still, as if even a thread of steam might tip her answer the wrong way.

"I'm not trying to rush you," he added, kissing her neck. At her silence he moved closer. "Are you considering it?"

A sudden image swam into focus. Barbanera gazing imperiously at Giancarlo. "Not tonight." It wasn't because of the cat. But she felt relieved when she said it.

He nodded and threaded her arm back through his. "There's time."

A noise from down the road caught her attention.

A kind of rhythmic slapping echoed within the tunnel. "What is that?" Stella asked.

"Somebody is coming," Giancarlo said, peering into the darkness.

"Now? By foot?"

He didn't answer, but gestured for her to stay put while he strode toward the sound. Stella heard a mangled shriek and then her name. "Stella!" Giancarlo called.

Stella ran toward his voice and found him supporting a man, half carrying him up the tunnel's stairs.

Leo—out of breath, sagging, shoes scraping stone as he leaned on Giancarlo.

"Leo?" Stella peered into his face. "Are you okay? What happened?"

He shook his head. "I need to get to Marta's. I was supposed to tuck Ascanio in. I promised him a race car story. She'll be worried sick. I don't have my phone."

"I'll text her," Stella said, reaching into her purse.

"No," Leo said, shaking his head as he gasped for breath. "It doesn't matter. I'm almost there."

Giancarlo lifted Leo higher against his side so his feet could find purchase on the cobblestones. Stella moved to Leo's other side. "But Leo, what happened? Did you get into an accident?"

He shook his head, muttering incoherently.

"What?" Stella asked, noticing Leo's clothes streaked with mud and grass stains, his face white and also dirtied. He smelled sharp, chemical.

Stella recognized the smell of panic, tainted by something more. "Leo!"

"I…I…" Leo started. "I hardly know. It happened so fast. But I think someone tried to run me over."

"What?" Stella and Giancarlo said in unison.

"I know it sounds crazy. But I was bringing the *porchetta* van home from the mechanic—"

"It's getting fixed again?" asked Giancarlo at the same time Stella sharpened, "At this hour?"

"I need the truck for the market tomorrow. I couldn't pick it up earlier because I needed a ride. Marta dropped me off after dinner; Rocco said he'd leave the keys in the van. I was on my way back when I ran out of gas." Leo's voice sharpened with annoyance. "Which means Rocco did not fix the gas gauge and yet somehow I got charged for it."

"So," Stella prodded. "The van ran out of gas. Then what?"

Leo didn't answer. Stella wondered if he'd heard her, maybe he was too caught up in the memory. Finally, he said, "I got out. I walked. What else could I do?" He tripped over the cobblestones and Stella felt Giancarlo hitch him higher.

Leo's voice, shaky in the darkness. Stella had never heard him sound so small. "That's when it happened. A few kilometers down the road, by the bend with the stone barn and the horses. A car came barreling down the road. I waved, thinking maybe they'd pick me up. But…but…"

Stella's throat tightened.

Beside her, Leo shivered. "It veered right toward me. I thought to pick me up. But then…it sped up. So fast. Right at me."

She inhaled sharply. "What did you do?"

"I dove off the road."

"Down the mountain?" Stella whispered. How did he survive?

"I got lucky, somehow. A tree stopped my fall." He put his hand against his ribs and winced. Giancarlo clocked the motion and exchanged glances with Stella. Broken rib?

Leo shook his head, as if hearing their concern. "It's my hand I'm worried about. I hope it's not broken again. Since the accident, it's prone to re-injury."

Giancarlo whispered low, "I watched that race. You were lucky it wasn't worse."

"You were there?" Leo regarded Giancarlo with surprise.

Giancarlo nodded. "I think everyone in Umbria showed up for at least one of your races. Never seen anything like it, the way you controlled the track."

"Well, that's over so I'm not sure what good it does to talk about it," Leo snapped. Instantly contrite, he said, "I'm sorry. I know I should be thankful that I lived through that accident. But thanks were difficult when my hand was so full of pins it looked like a hedgehog."

Giancarlo said, "Don't apologize. Nothing like it when an injury takes you out. It's the sound that sticks with me. I would have bet money my knee exploded."

Stella said, "Okay, but Leo. Tonight? After you dove off the road?"

"I waited there for what seemed like hours. Not moving. I . . . I was scared to go back up there," he said before switching to a defensive tone. "You would be too! If someone had nearly mowed you down."

Giancarlo lifted his hands. "No argument from me."

Stella said, "You did the right thing."

Leo shook his head. "I crept along below the road until I was sure the car was gone. Then I climbed up the rest of the way and started running. It wasn't until I was halfway here that I realized the fall must have thrown my phone from my pocket."

Outside Marta's door, Leo withdrew his arm from Giancarlo's neck. "I got it, thanks," he said before murmuring, "She's going to be worried sick."

Stella held out a hand. "Wait! Can you remember anything about the car? There aren't that many on the road to Aramezzo at this hour. Do you remember what kind of car it was?"

Giancarlo's eyes widened at her question before he said with a grin, "And now, ladies and gentlemen, she's got her eye on the net."

Leo didn't seem to hear him, his eyes closed as he thought. "No, it was just a car. Actually, hang on. It could have been a truck. The headlights were higher. But I can't be sure. It all happened so fast. Maybe after I settle down..."

Stella nodded. She put a hand on his arm. "I get it. Of course. Maybe tomorrow..."

Leo said firmly, "Tomorrow I'm going straight to the carabinieri. They need to know there's a killer on the road."

SATURDAY

Stella couldn't sleep.

All night, she tossed and turned, the words ringing through her mind: *A killer on the road.* By early morning, Barbanera had enough and stalked to the kitchen.

A killer. On the *road*. The words continued to swirl until they lost all meaning.

Might Leo have over-interpreted someone swerving toward him? Maybe someone had looked down at their phone, yanking the wheel when they glanced back up because they saw the edge of the road approaching.

Or maybe someone had attempted to mow him down.

Her thoughts slid to Roberto and Romina, the memory of their arrest overlapping with Leo's story.

The situations were entirely different, but one thing she'd learned in the kitchen—timing is everything. It can't be a coincidence when two ground-shaking events happen on the same day. They had to be connected.

Did one person have it in for all of them? Or perhaps they were both intentional, but unrelated, with different perpetrators. Or were they all accidents—a bag delayed in pick up? A mishap at the wheel?

Stella sighed and threw back the sheet. Her eyes ran over the half-unpacked boxes and papers she kept meaning to file, finally landing on the faded coverlet she'd tossed over her pile of clothes on the chair when the heat began its dramatic rise. Did Anna Maria make the coverlet, too?

Too early to go to Bar Cappellina for coffee.

She stopped.

No Bar Cappellina for coffee. Not for some time.

Barbanera leapt from the sofa and met her in the kitchen, rubbing against her legs for a moment, as if apologizing for leaving her alone with her thoughts. "It's okay," she scratched his head. "No use in us both being awake."

She spooned the last of the chicken liver into a chipped saucer with a raised pattern of flowers around the edge, before pulling a neatly-labeled container from the stack in the freezer to defrost for his lunch.

As she spooned coffee into the silver moka with a metallic clink, Stella thanked her years of cross-checking ingredients for instilling habits that overrode her innately disorganized state.

"Mess," that was the word her mother used. Or "disaster."

The coffee gurgled in the moka pot.

Stella's mother never failed to comment on how Grazie, two years younger than Stella, could clean her room in fifteen minutes while Stella could be found an hour later with her head in a toy bin she'd forgotten about, trying to fit a Barbie into a dress she'd made from an orphaned sock.

Stella checked the clock and groaned. Still too early to head to Domenica's.

Domenica would have found something that would help them free Roberto and Romina. She had to.

She opened the shutters to gaze out on the hills, barely illuminated by the weak sunlight. Her hand ran down the wooden slats. With a sigh, she latched the shutters closed.

How had Leo and Marta weathered the night?

Would Leo's history driving race cars make last night's vehicle assault particularly difficult for him? Kind of like if her bin of flour exploded, choking her with plumes of gluten. She smiled a little at the image.

Anyway, maybe it was the opposite. Just as she shrugged off burns and cuts in the kitchen, maybe Leo was so used to the adrenaline of the racetrack, he'd easily move beyond the moments of terror and settle back into his languid life in his *porchetta* van.

She hoped so. Mostly because he needed to collect himself, to offer up details he couldn't last night. But also because she'd grown to rely on those sandwiches of herbed and rolled and roasted pork as part of her Saturday ritual. She supposed that with the van on the side of the road, she couldn't hope for her favorite Saturday lunch, even if a good night's sleep helped Leo feel like his usual self. Maybe next week.

And maybe next week, Roberto and Romina would be back where they should be, at the De'Longhi espresso machine, caffeinating the masses of Aramezzo with their customary warmth and a little something sweet on the side.

She knocked back her coffee, sputtering and choking until Barbanera picked his head up and regarded her, food falling from his black chin. "I'm fine, I'm fine," she assured him.

He watched her for another moment as she grabbed a cup of water and swallowed, taming the cough.

Before her thoughts could enter challenging waters, she decided to complete the preparations she'd meant to do yesterday. Nabbing a *panna cotta* from the fridge, admiring its faint jiggle, she moved around the house. Taking a bite, eyes closed to savor the nuanced flavors anchored by creaminess, she stripped the beds and changed the towels.

She changed her clothes and packed a few *panna cotta* in a basket lined with a napkin. Stella imagined her mother's younger sister sewing the cloth's edges by lamplight, on the same spot on the couch where Stella read her Italian murder mysteries. Would Barbanera have curled beside Anna Maria like he nestled against Stella? Stella always assumed she'd been the one to tame the beast, but maybe his wildness had been grief at losing Anna Maria.

Stella stepped out into the morning, already bristling with heat. Barbanera appeared at her knees, lifting his head as if smelling which way the wind blew, then whirled back into the house to trot to a shadowy corner.

She nodded at Luisella, who dropped a bag of recycling at the foot of the steps. Luisella's eyes slid past Stella. Stella started to greet her, but Luisella turned into her house. The sound of the door latching filled the quiet street.

Stella adjusted the basket over her arm. Well, same dish, different day. The woman was nothing if not consistent.

At the bell's jangle over the bookshop door, Domenica whirled to face her with wide eyes. "Stella."

"Domenica?" Stella took in Domenica's wild hair and wan face. "Have you been up all night?"

"Have you?"

Stella nodded grimly. "Pretty much. What did you find?"

Domenica grumbled. "I'm stuck in a loop. This government database. Everything I try, like hurling leaves at an attacker. Nothing penetrates past the arrest warrant."

At the sight of Domenica's cowlick from where she'd pulled her hair all night, Stella's heart squeezed. "You'll get there."

Domenica rubbed her eyes. "A time or two I thought I was in, but then I hit another roadblock." She dropped her gaze to her hands, worrying over each other in her lap. "I failed."

"Hey, hey," Stella said, dropping the basket of *panna cotta* jars on Domenica's desk. "You didn't fail. It's the government's fault. It's really got some nerve setting up barriers to intrusion."

Domenica smiled weakly.

"I brought you *panna cotta*. I figured you'd be hungry."

Lifting the napkin, Domenica said, "I'm not sure what it says about me that you assume I'll eat three."

Flopping into the faded pink armchair, Stella said, "Matteo will be along soon."

Domenica pulled out a spoon from the jar of utensils next to her coffee pot. "Anyway, I sure hope you had better luck."

"I've been working on it and have some thoughts. But then I got derailed."

"By dessert workshopping." Domenica lifted a spoonful of the wobbly *panna cotta* to her mouth and closed her eyes. "Orange blossom?" she guessed.

"Orange zest. And bay leaf and peppercorns. But that's not what derailed me."

Domenica opened her eyes. "Sounds serious."

At the sound of the tingling bell, they darted fervent looks at the door.

"Matteo," Stella said, relieved. "Just in time."

He rushed in, out of breath. "Did you hear?"

Domenica's eyes narrowed. "Hear? Hear what?"

Stella said softly, "Leo?"

He nodded, eyes bulging.

Stella sighed. "Word gets around. Giancarlo, I suppose?"

Shaking his head, Matteo said, "I haven't seen him. Flavia over-heard Marta telling Orietta. She stopped me outside her flower shop this morning."

"Does anyone want to brief the old lady in the corner?" Domenica seethed.

"Sorry, Domenica," Stella said. "I was going in chronological order so hadn't gotten to this part yet. Last night, Leo's truck ran out of gas on the road to Aramezzo. While he was walking home, a car tried to run him over."

"*Tried* to run him over?"

"In that they didn't succeed. Leo flung himself off the side of the road.

Got beat up in the process, but he's mostly okay."

Domenica said, "Leo better go to the police."

"He said he would." They sat in silence for a few moments. Then Stella looked around. "Where's a cat when you need one?"

"Having breakfast," Domenica said, distractedly.

"Matteo," Stella remembered, "There's *panna cotta* in the basket."

He pressed his hand to his stomach. "Too nauseous."

She frowned. "Too nauseous?"

"This whole Leo situation. It's too intense." He cast his eyes on the basket. "What kind?"

"Orange, bay, and black pepper."

He nodded in thought. "Sounds either disgusting or fabulous."

She smiled wanly. "I guess I made haute cuisine *panna cotta* then. That's the line one walks."

Domenica waved her hand. "It's fabulous. Now, Stella. You've had all night to think about it. What have you come up with?"

"I've been spinning more than thinking, but last night at dinner..." Stella took a breath. "Vincenzo seemed thrilled about the arrest."

"You ruled out the trattoria because they're closed during the day," Matteo reminded her.

Domenica shook her head. "Besides, Adele adores Romina."

"Adele does. Her husband does not." She turned to Matteo. "Anyway, listen. I ruled out the trattoria but Vincenzo could have used the bar as the drop site. I think he might have wanted to shut down the bar. At dinner, Vincenzo said they're going to extend their hours."

Matteo and Domenica exchanged glances. Matteo reached for a *panna cotta*. "Seems pretty flimsy."

Stella pushed on. "There's more! Then after dinner, I found a box of espresso cups. Lavazza, like Roberto and Romina use."

"People buy cups, Stella. All the time," Domenica said.

Stella shook her head. "These were Lavazza. Which means Adele and

Vincenzo switched their supplier to Lavazza. Since they already have the cups, they must have switched to Roberto and Romina's supplier some time back."

Domenica's chair squeaked as she shifted. "That doesn't prove anything, right? Their coffee wasn't great, it makes sense they wanted to change suppliers. Maybe they were copying the bar, not trying to replace it."

"Their coffee is not great because Vincenzo doesn't know how to work the machine, but that's not the point," Stella said. "The box was burned."

Matteo said slowly, "Like they wanted to hide it."

Stella nodded. "Giancarlo asked Vincenzo about the cups, and Vincenzo practically admitted he had advance warning that he'd have an uptick in coffee sales. Since he's not the sharpest knife in the drawer, is it so impossible to believe Vincenzo got tangled in something bigger than he knew?"

Attila jumped onto the desk and Domenica petted him absently. "Okay, that is suspicious. But let's consider. We're talking about Vincenzo. He's pretty easily led to all kinds of strange statements. Is it possible Giancarlo set the stage and Vincenzo, being Vincenzo, walked onto it?"

Stella closed her eyes. The hum of the cicadas grew louder. "It's possible," Stella conceded.

Matteo nodded. "The guy hardly makes sense half the time."

"An unreliable narrator," Stella muttered in English.

"What?" said Matteo, his eyebrows furrowed.

Stella shrugged. "It's true the man is all foam, no flavor. Still, it's a lead. How do you feel about doing a little espionage work?"

"You mean rooting through trash?" Matteo grumbled.

"I tried to do it myself yesterday but the bins weren't out."

"And that would get tongues wagging. The American rooting through everyone's trash," Matteo said with a sigh. "Sure, I'll go through their trash when I pick it up on Wednesday. Just another perk of the job, right?"

"And the mayor," Stella said with a nod. "Veronica, too."

"The mayor? Veronica?" Matteo asked as his wide eyes grew wider.

Stella nodded. "They were so weird during the bust, didn't you notice?"

"I guess," he hedged. She'd forgotten how fervently he avoided the mayor's notice.

"And with their new car. And remember how Veronica was playing around with buying Villa delle Acque?"

Domenica frowned. "That's just Veronica. Always trying to impress."

"Exactly. What if she needed more money to impress?"

The room grew quiet. Matteo took a nibble of *panna cotta* and sighed faintly. He looked up. "Maybe you should watch Luisella."

"Luisella? Why?" Stella blinked in surprise.

"You heard Veronica's story of Luisella's reckless driving," Matteo said. He turned to Domenica, explaining, "Apparently she almost hit Veronica's dogs."

"Oh, come on Matteo, you know that's all toothless," Stella insisted.

Matteo shrugged. "Maybe it is. Maybe it's not."

"What would Luisella be doing out so late?" Stella muttered. "I don't see it."

Domenica said with a smile, "That's because you're fond of her."

Stella said, "I wouldn't say I'm fond of Luisella."

Harrumphing, Domenica said, "Are you kidding? Whenever that woman says the vaguest pleasantry to you, you crow about it all day."

"I don't crow. I never crow," Stella said crossly.

"Then tell us why she couldn't be a suspect."

Stella said, "She's been wearing the same few suits on rotation since I arrived and she seems perfectly happy with her battered Fiat Punto. And why would she have it in for Leo to run him off the road?"

Matteo protested, "Agreed on the Mafia, but why do the two events need to be connected? Maybe she's just a terrible driver."

"She never leaves Aramezzo. You think she's suddenly taken up moonlit joyriding?"

"Maybe she has a lover," Domenica said simply.

Matteo dropped his spoon and it clinked against his empty *panna cotta* jar. Stella paused mid-breath. They turned to Domenica like sunflowers toward an August sun.

"What?" Domenica shrugged.

Stella looked at Matteo as if to ask if he wanted to field this one.

"All you," he said, gesturing to the floor as if it were a stage.

"Domenica," Stella began. "Why reach for the most outlandish possibility? You could have said visiting an ailing sister, or picking up something so far away she had to return at night."

"Maybe she is picking up something. A lover."

"Domenica!" Stella gasped.

"Stella, you can be such a prude."

"Am not!"

Domenica grinned maddeningly.

Stella grumbled and said, "Domenica. When has Luisella shown any interest in male attention?"

"Why does it have to be male?" Domenica said, smugly.

Stella cast a furtive glance at Matteo before saying, "I was being all heteronormative again, wasn't I?"

"A bit, yes," Matteo said. "Though I agree with you. I mean, I'll never figure out how a woman who lived her entire adult life in New York City has gaydar so out of whack that you missed it in me—"

"How many times do I have to tell you, gaydar is reductive? And anyway, in New York, when people are out they are *out*."

"How many times do I have to tell you, I'm in no closet? But, Luisella? I'd be surprised myself," Matteo finished.

"Okay, okay," Domenica said. "I'm with you. But I don't like people making assumptions. And if Luisella wants to have a lesbian lover, I say have at it."

"Sure, fine," Stella said, exasperated now.

"I just don't think we can rule her out," said Matteo.

"Fair enough," Stella conceded. "I wonder if I can get her to talk to me."

"Bring Barbanera," Matteo said. "She has a soft spot for that cat."

"And something to eat," Domenica nodded. "Without Bar Cappellina I have no idea what she's eating for breakfast."

"Then I better get cracking," Stella said, rising.

Just as the bell over the door jingled again.

Cosimo shuffled into the bookshop, oblivious to the collective flinching in what Stella considered their Scooby gang. Hurriedly, the three of them hunted for books and cats to fling across their laps.

Stella grabbed a book from the table beside her and flipped through it, announcing, "I agree with Domenica. I keep picturing the main character of *The Goldfinch* as female. You don't?"

"Well, I'm only halfway through, and maybe it's different in translation," Matteo said pertly. From the corner of his mouth, he whispered, "That's a book of table etiquette. And it's upside down."

Cosimo bundled in, eyes bright. "Did you hear the news?" Spying Domenica's empty jar, he paused to peer into the basket. "*Panna cotta!*" he squealed, like a child opening a birthday present.

"Take one," Stella said, as Domenica plucked a spoon from the jar beside the hot plate and handed it to him with a square cloth napkin. Stella offered Cosimo her seat while she perched on the desk. Domenica stared at her but then accepted the intrusion.

"How delightful! Exactly what is needed on this tragic day." Cosimo spooned a bite with great flourish. He intoned cheerfully, "It is a dispiriting time, to be sure. But I am certain it will all fall right in the end, even if that looks different than any of us expected. I only wish the same could be said of the young woman." He raised a spoonful of the quivering *panna cotta* to his lips.

Stella practically fell from her perch on the desk. "Young woman? What young woman?"

"I rather wondered if she might be a guest of yours, Stella." He glared at the jar as if trying to identify its flavor profile before digging out another bite.

"The Copelands don't arrive until later today, and why when trouble falls do people always suspect my guests?"

Domenica shot a glance at her. Meanwhile, Cosimo merely shrugged and scooped out another bite. "She's not from here," he said, as if in answer to Stella's question.

Stella put a hand to her head.

"Cosimo, who is not from here? What happened?" Matteo asked with enviable patience.

Cosimo lowered the jar. He regarded the faces watching him intently. "I left early this morning when a colleague in Pissignano called to inform me that a vendor was rumored to be arriving for the antiques market with pieces of an ancient statue. A statue of Cybele, in point of fact."

"Cybele?" Stella asked. "The goddess who had a temple here, underneath the church to Santa Chiara?"

"You remember your lessons," Cosimo said fondly. "Of course, given how the blend of her power with Santa Chiara's led your cat to you, one can hardly be surprised."

Stella prompted, "So you left when you got the phone call…"

He nodded into his *panna cotta*. "I did, most certainly. Full of the mission! Can you imagine? The fair is tomorrow, I had to find this vendor before these precious remnants wound up piled on a table with old Roman coins."

Stella shifted on her perch and drummed her fingers on the desk. Domenica cut a glare at her and Stella stopped, instead tugging at the pendant of two intersecting coils that Cosimo insisted she wear to ward off the evil eye. She had never grown to like the charm, but still tucked it into her shoe when she and Matteo visited a swimming hole in the rippled hills of Monte Subasio.

Cosimo sighed lustily as if aware he was losing his audience. "Imagine my surprise when I almost ran over a body."

Stella's fingers tightened around the edge of the desk.

Matteo turned to stare at her, the whites of his eyes shining in the dim light.

Cosimo glanced around, rather like Barbanera when he caught a grasshopper.

"A . . . body?" Matteo said, haltingly. "Like . . . human?"

Chuckling warmly, Cosimo said, "I'd hardly classify the discovery of a dead porcupine as a tragedy, Matteo."

"But . . . who?" Domenica said. "Did you check?"

"Tell us what happened," Stella insisted, growing impatient. "Blow by blow."

He shrugged, adjusting the napkin over his lap. "Of course I checked. Even though it meant delaying my trip. Really, if these remains can be put together into a recognizable statue, it would set us forward immeasurably in our understanding of—"

"The body, Cosimo," Stella said, practically hissing like a teapot.

"Ah, yes. Of course, that would be the salient information for a woman like you." Stella flinched but the sting faded when she caught Cosimo's eyes, one blue and one green, crinkled in merriment. He went on, "I slammed on my brakes, as I said. At first, I assumed it to be a deer. But when I got out and approached, I quickly surmised it to be a woman."

"Dead?" Matteo's voice ratcheted up.

Cosimo nodded seriously. "Hence the word body, my child. Though I did call an ambulance just in case."

Stella felt Attila nudging her hand. She closed her eyes, running her fingers through his fur. She swallowed hard and asked, "Do you know who?"

"Decidedly not. Which is why I asked if you had guests." He ran his spoon around the inside of the jar, the faint sound filling the still bookshop.

"She wasn't as lucky as Leo," Stella said softly.

"Poor woman," Domenica murmured.

"Leo?" Cosimo frowned. "What does this have to do with Leo?"

Matteo said, "Leo was coming home last night when a car swerved toward him, almost hit him."

Cosimo paled. "You can't be serious. Leo? Who would want to hurt Leo?"

Shrugging, Stella said, "Who would want to hurt the woman in the road?" She straightened. "*Madonna mia.* My guest. They're supposed to arrive this afternoon, but what if they came early?" She turned to Cosimo. "Can you describe her at all? No, wait," Stella stopped herself. "I don't know what she looks like."

Cosimo offered, "Luca should be at the spot by now though, and I would assume he'll search enough to find—"

Stella sprang from the desk. "How far down the road, Cosimo?"

"Not far, at the first bend. If you wait, I'll drive you. The road should be clear soon, and I simply must—"

"No time!" Stella bolted to the door.

"Stella!" Domenica called after her.

"Not now, Domenica!" Stella said over her shoulder as she yanked the door open. "I have to see if it's Cindy Copeland."

"But Stella," said Domenica, "Signora Copeland is arriving with her husband, isn't she? Why would she be alone on the road?"

Stella whirled around to say, "Maybe there was an accident. Maybe she got thrown clear of the car."

"There wasn't a car," mused Cosimo.

But Stella's footsteps faded as the door banged shut.

       Stella didn't have to search for the body; the spinning lights of the police car and ambulance announced the location. She slowed her steps. Would there be gore? She minced her way forward. The woman lay curled in the road like a huddled shadow.

"Luca," she said as she approached him, leaning against the police car to scribble into his little notebook.

"Stella," he said grimly. He crossed his arms and looked over her shoulder. "Who told you?"

"Cosimo," she said.

"Right, Cosimo," he said before she finished the word.

"Listen, I'm sorry about yesterday. It got out of hand and I—"

"Forget it," Luca said, his expression hooded. "I have."

Her eyes searched his for a moment before she dropped them to the ground. With a sigh, she gestured to the body. "So, yeah, I need to make sure that's not my guest."

Leaning backward a touch, Luca called to Salvo, his voice clipped. "Salvo! Any identification?"

A tall officer with an impressive mustache emerged from around the far side of the police vehicle. "Negative."

Stella paused. "Nothing in her wallet?"

"No wallet. Or purse. Or even a phone."

Luca said, "Pockets?"

"Empty."

Luca and Stella said nothing. She adjusted her bandana. "You heard about Leo?"

Luca shifted his weight and fixed his gaze over her left shoulder. "He came in this morning."

"Does he remember anything about the car?"

Luca shook his head, still not looking at her. "His memories are pretty jumbled."

"Understandable," Stella said. She gestured vaguely. "I mean, that could have been him."

They stood side by side, watching as a man and woman leapt from the ambulance with a stretcher.

"Okay if I get closer?" She asked, unsure if she was asking for permission or hoping to get a sense of how grisly she should expect to find the scene.

He seemed to read her thoughts, even though he avoided her gaze. "It's tame as these things go. But unless you've seen a photo of your guest, I'm not sure how you'd recognize her."

"Maybe something will click," Stella said softly.

Luca called to the paramedics, "Hold up. Let Stella see if she can identify the body."

They paused. Stella recognized the paramedic from the murder at the villa just a few weeks ago.

As she approached, Stella ran through everything she knew about her guests. James Copeland's email address was from the Mayo Clinic, so he was probably a doctor of some sort. But that would hardly translate into something on his person, let alone his wife's. She wished this couple had come for a cycling tour as many did, so she could at least look for prominent leg muscles. Though that would only help if she wanted to pull up the woman's pants. Which she didn't.

The name . . . Cindy Copeland. Stella imagined her to be blond, probably based on memes of little Cindy from the Brady Bunch.

Her mind still whirling, Stella stood over the body, summoning courage to look at the face. Young, mid-twenties, she'd guess. Fine features, almost delicate. Beautiful, though the kind of beauty that the bearer rarely appreciated. Stella took in the brown eyes, wide in horror.

The neck at an awkward angle. The clothes that covered every inch of her body other than her hands and face.

Stella leaned closer. The wind shifted and with it, Stella smelled something musky and spicy. She crouched over the woman. What was it? A sudden image rose in her mind of her mother, every Friday, complaining about the fish she never wanted to cook, though her husband insisted on meatless Fridays. He wanted to keep his wife's Italian traditions alive for their daughters. Her mother complied, even as she grumbled that her own parents never kept fish Fridays. As soon as the meal was over, she would light . . . incense!

But no, this was more than incense. Stella closed her eyes and inhaled slowly. "Oh, boy," she heard the paramedic mutter from behind her. "Here we go again."

From further away, Stella heard Salvo say, "Let her work!"

For a second Stella warmed to the mustachioed officer until she remembered how he strutted around like he'd cracked the last case, when she'd done the work.

Loudly, the paramedic said to his partner, "Waste of time. Salvo solved the last case. And he didn't do it by sniffing."

Under his breath, Luca muttered.

To which Salvo said, "What's that, Luca?"

"Nothing," Luca said.

Shut them out, Stella ordered herself. Just breathe.

The spicy musk scent floated high in her nose. But grounded by something else. Something sturdy. Like earth. Or no . . . *stones*. Stella rose quickly, her eyes running once more over the woman's face.

"Church," she said, rising. The image came to her cleanly, as if carved from marble. Don Arrigo lighting the incense as he welcomed Stella, who arrived early to catch a few moments of silence before services began. Her voice sure now, she said, "She came from church. Recently, I'd guess."

Luca and Salvo approached. Salvo saying with a teasing tone, "Does church have a smell, Stella?"

Stella blinked to bring herself back to the moment. She turned to the officers and the paramedics. "It's not Cindy Copeland. It's not my guest."

"How can you be sure?" Salvo's eager eyes belied his showy frown of doubt.

Stella felt Luca's gaze on her. She looked at him and he looked away. She said, "Her hair. It's a few inches long. My guest asked if I had a curling iron. May I?" She gestured at the woman's neckline, where she saw what looked like a thin rope.

Luca nodded, leaning forward despite himself.

Stella pulled back the neckline to reveal a wooden cross. Straightening, Stella asked Luca, "Do you know where Leo was almost hit?"

Luca nodded. "Based on what he told us, I'd say it's a kilometer or so down the road."

"I guess if I hit the *porchetta* van, I've gone too far."

"Unless Leo picked it up. He said Mimmo was bringing him a can of fuel so he could get to the market."

Stella frowned. "Mimmo? Since when does our charmingly crotchety hunter do favors for Leo?"

Luca said, "Marta."

Stella nodded. Yes, Mimmo was short on affection, but he cared a great deal for Marta and Ascanio, taking on an almost uncle-like role with the boy. "Leo was able to roast a pig with all this going on?" Then she remembered, "Oh, right, he probably cooked it yesterday in the drum roaster."

Luca shifted his weight again. Finally, he said, "Well, if there's nothing else—"

Just as Stella said, "Okay, well, I'll go check out the van."

His jaw working, Luca nodded and then began writing in his notebook.

From behind her, she heard Salvo call, "Don't you want to examine this area? See if anything looks out of place?"

She turned and walked backward. "It looks like you've got it covered."

Luca looked from one to the other, his eyes narrowed.

Stella found the *porchetta* van pulled against the hillside. Luckily the road was wider here to accommodate its bulk on the wrong side of the road. Walking around the van, Stella wondered what she was looking for. It's not like a near hit-and-run would leave clues. Still, criminals weren't always masterminds. She wouldn't put it past a masochistic driver to also be a litterbug.

But the only thing she noticed was a crumpled bag of Fonzies behind the van that, given the faded coloration, had probably been there for some time. Fonzies. What a word for not-particularly-cheesy cheese curls.

Stella walked down the road to collect the bag. As she straightened, bag in hand, she remembered the place farther down where the brush parted to reveal a small shrine. She'd passed the shrine a hundred times by now, but hadn't paid attention to it. Cave-like shrines were common on Italian roads.

She approached this one, then ran her hands over the glossy pools of melted wax. Like most, this one featured a statue of a Madonna surrounded by votive candles, strings of rosary beads, and a few faded photographs—personal leavings, which gave the shrine an air of longing, a beseeching quality that caused tears to well in Stella's eyes. The people who left these remnants of devotion, what suffering did they carry to the shrine? What peace did they find here? What did they carry home?

Stella reached to touch the hem of the Madonna's dress. Tucked behind the statue were layers of old prayer slips—rain-blurred ink, wax-stuck corners. One newer card slid free when she brushed the flowers aside; scribbled words bled across the bottom: blue smudges, and beneath them, a harsh scratch of green ink. She stuffed it back before anyone caught her loitering.

She looked down at the Fonzies bag and fought a desire to shove the snack bag into the niche.

A tractor growled in the distance.

Stella continued to scan the bushes beside the van, lifting her nose, wishing for the scent of *porchetta*—the pig skin crackling into shattering caramel, the herbs tucked within the roll of juicy meat. She knew she wasn't the only one to thrill at signs all over the region, "*Oggi porchetta.*" *Porchetta* today. Thinking of the sliced meat, packed into a crusty roll with a fall of sea salt, her stomach rumbled.

Stella frowned at the lack of scent around the truck. It clung to Leo like an aura, shouldn't it be around the truck? Then she remembered that the van had been in the shop for some time. And he didn't cook the *porchetta* within the truck—he just sliced and sold it from there along with *prosciutto* and other cured meats.

She drew in a full breath and a chemical sting caught in her throat. She coughed and stepped back to the grass. Warming asphalt, motor oil, gas, cleansing fluid, and bleach maybe, or some other harsh cleanser, these did nothing for one's palate.

A roar from down the road, and Stella leapt to the side to hug the hillside.

To her surprise, the car stopped beside the van and a man leapt from the driver's seat, belting out the opera playing full volume from his car speakers. A sharp scent of tree sap and musk followed him.

Stella pushed herself from the hillside, putting herself in the driver's line of sight as he opened the trunk of his car.

He startled at the sight of her before a grin broke across his face. Raising his voice above the music still spilling from the car, he said, "You don't look like the kind of woman who typically stands around the side of the road." Stella realized he meant sex workers, who often lingered at intersections, in search of work. She frowned. He chuckled, "Don't worry, you're as pretty as any of them. Just need different clothes is all."

Stella resisted the urge to step backward, to turn away. Instead she muttered a sharp retort, but kept it under the volume of the music.

He drew a pair of latex gloves from his pocket. Catching Stella's eyes on him, he smirked as he stretched the gloves over his hands. "Can't smell like gas fumes all day. Gets in the way of the money I spend on cologne."

Too much money for that blur of chemicals, Stella thought to herself.

He pulled a gas can out of the trunk and jogged to the van, singing along with what Stella guessed was *La Traviata*. Or maybe *Tosca*.

In the breath between lines of the song, Stella raised her voice to be heard. "Do you know the owner of this vehicle?"

"Leo? Sure." He flicked open the gas cap door. "And here I thought you were mute. Which would not be a deal-breaker." His open-mouth smile made her feel slightly nauseous.

"Leo was going to have a friend bring him gas."

The man gave Stella a once over, letting his eyes stutter over her. One eyebrow furrowed hard in concentration. "And you, you are this friend?"

"Me?" Stella let out a snort. "No. Mimmo."

"Ah." The man shrugged before aligning the nozzle of the gas can into the mouth of the tank. "I guess I beat Mimmo to it." He closed his eyes and swayed to the music, his face tilted back to catch the sun's rays as gas poured into the empty tank.

"How did you know he was out of gas?"

He opened his eyes. "What do you mean, how did I know? He called me last night to give me an earful, complaining about my shoddy workmanship." Ah, the mechanic. "I told him I was, you know, *occupied*." He leered and Stella shivered in distaste. "I was telling him I would come in the morning when I heard him shouting at someone to slow down. Then the line went dead."

Stella watched him for a moment, processing.

A vulpine smile stretched across his face. "So you are waiting for me, I expect."

"What?"

"It's no crime. You wouldn't be the first to want a little taste of Rocco."

He adjusted the gas can in an awkward way, bending his elbows close to his body.

He'd been talking to Leo when the near miss happened. He might have heard something useful—if only he weren't so busy trying to make his muscles pop. Which gave her an idea.

"I'm just out for a stroll. Before it gets too hot."

"So running into me, lucky then, huh?" He glanced down at his arms, presumably to make sure the tattoo of barbed wire that encircled his bicep bulged properly.

"My luck or yours?" Stella said on impulse.

Immediately, his smile vanished. His eyes narrowed and he ripped the gas can out of the tank.

Okay, then. Not a man who favored women who held their own. She tried a different tack, making her limbs look fragile but fearing she was doing an unfortunate imitation of a rag doll. Her voice breathy, she said, "You're done already? Wow, you did that so fast!"

He muttered and strode toward his car.

Stella couldn't do this anymore. She straightened and said, "When Leo called you, did he say anything about the car coming toward him? Or anything he noticed after the van ran out of gas?"

Rocco stopped. "What are you, some kind of detective?" Stella must have hesitated a beat too long because he nodded knowingly before tossing the gas can into the trunk. "Stella, right?"

She blinked as he slammed the trunk closed.

"Have a good day, Stella."

He yanked open the car door and slid into the driver's seat, barely closing it before he screeched off, leaving a trail of rubber. Using the bare thread of the road's shoulder, he flipped the car around. Stella flung herself back to the hillside to avoid the edge of his curve. He lifted his fist out the lowered window, his baritone mixing with the opera as he flew down the hill.

Stella looked down and realized she still clutched the faded bag of Fonzies.

No wonder Leo's van was always in the shop. This Rocco didn't seem particularly detail-oriented, except when it came to protecting his bad cologne.

Trudging back up the hill, she looked for the spot where Leo might have had the encounter with the truck or car. Nothing. Something about that tugged at her memory.

The ambulance passed, taking the woman's body down the hill. No sirens. No emergency.

What had the woman been doing on the road so late at night?

Something about the woman's hair stuck with Stella. She knew many women, herself among them, who didn't bother with trendy hair fashions or styling products. Who had time for that when there were eggs in need of beating into airy peaks? But something about this woman's hair suggested more than disinterest. Her hair practically looked sawed off. Maybe cut with kitchen shears? Some kind of punishment? Stella winced.

Her thoughts turned to the wooden cross around the woman's neck. The ill-fitting clothes. Like spices in warm butter, an image bloomed—a woman in black and white. Singing. No, that wasn't right. That was from *The Sound of Music*. But close...

A nun.

It had to be.

It still didn't answer the question of why a nun would be walking to Aramezzo. From presumably Assisi, which thanks to Saint Francis giving his seal of approval to a cadre of female followers, was home to several convents. At least.

Panting now, and wishing for a bottle of water, Stella waved at Luca, looking impossibly fresh in his pressed uniform and aviator sunglasses. Stella scanned the ground. No marks or clues of any kind.

She caught sight of Luca waving her over and she trotted toward him, aware of the sweat pooling under her t-shirt. What a day to choose a black one. They started to speak at the same time, then Luca waved her on. "Ladies first."

A cursory glance at her phone reminded her of the few hours she had before her guests' check-in. "Any vehicles abandoned on the side of the road, other than the *porchetta* van?"

He shook his head. "You suspect she had car trouble?"

"It would be a staggering coincidence. But somehow more probable than her walking in the dark to take in the night air."

Cocking his head to the side, he said. "True."

"I guess we know it happened after Leo's incident, right? Or he would have stumbled right over her."

Luca frowned. "Maybe. But it was dark. And he may still have been below the road."

Stella nodded. Then reminded him, "Your turn."

"What? Oh! Right. I wanted to know if you found anything."

"Just this," Stella held out the Fonzies wrapper still in her hand.

"So I'd guess we're looking for a snack hound," Luca said, trying not to smile.

"Probably doesn't eliminate a lot of suspects," Stella said, watching the corners of his mouth tug upward.

"Just those who keep off the snacks." He grinned, a grin so different from Rocco's. So full of warmth and humor. Her gaze snagged on the way his front tooth overlapped its neighbor.

His laughter faded, but he kept his gaze trained on Stella.

Who kept her gaze trained on him.

The moment grew charged.

At once, they both startled and backed up.

She cleared her throat. "Anyway, the bag is faded." Knowing how Italians were irrationally fond of their Fonzies, she didn't add that the musty hay smell of the bag had dissipated long ago. "Probably there for some time."

He nodded and started to turn away.

To her surprise, her heart tugged. She reached a hand toward him. Closing her hand into a fist, she dropped it to her side and said, "Luca?"

He turned, eyebrows lifted above the line of his sunglasses. "I wanted to say . . ."

"Yes?" His eyes found hers and held them.

"Um. I ran into Leo's mechanic. Rocco."

Luca waited.

Stella went on. "He filled the tank. In case you see Leo. He can tell Mimmo to save a trip."

Luca nodded once and then turned back away, muttering to himself about dental records.

Stella wondered if she should tell him her theory that the woman was a nun. Or was that just her trying to prolong the conversation? Their interaction was a palate-cleanser after Rocco.

Luca caught sight of her, standing with her eyes unfocused. "Do you have something else?"

She shook her head.

He watched her for a moment before he turned away, pulling out his notebook and pen.

A smell, that wasn't enough to go on. She couldn't keep him all day with hunches. She shook her head and then turned to walk back up the hill, the sun beating on her shoulders.

Once on the ring road, Stella heard her phone pealing in her pocket. She pressed herself into the narrow band of a wall's shade to accept Matteo's FaceTime call.

"Stella? Where are you?"

She turned the phone so he could see the bakery, broiling with the wood-burning ovens. No wonder the bakers wore nothing but white boxers and undershirts. "Outside Antonio's."

From a distance, Stella heard Domenica's voice. "Stella? What happened?"

Matteo propped his phone in front of the two of them. "Okay, go."

"There's not much to say," Stella began slowly. "It's as Cosimo said. A woman in the road. Not my guest."

"Who was she?" Domenica asked.

"No identification. But," Stella hedged. "This is going to sound weird, considering the woman was wearing regular clothes. But I think she was a nun."

"Why would that be weird?" Domenica got so close to the screen, Stella only saw her eyebrow. Despite coaching, Domenica had never mastered FaceTime. Or texting, when it came to it. She still signed her few texts, "*Cordiali saluti*, Domenica." Kind regards. In a text.

"I don't know. Odds, I suppose," Stella said.

Domenica's eyebrow still filled the screen, but Stella heard Matteo say, "Odd in Manhattan, maybe. Not here, a stone's throw from Assisi."

"I'm headed to ask Don Arrigo—Domenica? Can you back up? This up close and personal view of your hairline is a little unnerving."

"What?" Domenica said. "I'm trying to see you. You're in the dark."

Matteo flicked at the screen and muttered, "I keep the brightness down so my battery lasts longer. Stupid old model drains too fast."

"It could be me. I'm struggling to stay in shadow," Stella said. "It's beastly out here."

"Rain tomorrow," prophesied Domenica, now filling up an appropriate amount of screen. "What are you seeing Don Arrigo for?"

"I'm not sure. Maybe he can use his contacts to figure out what order the nun is from? So we can get a bead on the missing woman a little faster?"

Matteo's face froze for a beat as he said, "What makes you sure she's a nun?"

Stella sighed. "Wooden cross. Smell of incense. Also severely cut hair, but that could be a commentary on the beauty industry."

Matteo muttered to Domenica, "Luca and Salvo would have missed the incense."

Domenica nodded. "With just the cross, no incense, she could be any sort of devout woman."

Matteo nodded, "Though even with the incense, she could be a devout woman who lights a lot of incense, right? Stella, how do you know—"

"I just do," Stella said, nodding to herself. "Okay, I gotta run."

"Wait!" Matteo held up his hand. "We weren't so much asking for an update as wanting to give you one. Or two actually."

Stella peered around. The streets seemed empty. But who could be lurking behind curtains? Lowering her voice, she said, "I'm switching to audio."

As she pressed the icon to remove video, she heard Domenica ask, "Where did she go?"

"Right here," Stella said. "Walls have ears and all that."

"She can't see you," Matteo told Domenica. To Stella he said, "She's nodding."

"I am not!" Domenica protested.

"So what's the update?" Stella asked.

"Right. Domenica, you go first."

"Stella? I'm in."

A sudden rush of relief filled Stella.

"Stella, did you hear me? I broke into the DIA system."

"I'm here, Domenica. Good work. What did you find?"

"Roberto and Romina are being held at Costarella."

"Is that supposed to mean something to me?" Stella asked.

"It's in Abruzzo. It's a prison that houses a lot of Mafia members during processing."

She started to think of Luca, then stopped. No way to explain without tangling Giancarlo or Domenica. "Has Matteo heard anything else from Giancarlo?"

"No, but Stella that's not all. I accessed the informant's notes. The drug runner has a long history of Mafia-related suspicious activity. Which apparently led the DIA to Roberto and Romina."

"I can't believe this," Stella said.

She heard Matteo's low voice, "It makes no sense."

Stella went on, "Anyway, how can this informant know all this but not have a name?"

"Stella, I'm telling you what I know. Maybe the informant offered information as part of a bribe and then bolted when he or she realized the magnitude of the arrests. Maybe the informant assumed it was Roberto and Romina based on faulty evidence. Who knows?" Domenica's voice trailed off.

Stella sagged against the stone wall, a jagged corner biting into her shoulder. A black cat appeared at her ankles with something squirming in its mouth. Before Stella could see what it was or try to free it, the cat trotted away, tail held at a jaunty angle. The sound of a faint squeak faded in its wake.

Domenica spoke again, "All we know for sure is that the informant told the DIA the drug-runner lives in Aramezzo, owns a business to run drugs through, and has a past that connects them with the Mafia. The DIA went through the system and decided it must be Roberto and Romina. I expect the briefcase served as confirmation."

"Any chance you checked whether Roberto and Romina actually do have a criminal record? I'm not saying the informant is correct, but if there is a problematic past, I don't want to be caught flat footed."

"Stella, I can't do that. I told you. How can I ever banter with them about where to find wild asparagus or who caught the most recent sighting of the white goat if I know all their secrets?"

Stella paused. "Wait. White goat? What white goat?"

"The white goat, Stella. I'm sure you've heard of it. Breaks into gardens, some people think it's paranormal, some sort of goat-headed phantasm. Cosimo must have mentioned it. Anyway, the good news is Roberto and Romina have a lawyer. Ginevra Franco."

"Do you know her?" Stella asked.

"No," Domenica answered. "But that doesn't mean anything. We only have a few lawyers in Aramezzo, none who would be equipped to manage a case like this."

"Okay," Stella said. "At least they've got someone in their corner."

"We thought you'd want to know," Matteo said. "My turn. It's probably nothing, but when I went back to work after you left, I spotted the mayor. With his wife. They were in the tunnel, and it sounded like they were listening to a voicemail. They seemed pretty tense. Whispering fast, like they were nervous or scared or angry."

"Which one, Matteo? Nervous or scared or angry?"

"It's hard to tell in a whisper!"

Stella heard Domenica in the background. "I think urgent would be the right word. Captures all three."

"Fine. Urgent. I did hear something about going to the bank."

Stella frowned. The bank?

Matteo went on, "Like I said, it's probably nothing. Maybe a fraud alert on their credit card. Who knows. But since tailing them is my job and all, I wanted to tell you."

"Thanks, Matteo. I don't know what it could mean, but more information is better than less, right?"

She heard Matteo exhale. "That's what we figured. Today was recycling, and their bag just held bottles—no luck there. We'll have to wait until Wednesday for trash. The trattoria gets daily trash pick up, but I went through it and nothing."

Stella's heart sank. Wednesday. "Thanks, Matteo," Stella said, noticing her hair had gotten caught in a bushy vine. She pushed herself away, swatting at the leaves.

"Okay, I better get back to work. The streets aren't going to sweep themselves."

Stella signed off, agreeing to stop by after her guests were safely received.

She slid the phone into her pocket, her gaze darting around the street. Movement stirred in the apartment above—maybe only a breeze billowing the curtain. A breeze that blew too high for Stella to feel. She straightened her scarf and jogged the rest of the way to the church.

Entering the church, Stella felt the tension ebb from her shoulders. The dimness of the soaring interior amplified the coolness of the stone walls. It reminded her of Bar Cappellina. Stella always forgot the bar was once a chapel. A bird fluttered in the rafters.

Stella drew a deep breath of incense-tinged air. Less frankincense than the lemony scent she'd caught on the nun, and none of the costly benzoin, if the absence of vanilla notes was any indication. This one smelled more woodsy.

Pushing through the door to the church office, Stella noticed the empty secretary's seat. Don Arrigo popped his head out from his work area. In his gravelly voice, he called out, "*Buongiorno*, Stella! What brings you here in the heat?"

"Out of the heat, actually. It's so cool in here!"

"Medieval air conditioning at its finest," Don Arrigo agreed.

"Still haven't filled your assistant position?" she said, gesturing to the empty chair.

"Shockingly few applicants, if you can believe it. Given the low pay and zero perks." He grinned.

"Plus a total absence of workplace intrigue." She grinned back.

Chuckling, Don Arrigo said, "You'd be surprised at what the aged of our community admit in the confessional."

"Do tell." Stella clasped her hands before her.

"Never," he said, the smile creasing the corners of his eyes. "But what brings you in?"

"Remember some time ago, you said you'd tell me a story about our local nuns?"

He frowned in thought. "Which nuns?"

"Something about a kitchen garden."

Don Arrigo's face cleared. "Ah, yes! The cloistered nuns that lived here in the early part of the century. But what is bringing this up now? Isn't there a mystery in need of revelation?"

"There is. I'm trying. But then something came up."

"The body in the road?"

She paused. "One thing about Aramezzo's gossip train, you can count on it making all the stops."

"Especially with Cosimo at the engine."

She smiled. Then she asked, "Don Arrigo, you can't for a second believe the DIA has the right suspects."

"Of course not."

Stella breathed a sigh of relief. "Which means, either the government made a huge blunder—"

"It's been known to happen here."

"In my country, too," Stella nodded. "But either it was a mistake, or they were framed."

"Which raises the question—who would want to hurt them?"

"*Esatto*," Stella breathed. Exactly.

He shook his head. "I can't think of anyone. Here, let's go into the side chapel. The pews will be empty and it's a little cooler."

Walking into the church, Don Arrigo gestured to a pew far from the portrait of Mary that bore an unsettling likeness to Stella's mother. It no longer rattled her. In fact, sometimes after services she lingered in front of it, trying to feel the maternal radiance she never felt from her mother. But right now, she didn't need the distraction.

"Do you know the person in the road? I hope it wasn't your guest?"

Stella shook her head. "No. I think . . . I think she was a nun."

"A nun!"

"Yes. I remembered you were going to tell me about the cloistered nuns here and I realized I don't know anything about where nuns live or how they live or if it's strange that she was out on the road in the middle of the night."

"If she were cloistered, like the nuns here ages ago, yes. Cloistered nuns rarely leave their convents. In fact, they have little contact with the outside world. But few convents are cloistered nowadays."

"Why?"

Don Arrigo shrugged and plucked at the crease in his black dress slacks. "It's not a sustainable model. The church is languishing financially anyway, what with decreased participation, so to fund a group of nuns whose life revolves around prayer, reading, and contemplation, without offering direct help to the community that's paying for its food and cloth, it's gotten to be a bit of a hard sell. Last I heard, there are only about five thousand cloistered nuns in Italy. Though there are three cloistered convents in Assisi, so they still do have a presence."

"Cloistered nuns pray and read and contemplate all day? That's all they do?" She cocked her head to the side. She could barely sit still long enough to check her email.

"Behind closed doors, who can say? But that's the stated intention. Some cloistered nuns make candy or cloth to sell through the wheel. But many orders find even that amount of contact too much contamination from the outside world."

"Wheel? What wheel?"

"You haven't seen it?" Don Arrigo jumped up. "Follow me. It's just around the side of the church."

Stella hurried to keep up with his long strides. "What did the nuns sell?"

"As far as I know, nothing, though the records are poor and disorganized," Don Arrigo said, holding up a hand to keep the direct sun off Stella's face. "The best I can tell, our nuns used the wheel for taking in mending. And of course, collecting babies."

"Babies?"

"You haven't heard of this? Desperate young mothers put their babies in the wheel and then rotated it until the wheel faced the inside of the convent. The inside of ours faces the kitchen. The mother dashed away, knowing that the church would find a home for her child."

"But that's awful!"

Don Arrigo slowed his steps. "I'm not sure it's any more awful than overrun orphanages."

"But a mother, leaving her child that way, without a thought..."

"Oh, I'm not sure it was ever without thought. An unwed mother, back in the day, she had no options. Certainly none that involved her raising her child with any sort of financial stability. Here, I'll show you how it works."

Stella stood in front of a wooden door, like a hatch in the wall. "This?"

"Open it."

Just then Stella noticed a small wooden handle. She tentatively put her hand on it, imagining mothers standing just this way with a newborn in their arms.

"Go on. Pull," Don Arrigo said encouragingly.

She did and when the door creaked open, she noticed a kind of carousel filling the space, with panels from bottom to top. She put her hand on the floor and it rolled around with a wooden groan, sending up a cloud of dust.

"See, people put clothing that needed mending with some coins in the outward-facing segment and then rotated the wheel. A nun accepted the clothing and the money, and pushed forward a receipt. At the appointed time, the person came back with their slip, and exchanged it for their mended clothes. On the other side you can see the arm for the bell that would ring out in the convent when the wheel turned."

"Is that how the nuns got their groceries?"

"Ha, I never thought of it," said Don Arrigo. "Maybe small items. But there's a vestibule where trusted vendors could enter and leave purchases."

"What if they needed a plumber?"

"They only used church-vetted providers who would meet with the Mother Superior, who led them to the leak."

Stella considered. "I don't know. It feels like training already anxious people to become even more anxious." She rotated the wheel for another moment, back and forth, before brushing the cobwebs off her hands. "I guess it's better than I pictured, since people were used to the wheel leading to a human, not just into the ether. But I still can't imagine anyone leaving their baby in one of these."

"And yet they did," he said, his voice trailing off.

"Don Arrigo? What do you . . . *recently*? People left babies here? Who? Who left their babies?"

"Stella, you know I can't tell you—"

"Did someone tell you in confession? You can't say because of your vows or whatever?" Stella suddenly cursed her lack of knowledge of church lingo.

Don Arrigo closed the door and gestured to Stella to step back round to the front entrance of the church. "I hope I don't need a vow to keep people's private information private. Stella, how could people trust me if I blabbed their family secrets?"

"Oh," Stella said, chastened. "Of course. I get it." Still, she felt overcome with curiosity. Someone in Aramezzo had to have been left in the carousel, right? If it was someone aged and gone, why would Don Arrigo be so circumspect?

She stopped walking. "Wait, was it someone in my family?"

Don Arrigo smiled. "You must have comprehensive birth records going back centuries."

"I don't, though. Remember? The house was ransacked. At least once, when my mother was on her way to the States. And I'm beginning to think again after my aunt passed away, given how much is missing. Photos, documents. The jewelry Cosimo and I searched for. There's no evidence of our family history."

"Except the painting," Don Arrigo gestured to the niche at the far end of the church.

She blinked. "What?"

"Valerio Pellegrino, the artist who frescoed the Madonna," Don Arrigo said, "was long familiar with your family. I thought you knew."

Stella's eyes widened. Adjusting her green scarf around her curls she said, "I thought maybe the resemblance was my imagination." And Cosimo's, she remembered.

Don Arrigo chuckled. "On the contrary. It's so much a part of town lore that no one finds it interesting. But when I came to work here, the previous priest gave me an intensive tour of the church's art and architecture. Along with a ream of copious notes."

"I thought you said there weren't records of the church's history."

"Ah," Don Arrigo flushed and stared at the stone floor. "Truth be told, we know an extensive amount about the church. It's the nuns no one thought to chronicle."

Stella frowned.

Don Arrigo waited.

Stella waved her hand. "Go on."

He nodded. "Anyway, as an apprentice, Pellegrino fell in love with what I believe must be your great-grandmother. Rumor goes they wanted to marry, but her parents forbade it."

"Because he was an artist?"

"Lower than an artist. An apprentice. When the church commissioned Pellegrino to fresco the niche, he used your great-grandmother as a model. The romantic in me thinks this was his way of tying them together."

She nodded slowly.

Removing a handkerchief from his pocket, he mopped his brow and said, "Before we sit, do you want to see the cloisters?"

Stella perked. "People can see them? No nuns living there?"

"Just me, I'm afraid. I've often wondered if we could rent out the rooms like some former convents do. Or create a kind of residence for adults who require extra support. But all that takes more hours than I have. And so I kick around in a house far too large for me and God."

"Where did the nuns go? Did they just die out? Or did they stop being funded, like you said?"

He hesitated. "Both of those are explanations for why some cloistered convents shifted to more open models. But I'm afraid that's not the case in Aramezzo."

Stella looked up at him, curious, but he kept his eyes straight ahead and frowned, pausing for a moment before walking through the church to the far end, where the air was stale and cool.

He pushed open a door and the scent of rosemary rushed around them. "Oh my!"

Before her lay a courtyard filled with magnificent rosemary bushes, blurred with amethyst-hued flowers among which bees and butterflies capered. She'd seen impressive rosemary bushes in her time, but these were a thing apart. Full, rich, with gnarled roots like ancient olive trees. "The nuns planted these?"

He put his hands in his pockets and nodded.

"Do you cook with it?" she asked, running her fingers through the branches, releasing the scent over her fingertips and into the air.

"If you call what I do cooking, yes. A frittata here or there. Some pasta and vegetables."

"I bet it tastes different. Rosemary this well established."

He smiled. "I always thought so, but I don't have your palate."

She drew in a breath. "It's so floral it veers into lavender. But with that piney edge of rosemary."

He nodded. "Yes, that sounds right. You are welcome to some anytime."

Stella watched a butterfly alight on one branch after another before she said quietly. "So the nuns?"

"They lived around the edge of the courtyard. See the doors?" He gestured to the doors lining the portico that framed the courtyard. "That one leads to the communal space. The old hall we use for church events. You came to the blessing of the Easter breakfast?"

She nodded, remembering the line of women carrying wicker baskets filled with hard-boiled eggs, new wine, bread, and cured pork to be blessed before breaking fast. She had dismissed Matteo's remark that the blessed eggshells couldn't be tossed in the trash as trash-man humor, until she saw the display of burning shells.

"Then you've seen the hall. You just came at it from the offices. Which were built later."

Stella waited.

"Yes. You'll have noticed my avoidance." He sighed. "It's a dark period of our history. After the earthquake in 1943, the pipes running under the courtyard got disrupted. Workmen came to fix them…"

She said nothing.

He said, "They had to pull up a few of the rosemary bushes. There," he gestured vaguely to the far end, facing the valley. "They found…" He looked into the distance.

Stella waited.

He closed his eyes. "They found skeletons."

"Skeletons?" Stella's voice went up before she lost her voice all together. The word hung in the air between them. Finally she said, "Like an old burial ground?"

"Of sorts. Only of women. And . . . and babies."

"*What?*"

"I'm afraid so," Don Arrigo said. "Three women buried with presumably their infants. And two pregnant women."

"I . . . I don't understand."

"Let's go back in." He turned on his heel. Once settled back into the pew, Don Arrigo said, "We can't know for sure. There was nothing in the records. Though records can be falsified. And they tested the rest of the courtyard . . . no bodies. The theory is that over the course of the convent's history, nuns got pregnant. Perhaps they died in childbirth or while pregnant. But there are rumors of something darker."

Stella's mind raced—something being slipped to pregnant nuns, forcing them to expel a child. Stella shivered. "But . . . how did the nuns get pregnant? In the cloisters . . . cut off from the world?"

He stared down at his thumb running over his knuckles. "Apparently there was a period of time when it was a badge of honor for a young man to deflower a nun."

Stella closed her eyes to block out the image.

Softly, Don Arrigo went on. "There weren't many nuns here when the bodies were found. They were shaken by the discovery and the Bishop moved them to Assisi to live out their days with a Poor Clares order there."

She checked the time on her phone. "Does the short hair of the woman I found mean she was a cloistered nun?"

He shook his head. "Not necessarily. Many nuns choose short hair because it's easier to care for underneath the wimple. And while some cloistered nuns have rules about hair, not all do. Those rules are largely kept from the public, so I don't know."

Nodding, Stella said, "How many convents are in Assisi?"

"Eighteen," Don Arrigo said. "And eight monasteries."

Stella fought the urge to ask why the numbers were so different. "Eighteen. Would they talk to me, do you think? Tell me if they are missing a nun? Would that depend on whether or not this nun was cloistered?"

He shrugged. "Good question. As I said, different convents have different customs, and they don't post the rule book. But they'll certainly talk to me."

Stella leapt up. "Can we go now?"

Shaking his head, Don Arrigo chuckled. "Always ready to jump into the fray. But I think it's best for me to make some preliminary phone calls."

"Right, of course. Anyway, I need to get ready for guests." Stella rose. "Thank you so much for talking to me, and for offering to make those phone calls." The thought of women buried beneath the rosemary loomed in her mind. "You'll call me when you hear anything at all?"

"The very moment," he said with a smile. "Godspeed, Stella. Be careful."

"Aren't I always?"

Don Arrigo regarded her steadily. "Categorically . . . no."

She laughed self-consciously. "Okay, fair enough. But I'll try."

With seriousness and warmth in his eyes, he said, "Please do, Stella."

Stella stopped laughing.

He went on, "Now, of all times."

As she turned down the tunnel that led to the second tier of Aramezzo, Stella spotted a newspaper sticking out of a city trash receptacle. A newspaper! That would at least give her an understanding of the raid and maybe Roberto and Romina's place in it.

She pulled the newspaper out of the trash. A national one, not regional, so it focused on the large-scale nature of the raid. Her eyes darted until they landed on Umbria. Pulling out her phone, she snapped a photo of a paragraph that referred to the area around Perugia being headed up by a Salvatore Mancini. And that a Mancini associate had turned informant, likely cutting a deal to lessen gun-running charges.

Not much. But context.

She stuffed the paper back into the trash, startling a seagull who screeched into the quiet. With a leap, it rose from its perch and circled lazily before turning over the mountain, perhaps back to the sea. Stella watched the sky until the bird disappeared against the unyielding blue.

Giancarlo waited on her stoop, hands loose between his knees, gaze fixed on some distant point. He smiled when he saw her and rose to standing. "Matteo told me about the woman in the road. Never a dull moment, eh?"

She shook her head. "And people vacation in Italian villages for peace and quiet."

"There's usually plenty of both."

"I must have brought all my jangly American energy with me." She spoke the words lightly as she turned the pendant in her fingers.

"Hey," Giancarlo said, catching her fidgeting hands in his strong ones. "You know that's not true."

She sighed and dropped onto the step. "What a morning."

He looked up at the blistering sun. "And barely half done," he said before sitting beside her.

She loosened her shirt from her sticky body, waving it to create a whisper of breeze. "I hope you're not here with more bad news?"

He smiled. "Thought you might need a hand. You can't have had time to prepare for the Americans."

Stella's eyebrows flew upward.

His smile broadened. "Juggling is not my only skill, you know."

For an instant the image of a clown leapt into her brain. Then she realized: soccer, not circus. "I don't doubt it." Though she did—did soccer stars even know how to run a load of laundry?

"Also, I wanted you to know about the raid. It turns out, it was nation-wide, and the section that Roberto and Romina are caught up in is headed up by—"

"Salvatore Mancini. It was in the paper."

"Right," he said. "Also goes by Lupo. An informant tried to draw him out, but all he learned was that the smugglers ran their own operation."

"Did your source tell you what makes Roberto and Romina suspect?"

He pulled out his phone and started typing. "I'll ask."

She nodded. "So how does the tracker fit in?"

Slipping his phone back into his pocket, Giancarlo said, "My guy says they started tracking bags to guide them to distant arms of the organiza-tion. They'd just started tracking the Aramezzo wing."

She thought aloud, "The government needed proof, down to the small fish. The anchovies of the Mafia world."

"Right," Giancarlo grinned. "The anchovies."

Stella's phone rang and she drew it from her pocket. Seeing the American phone number, she said, "Hello, this is Stella."

"Oh, Stella, thank goodness. It's James Copeland. My wife and Google Maps are in perpetual disagreement, and we've accidentally taken the scenic route."

"Oh no!" She rose to standing and Giancarlo straightened, his face alarmed. Stella shook her head and held up a hand to stay him. "Can I help point you in the right direction?" Stella silently prayed he'd decline. In a region like Umbria where the roads seemed scribbled by a toddler with a fresh crayon, she had a hard time pointing north.

"A gentleman at the gas station took out a map and showed us where we went wrong." Stella breathed a hopefully inaudible sigh of relief. "We're all set, but I wanted to let you know we'll be late. I think probably another couple of hours."

"So good of you to let me know. You must be so tired of driving! Are you hungry? Can I have something waiting for you?"

She heard Mr. Copeland conference with his wife for a moment. "That would be fantastic, thank you. Cindy wanted to stop for lunch, but I reminded her that we travel for the sights, not the sandwiches." He chuckled at his own joke.

"Let me know when you pass Assisi, and I'll meet you in the parking lot."

Hanging up, she turned to Giancarlo. "I better get moving. Thanks for the insights, it's been helpful."

He rose. "I can help."

"Help?"

He smiled that slow smile. In English he said, "I got time."

She grinned. "Okay, then. You may be a beast on the soccer pitch, but let's see how you do with furniture wax."

"Little do you know, my grandmother had me wax her table every week. Took years to wash the stink of honey off my hands."

"There are worse things," Stella laughed and opened the door, calling hello to Barbanera, who remained hidden in whatever cool corner he'd found. Closing the shutters had worked after all.

"Like what?"

She cocked her head to the side. "Deer horn salt is pretty nasty."

"Deer horn salt?"

"A leavening agent used mostly in Sweden. My friend Anders makes cookies with deer horn salt for Christmas. Smells like someone relieved himself in the oven. Only worse. Like skate gone bad."

"You're pulling my leg. Why would anyone cook with that?"

She shrugged before walking into the kitchen. "The ammonia smell cooks out and the crisp on those cookies . . . impeccable. Want to help me make focaccia?"

"You have enough time?"

"I made some the other night to bring Basilio and doubled the batch."

"Basilio . . . the kooky farmer?"

"He may be kooky but he knows his trees. Takes them quite seriously, to which I relate, as a person who can take what other people find mundane too seriously," Stella smiled.

"You are anything but mundane," Giancarlo said, his eyes steady.

Stella laughed. "Anyway, when I arrived last fall, my trees bore hardly enough olives to press for oil. Now the boughs are heavy with little baby olives thanks to Basilio. He came by last week to show me how to remove suckers." She pulled the bowl of dough out of the refrigerator. "I need to let it warm a bit. Maybe you can start the fire?"

"Where are your matches?"

Stella moved easily around him and pulled open the drawer. He drew out the matches and caught her hand, kissing it briefly before stepping outside where Stella heard him filling the outdoor oven with wood. In the quiet, Stella drummed her fingers on the wooden kitchen counter, as she searched her palate's memory.

The anchovies of the Mafia world.

She closed her eyes, remembering a train, in France, not Italy. The smell hit her before the image—sweet and smoky and savory. *Pissaladière.* A French tart with caramelized onions, olives, thyme, anchovies. With her local onions from Cannara. She'd soak the anchovies in milk to soften their bite, leaving a silky, umami oomph that even preserved-fish-avoiding Americans would appreciate.

She turned the heat under the pan and began peeling onions. Giancarlo came back, casting a quizzical look at the onions. She told him her plan and his eyebrow furrowed. "That's not focaccia."

"So it's not traditional," Stella shrugged.

He didn't answer, stalled by the sight of Stella's hands flying over the cutting board, leaving thin ribbons of onion. She swiped at her eyes. "Stupid onions."

Chuckling, Giancarlo moved to her and ran the pad of his thumbs over her cheek. "There, there. It's not worth crying over."

"Easy for you to say," Stella said, sliding the onions into the waiting pan. "A big burly soccer player like you."

He grinned. "Soccer players aren't burly."

She shrugged. "I told you, I don't know anything about soccer."

He stuck out his chest. "Would you call me burly?"

Her eyes ran over him. While she looked like the Sunday comics drenched in spilt water, the colors running into each other, Giancarlo had nothing but small beads of perspiration at his hairline. Maybe she should exercise more.

"Stella," he said, lifting her chin to look into her eyes. "Don't worry. I love that you aren't a soccer fan." He went on with a sigh, leaning against the counter with his arms crossed over his chest. "It's refreshing actually."

"Get tired of all those crazed soccer fans tossing their underwear at you?"

Giancarlo smiled self-consciously. Did women actually do that? Stella shook the pan until slices of onion danced in the air, sending the sweet scent into the air. "While these caramelize, let's see those waxing skills of yours."

They chatted as they waxed the table, gathered thyme from the garden for the focaccia, soaked the anchovies in milk, and folded the last of the laundry. Stella laughed at Giancarlo's stories about being the only Italian on his team and he had many questions about the summer she worked at Olive Garden.

Spotting the spice jars on the wooden counter, Giancarlo opened one and held it out. "Do you know what it is?"

Even before the lid's removal filled the room with the scent of licorice, Stella knew the jar contained anise seeds based on its place in the order. But she shook her head. "Miles to go. Let's get the focaccia in the oven."

"Oh, come on. I bet you can't. How about this one?"

He opened the spearmint and held it out.

She smiled vaguely before walking outside with the focaccia.

Giancarlo followed behind a beat later.

He said, "When do the guests—"

Just as she said, "This heat reminds me—"

Giancarlo leaned against the wall and gestured for Stella to speak. She told Giancarlo about her initial surprise seeing the bakers in their underwear, then instantly flushed, hating her habit of filling silence with mortifying content.

"Maybe you can borrow the outfit on hot days?" Giancarlo said, one eyebrow raised.

Stella laughed.

"Or you can buy bread, like everyone else. It's much easier."

She looked at him out of the corner of her eye, wondering if he was joking.

"What? Antonio makes good bread."

You could take the boy out of Umbria, but you couldn't take Umbria out of the boy. Locals bordered on the obsessed with the bread that travelers, even Italians from the north or south of Italy, found dull and bland, thanks to its lack of salt. She wondered if Umbrians loved their bread so fiercely only because they'd defended it for generations—repeating until they believed it themselves. Though Stella did have to admit it had been growing on her, and not just as a vehicle for olive oil and salt. She'd found herself popping cubes of it into her mouth when she made *panzanella*, the bread salad with red onions and tomato that Stella liked with a little young basil.

Stella asked, "Does your family have an outdoor oven?"

He shook his head. "But our neighbor always asks if we have anything to throw in when he lights his."

Stella peered into the oven with a practiced eye. The door squeaked as she closed it again. A few more minutes. "My neighbor, Alvaro, the one with the chickens, always shares a bottle of his homemade wine when we are both out here cooking."

He frowned. "Is it any good?"

Stella paused. "It's unruly. But also wonderful." She went on, "Alvaro showed me a zucchini plant in the corner of my yard that comes back every year. Like magic!"

"Not magic," he said. "Seeds from rotting zucchini come up again the next year."

"Magic." Stella shrugged. She opened the oven door and nodded. Shoving the peel under the crust, she said, "Maybe I should have made zucchini blossom focaccia instead."

Giancarlo came behind her and pressed his face against her neck. "They'll love it."

She leaned against him for a moment, drinking in his scent of woodsmoke from starting the fire. "I...I have to get this in the house."

"Let me," he murmured against her ear before stepping around her to take the loaded peel with the casual grace of plucking a wildflower. Once he placed the focaccia on the counter, he put the peel beside it and drew Stella closer.

"I'm so sweaty," she whispered.

"You call that sweat?" He smiled and put his hands on her waist.

She smiled back at him before closing her eyes to breathe him in. He moved his hands to her cheeks, tilting her face up to kiss her softly.

Pressing closer to him, the kiss grew in strength. One of his hands worked into her hair as the other dropped back to her waist, wrapping behind her to draw her tightly against his heart. Heat surged through her, the energy between them crackled.

Bang!

At the hard, cracking sound they leapt apart, disoriented.

"What...what..." Giancarlo looked around, confused.

Stella pointed at Barbanera sitting on the edge of the table, a salt shaker on the floor. "He knocked it off the table."

"On purpose?" It seemed an odd question, though with Barbanera, a reasonable one.

She shrugged with a half-smile.

"He doesn't like me," Giancarlo said mournfully, staring at the cat, now flicking the edge of his tail.

Stella touched Giancarlo's arm softly.

He reached for her, and she danced lightly backward. "No more distractions." Barbanera continued to glare from the table. "I better get him down. Guests don't like cat hair with their breakfast."

Barbanera blinked at her and jumped down with a stretch before trotting into Stella's room. She heard the thunk of him leaping on the bed.

She dragged a hand across her forehead before checking her phone. "I think I have time for a shower."

"Want some company?" Giancarlo said, eyes locked on hers.

She breathed in a ragged breath, torn. Finally, she said, "I don't have time."

He checked his watch. "You have almost an hour."

After a pause, Stella said, "I have to budget extra time. You know…"

"Aramezzo," he finished with a grin.

"Exactly. Every errand takes three times as long as you expect."

"You know, you can tell people you're in a hurry. I do that all the time. Nobody minds."

Stella wondered. Did they really not mind? Or did Giancarlo move around their hurt feelings like he might dodge a defender on his way to the goal? As for her, she enjoyed the novel sense of having a community expect her engagement.

She hitched her thumb over her shoulder. "So I'm gonna go."

He nodded, resigned. "But I'll see you later?"

"I hope so."

He wiped at a smudge under her eyes and touched his nose to hers. "I'll make sure."

If Luisella hadn't rubbed her fingers together to call Barbanera, Stella would have walked past her. *Something's wrong.* Luisella wasn't one for loitering on steps, let alone kneeling. Yet here she was. Kneeling.

"Luisella. *Buona sera.*" Stella took a breath. Was this her opportunity? Was there ever an opportunity with Luisella? The woman resembled nothing so much as a stubbornly closed clam. She wished she'd brought something to eat, like Domenica suggested.

"He's not afraid of the rain?" Luisella's skirt rustled as she stood.

"What rain?" Stella gazed up at the sky.

Luisella gestured. "A mackerel sky. You know, when the clouds look like fish scales, get out your rain pails."

Stella squinted. The sky did look clotted. "Like Barbanera's fur," Stella chuckled.

Luisella smiled. She crouched again and called Barbanera with the whispery, whirring sound people used to call cats to dinner.

Stella held her breath, hoping Barbanera would behave. As a cat, his charm often got lost in translation. The cat looked up at Stella. She wasn't sure if she should encourage him to go to Luisella or act like she would hate that. Her black-chinned, one-eared cat was nothing if not contrary. Before she could decide, Barbanera jogged toward Luisella, tail held at an alert, friendly angle.

What a vixen, Stella thought, as Barbanera wound around Luisella's ankles.

Luisella laughed, the sound creaky as if from disuse. "I can't believe he's acknowledging my presence."

Affecting a casual air she most certainly did not feel, Stella shrugged. "It takes him a bit to warm up." She hesitated, letting Luisella caress the side of Barbanera's face. The beast leaned into her before looking up at Stella.

Did he wink?

Stella asked, "You must have known Barbanera for some time. Was he affectionate with my aunt?"

She expected Luisella to go straight-lipped and whirl into the house, but the woman seemed fairly bewitched by Barbanera's silver-spotted fur as he wound between her legs. "Anna Maria called him the feral beast. Always skulking around. The most domesticated thing he did was leave dead mice in the fireplace. Anna Maria didn't mind his wildness, though. Kept food out for him and left the back door ajar when it rained."

Stella took advantage of the conversational gate left open, as Anna Maria left a way open for Barbanera. "Luisella, I wanted to ask—"

Luisella rose with a sigh. "I've been waiting for this."

"You have?" Stella started.

"I'm actually surprised it took you this long. Given how nosy you are." A slight smile softened Luisella's tone.

Barbanera went back to making figure eights around Luisella's ankles. "*Che dolcezza*," Luisella murmured, leaning down again. Such sweetness. Stella watched the display in silence.

Luisella sighed. "But I don't know anything about why your mother ran from Aramezzo. Anna Maria never said."

"Oh!" Stella said, the batter finally coming together. "Well, I know that. She left to marry my father."

Luisella straightened and gazed at Stella without blinking. "Right. To marry your father."

"That's right," Stella confirmed. "Unless..."

Luisella stiffened. "I've said too much already."

"You haven't said anything!" Stella groaned inwardly. So much for not scaring off her neighbor.

But Luisella didn't back up or whirl away. Instead she widened her eyes and Stella got a glimpse of the ingenue she must once have been. "Haven't I?"

Stella tamped down her irritation at the conversational circles. "Listen, Luisella, I was wondering. When was the last time you left Aramezzo?"

Luisella stiffened. "Thursday. Why?"

Thursday, the day Veronica reported the near miss with her dogs. Relief loosened Stella's shoulders.

Thursday put Luisella safely at home during last night's murder and near-murder. Unless . . . might Luisella be lying? After all, if she hit someone in the road, or even almost did, would she really volunteer that she'd been at the scene of the crime?

Clearing her throat, Stella said, "Oh, just I heard about your almost hitting Veronica's dogs, but I didn't think that could possibly be true."

"Why not?" said Luisella without a glimmer of irony. "She lets those dogs run everywhere. Easy enough for one to get trapped under a car's wheels." She muttered something about how it would likely be better for the dogs to get away from their mistress's talons.

"Oh," Stella's stomach dropped. "And last night . . . is there any chance you popped out for a bit?"

A stormy expression clouded Luisella's face. She picked at invisible lint on her dress. "I have things to attend to."

She spun on her heel. Before Stella realized she was gone, the door latched firmly behind her. No curtain flicker suggested she'd lingered to listen.

"Well, Barbanera," Stella said to the cat, who sat down and glared at the door. "I guess that's that."

The jog to the parking lot for a guest's arrival had become fairly routine—the waving at any unfamiliar car, which surely proved to be visitors to Aramezzo (except that once when it turned out to be the mayor and his wife returning from the Mercedes dealership in Perugia). She'd help unload the guests' bags and then give them the spiel about how people had been living on this outcropping over the valley since Etruscan days, though the city as it stood now was built in the Middle Ages. She'd point out what she was never able to accurately convey in her booking email—the curious wedding cake shape of the town, so unlike most hilltop villages built along the ridge of a mountain.

Over the months of running the bed-and-breakfast, Stella had learned that even if guests arrived cranky and dismissive of Aramezzo's three ring roads that divided the town into tiers, and even if they waved off the view from the parking lot, a good night's sleep was enough to prompt them to gasp in pleasure at their first breakfast in the garden, with the rolling terraces of olive groves swooping down to the green valley before yanking up in the distance into peaks that punctured the liquid-blue sky.

Or maybe it was the *cornetti* she served with homemade jam, usually from whatever fruit her neighbors had left in baskets by her door. Most recently she'd preserved plums from her own trees—small plums, hardly bigger than cherries, their thin skin barely containing tart juices that sang with an almost five-spice flavor. She'd asked every passing neighbor and even called Basilio to identify the plums on her tree. Everyone shrugged and said, "Aramezzo plums."

She'd looked it up and could find no such designation. Then again, Basilio insisted the Umbrian valley had once been a sea, even bringing her a seashell he'd found while foraging asparagus. When she mentioned to Basilio that she'd found no online evidence for this long-ago sea, he pointed across the valley. "Trust your eyes."

"The olive trees? What about them?"

He'd shrugged. "The past is in the leaves. See the color?"

Suddenly, Stella wondered how she'd missed it. About one-third of the way down the mountain, the leaves of the olive trees darkened. "Is it a different kind of tree?"

"A different kind of soil. Chalkier. From the shells breaking down.

Where the sea was."

Part of her assumed this must be an elaborate joke on the naive American woman, except Basilio wasn't inclined to joke, especially about trees. Anyway, she'd taken a walk around the hills to the groves and found the line of trees. Kneeling in the soil she found a clean line where the soil got whiter and drier.

The world was full of marvels, and Umbria was a teacher.

Her guests found the story fascinating, prompting some to draw out their phones for a spot of research. She didn't know why—the whole point was that the plums and the soil left no internet footprint. The only way to understand this region of her forebears was to run one's hands through the soil and taste the fruit.

Trust your eyes.

In any case, she'd grown to love serving that first breakfast with a side of storytelling. She felt the guests' very vibrations shift to a lower amplitude as they listened, sipping their coffee and slathering plum jam over *cornetti*, Italy's answer to the croissant.

Not all guests, of course. Some bikers only wanted to discuss road conditions and some pilgrims only wanted to know how to reach Eremo (the forest outside Assisi where Saint Francis prayed) and some tourists only wanted to know how to make a reservation at the Perugina chocolate factory. But some travelers lingered and smiled softly, shaking their heads in wonder when she told them the tale of Santa Chiara calling the wild cats to Aramezzo.

As an unfamiliar car rounded into the parking lot, gravel crunching under the tires, Stella breathed to quiet her brain's clattering. She hoped these guests were low-maintenance. Even if they were the worst kind of travelers—those who complained that Italian food was better in the United States, or the ones that wiggled their eyebrows leeringly when asking if the floorboards on the steps squeaked in the night. All that she'd happily take if their self-sufficiency left her space to think.

Stella straightened the green scarf, her fingers catching on her curls. She wished she'd washed her hair, but while her brief beauty routine would only have cost her a mere thirty seconds, her Italian neighbors would have lost their minds if she'd stepped outside with wet hair. She still didn't understand the rationale, but it was simply not done, like asking for parmesan with a fish dish. Even in small-town Italy, residents seemed to care an outsized amount about *la bella figura*.

She walked to the car, Barbanera trotting in front as if to show her the way. He rarely accompanied her on guest pickups; a shame as his presence broke the ice better than the view.

The man, Mr. Copeland, dressed in khaki-colored tailored shorts and a peach linen shirt, did a double-take at the sight of the dog-sized cat. He took off his sunglasses and remarked to the woman climbing out of the rented Renault in a cream-toned sundress and buttery sandals. The woman smiled vaguely in Stella's direction before turning to take photos of the valley.

"*Buongiorno!*" Stella called. Her eyes darted toward the sun sinking into the mountains the way she sank into a warm bath at the end of a day of stripping wallpaper. It was probably more accurate to say *buona sera*, but she'd noted Italians were loose with these rules and anyway, her guests would hardly notice.

"*Buona sera*," Mr. Copeland said with a raised eyebrow.

Stella stalled. His accent was quite good.

"That's quite a *gatto* you have. With only one . . . er . . . *orecchio!*"

"Indeed. He came with the place." Stella avoided telling the story of how Barbanera lost his ear. "Your Italian is excellent."

His easy laugh filled the parking lot as he drew two suitcases from the trunk. "People tell me I can get by with English, but where's the fun in that?" He glanced at his wife. She averted her eyes and aimed the phone at Barbanera, who had jumped on the hood like a model across a sports car. The cat certainly was pulling out all the stops today.

"*Piacere*," Stella said to Mrs. Copeland.

The woman mumbled, flushing a shell pink.

Mr. Copeland said, "We make a good team. I do all the talking and she takes all the pictures. I'll send you the best ones so you can update your listing."

Stella waited for Mrs. Copeland to chime in. When she didn't, Stella said she'd be only too delighted to replace the photos on her website, which she'd taken with her outdated iPhone.

Mrs. Copeland turned and opened her mouth as if to say something, but then turned back to Barbanera, now lolling over the hood of the car luxuriously.

Her husband volunteered, "That's your problem. You can't beat the camera on a Galaxy. You should see Cindy's phone. The lock screen is gibberish to me; it's so full of all the apps she needs at a moment's notice." He grinned at his wife, who had put down the phone to reach out to Barbanera's nose. The cat sniffed Mrs. Copeland's fingers and then rubbed his face against her hand.

"Something to think about," Stella said with great cheer. Though she didn't care enough about pictures to switch phones.

"But beware! You may become a photophile like my wife. We don't cover nearly as much ground as we would if she didn't stop every few minutes to take pictures."

Mrs. Copeland flushed before stashing her phone in her purse with a snap of the clasp.

Mr. Copeland chuckled. "I'm kidding around, Cindy. You know how much I enjoy your little hobby." As an aside to Stella, he said, "Honestly, she's very talented. And this might be her first endeavor that doesn't lead to our house reeking of botanical extracts."

Mrs. Copeland's jaw tightened.

Stella paused. "I like botanical extracts."

He grinned. "The artisanal soap phase was one of my favorites. Because," he said with mock seriousness, "mass-market soap is basically detergent."

Stella tried to remember which soap she'd put out in their bathroom, then gave up. At least she'd left a sprig of lavender on the bedside table.

She launched into tour guide mode, pausing when Mrs. Copeland stopped to take a photo of a dark alley with light spilling at the far end or a wash of jewel-toned wisteria tumbling down a wall. The woman's studied lack of response reminded Stella of Barbanera, curled into a tight ball, his single ear giving the only indication of his listening.

"If you go the other way out of this tunnel, you'll find an *alimentari* if you want to pick up iced tea or snacks."

"And up the tunnel? What's on the second ring?" Mr. Copeland asked, pausing to dab his forehead with a linen handkerchief.

"That's where you'll find most of the shops. The bar, the bakery—"

"Bakery?" Mrs. Copeland said.

"Now you've got her attention," Mr. Copeland said, chuckling.

His wife studied the suede of her shoes.

Stella smiled encouragingly. "Yes, Antonio is famous around here for his bread, both Umbrian loaves and also *torta al testo*, a kind of flatbread used for sandwiches. I'll make some of those for your picnic tomorrow at the Piano Grande."

Mrs. Copeland said, "Umbrian bread is utilitarian, I think. I mean, that's what I read. Like, it's pretty . . . sturdy? Sorry, never mind, I'm probably wrong." Mrs. Copeland waved her hand as if to scatter her words before anyone could hear them.

Stella's eyes widened.

Under his breath, Mr. Copeland said, "Yikes."

Stella said, "You nailed it. Traditional bread here isn't salted, so it doesn't retain moisture. Which is why we have so many recipes using dry bread."

Mrs. Copeland stared at Stella for a moment before dropping her gaze to the ground.

Mr. Copeland said, "Is that where we get pastries? Antonio's bakery?"

"I'm afraid not," Stella said, thinking through the contents of her freezer. "But I do have *cornetti* for the morning."

Mrs. Copeland looked up. "We read about your *cornetti!*"

"You did?" Had she hosted a food critic and missed it? Weird. In her New York days, she'd developed a sixth sense for spotting a critic.

Mr. Copeland sighed, "In your reviews."

Ah, okay, she hadn't totally lost her critic radar. "Since you like pastries, tomorrow I'll direct you to a wonderful bakery in Norcia on your way to the Piano Grande. Which, by the way, is at peak color right now, all those blue lentils and red poppies."

Stella unlocked the door and handed the couple the key. After registering their documents and collecting their payment information, she led them up the stairs and opened the shutters, smiling at Mrs. Copeland's intake of breath. "It's like a Giovanni Fattori," she said softly. "All the yellow ochre and sap green. Che be-ya."

Mr. Copeland laughed. "What creative pronunciation! *Che bel-la!*"

Stella shifted her weight. "Take your time getting unpacked. I have a bottle of wine and a tray of focaccia on the board next to the door that leads to the terrace. Help yourself and bring the tray to the kitchen when you're finished. Would you like me to make reservations for dinner tonight or would you prefer to eat here?"

Mrs. Copeland lifted her suitcase onto the bed. Mr. Copeland turned to Stella. "Let's eat here tonight. Sound good Cindy?"

At Mrs. Copeland's nod, Stella said, "Wonderful! Any new dietary restrictions or aversions since you filled out the online form?"

They shook their heads, Mrs. Copeland darting a look at her husband.

Unsure, Stella said softly to her, "Is there something you'd particularly enjoy?"

Mr. Copeland opened his suitcase with a frown. His wife watched him hopefully for a moment and when he didn't answer, she muttered,

"Something local?"

Stella felt her heart would burst. It created such difficulty when guests asked for something like linguine and clams and Stella had to tell them that yes, Aramezzo was only an hour from the sea, but inland and seaside Italy were worlds apart in their culinary habits. She could only get clams from the Assisi fishmonger on Tuesdays, unless she ordered them in advance.

"Absolutely." Stella looked from husband to wife before turning and closing the door behind her with a sigh. Barbanera appeared at her feet with a meow.

Thank the bed-and-breakfast gods these guests looked to be the easy sort. With her Roberto and Romina behind bars and a dead nun to identify, Stella already had plenty on her plate.

As Stella walked to Cristiana's, she decided on pasta with *tartufata* sauce. A simple dish that would take minimal time, as Cristiana stocked wonderful jars of *tartufata*, with the perfect blend of black truffles, mushrooms, olive oil, and garlic. Even her foodie guests, well-versed in truffles, were still surprised at *tartufata*.

The jar of sauce nestled in her basket, Stella lingered in front of the shelf of pasta. Of all her guests, Americans expressed the most enthusiasm for unusual pasta shapes. Such an easy way to delight, since the pasta aisle in the grocery stores around here rivaled the length of the cereal aisle back home.

She picked up a box of *strozzapreti*—the short, slightly curled shape had a satisfying chew. Remembering the name meant "priest killer," she shivered and put the box back on the shelf. At the sight of a packet of *umbricelli*, Stella remembered last night's pasta with greens. Those greens would work with *strozzapreti*'s curl and springy texture. She picked up the box of *strozzapreti* again and studied it as if evaluating the risk of bringing it home, before dropping the box into her basket.

For tonight's *tartufata*, though, she considered a packet of *strangozzi*. The flat and rustic strands would ground the *tartufata* without complicating the dish. Perfect. Even if the word *strangozzi* translated to "strangler." What was it with Umbrians? Maybe they shouldn't be surprised by all these murders, it seemed like they had constant nudges to resort to violence.

On her way past the drink section, she picked up a container of ACE juice. Guests enjoyed the blend of carrot, orange, and lemon and often expressed amusement at a juice named for vitamins A, C, and E.

No basket of greens by the counter, but she had time to stop at Pia's *fruttivendolo*. Maybe she'd find melons to pair with *prosciutto*. Too often dismissed by Americans thanks to their ubiquitous presence on antipasti boards, the local version astonished guests: musky melons at peak ripeness paired with Umbrian prosciutto, saltier and touched with grassy, floral notes from its long curing in stone cellars. That reminded her— she'd ask Cristiana for *prosciutto*, too.

As she debated hand-cut or machine-sliced prosciutto, she noted a woman standing stock-still in front of the tuna cans. It took Stella a moment to recognize the woman as Marta, even though her friend carried her perennial scent of lavender flowers. Marta's hair, too, looked the same as ever—the delicate curls plaited into braids that she wound around her head, a few wisps loosened at her temples.

She held her body stiffly, as if movement caused pain. This must be why Stella didn't register her.

She touched Marta's arm and Marta jumped.

"Sorry!" Stella said. "I didn't mean to interrupt."

Marta smiled when she saw Stella. "Not much to interrupt. I don't even need tuna, really." The smile fell quickly from her face, her usually mobile mouth was drawn. Her face, wan.

Stella nodded. "What do you need?"

Marta looked around, blinking. "Honestly? I think when Ascanio's grandparents offered to keep him for the afternoon, I just wanted to get out. It's been a lot."

Stella nodded again.

Marta dropped her eyes. "That poor woman. It could have been—"

"I know," said Stella softly. "How is Leo?"

Marta smiled. "Keeping a brave face. You know Leo!"

Stella inclined her head "Yes."

Marta dug in her purse, "You have to see this photo I took of Ascanio riding Leo like a pony." After a moment, she said, "*Madonna*, I left my phone on the table." She closed her eyes, lips pressed together.

As if from a distance, Stella heard Cristiana chase a cat out of the shop. Softly, she said, "And Leo went to work today?"

"That brave face." Marta sighed. "I'm just glad the van didn't break down again. I think he needed a normal morning, selling *porchetta* like always."

Stella reached to touch Marta's arm. "His *porchetta* gets better every week."

Marta's face lit in its first true smile. "Thanks to your tip about rubbing lemon juice on the skin."

"You told him about that?" Stella had worried her blurted idea sounded like criticism when she and Marta and Ascanio feasted on *porchetta* sandwiches and iced tea and chips before Ascanio tore off to conquer the playground.

"He told me it sounded weird—you know men resist anything that's not their idea." Marta rolled her eyes with a laugh. "But he asked around and found out that you're right, lemon juice tightens the pork skin."

Ah. That's why the ends of the pork were more caramelized last week.

Marta gestured to Stella's basket. "Guests in town?"

Stella looked at her basket. "How do you—?"

"You never drink juice."

With a grin Stella said, "Why drink fruit juice when you can drink juice squeezed from coffee beans?"

Marta's face froze. At the counter someone clanked two bottles of wine. "Roberto and Romina . . . do you know anything?"

"Not much," Stella admitted.

"But you're working on it?" Marta's eyes pleaded.

"I'm working on it," Stella assured her. Which reminded her, "You don't have any idea who might want to frame them, do you?"

"Roberto and Romina? No way. No one."

Stella nodded. "How could they have enemies?"

Nodding, Marta said, "That's exactly what Leo said. We think the government is trying to increase their arrest record or something."

"Or Roberto and Romina were accidentally framed. Like someone was using the bar as a drop point, and had no intention of pinning it on them."

"Oh, I guess that's possible." Marta smiled. "I guess that's why I'm not a detective."

"Neither am I," Stella reminded her.

Marta thought for a moment as the refrigerator let out a low hum. "But that means someone in Aramezzo is working with the Mafia."

"You know about that?"

Marta shrugged sheepishly. "I admit, I eavesdropped on Luca talking to Salvo."

He knows.

Slowly, Stella said, "I've been trying to figure out if anyone in town has fallen into a lot of cash."

Marta laughed bitterly. "Not me, that's for sure. Wool and lavender are not moneymakers. And Leo can't even afford a new van."

"I always figured Leo sat on a pot of racing money."

Marta opened her mouth, but then closed it and looked away, fiddling with a pack of tuna mixed with vegetables, before dropping it back into place with a small click.

"Marta? What is it?"

After another pause, Marta said, "Please don't tell anyone, Stella. I once mentioned it in passing to Mimmo. Leo got so angry. Anyway. It makes sense that Leo doesn't want this to be common knowledge, right?"

"I don't know," Stella said softly. "You haven't told me anything."

"Oh, right," Marta laughed uneasily. "It's just that Leo didn't make as much racing cars as you would expect. If it wasn't for the *porchetta* business his father handed down, he'd be broke."

She thought aloud, "How can that be? Aren't those purses huge?"

Marta said, "But Stella...getting a car around the track costs money. The expensive car...let alone all the parts and the staff. A first-place finish barely covers the cost of putting the car on the track. A less than second place finish becomes a loss."

"His sports car..." Stella began, unable to think of the make.

"Oh, that impractical thing," Marta laughed. "Alfa Romeo gave it to him as part of a sponsorship package. He would have rather had the cash."

"No wonder he quit," Stella said.

"Oh, if it wasn't for the injury, he would have raced forever. It was his antidepressant." Her voice trailed off.

"He's depressed?" Stella said, moving closer and dropping her voice.

Marta stammered, "I...I didn't say that..."

Stella put her hand on Marta's arm. "This is between us, Marta."

Marta exhaled, closing her eyes in relief. "It's not my story to tell."

Stella remembered the night before, Leo cradling his hand, his saying he didn't think it was broken, but the fall had activated an old injury. His vulnerability, it made her warm to him. "His arm. Is it okay, after last night?"

"His hand, actually." Marta frowned. "It's a little numb and tingling. He'll need to see his doctor next week." With a start, Marta rustled in her empty purse. "Stella, what time is it?"

Stella pulled her phone out and showed Marta the time.

"Oh no! He'll be getting back soon and if I'm not home…"

"He'll worry about you. I get it," Stella said.

Marta looked momentarily confused. "Right. Thanks for listening, Stella."

"Anytime."

"Oh!" Marta said. "I completely forgot about the article."

"The article about the murder at the villa? Domenica showed it to me, you and Leo looked fantastic. Wise journalistic choice not to include one of me, all disheveled."

"You were gone by the time the press showed up," Marta reached into her purse, "But I don't mean that one. Oh, I bet it's still on the table. With my phone. Where is my head these days?"

"Marta, what article?"

"Didn't I tell you? The article about Giancarlo in *Il Messaggero Umbria.* I clipped it for you."

"Oh, right." Marta had mentioned it last week, but Stella hadn't followed up. Was it stalking to read an article about a man you'd just started dating?

"I'll take a photo of it when I get home and send it to you. You okay waiting for the hard copy?"

"More than okay." She was hardly going to keep a scrapbook.

Marta pressed her cheek against Stella's. "Be careful if you go on the road, okay?"

"You too." Stella said, breathing in Marta's scent of lavender as they pulled apart from their embrace.

Marta gave her one more smile before walking out of the *alimentari.* Stella called to her receding back, "No tuna?"

Marta shook her head. "I think I needed people. With the bar closed…"

Stella's heart clenched. She brought her basket to the counter and asked Cristiana if she'd heard of anyone having a problem with Roberto and Romina. Cristiana's face fell. "No one. We've been talking about it all day. It doesn't seem possible."

As she walked toward the *fruttivendolo*, she felt her phone vibrate and checked the screen. Huh. Don Arrigo rarely called. Did he have information? "*Ciao*, Don Arrigo."

"*Ciao*, Stella. I have information."

She smiled. "Shoot."

"What?"

She rolled her eyes at herself for lapsing into English. She switched back, "Go ahead."

"Okay. There is a nun missing from the Sisters of the Sacred Heart. Do you know it?"

"What do you think?"

He laughed. "It's the Augustinian convent on the edge of Assisi. The Mother Superior said that one of their professed nuns didn't show up for morning services."

"Professed nun?"

"It's the stage after novitiate. Professed nuns have taken the vows of poverty and chastity, but their commitment is not yet permanent, as it is in the perpetual stage."

"If you say so," Stella said vaguely. Who knew convents had this much jargon? Worse than a kitchen!

"Anyway, Mother Superior Maria Teresa said that she figured the nun wasn't feeling well. She'd been complaining of stomach pains. But when she didn't show up for lunch either, she sent a novice to check on her."

"And she was gone? The professional nun?"

"Professed nun," she could hear Don Arrigo smiling. "And yes."

"Is the order a cloistered convent?"

"It is not."

"So they're allowed to leave?"

"Yes. But there's more."

Stella waited.

And waited.

"Don Arrigo?"

"I'm not sure how to say this. It might not carry the same weight to a civilian than it does to someone of the cloth."

"Try me."

"She left her habit and wimple behind. In a pile."

Stella imagined the clothes, cast aside on a cold, stone floor. "That does sound drastic."

"Right," Don Arrigo sighed. "You get it."

"Though she still wore a cross. If that's her, of course."

"I'm waiting on a few more calls. But I think the odds are high that the nun you found is Sister Elena."

Stella remembered the woman in the road, bent at such an awkward angle. "But … the clothes she was wearing. Did she have clothes for, I don't know … non-nun days?"

Don Arrigo chuckled. "Such a heathen you are, Stella."

"Hey!"

"I'm only joking. I'm not sure about her wardrobe. Like I said earlier, that varies from order to order and really convent to convent. But the Mother Superior did say that it looked like their boxes of clothes for the poor had been ransacked."

"Did you tell her about the woman in the road?"

He paused. "I didn't. Which did lead to a lot of questions about why I was asking and how I knew. But I didn't feel like I should be the one to divulge that news."

"If it's news."

"Right. That too."

"But it is a lead," Stella said, thoughtfully. "I need to visit the convent. What's the name again?"

"I'll text it to you," Don Arrigo began. "Have you filled Luca in?"

"Not yet." She imagined Luca's eyes narrowing at her interference. But he'd be angrier if she continued behind his back. "But I will."

Don Arrigo paused. "Okay, I'll let you know if I hear anything from the other convents."

"Are you sure I can't call them myself?"

"I'm sure," Don Arrigo said firmly. "These houses are skeptical of strangers. Consider me your foot in the door. I promise it's top priority for me."

"*Grazie*, Don Arrigo."

"That nun," he said softly. "What could she have been running to?"

"Or," countered Stella, "What could she have been running from?"

Leaving the *fruttivendolo* with greens, a melon, and a spectacular head of lettuce, frilled like a sea creature, Stella caught sight of Luca at the edge of the piazza, his hands in his pockets. If Stella didn't know better, she'd have assumed he was having a lovely moment, contemplating the robust beauty of the valley.

But the tense rise of his shoulders gave him away. As did the tightness of his jaw when he turned his head and she caught his profile.

Something about his stillness forced her to watch him a few moments longer.

He caught sight of her and startled. "Stella! What are you doing?"

She looked around, hitching her grocery bag higher on her arm. "What people do in a crisis. Shop for dinner guests." She sighed. "Isn't that weird?"

He shook his head and looked back over the view. "So weird. I was actually just thinking about that. I'm supposed to be processing requests for new identification cards. But I can't work through the paperwork any better than the arrest or the dead woman." He kicked at a loose cobblestone. "Useless."

She sighed. "Tell me about it."

"And why are so many old men losing their identification cards all of a sudden?"

With a shrug, Stella said, "Maybe all the action around here these last few months makes it hard for them to focus, too."

They stood in silence, staring out over the valley as a rising wind shuddered in the trees.

Luca dropped his head and rubbed his eyes. "We can't accept reports of a missing person until tomorrow. Until then … this woman is dead and somebody has to be looking for her. Panicked, probably. And I can't do anything."

His forlorn tone reminded Stella of her sister, Grazie, mourning a shriveled dandelion crown.

"Stella?"

She gazed out over the fields. The poppies were fading now, the red replaced by a bloom of purple. It couldn't be lavender, could it? The Piano Grande had purple lentil flowers, but they wouldn't get lentils here, could they?

"Stella? Don't go vanishing on me," Luca said softly.

The kindness in his voice broke her reserve. "The woman in the road …"

"*Madonna mia*, did your guests never show up?"

She shook her head impatiently. Now that she decided to tell him, she needed to get the words out. "No, Mrs. Copeland is alive and well. And waiting for dinner." Stella lifted the groceries.

"Oh, right. You said. Sorry, my head is all over the place."

"I think the woman in the road is … was … a nun."

Luca frowned. "Jumping to conclusions isn't helpful right now, Stella."

"I don't jump. I never jump." Stella hugged her grocery bag to her chest.

He rubbed his eyes again, muttering to himself, "I'm drowning in variables. Just give me one damn constant."

Stella shifted her groceries to her other shoulder. "I don't work that way."

"I know," Luca said, waving his hand. "You take in all this chaos and put it in the matrix of your brain and somehow a reasonable notion comes out. Good for you."

Stella stared at him.

Luca pressed his lips together. "If you thought she was a nun, why didn't you say so this morning?"

"Because given how . . . awkward things have been between us," Stella said as Luca looked away. "I wasn't sure you'd listen! Imagine that!"

"So why are you telling me now?"

Stella hesitated. "Don Arrigo called around to a few convents. One order is missing a young nun."

"Don Arrigo called . . ." Luca's expression shifted from surprise to suspicion. "You put him to work."

"What? No. Not exactly," Stella fought to keep the defensiveness out of her voice.

"Not exactly? I can picture how this went down. You played helpless like always and got someone to do your dirty work."

Her breath caught.

He continued. "You overstepped, Stella." Under his breath, he muttered, "Maybe Captain Tribuzio was right. You have no idea what your place is."

Stella went still. She set her bag on the cobblestones and looked up, her voice ragged. "My place?"

He shook his head. "Don't take it out of context."

"Pretty sure I've got all the context I need, thanks." She picked the bag up and flicked a glance toward the road.

He sighed heavily. "Listen. You need to watch the line. Leave the heavy lifting to the professionals."

"Heavy lifting."

He smiled, as if relieved she got it. "Yes! Just don't insert yourself into an investigation."

"You were investigating convents?"

He sighed. "No. Obviously, not. But don't you see? If you start asking questions, it makes it harder when I have to go in asking questions. Convents hardly throw their doors open. How is it going to look when I show up, a day after a priest called asking after a missing nun?"

"Oh," Stella said. "I guess I hadn't thought about it that way."

"Of course you didn't," Luca said. "Because you never think. You're all reflex, no reflection."

"That is unfair."

"Is it? At the merest hint of drama, you come flying down the road."

"I had to know if it was my guest!"

"Why? Why did you need to get a jump on officials?"

"Because," Stella said through gritted teeth. "Because if it was Mrs. Copeland, it raised all sorts of scenarios. Her husband trapped, injured, maybe worse." Stella shook her head to clear the welling tears.

At the panic in her voice, Luca softened and took a tentative step toward her. He stopped and rubbed his neck. "Hey. Hey, Stella, I'm sorry. I should have known."

Stella refused to meet his eyes. This wasn't the moment to drown in memories of the car accident that left her fatherless and a sister to no one. "Should have known that maybe I acted because I was terrified of what might happen if I didn't?"

"Well…"

"You treat me like a bloodhound. Good for the nose, but when I tell you my concerns about what it all means, you send me away like I peed on your carpet." Stella winced at the harshness of the words in the rising wind.

The lettuce worked its way out of the bag and fell to the ground. She picked it up angrily.

Luca stared at Stella. "You know that's a dramatic retelling of events."

"Is it?" Her hands gripped the lettuce, bruising the tender leaves.

"It is," he said firmly. "I'm not criticizing your hunch. I am irritated that you had Don Arrigo call around to convents. Get a hold of yourself."

Stella froze. "'Get a hold of myself'?" Stella laughed through the increasing pressure of tears. "You realize you're one step from telling me I'm hysterical. Do I faint next?"

He flinched. Jaw tight, he took a slow breath. "You say you're terrified of what might happen if you don't act? Well, maybe one day you'll cause more damage by acting than if you'd just stood still."

The grocery bag slipped off Stella's shoulder and hit the ground, the melon rolling to Luca's feet with a small thud. She snatched it back and pushed it back in the bag, her hands tangling in the straps. Finally, she yanked the bag up to her shoulder.

He stopped her from whirling around with a hand on her arm. She yanked it back and the grocery bag fell off her arm again, this time with an alarming crash as greens spilled across the piazza. "Don't touch me!"

"Stella, come on. Let me help."

"Don't bother!"

He opened his mouth to say something but then turned on his heel and strode away.

She fixed her eyes on her groceries, scattered. For a moment she held herself utterly still and then began shoving the juice and pasta and greens into their bags. To add to the indignity, her crouched position pushed her phone out of her pocket and though she tried to catch it, it slipped through her fingers to clatter onto the cobblestones. Holding her breath, praying that she didn't crack her screen again, she turned the phone and felt a wash of relief. No new cracks.

But there was a message from Marta. Bringing the bag up to her shoulder again, she noticed Marta sent the article about Giancarlo.

Giancarlo.

Steady Giancarlo.

They hadn't reached full trust yet perhaps, but he would never goad her in the piazza and then walk away when she was surrounded by groceries. A small voice reminded her that she all but told Luca to leave. She lifted her chin, ignoring the sting.

A raindrop hit her cheek.

Stella opened the article.

The rain fell harder and Stella decided to put her phone away and read the rest later. Then her gaze snagged.

She dropped her bag of groceries. But this time, eyes glued to the screen, she didn't notice.

SUNDAY

The sound of rain worked its way into Stella's fitful sleep. After a fractured dream of looking under couch cushions for something lost but unnameable, she threw back the covers and gave up.

She rubbed her eyes.

Roberto and Romina...

Leo...

The nun...

Giancarlo.

Should she talk to Matteo about Giancarlo? Her thoughts returned to the article that upended her evening. She'd cooked on autopilot and only smiled when Mr. Copeland suggested that the pasta could use some saffron. Then he laughed at his wife's empty plate, saying that she clearly didn't think the dish needed any alteration, adding, "I guess vacation agrees with you!"

Stella stood up and opened the windows, wondering at the rain. The old wives had it right. Funny, neither Domenica nor Luisella were actually wives. Perhaps never had been—Domenica avoided the subject and Luisella avoided all subjects.

Checking the clock, Stella realized it wasn't yet time to start breakfast. But she could get ahead of the day's cooking. She stared at the rain for a moment before climbing back in bed, turning the pages of her mystery novel until she found where she'd left off the night before. Barbanera curled beside her, she tried to lose herself in crimes and clues, but all of it fell flat.

She tossed the book to the side.

Her hand itched to pick up her phone, to read the article again.

Instead, she got up and made her bed, trying to focus on each step of the process, like she might focus on measuring flour. She willed the meditative state brought on by cooking, focusing fully on process to allow her creativity to roam and wander.

Nothing happened.

She flopped on the bed, trying to still her racing heart.

A warm shower, she told herself. She scrubbed her hair, deciding she had plenty of time to dry it.

By the time she entered the kitchen, clean if not refreshed, it was only a little ahead of schedule.

She heard Mr. Copeland on the phone, speaking softly on the stairwell. "Is there sign of diaphragmatic herniation…and there's no way to move her to…no, of course, I hadn't considered the security risk…yes, I can be ready…what time?"

Diaphragmatic herniation?

As she released the fire under the moka for coffee, Mr. Copeland came downstairs. "Stella, I wonder if I could ask you a favor?"

"Of course," Stella said, drying her hands on the towel. "A shame about the rain, but I can direct you to some great museums."

As if to punctuate her sentence the rain drove harder, practically clicking against the pavement. Hail?

Mr. Copeland glanced at his phone. "I've been called away on a rather urgent matter."

"I hope everything is okay?"

"Yes. In a way." He paused, pushing his iron gray hair off his forehead. "You see, I'm a thoracic surgeon."

She nodded.

He hesitated. "I can't say too much…but there's been a major Mafia bust."

Stella worked to keep her face neutral. "Is that so?"

"Yes. And in the process, a high ranking US federal agent has been shot. With my experience in diaphragm repair, they need me to come in."

"What would they do if you weren't nearby?" Stella asked, curious now.

"Fly her to the Landstuhl Regional Medical Center in Germany, but transporting a person in critical condition isn't ideal. Easier to move me to her."

"Okay," Stella said. *What does this have to do with me?*

"I can't take my wife," Mr. Copeland said, his gaze glancing up the stairs, where Stella could make out a slow shuffle across the floorboards. "I…You…Well. She's not confident on her own."

Stella nodded uncertainly.

"A helicopter is meeting me in Perugia in an hour and I'll be gone at least a day. Two or three, if the lungs are lacerated. Cindy's been so looking forward to this trip, she loves Italy. You should see our house— paintings of Venice and ceramics from Deruta everywhere. I can't bear to think of her seeing nothing but the four walls of our room."

He looked at Stella beseechingly, as if willing her to understand, to help.

"You want me to show her a good time?" She blurted.

Mr. Copeland exhaled in relief. " I know it's a lot to ask, and of course I'll pay extra for your tour guide services."

Stella's mind raced. How in the world could she take on a charge when she was already in the weeds?

His eyes flicked back to the stairs. "I wouldn't ask, except I told her I needed to leave and…well, would it be possible?"

Stella's hands gripped the counter. "Of course."

An hour later, Stella regretted her acceptance.

Mrs. Copeland was perfectly polite, but Stella's every question landed with a thud. Using her most encouraging tone, Stella tried to get Mrs. Copeland talking about where she lived, her children, if she had cats, but the woman answered in single syllables while studying the pot of jam. Then she stared at her phone, rearranging the order of apps on her lock screen. Pouring Mrs. Copeland another cup of coffee, Stella noticed that Mr. Copeland hadn't been kidding about all her phone camera functions. The number of settings on Mrs. Copeland's lock screen made it look like hieroglyphics.

As soon as Mrs. Copeland finished her last bite, she leapt up to clear the table.

Stella said, "Please, allow me. Why don't I clean up and then we can go to my friend Cosimo's antique shop?" Older Americans loved "antiquing" and found Foro Antiquariato a treasure trove of delights. Though her guests rarely spoke Italian, and Cosimo's English was limited to numbers and the jovial pronouncement—which he always offered several decibels louder than necessary—"Very *old*! Very good!," guests often remarked in their reviews that their visit to the antiquarian ranked as one of their trip highlights. Somehow forging an understanding over dusty relics made for a memorable experience.

At Stella's proposal, Mrs. Copeland shrank back against the stairwell. She held up her phone, "Oh, I can't take rainy-day photos until I get the perfect app. I'll stay behind and research. I have to edit the photos I took yesterday, anyway."

Stella floundered. If she left Mrs. Copeland behind, would her husband assume Stella had ignored his request? "Cosimo is a hoot. You'll have a good time. And his shop is dry, with plenty of curiosities to photograph."

You can't keep hiding behind your camera, she thought but did not say.

Mrs. Copeland shook her head. "But what if he says something to me in Italian?"

Stella stared. Cosimo was well known for telling anyone who would listen, whether they understood or not, all about his shop—from the fact that it sat on a former worship site to how he sourced the glass for his windows. "He'll definitely say something to you in Italian. He doesn't know much English. But you'll love him, trust me."

Mrs. Copeland stared at her shoes, muttering that he might be insulted if she didn't answer properly.

Stella wanted to explain that it was almost impossible to insult Italians. When she passed old men playing cards in the piazza, they regularly chided each other for poorly thought out moves. No one took offense.

Watching Mrs. Copeland's struggle, Stella's heart twisted. She knew all about being a stranger in a strange land. Weirdly, she realized, she felt less a fish out of water here, in her mother's ancestral village, than she had growing up in her own home.

She wondered if Mrs. Copeland felt the same.

Stella adopted an encouraging tone, "You don't have to say a word. I'll do all the talking. And if it's not for you, we can go to the bakery. Didn't you want to try a loaf of real Umbrian bread?"

Barbanera sauntered out from the kitchen, licking his lips from the breakfast of roasted chicken and bone meal pureed chunky style, served on a pink saucer rimmed with darker pink, the same shade as the flowers that marched across the matching tea cup.

He walked to the front door, his tail waving like a flag.

"Is he coming?" Mrs. Copeland asked. "In the rain?"

Noticing that the rain's thrumming had faded, Stella said, "I think it's stopping. Knowing Barbanera, he knows exactly where I'm going. Cosimo always gives him a cat treat."

Mrs. Copeland held her breath for a moment. "Okay, okay," she said quickly, as if trying to talk herself into it. "I'll go."

"Great! That's wonderful!" Where did this Mrs. Rogers Neighborhood persona come from? And how could she persuade it to take a hike? This much cheery encouragement made her head spin.

Despite the grating tone of her own voice, Stella found herself animatedly pointing out Aramezzo's landmarks. Mrs. Copeland warmed to Stella's descriptions of the shopkeepers of each business they passed, though when Bruno stepped out of his *macelleria* right as Stella was telling her about how he hand cured *capocollo* from his brother's pigs, raised semi-wild in a large enclosure on Monte Subasio, Mrs. Copeland wandered away to take photos.

The butcher gave Mrs. Copeland a curious glance before telling Stella that he'd made sausages and had a batch of her special request—pork sausage with a splash of amaro. He raised his eyebrow. "I fried two up for our dinner last night. Stella…*complimenti*. I take back my jokes about drunk sausage."

Stella grinned.

"You got some more culinary surprises in there?" he said, pointing to her basket.

She laughed. "Cosimo is always in a better mood if I bring him something I'm working on. Two pots of jam."

Noticing the butcher staring hard at her basket, Stella said, "I bet Benedetta would love the apricot with lavender. Here, take this one."

He broke out in a grin. "Cosimo won't mind?"

"He doesn't know he's getting any, so he'll be quite satisfied with plum."

One of their longest conversations.

Bruno strolled back into his shop, whistling. Stella chuckled, remembering his little flute. For such a scowling man, he sure delighted in ethereal music.

Mrs. Copeland inched back, muttering, "These stone walls are fascinating."

"The walls?" Stella frowned.

Mrs. Copeland fixed her stare on a spot over Stella's shoulder and said all in a rush, "I read how the walls around here are from different eras, with Roman foundations, and then mostly Medieval with Renaissance additions and modern repairs. Like a layer cake, I guess. Though like no cake I've ever eaten. Too bad about the vines growing out of them. Vines aren't as dangerous to walls as old cannons, I'd say, but they can take down a wall over time."

When she paused her recitation, Stella said, "Huh. That's interesting."

Mrs. Copeland startled and clapped her hand over her mouth. "I went on and on, didn't I? James warned me against delivering bizarre factoids."

Stella blinked. "No, I mean it." She did. Even though the delivery was a little . . . intense. Stella had a sudden image of Mrs. Copeland as a child on the edge of the playground, struggling to make friends by explaining to kids that bananas are berries but strawberries aren't.

Ten minutes into their visit, Stella realized that Cosimo would have no more luck than she or Bruno when it came to warming Mrs. Copeland. Even when Stella tried to inveigle the woman in conversation about Aramezzo's mystical history, with Cosimo pointing out charms and talking about the unexplained rock formations on Subasio, Mrs. Copeland only smiled vaguely before wandering to a corner, snapping photos of an old lamp.

She went outside to wait for Stella.

Cosimo shook his head, his candy-floss hair standing out about his head more than usual. "A bit of a dud, your Signora Copeland. How is the husband?"

Stella sighed. "He's got some bitter undertones, but he's easier to talk to. More outgoing."

"They say opposites attract."

"I suppose."

"I hope babysitting isn't getting in the way of helping the police solve these mysteries. Goodness, Aramezzo is busier than Palermo these days." Cosimo chuckled to himself.

"The police don't want my help," Stella said irritably.

"And when has that ever stopped you?" Cosimo asked, his voice warm with affection. His next words were cut off by Leo emerging from a side room.

Leo stopped when he saw Stella. "*Buongiorno*. Everything okay, Stella?"

Her voice warm, Stella said, "I should be asking you that."

Leo gave a tight laugh. "Sorry, I guess it feels like everyone is in some jeopardy. I'm pleased when I see anyone walking around, normal-like. Even this guy," he jerked his thumb toward Cosimo with a smile.

Cosimo smiled back, "Keep that up and maybe I won't let you root through my unsaleables. Did you find what you were looking for?"

Leo held up a lamp. "This will do." He turned to Stella, "Orlando knocked over Marta's lamp. That dog has no manners."

Cosimo frowned. "I thought you broke it when you were letting Ascanio ride you like a horse."

Chortling, Leo said, "And I thought we agreed to keep that part between us." Waving goodbye, he strode past them toward the door. "Good to see you, Stella. Thanks again, Cosimo."

As he walked away, Stella lifted her nose. Since Roberto and Romina got hauled away, it seemed she smelled coffee everywhere. This aroma of coffee that Leo wafted behind him, it smelled rounded and sweet. Better than what she got her moka to produce. She'd have to ask Marta where she got her beans.

Outside, Leo stopped to greet Mrs. Copeland who yanked her phone from her pocket and ran to the piazza to take photos. Leo watched her for a moment before shrugging and striding away.

Cosimo chuckled.

Stella said, "It's nice you and Leo get along so well now..." Her voice faded as she noticed strangers filing stiffly into Trattoria Cavour.

Cosimo said, "I always liked the boy, just thought his *porchetta* could use a little more flavor. Like his father's."

Now Stella remembered, it wasn't Cosimo who had a problem with

Leo, it was the other way around. It was Leo who considered Cosimo—what was it? Ah, yes. "An old fart."

Cosimo continued, "He's matured quite a bit since dating Marta, don't you think? He used to be so arrogant, peacocking all over town. Ah, the power and profundity of love."

Stella felt like she had to get going before Cosimo used this as a segue to ask winkingly about Giancarlo."Powerful, yes. Profundity. Anyway, I need to chase after my guest."

"Here's a notion. Why don't you take your *musone*—"

"My what?"

"*Musone*. A person who dampens the mood."

"Like a stick in the mud?"

"If you like," Cosimo said expansively. Easy enough for him to be breezy, he wasn't juggling a guest and an investigation. "Take her to Domenica's."

"You don't think Domenica would overwhelm her?"

Cosimo grinned, his two different-color eyes flashing with humor behind his thick glasses. "I think she just might."

Domenica studied Mrs. Copeland as they shook hands. As Mrs. Copeland fussed over which seat she should take, Domenica handed her a basket of books and showed her how to shelve them.

Mrs. Copeland flushed faintly before shifting the basket to her other hand. For a moment it looked like she might put the basket on the desk and stroll out, but then she hitched the basket into the crook of her elbow and disappeared into the rabbit warren of stacks.

"She must understand more Italian than she lets on," Stella said quietly.

"She doesn't." Domenica settled into her chair at the desk.

"But she did what you asked."

"Listen, when you work at a refugee settlement like the Shousha camp in Tunisia, with people from every language family arriving en route to Sicily with eyes on the European Union, you learn that charades is universal."

Stella opened her mouth, but then shut it. Tunisia? Refugees? Sicily?

"One day I'll tell you the stories. You'll love the one about Sister Paola who managed to outwit a customs officer using only a crucifix and a tin of sardines." Domenica smiled fondly at the memory before shaking her head. "Your distractibility is rubbing off on me. Tell me what you've learned and I'll tell you what I've learned."

Nodding, Stella said, "First of all, I saw a bunch of strangers filing into Trattoria Cavour."

Domenica pushed her glasses higher on her nose. "Strangers?"

"Well, I didn't know them. We need to ask Matteo to keep an eye on the restaurant today, to watch when they leave. He might recognize them."

Nodding, Domenica said, "Okay, noted."

Stella glanced back into the stacks. "Should we be talking about this with her in earshot?"

"Signora Copeland," Domenica said loudly. In a few moments the woman appeared from behind a bookshelf.

"Cindy, please."

"Cindy. Make sure you watch out for the nest of live rats in the corner of the baking section." Domenica kept her face expressionless, her hands clasped in her lap.

Cindy looked from Domenica to Stella.

Finally, Stella said in English, "Domenica said the books are dusty. Be careful of your dress."

Cindy nodded uncertainly and escaped back into the stacks.

"See?" said Domenica. "So when is the husband coming back?"

Stella shrugged. "Depends on how well the operation goes, I suppose."

Domenica looked toward the stacks, where the sound of books

sliding onto shelves punctuated the silence. "What's he like?"

Stella shrugged again. "He told me I should add saffron to the *tartufata*."

"Ah," Domenica said. "That makes sense."

Stella scowled. "You agree with him?"

"Of course not," Domenica said. She took off her glasses and cleaned them on her scarf. "By the way, Giancarlo came in last night, looking for you. He said he'd stopped by your house, but you weren't home and didn't answer his calls."

Stella kept her face blank. "Okay. Thanks."

Domenica narrowed her eyes. "Everything okay there?"

The bell over the door jangled and Stella lunged to cover the computer, then realized it was already covered.

"Nice. So steady," muttered Domenica under her breath as Luca walked toward them.

Without preamble, Luca said, "I spoke to Don Arrigo. He said the Mother Superior is willing to talk. The one from Sisters of the Sacred Heart. Don Arrigo believes she'll be more forthcoming with a woman in the room."

"And?"

"And what? None of our female officers are on today."

"All two?" Stella frowned in pretended confusion. "What are the odds?"

"*Madonna mia*, Stella," he said softly, shaking his head.

"What? It's math. Is math hysterical nowadays?"

His eyes flicked to Cindy, who had emerged from behind a bookshelf. Quietly, Luca said, "I never said hysterical. You know I wouldn't say that."

She kept her face deliberately blank, her toe tapping the floor. Peace offering? Or trap?

He held her gaze for a beat. When he spoke, his voice eased softer. "If you're done dressing me down in your head, will you come with me?"

"Where?"

"To the convent," he said, a smile just touching his mouth. "I did mention it."

"All the women in Aramezzo, and you picked me. Should I be flattered?"

"Don't read too much into it," Luca said, rubbing his chin. "And I'm only asking if you promise not to bite my head off on the way."

"I'll consider it," she said, her lips betraying a smile.

"Promise?" There was a flicker in his eyes. She glanced at Domenica, who was smirking at them. And just like that, Stella saw it clearly: he wasn't picking a fight and she didn't need armor. Then she remembered. "Oh, I can't. I told Mr. Copeland that I'd look after his wife."

Luca regarded Cindy Copeland for a moment. "She's got two legs and two arms and she looks functionally intelligent. Why can't she stay on her own?"

Stella shook her head. "It's too much to explain. Take Domenica."

"Am I not to be consulted?" Domenica interjected. "Because I have no interest. I'd rather stay with Cindy."

Cindy's eyes widened at the sound of her name.

Stella hesitated. "You're willing to stay with her?"

"It's hardly babysitting. Go. Have fun," Domenica grinned knowingly.

"Mrs. Copeland," Stella said. "I—"

"Cindy, please. And I can stay here while you do your errand."

Stella rocked back on her heels. "You . . . you understood all of that?"

"Enough," Cindy said before adding, "Charades" just as Domenica said, "*Sciarade*." The two looked at each other with quizzical expressions and then burst into laughter.

Domenica waved Stella off. "See? Now go on. We'll be fine. Oh!" She said, straightening. She rummaged in the drawer of her desk. "This book I just got in about advertising in the 1950s—the industry's golden age."

Cindy's face lit up. Within moments the women were hunched over the desk. Stella could hear snatches of their conversation. "That's a cigarette," said Cindy.

"Cigarette," repeated Domenica without a trace of an Italian accent. "*Cigaretta*."

"*Cigaretta*," repeated Cindy carefully. She looked up, from Stella to Domenica and said, "Did you know that doctors actually used to prescribe cigarettes to patients? Beer, too. It makes me wonder what things we currently assume are healthy will be found to be poison in a few decades." She flushed bright red, then dropped her gaze to the desk.

Domenica's chair squeaked as she changed position. In Italian she said, "Society's perception that cigarettes make men seem burly and women seem elegant is strange indeed."

Domenica and Cindy smiled at each other, and Stella wondered how much they understood the other. It didn't seem to matter as they hunkered over the book once more, their heads close together, the steel grey and the ash blonde.

Stella said, "Domenica, will you let Matteo know I've left. And remind him about that other thing?"

Domenica didn't look up but waved her hand to show she'd tell Matteo about the strangers at Trattoria Cavour.

"Well, I guess my work here is done," Stella muttered. She looked for Barbanera, forgetting he'd followed the butcher into the *macelleria* in hopes of scraps.

Stella followed Luca out. In silence, they walked to the parking lot, where he unlocked a truck. "Not your usual vehicle," she said.

"Long story," Luca said. He opened the door for her and she recoiled from the wave of heat surging from the cab of the truck. An irrational part of her wanted to hold her breath as if diving into a pool. She slid in and drummed her fingers on the door handle, waiting for him to crank up the air conditioner.

They rode in silence until Luca pulled the truck onto what appeared to be a farm road. "Can you open the gate?" he asked, gesturing at the barrier before them.

She turned to stare at him. Why were they entering a farm?

He sighed and hopped out of the car—opening the gate, then driving forward, and then closing the gate again before sliding back into the driver's seat.

"Is this private property?" Stella asked.

"Call it a shortcut."

"I'm supposed to trust that you didn't bring me out here to kill me?"

His lip twitched. "So dramatic."

She looked away and smiled. "Are you going to explain why of all the women in Aramezzo you chose me for this mission?"

He thought for a moment. "I didn't want to get anybody else up to speed."

"Plus, you remembered my unerring ability to look before I leap."

He tried not to smile.

She stared out the window at the horses. What farm was this?

"You're good with people," Luca said. "It's the flip side of your recklessness."

"Recklessness?" Stella said.

"Don't start. You know what I mean. You go in heart first. It's not always great for detective work—"

"Need I remind you—"

"No, you needn't," Luca said with a small grin. "Yes, you've been helpful. Last case notwithstanding."

At the mention of Salvo, Stella narrowed her eyes and glared out the window.

Luca went on, "I'm not saying you don't have a talent for it. You do. You have great intuition, above and beyond your ability to sniff your way through anything."

Stella pressed her palms together in her lap.

He sighed. "Yes, I know you're more than a bloodhound. That's what I'm trying to tell you. And failing, obviously."

"Keep going and we'll see," Stella said, grinning out the window. "The part about my fabulous intuition isn't so bad."

He chuckled. "Sure, you lack restraint and I get irritated when that makes you horn in on my work, but I'd have to be an idiot to miss how people trust you."

Her fingers tightened on her lap and she looked out the window. They drove in silence for a few minutes and then she yelped. "I know this road! Or at least I know this stand of trees. But I usually see it from the other side."

Luca stopped at a gate. This time Stella hopped out, opened it, and closed it behind them. Once she was back in the car, he said, "A shortcut. As I said."

"Why don't I know about it?"

He dropped his head to regard her over the rim of his sunglasses. "If I had a euro for everything you don't know—"

She scowled, but at the sight of his eyebrows rising, she broke into laughter.

He smiled. "The road isn't private, but since the whole area is mostly used for grazing, it's not maintained. Gravel and potholes are murder on a car's undercarriage."

"That's not such a long story," Stella said. "But whose truck is this then? I haven't seen you with it." She looked around. "Though it does look familiar."

"My father's. He took my car. It's more comfortable for taking his brother to the oncologist. And Salvo has the cruiser."

Oncologist.

"Cancer?" she asked softly.

He nodded, his lips tight.

Quietly, she said, "I'm so sorry. Really, Luca. I'm sorry. It's hard to lose someone before you know that's a possibility, but I bet it's just as hard to worry you'll lose them."

He said nothing. When he finally spoke, his voice shook before it found its bearings. "We found out last week. They caught it early, but. You know. Anyway. Thank you. For saying that."

He pulled into a parking lot and cut the engine. "*Eccoci qua.*" We're here.

A three-wheeled truck trundled down the road. Luca and Stella both watched until it disappeared around the bend.

Tentatively she asked, "Are you close? You and your uncle?"

He nodded, his eyes fixed on his hands gripping the wheel. "Not as close as he is to my brother. But yes, pretty close." Luca cleared his throat. "Okay, I'm taking the lead. Stella, listen. *I'm taking the lead.*"

"I'm sorry. I didn't mean to pry." She wiped at the perspiration beading on her forehead.

He turned to her, his gaze steady. "It's not prying. Later I can tell you all about how my brother has always been a better student than me, and he and my uncle bonded over their love of World War II history. For now, though, we just need to get out of this hot car."

She nodded. "You're in charge. Got it."

"But if you notice anything amiss, let me know, and if appropriate, I'll hand the reins to you."

She leaned forward, her shirt sticking to her back. "Does Captain Tribuzio know you brought me?"

"Stella, I could hardly bring you if he didn't approve it."

Her eyebrows lifted in surprise.

He sighed. "I may have told him that Don Arrigo mentioned that some of the nuns, especially the new ones, come from English speaking countries and so we needed not just a woman, but an English-speaking one."

She shook her head, muttering, "I swear, I never thought my language ability would be currency."

"Language *is* currency, Stella. No two ways about it." He climbed out of the car.

They walked in silence, heat waving off the stone walkway. Luca watched Stella for a moment before gesturing at the heavy wooden door. "Ladies first."

She knocked and smiled at the young nun who opened the door. The nun introduced herself and ushered them to the Mother Superior's office. "The Reverend Mother will be with you shortly." She closed the door and Stella and Luca sat in silence. Stella inhaled. Definitely more frankincense than the one in Aramezzo's cathedral. And more of benzoin's vanilla and balsam notes.

Luca watched her. "Incense match?"

"Not a bloodhound," Stella reminded him lightly.

"I didn't—" Luca started and then clenched his jaw and looked away.

"I'm kidding," Stella said. "Sorry. My delivery is bad. I guess I'm nervous. I went to Catholic school for a few years. Not a great experience. To tell you the truth, I find nuns a little terrifying."

He looked at his hands and chuckled. She switched gears. "So what do you want to get out of this meeting, anyway?"

"A photograph of the nun. To identify her."

Stella lifted her eyebrows. "That's it?"

"You want to know more than that?"

She stared at him, uncomprehending. "I want to know what kind of nun she was. If she showed up on time to meals. If she followed the rules. If she cried at night. If she picked at her food. If she read books."

He considered. "Why does it matter in a hit-and-run?"

She looked away.

"You don't think it was a hit-and-run."

She said nothing.

Luca said, "Yes, the person almost hit Leo. And then hit the nun. But there's nothing to imply it was intentional. Reckless, yes. Intentional, no."

Reckless. It's how he had described her.

Finally, Luca said, "You disagree."

After a few moments, when the only sound was the deep ticking of the clock in the corner, Stella said, "The person didn't stop. Either time. Once for Leo and once for the nun. Didn't stop. That's not reckless. That's malevolent."

"You don't know about drunk drivers, how they—"

"Don't I?" She turned to gaze at him steadily.

She saw the dawning understanding in his eyes. "Oh, Stella. Of course you know."

She pressed her lips together and stared at the desk in front of them. How could a room in a convent feel so much like purgatory? She'd never get out. She ran a finger around her collar, loosening it. Fighting for air.

"Stella? Are you okay?" Luca leaned toward her.

She gave a vehement shake of her head. Her thoughts swam wildly, reaching for a handhold to pull her into the present. The fall of wisteria, the smell that exploded when she popped the lid off the *tartufata*, Barbanera winding himself around Luisella's ankles.

Luisella.

Who almost hit those dogs.

Slowly, as if working through her thoughts as she spoke, Stella said, "An impaired driver, a drunk driver ... they can tell when they've hit something. Even a squirrel. Let alone a human. A drunk driver would have hit the brakes. If not before impact, at least after, to figure out what happened."

"How do you know they—"

She turned to him. "Whoever it was left no rubber on the road. Did you notice? No skid marks."

Even in the dim light, Stella noticed him pale. She went on, "Something about that bugged me at the time, but it didn't snap into place until just now. Whoever hit the nun, they didn't stop to wonder what they hit. Which means they meant to hit her."

The door opened, and a woman entered with a rustle of fabric, her broad smile creasing her already lined face. "I'm sorry to have kept you waiting."

Stella ordered her thoughts, skittering around her brain like peppercorns in boiling broth, to settle, settle, *settle*.

Images crashed around her. The nun, hit and left like an animal in the road. The memory blurred to Roberto and Romina being carted off. They were part of this, they had to be. The timing couldn't be coincidental.

She arranged her face into calm as the nun sat at the desk, arranging her habit around her before clasping her hands on the desk. "I'm Mother Maria Teresa. Now, I hear you may have news of our Elena?"

Luca darted his eyes to Stella as if reminding her to hold her tongue.

He needn't have bothered. Stella never felt less like talking in her life.

"Reverend Mother. Thank you for seeing us. I'm so sorry to bring you what might be bad news. Early yesterday morning, a motorist discovered the body of a person we believe to be a nun on the road leading to Aramezzo."

The smile dropped from her face, but other than that, the nun's expression didn't lose its neutrality. "A ... a body? Don Arrigo ... he didn't mention that." She shook her head. "This is shocking. I'm sorry, I don't know what to say. You think it's Elena?"

Stella studied the nun, who, for all her stammering, didn't look surprised.

She tuned in as Luca said, "We may need someone from the convent or someone from her family to come and identify the body. But in case it's not the same woman ... do you have a photo of Elena?"

The nun shook her head sadly before remembering. "Wait. Yes. Schoolchildren came in last month to assist us in feeding the poor. The teacher sent us photos. Now where are they?" The nun rifled one drawer, then another, before returning to the first and pulling out the same papers with trembling hands.

Luca checked his watch, then looked back at the nun.

Finally, Mother Maria Teresa withdrew an envelope from under a pile of rosary beads. The nun opened the envelope and thumbed through the photographs within. She stopped and pulled one photo close to her eyes for a moment before holding it at arm's length, muttering about needing a new glasses prescription. Then she pushed the photo across the table. "That's Elena. The one with three children around her. Children love Elena."

Stella and Luca jerked forward to lean over the photograph. They glanced at each other. Stella nodded. Even with the habit and the animated expression, it was the same woman. Same fine features, same high cheekbones. Luca nodded in return, picking up the photograph. He cleared his throat. "I'm sorry to tell you, but this is the same woman we found outside of Aramezzo yesterday morning."

The nun choked on a sob and pressed the back of her hand against her mouth. "I had prayed for it not to be..."

Before she could stop herself, Stella said, "You thought it might?" She darted a glance at Luca whose gaze was trained on the nun.

"Not so much thought as...as...feared. When I heard from Don Arrigo. Why would a priest from another town call me to ask if a nun was missing if not with dire news?"

Luca gave Stella an almost imperceptible nod, so she continued. "Was there anything about Sister Elena that gave you reason to believe the body we found might be her?"

"Well," Mother Maria Teresa began, "I mean, Elena disappeared."

Leaning forward, Stella said, "This can't be the first time a nun has left the convent, surely?"

"No. Of course not. Our world isn't for everyone, and often young nuns romanticize convent life." The nun caught Stella's widened eyes.

She smiled. "It may prove impossible for you to imagine, but some women crave our quiet and predictability, our life of service. Perhaps because they are born to it, or perhaps their childhood was tinged by enough chaos to make our routines a balm."

Stella nodded, thinking. "When nuns disappear, where do they usually go?"

"Home," the nun said simply.

"Then why didn't you assume that's where Elena had gone? Why leap to the conclusion that the body was her? Rather than what history has taught you—that errant nuns are to be found in their childhood beds?"

"Oh, er...well. I don't know, really. I suppose that phone call."

Stella thought for a moment and then said, "Is Elena's family from Aramezzo?" Luca flicked a smile in her direction and leaned back in his seat. "Is that why when a priest from Aramezzo called, you figured it to be related to Elena's disappearance?"

"No," the nun shook her head gravely.

"Then why didn't you assume Elena skipped home, like the other nuns?"

Mother Maria Teresa sagged for a moment and then straightened. "If you must know, Sister Elena didn't come from the kind of home women long to return to." Her voice trailed off.

"You don't sound certain, Reverend Mother," Stella said. Luca shot her a warning look. She pressed on. "Might there be more?"

"No," the nun clasped her hands in front of her. "I'll not sully Sister Elena's good memory by telling tales of her estrangement from her family. They moved house long ago, she didn't know where, and that's all I know of that."

Stella registered the dismissal. She and Luca stood in unison. Luca drew the photograph closer, studying the image of the beaming nun. He clicked the edge of the photo on the desk. "Can I take this photo for our file or would you prefer I photograph it?"

Mother Maria Teresa waved her hand. "Keep it."

Luca nodded and pulled out a business card. "If you think of anything else, please call me. Given what you've said about Sister Elena not having family for us to contact, there is a possibility we'll need to arrange with you to identify the body."

"Because there is no one else," Mother Maria Teresa said softly, staring at her hands folded on the desk.

"Because there is no one else," Luca confirmed.

"Do you need assistance finding your way back?" Mother Maria Teresa asked, uncapping a fountain pen and writing notes in the margin of the paper in front of her. The green ink shone wetly in the dim room.

"*Grazie*, Reverend Mother, but no," Luca said. They turned and walked into the shadowy corridor.

"She's hiding something," Stella whispered, as soon as they were out of earshot.

"Not now, Stella," Luca muttered.

"Luca—" She started to say more, but he put his hand on her back to propel her to the front door. The warmth of his touch loosened her knees, and she stumbled. He caught her elbow, brushing against her hip, and she stiffened her muscles to keep from leaning into him.

He muttered into her ear, "You may be right. But it won't do to antagonize a nun. Especially one with her power."

From around the corner in front of them they saw the flick of a black habit. As they approached, a face peered out before darting a look over her shoulder. In the low light, they couldn't make out features, just her diminutive size. The tiny nun crooked her finger and pointed to an empty room behind her.

Stella and Luca exchanged glances and followed the nun. Once in the sunlit room, the nun hurriedly closed the door behind them with a sigh. Now Stella could see her face, she noted the youthful bloom on the nun's cheeks, the unlined forehead. A young nun, like Sister Elena.

The nun checked the closed door and then said in a whisper, her gaze fixed on Stella, "I don't have much time. You're here about Sister Elena?"

Stella and Luca nodded. The nun closed her eyes. "Is she okay?"

Luca inclined his head to Stella. Who said, "I'm afraid she was hit by a car."

"She's . . . she's dead?" The nun asked, lifting her hand to her mouth.

Stella could only nod.

"Oh, *Dio mio*," the nun said, shaking her head. "When Elena disappeared, I thought I smelled trouble." Slowly, she added, "You have to talk to Sister Serafina."

"Sister Serafina," Stella repeated softly.

The nun chewed at a cuticle. Suddenly aware of her action, she whipped her hand away from her mouth. "Nasty habit," she said with a forced laugh. "Sister Serafina shared a room with Sister Elena. She hinted once or twice that Sister Elena had her fingers in the wrong pots."

Stella caught her breath. "What kind—" she started to ask.

"I don't know," the nun said fervently. "I tried to get Serafina to tell me, but even when Elena went missing, she couldn't get the words out. I begged her to at least talk to Mother Maria Theresa . . . the secret was killing her. I don't know if she did. I hope she did, but I worry she didn't."

"Do you think she'd talk to us?" Stella breathed, hardly daring to hope.

The nun cast a quick glance at Luca. "She's not here. She went with a group of sisters to the hospital to provide comfort to patients and their families."

Stella didn't look at Luca when she said, "We think Elena may have been killed."

The nun went as white as her wimple and let out a sound like a small cat.

Stella felt Luca stiffen beside her and knew she didn't have much more latitude. "We need to know everything we can so we can find the person who did this."

Luca mumbled, "If someone—"

"Luca, give me your card," Stella said, ignoring him.

The nun shot a look at Luca and then brought her fingers to her mouth again, nibbling at her nail. "I don't think—"

Stella took the card from Luca, her eyes sliding past the 333 that prefaced many Italian mobile numbers, staring at the rest. "312 22 22? Is this real?"

"You know my number," he said.

She shook her head. "No, you put it in my phone ages ago."

"Stay focused," Luca said, eyeing the door.

Stella grabbed a pen from the table, flipped the card over and uncapped the pen. She paused for a moment, staring at the pen, but then started writing when she saw the nun glancing over her shoulder. "Here's my number. Sister Serafina can call Officer Luca, or she can call me, whichever is more comfortable. We'll keep anything she says confidential. But tell her anything she can tell us, even if it doesn't feel important, could help us find Elena's killer."

The woman looked at the card in her hands. A clock ticked in the distance. Large, judging by the resonant thunks of the pendulum.

Stella hesitated, the scent of incense prickling her nose, underscored by the aroma of creamy mushrooms. She took a breath and said, "Whatever Elena did, it wasn't her fault. It was his."

Luca's head snapped toward Stella.

The nun's eyes widened.

Stella went on. "Have Sister Serafina call me. Please. For Elena."

The woman tucked the card into a pocket in her habit. "I'll try. I will. But now, you need to go before anyone realizes..."

Stella moved around the nun to stand by the door. "Hang back." She stepped out of the door and nearly knocked into the Mother Superior.

Stella froze for a moment before launching into speech. "Oh, hello! Can you believe we took a wrong turn? We should have accepted your offer of a guide after all! But I hope it's okay, I used that as an opportunity to admire the convent. I'm from the States and we just don't have places like these. Really special, these are. Love the stonework." Stella gestured vaguely behind her, at walls of stucco, not stone.

The older nun's eyes narrowed. "Why did you have the door closed?"

"Should I not have?" Stella asked laughing in what she hoped was an airy manner, though she feared she sounded manic. She grabbed Luca's hand and pulled him out of the room, pulling the door shut behind her. "We live in the country, you know. Leave a gate as you found it. So we closed that door to go to the other end of the room, but when we realized we shouldn't be walking without permission, we turned back."

The nun glared at Stella.

"Anyway," Stella babbled on hoping to distract the Reverend Mother from opening the door and finding their young friend. "You've got something great cooking for lunch today. Mushroom lasagna? One of my favorites! I hope you enjoy it."

The nun lifted her nose and sniffed and then looked back at them, but Stella and Luca had already disappeared around the corner and out the door.

Stella's mind whirred so frantically she didn't notice the passing landscape. Once in a while, she darted a look at Luca, but his eyes were fixed on the road, his jaw working. Would he tell her off for overstepping? She thought of his hand on her back as he guided her into the passenger seat.

"How did you know?" he asked.

She turned to him, eyebrow furrowed.

"You said it was 'his' fault."

Not the time for a treatise on the patriarchy. "I took a shot."

He slowed as they approached the part of the road where Leo's van had stalled. She saw his eyes scanning for skid marks. Her eye caught on the shrine. "Stop!"

The sudden braking lurched Stella forward, but she hardly noticed as she flung off her seatbelt and threw open the truck door. The smell of dust and olive leaves rose around her. She could hear Luca's voice behind her as she approached the niche carved into the cliffside. "Stella, can you pray later?"

She reached into the niche, her fingers brushing artificial petals and the sharp corners of rosary crosses. For a moment she worried it was gone, taken, but then she felt the edge of cardstock. She drew out the prayer card just as Luca drew up beside her. Her eyes ran over the message inked in blue. *Purity and silence in the face of temptation.*

And then the postscript in green ink. *Perdonami.* Forgive me.

"Stella?"

She held out the prayer card. "I found this yesterday."

Gingerly, he plucked it from her hand and examined both sides. "What am I supposed to be seeing?"

"Do you see the part that says *'perdonami'*?" He took off his sunglasses and scanned the card.

Stella took out her cell phone and dialed, her heart in her throat. She waved down Luca's protests to explain as the connection snapped open. "Don Arrigo. Thank goodness."

"Stella? Are you okay? Did you go to the convent?"

"I did and I have a question. What kind of ink do church officials use?" She turned away from Luca trying to get her to explain.

"What kind of ink?" She heard the confusion in Don Arrigo's voice. "I don't understand."

"Color, ball point, whatever. Is there a standard?"

He hesitated. "Ball point or gel, the archival kind that resists smearing."

"What about fountain pens?"

"Only for ceremonial documents. Fountain pens aren't uncommon then."

Stella nodded.

"Stella? Want to fill me in?"

"In a minute. How about color of ink? Is there a standard color?"

"I use blue, mostly. Black for official documents."

"Is that typical?"

"I've never really thought about it. Give me a second." She heard him shuffling papers.

Don Arrigo again. "Yes. Blue and black. Mostly black."

"Never green?" Luca gave a low whistle.

"Green? No. I don't think I've ever seen green ink on a church document. Or any documents, when it comes to that. It's not a very common color, is it?"

"So use of a green *fountain* pen would be even more unusual."

"I mean, unusual, but not impossible. It would be a stylistic preference, not a church-mandated one. Kind of like how C.S. Lewis used green ink."

"C.S. Lewis? The guy who wrote those Narnia books?"

"Correct, though he also wrote extensively on theology." He paused and added gently, "Which I'm happy to speak with you more about, but I'm guessing you have weightier matters to attend to?"

She shook her head. "Right! Okay. Thanks for your—wait! Do you know anyone locally who prefers green fountain pen ink?"

"I don't." She heard him chuckle. "But it's a habit I might pick up. It would give my documents a dramatic flair, don't you think?"

She smiled and signed off before turning to Luca who said, "I got it. The ink on this card—green, like what the Reverend Mother used."

She nodded. "Not common, according to Don Arrigo."

"In the church perhaps, but anybody could have left this prayer card. It doesn't have to be someone with a church affiliation."

"How many regular people use fountain pens?"

He frowned and stared at the card.

She went on, "Also, see how the first message is in blue ink? But the second, the part that reads 'forgive me' is in green, like somebody added it on impulse." Stella thought aloud. "For the Reverend Mother, the use of a fountain pen would mean tradition, dignity, connection to old ways. The green, her personal preference."

Gently, Luca said, "But why in the world would the Reverend Mother leave this prayer card here?"

"It's the closest shrine to where the nun was killed."

"But you found it the day we found Elena. Which means the card was here when she died."

She stared at Luca, willing him to understand.

"Oh, no, Stella. No, no, no, no. You can't be serious."

She shrugged. "What if the Reverend Mother killed the nun?"

"Stella, please. Why in the world would she want to do that?"

"Don Arrigo told me some stories about nuns that led me to believe nuns capable of anything."

Luca paused. "The skeletons?"

"The skeletons."

Luca said, "That was a long time ago."

"And you feel humanity has only become more beatific since then?"

He pressed his fingers to his eyes. "What kind of motive, Stella? It doesn't make any sense."

Pressing her lips together, Stella had to acknowledge he had a point. "I don't know yet. Maybe if Sister Serafina calls."

He ran his fingers over the edge of the card. A mourning dove called from the olive trees swaying in the hillside above them. "I can't take this to Tribuzio."

"I know." She took the card from him and tucked it back behind the Madonna. They walked to the truck in silence. Without a word, they buckled in and Luca drove up to Aramezzo, pulling his grandfather's truck into the parking lot. He kept the engine running.

His phone buzzed and he checked the screen, studying it for a moment before flipping the phone back over and looking back out the window.

Lilliana?

Stella broke the silence. "The nun was walking to Aramezzo. Don't people do walks for religious reasons?"

"Pilgrimages, yes," Luca nodded. "But if she was doing a pilgrimage to Chiesa di Santa Chiara di Aramezzo, Don Arrigo would have known about it. And she certainly would have asked permission from the Mother Superior. Who didn't mention it."

"Maybe she didn't mention it for a reason."

He took a breath. "Don't take this the wrong way. But please, don't let your imagination run away with you."

She shrugged. "I am logic girl. The nun was walking. Maybe the reason why is important."

"Maybe she knew someone in Aramezzo," Luca guessed. "I'll show her photo around."

"Oh, that's why you wanted the photo."

Luca nodded again, his eyes fixed out the windshield.

Finally, Stella said, "I sure could use a coffee about now."

Luca pressed his lips together, an almost smile. His hand moved to the key, but then went back to his knee. The air kept running and neither of them moved.

Finally, Stella said, "Luca?"

"Hmmm?"

"I want to be on the same team."

"Okay." He took off his sunglasses and turned to face her.

"I can't trust you if when I tell you a theory, you get angry that you didn't think of it first," Stella said,

His eyes narrowed.

She waved her hand. "Sure, you'll call it my flights of fancy or my insistent need to overstep. Which, well . . . maybe you're right. I see how I can get in your way."

He exhaled.

"I need to know that you're a safe place to land," Stella said. Her thoughts flitted to Giancarlo.

"You don't feel I'm safe?" Luca said softly. "The prayer card. I don't remember biting your head off."

She nodded but didn't answer, thinking through those awkward moments between them that sailed south.

"You solved the murder at the villa, didn't you? Not Salvo," Luca said with a sigh.

Stella watched Orietta, the pharmacist, staggering under the weight of a bag of potting soil.

"Stella?"

She shrugged, watching Orietta struggling under the bag.

Softly, he said, "Why didn't you tell me?"

Stella ran her teeth over her bottom lip.

He watched her in silence.

She stopped and turned her gaze to the window.

So lightly she wasn't sure it happened, he touched her hand. She looked at him. He looked at her and said, "You have something to tell me. I can listen."

She took a breath and without citing her sources, told him what she'd learned from Giancarlo and Domenica—why the government considered Roberto and Romina suspects in a Mafia drug running operation, what with the informant's information about the suspects' access to money laundering, and something shady in their history.

Luca nodded as he listened, his eyes fixed on hers.

At the end of her recitation, she paused. "I want to know what Roberto and Romina were doing when Romina's sister Lavinia was running the bar. The way Domenica tells it, they went completely off the radar. Why?"

Luca thought for a moment. "Weren't they with Roberto's family?"

"Where's that?"

"Sicily."

"Sicily? Like the home base of the Mafia?" Stella's voice went up an octave. She shook her head and said, "It feels like I'm talking about the north pole. Like Santa Claus is real."

"Sicily is big. The odds are low that his family is remotely involved with organized crime. Plus, I think they were becoming grandparents then."

"According to the movies, being a grandparent doesn't rule one out from being a godparent, if you know what I mean."

"I don't."

She shook her head. "It doesn't matter. I can look into Roberto's family. No need to waste police resources on a wild goose, right?"

"Stella, these expressions are baffling. But I appreciate your candor. So I'm going to tell you something, in case it proves relevant for Domen—I mean, in your thought process."

Stella arranged her face to appear suitably both confused by the reference, and ready to listen.

"But you can't tell Matteo."

"Why Domenica and not . . . I mean, why not Matteo?"

Luca's jaw worked.

Oh.

Giancarlo. He didn't trust Giancarlo.

Luca sighed. "The police raided Roberto and Romina's house."

"They did what?"

"Look, Stella, we were under orders."

"When was this?"

"This morning."

"And you're just now telling me?"

Luca scowled and held up his phone. "Stella, you are finding out about three minutes after I did."

She dropped her gaze to her lap before looking back up with a sigh. "Okay. What did they find?"

Luca closed his eyes.

"Luca?"

"Heroin. They found heroin."

"*Heroin?*"

He nodded.

She bit the inside of her cheek. "Do people still use heroin?"

"Stella."

"Sorry, sorry."

Luca paused. "I used to think it was pretty 1980's too, but heroin is a favorite of the Mafia—pretty much their exclusive domain in Italy."

"Heroin," Stella said, disbelief quieting her voice. "At Roberto and Romina's?"

"I'm afraid so."

The engine idled louder. "No way. Listen. There's another way this could have gone down."

"I'm all ears."

"No, wait, don't just dismiss me! Hear me out!" Stella caught herself. "Oh. Disregard."

Luca smiled and turned to face Stella more fully, his dimple flashing. Why did she always forget about his dimple? She'd noticed months ago that both dimples appeared when Luca was delighted. It occurred to her that she hadn't seen both dimples in some time.

She realized Luca was waiting for her to speak. "What if someone else in Aramezzo was running drugs for the Mafia. And when he—"

"Or she."

Stella smiled. "Or she." After a beat, she went on, "When the person regardless of gender realized the government was onto them, they framed Roberto and Romina. Meanwhile, the Mafia members who did not get picked up think there is some loose thread in Aramezzo. And they tried to run down that loose thread."

Luca thought. "Leo? A loose thread? The nun?"

"Okay that's where my theory breaks down. But maybe Leo and the nun were collateral damage and the killer was after someone else."

"You think the crimes are related."

She shrugged. "Two soufflés collapse, you suspect the oven."

He chuckled. "Not sure kitchens and crime scenes are close enough neighbors for that to work."

"Are you kidding? In both you follow the ingredients, trust your gut, and hope the whole thing doesn't blow up in your face."

"Nonetheless, you'll forgive me for not signing onto the theory that the Mafia has anything to do with Elena's death."

"Fair enough," Stella nodded. "As long as you're not mocking me for it."

"Never mocked a day in my life," Luca said with a grin.

Stella grinned back. "Anyway, it's easier to buy than Luisella driving around like a crazy person."

"Luisella?"

"I'm kidding. Mostly. Just remembering Veronica and the dogs."

"Oh," Luca said, chuckling. "I heard about that."

"Besides, Leo said the headlights were higher, like a large car or truck, right? So it couldn't have been her little Fiat."

"He did say that, but two minutes later he said the lights were car height. It's common with people in stressful situations. Adrenaline wreaks havoc on memory formation."

She nodded. After a few quiet moments, Stella said, "Well, I better get going. Need to relieve Domenica of her charge."

Luca looked as if he were going to say something, but then he killed the engine.

As they wandered toward the town entrance, a car came speeding up the hill. At the sound, Luca stepped between Stella and the oncoming vehicle. Her pace flagged briefly. She glanced up at Luca, but he said nothing, his eyes straight ahead. Mimmo parked his truck and jumped out, headed down the hill toward his house. Luca said, "You were right about coffee. I would kill for a cup."

Stella shivered.

"Sorry. Poor choice of words."

Stella caught sight of Matteo, sweeping the road by her house.

Luca murmured, "I'm trusting you."

She nodded. "Heard, chef."

He did a small double take and then chuckled before striding away.

Matteo raced up to her. "The convent. What happened?"

She told him.

"And that was it?" Matteo asked. "That's all you know?"

"I mean, I don't *know* more. But I have suspicions." She thought of the prayer card.

"Care to elaborate?"

"Not at the moment, no," Stella said. She needed to cook.

"What self-control." Matteo grinned and went back to sweeping.

Stella laughed. "Self-control is generous. I'm overwhelmed by which thread to pull."

Matteo wiped the sweat from his forehead with his sleeve. "I'm sure the guests don't help."

"Mrs. Copeland!" Stella remembered with a start. "I have to get to Domenica's."

"She's not there."

Stella stared at him. "What?"

Shaking his head, Matteo said, "She went to get drinks and snacks. At the *alimentari*."

Stella muttered, "How did Domenica talk her into interacting with strangers?" A mystery for another day. Right now, she had to pick up Cindy, when she really wanted to change out of her sweaty clothes. Could she cook with Cindy underfoot? She pressed her hands against her hot cheeks. "I better collect her."

"I'll walk with you."

"Did Domenica tell you about Trattoria Cavour? The strange men filing in?"

"I watched as long as I could but couldn't sweep the piazza forever. Giancarlo took over the watch."

Stella adjusted her headband. Carefully, she said, "That's nice of him."

Matteo stopped walking and leaned his broom against the wall. "What's with the iciness?"

"Iciness?" Stella's hand went to her forehead.

"Giancarlo said you haven't returned his calls."

"I've been busy," Stella gestured to the stone walls as a hum of cicadas rose around them. "You know that better than anyone."

He considered her with a frown. "There's something you aren't telling me. You're all armored up."

She looked down at her t-shirt sticking to her midriff, her jeans, her scuffed boots. "What armor?"

"That thing you do when you pretend nothing can get to you."

Stella pressed her lips together before whispering, "Please, not now. I can't do this now." She needed to cook, to get inside, to escape the blistering sun and the hot seat.

He snatched his broom. "So there is something."

Staring at the ground, Stella took a breath. "Marta sent me an article. About Giancarlo."

He blinked at her.

Dragging her toe in a half circle in front of her, Stella said, "I read it."

Matteo inclined his head. "Congratulations?"

Stella huffed. "The article, it mentioned his daughter."

"And?"

Silence stretched between them. Matteo's face fell. "He hasn't told you about Bierta."

"He has not." She folded her arms, bracing.

Matteo stabbed his broom at a leaf stuck between cobblestones. "She's not in his daily life. I get why he might not bring it up."

She tilted her head. "I asked him if he ever wanted children."

He said nothing.

"He deflected."

With a shake of his head, Matteo said, "Come on, Stella. Give him a break. He was twenty. One mistake. He's done right by her since."

"Gold stars all around." She shook her head hard enough to dislodge her scarf. "You know me. You know that's not what this is about."

"Then what is it about?"

She closed her eyes briefly, her scarf slipping further off her head. Then said, "A child is not a detail. What else is he leaving out?"

"*Madonna mia!*" Matteo snapped, his hands clenched. "You're willing to write him off after one mistake?"

Stella shifted her weight. "The thing of it is, I'm not sure it is a mistake. He stores stuff in meat lockers. I keep my spices on the counter."

"That's ridiculous and you know it." He shook his head. "So that's it. You cast off my friend like it's nothing."

"I didn't say—"

"Like it's *nothing*." Matteo turned his back, paced away and then strode back. "I didn't figure you would be this cold to my best friend."

Stella's chin trembled and she wiped at her eyes, hard. "Can't you see it from my perspective—"

He crossed his arms and glared at her. "While you're ranting about meat lockers and spices? No, I don't think so."

"He lied to me."

Matteo shook his head. "He didn't tell you. Not the same thing as lying."

"Well, I don't want to have to cross-check his stories." She set her jaw. "I can't trust him, and that's enough."

His eyes narrowed. "You don't see that maybe that's on you? The armor thing again? Why don't you examine yourself, here, Stella, instead of pointing fingers at everyone else."

"Oh, that's rich coming from you." She felt her scarf slip down her cheek and fall to the ground.

He stilled. "What are you—"

She felt a buzz in her pocket, but it barely triggered her notice. The words clawed up her throat. She should bite them back. Instead, they ripped out of her. "You're awfully involved in my love life. In Giancarlo's love life. Ever thought maybe it's because you don't have one of your own?"

The broom fell from his hand and he lunged to catch it. He straightened and glared at her. "Wow."

"That came out wrong."

"I doubt that's true," he said coldly.

"Matteo, if you just..." Stella faltered.

He turned away. And then turned back.

"What should I tell him? Giancarlo," he asked, quieter now.

She strengthened her voice. "Tell him exactly what he told me." She turned away.

A pause. Then, "Which is?"

"Nothing," Stella called over her shoulder. She walked toward Domenica's, blinking hard. She turned and watched as his back receded around the corner of Aramezzo. Her eye caught on her scarf, lying limp on the cobblestones. She swooped it up, tears welling in her eyes. As she retied it around her curls, she felt a press against her shin. Looking down, she saw Barbanera seated at her feet.

At least Giancarlo would leave soon and spare her the constant reminder of their doomed interlude. Thank the Madonna she never got involved with Luca, whose presence lingered everywhere.

The heartbreak of it all.

Barbanera leaned against Stella for a touch before straightening.

But wait. Her heart, it did not feel broken.

Stella frowned.

She had fallen for Giancarlo and yet... this was not heartbreak.

Heartbreak would mean never baking again. This was a soufflé collapse: disappointment, not devastation.

No time for this now.

She looked to Barbanera. Did he want to come in?

He gave a disdainful look at Domenica's door before turning and trotting off, tail held high.

Stella watched him until he jogged out of sight.

One thing felt certain.

She needed to cook.

Stella shoved open the bookshop door and blinked into the dim light.

Domenica looked up and pushed her glasses higher on her nose. "Something happened." It wasn't a question.

"Plenty," said Stella, dropping into the faded armchair, the cushion wheezing beneath her frame. "Where's Cindy?"

"At the *alimentari.*"

"How did you get her to go?"

Domenica shrugged. "I don't know. I guess I didn't assume she wouldn't."

Stella rubbed at the worn fabric of the armchair.

"Leo came in," Domenica said. "Looking for you."

"Me? Why?" Stella glanced up. Had she ever been this tired?

"He didn't say."

Stella nodded slowly. "I saw him this morning. How did he seem to you?"

Domenica watched Stella. "The feeling in his hand is coming back. He'll be okay."

"That's not what I meant."

Domenica nodded. "Smaller. Quiet. Not himself."

"Join the club," Stella said.

Frowning, Domenica said, "What's going on?"

Stella shook her head. "There's too much."

Domenica nodded, as if Stella had given an answer. "The convent?"

"Right. The convent. We confirmed the missing nun was the one in the road."

Domenica sighed.

"But it raises a bunch of questions. Apparently, the nun had some secret. I'm hoping her friend, Sister Serafina, calls. What are the odds, though? I mean, it would be easier to forget all about her old pal Elena, I'm sure."

Pushing her glasses higher on her nose, Domenica leaned back in her chair, studying Stella.

"Also, I have this feeling the Mother Superior is involved."

"Involved with what?"

"The nun in the road." Stella ran her hand over her forehead. "I know it sounds crazy."

Domenica looked baffled.

Stella shook her head. "When is Cindy coming back? I need to cook something." She pulled her phone out of her pocket to check the time. A voicemail. Stella's breath vanished with a squeak. She rose quickly and turned, pressing her phone against her ear.

"This is Sister Serafina. I wasn't sure I should call. But Beatrice told me I owe it to Elena. I don't know. I feel . . . responsible. For what happened. I should have . . . well. I'll try to call during Vespers."

Stella turned back. "It was the nun. And I missed it. All because of this stupid fight with Matteo."

"Again?"

"What do you mean again?"

Domenica rolled her eyes. "You two are like siblings. You squabble and make up and are inseparable once more and then squabble like it's the first time all over again. Can you call the nun back?"

"What?" Stella said, distracted by Domenica's characterization of her and Matteo's relationship. She looked at her phone. "Do nuns have cell phones? Elena didn't. I figured Serafina called from a communal phone."

"What's the number?"

Stella told her and Domenica whirled to her computer, flicking scarves away with one hand as she typed with the other. The sound of keys clacking filled the bookshop. "Yes. A landline. For the convent." She twirled back. "What did the message say?"

"That she feels responsible. And that she'll try to call back during Vespers, whatever that means."

"Evening services."

"Don't tell me you were a nun."

Domenica waved her hand dismissively. "I'm Italian. It's in the water."

The bell over the door jingled and Cindy rushed in, beaming. "I had the best time! Oh, *ciao*, Stella."

"*Ciao*," Stella said dully.

"Was your trip not successful?"

Stella remembered her role. Upbeat. Competent. Hands on the reins. "Very successful! And you? Looks like you got yourself something there."

"Oh!" Cindy said, setting the bag down and taking out a foil-wrapped chocolate. "Treats from Perugia! Like Hershey's Kisses, but with hazelnuts. Ancient Romans used to give hazelnuts as wedding gifts, as a charm for marital bliss, not to mention childbearing." As Cindy popped the Baci in her mouth, she said, "I'm long past childbearing, but can't any marriage be made more blissful? Wow, that's good."

At a break in the monologue, Stella nodded distractedly. "All right, well, I better get back. I have to make dinner." She turned to Cindy. "Are you ready?"

Cindy looked around surprised. "I guess I have some editing to do. I must have taken a zillion photos of doors. Then another zillion of laundry. Why do you think people are so attracted to doors and laundry? I think it adds intimacy to a photo."

"Great," Stella said in what she hoped was a bright tone. "I'll be back later," Stella said over her shoulder to Domenica.

"You better," Domenica said. "Come by when you've talked to the nun."

Once out on the street, the sun's glare woke Stella from what seemed a dream. "Wait here," she told Cindy and dashed back into the bookshop.

In a rush, Stella told Domenica, "Can you look something up when I'm gone?"

"Maybe," Domenica said.

"Two things, actually. One. Luca told me that they found heroin in Roberto and Romina's house."

Domenica blinked. "You wait until now to mention this?"

"I haven't exactly been sitting around drinking coffee." Stella said and then instantly felt contrite. "I'm sorry for snapping. I can't stand how little I know. Plus. This heat."

"I'm sorry, too. I didn't mean to sound accusatory." Domenica sighed. "I suppose we're none of us impervious. So what do you want me to do with this information?"

Stella thought. "I have no idea."

Domenica pushed the glasses higher on her nose. "You found it so shocking you wanted me to know."

Stella felt a real smile flicker across her face. "I suppose that's right."

"Okay then, what's two?"

"Two what?"

"You said there were two things."

"Oh, did I?" Stella frowned. "Once again, my head is a steel sieve."

Domenica leaned forward, watching Stella's face. "Stella, I think you need a drink of water. Have you eaten today?"

"Oh," Stella tried to remember. "No. At least, I don't think so."

"And you've been doing such a good job feeding yourself." Domenica sighed. "Eat. Rest up. We need your wits about you."

Stella shrugged. "Wits? What are those? No, Domenica, we need a stroke of luck."

"Luck favors the prepared mind," Domenica nodded.

Stella stared at Domenica.

"Louis Pasteur." Domenica gestured with her chin. "Cindy is waiting."

Stella stepped back outside and smiled wanly at Cindy. "So. Good day?"

"Oh, yes! Everyone is so *nice*!" Cindy stared at Stella as a grin stretched across her face.

"They're the best," Stella said flatly.

Cindy began chattering about how Cristiana at the *alimentari* had mimed picking mushrooms to explain a pasta flavored with porcini. Cindy had bought three packets to take home. Stella only half-listened and then stopped listening altogether when she noticed Leo walking away from her house. "Leo?"

"Oh, good. Stella. I'm glad I caught you."

Cindy looked from Leo to Stella, a look of recognition passing across her face. Stella remembered that Leo had tried to talk to Cindy earlier in the day. This time Cindy nodded at Leo before turning to Stella. "I'm going to go in and see if I can get ahold of James. He won't believe the day I've had!"

When the door closed behind her, Stella said, "How did the lamp work out?"

"Lamp? Oh, right. The lamp." He gave a wan smile. "It works. Sorry, I keep thinking of that woman, the one in the road. That could have been me." He closed his eyes and made a scoffing sound. "Not very manly, I know. You'd never know I used to race cars."

"Well," Stella said comfortingly. "I doubt those race cars jumped out at you in the middle of the night."

He opened his eyes. "I suppose."

"How is your hand?" Stella asked. "Such bad luck to fall on your injury."

"The bad luck was injuring it in the first place. You wouldn't understand this, but getting sidelined at the height of your career... it's rough."

Not the moment to tell him she had a vague idea of what it might be like to be yanked off your path. Gently, Stella said, "But it's better now? Your hand?"

"Sure," Leo said. He squinted at the wispy clouds crossing the sky.

Stella paused. "Do you remember any identifying details about the vehicle?"

"Luca just asked me the same thing. Sometimes I think I remember, but then... it all disappears. To tell the truth, I want to put it all behind me. Behind us. Marta gets anxious every time I run an errand."

"She thinks someone was out to get you?"

"Nah. But there's this crazy person on the road. Ascanio has a pediatrician appointment next week, I'm not sure she'll work up the courage to take him."

Stella surreptitiously checked her phone. "Domenica said you were looking for me?"

"Oh! Right. About Marta. Any chance you can stop by tonight? I haven't seen my parents since the accident, but Marta will be anxious the whole time I'm in Foligno. Ascanio distracts her," he said fondly. "But she could use a friend."

"Of course," Stella said. "Tell her I'll come by with dinner."

He put his hand on her arm. "Thanks, Stella." He walked away and then turned back. "Stella? You're not … investigating this, are you?"

"The lunatic driver?" Stella asked.

"No, there's nothing to investigate there. At the time I thought someone was trying to run me over, but I think that was the adrenaline. It makes more sense that someone fell asleep at the wheel or something. Bad luck for me, worse luck for that lady."

A swallow arced overhead, and Leo's gaze followed it over the rooftops. "I've heard things … well, you've probably heard the same things. If they really were caught up with the Mafia, you don't want to put a target on your back."

She furrowed her eyebrows. "A target?"

He shrugged, walking backward, without looking. "Some of those guys used to come to the track. You think faulty brakes are scary? It's nothing compared to what they're capable of."

"What do you mean?"

Leo paused in his walking backward. "I'd hate to have anything happen to you." He grinned. "Just when I'm getting used to you."

Her phone rang and she jumped.

He nodded. "I'll let you get that. But Stella? I hope you listen to me. Stay safe, okay? It's risky out there."

She nodded and drew her phone from her pocket. The number, the same as the last time the nun called. She touched the phone to accept the call. "*Pronto?*"

"Stella?" a breathy voice responded. "This is Sister Serafina."

"I'm glad you called."

Silence. Then, "I … I don't have much time."

"I'm listening." Stella gripped the phone against her ear.

"I think Elena was … involved. With someone on the outside."

Stella didn't ask her to clarify "involved." "How do you know?"

"The cell phone."

"You mean she had a phone? Why would that—" Realization dawned. "Oh. You don't have phones."

"Right. But she's had one for the last month or two. Not a flip phone either, which we're sometimes given when we do service outside the convent. This was a smartphone. She tried to hide it. Put it away quickly when I walked in. But I couldn't miss it. Especially because of her face when she shoved it under her pillow."

"Her face?"

"Red. Like she was caught in the act." Serafina hesitated.

"Serafina? What else?" Stella's knuckles whitened around the phone.

"Someone's coming," she whispered. After a moment she said, "Elena and the phone. She looked lost in a dream. When I caught her using it, but also … other times. I'd find her standing with a mop in her hand, staring at nothing, with this reverent look on her face. When I teased her about it, like she was taking our training too far, it's only mopping … she snapped at me."

"It does sound like new love," Stella said.

"I wouldn't know." Stella thought she could hear the nun smiling.

"Did you ever get confirmation? Like, did she let anything slip or confide in you?"

Stella could hear Serafina draw in her breath. "No, she didn't. But a week ago, she ran out of the room, late to lunch as usual. Well, not as usual, she'd always been so punctual. But since the phone appeared … she was late a lot. Anyway, I knew where she'd shoved the phone so I took it out."

"You know how to use a smartphone?" Stella asked.

With a tense chuckle, the nun said, "I haven't been sequestered since the Middle Ages. And they haven't changed *that* much."

"Got it, got it," Stella said with a grin, despite herself. "So what did you find?"

"Nothing." Stella's heart sank. "At first." Stella's heart soared. "I couldn't unlock it without her password. I figured her password couldn't be that complicated. But I tried all the most obvious candidates."

"How do you know the most obvious candidates?"

"I read a lot of spy thrillers."

"You're allowed to—" Stella began, then shook her head. "I'm sorry. I know you have limited time."

The church bells above her rang, echoed by the bells chiming at the convent.

"I didn't want to try more than two possible passwords in case the phone was set up to take a photo the third time. But right as I was putting the phone back under the pillow, a text came through."

"What did it say?"

"It was bizarre. I wrote it down, hang on." Her voice broke off.

Stella heard a commotion in the background. Footsteps swirling. And the chatter of excited women. Must have been some Vespers.

The nun's voice trembled. "I have to go."

"No! Wait! Tell me quickly . . . please!"

Serafina's breath quickened. Her words muffled, like she had the receiver smashed to her cheek. A piece of paper crumpled or uncrumpled. "The text said, 'I can't stop thinking about you. The way you look at me, the way you move. When I gave you my valise, I gave you more than I should have. You carry something of mine now. I can't wait to hold you, my innocent one. To take care of you. Forever.'"

"Valise? Like a locket? Is that an old-fashioned word for love or heart or something?" Stella actually wondered if it was a sexual euphemism but couldn't bring herself to ask the nun.

"I don't know!" Serafina's voice broke off as Stella heard the phone whoosh down. All she caught was, "The phone rang as I passed! Wrong number."

Click.

You carry something of mine now.

Elena wasn't found with romantic jewelry, just that rough cross.

Stella pictured Elena running late to Vespers. What had Don Arrigo said about morning services? She'd skipped them, complaining of stomach pains.

Stella sagged down on the steps, hands gripping the stone.

Luca had said that they needed a motive to connect the prayer card with the dead nun. A forbidden pregnancy, a need to erase evidence of the scandal. That would be a motive.

Stella shook her head. This had to be her imagination taking her for a joyride.

She forced her brain to march in order. *Valise.* She didn't even know how she knew the Italian word, *valigia*, it was so old-fashioned. She'd have to ask Domenica if "valise" meant something in dialect. Domenica would know, especially if the subtle meaning was remotely dirty.

Stella tapped the phone in her hand. The phone. What happened to Elena's smartphone? She wouldn't have left it at the convent.

She straightened—maybe Serafina wasn't concerned about being caught on the phone because the phone was forbidden. Maybe talking about Elena was forbidden. By the Mother Superior.

Mother Maria Teresa had to know more than she let on.

"Hey, Stella."

Stella squinted into the sun's glare. "Luca?"

"I'm glad you're here."

"Same." Stella took a breath. "I talked to the nun. The one who shared a room with Elena."

Luca's expression tightened. "You did? When was this?"

"I just hung up."

He nodded and dropped beside her on the step. "And?"

She filled him in as he listened quietly. Then he said, "I'm surprised you remembered that whole text."

"I'm glad I had a reason to repeat it so quickly. I feel like it's jumbling even now."

"I'll write it down," Luca said, getting out his notepad.

After a pause, she said, "I'm stuck on the word *valigia*. Does it have a dialectical meaning I don't know?"

"Not unless it's archaic. I thought it meant a holder of some kind."

She nodded. "Also, the bit about carrying something of his, the taking care of her. Could he be referring to a pregnancy?" She tensed.

Luca gave a low whistle. "With the Mafia raids, the medical examiner's office is backed up. We won't have autopsy results until tomorrow morning at the earliest." Luca studied his hands, folded on his knees.

"The ink. The possible scandal," Stella ventured. "Plus, didn't the Mother Superior feel off to you?"

He considered. "One thing I've learned, there's never an elegant way to accept this kind of news."

She nodded. "I'm wondering about the phone. The one Elena got the text on. Where is it?"

"What do you mean?"

"Well, wouldn't she have brought the phone with her when she ran from the convent?"

"Probably."

Stella asked, "Then where is it?"

They exchanged glances and stood up.

As they jogged down the street and through the town gate, Stella felt her stomach growl. She ignored it.

The heat pressed against Stella's skin.

She ignored that too.

As they approached the spot, he said, "If we can't find the phone, then we have to assume someone took it, which means there's reason to believe it's a homicide, not an accident."

Her steps slowed.

He did a double take when he realized she wasn't next to him. Turning, he said, "Stella? Did you get a cramp?"

She shook her head. "It's nothing."

"It doesn't look like nothing. It looks like something." Luca leaned toward her, his voice soft.

Stella felt her own voice soften. "I guess I'm glad we're stirring the same pot."

He regarded her quizzically for a moment before smiling. "Me too."

Their gaze held.

Stella turned away, her eyes scanning the spot where they found Elena. "It couldn't have landed in the road or we would have seen it."

Luca nodded. "Let's check the hillside."

"Good thing the grass is short."

He grinned. "It's fresh-cut hay."

"Right, right, I knew that," she muttered, walking methodically up and down the hillside.

After fifteen minutes of sweeping the hillside, they stopped.

Stella shook her head.

Luca shook his head too. "I'll come again with a metal detector. But it doesn't look like it's here."

Stella slumped onto the ground, the cut hay prickling her through her jeans. "That poor woman."

As Luca dropped beside her, his sleeve brushed hers. They sat in silence, gazes fixed over the valley. Finally, Luca inhaled deeply and said, "Listen. I came by because I have some bad news. And I'm procrastinating telling you."

Her stomach clenched.

"I looked up Roberto's family. It turns out...I don't know how to say this."

"Mafia?" Stella said in a small voice, her body still.

Luca nodded. "Apparently in Sicily it's an open secret—his family is known for its ties to organized crime."

After a pause, Stella said, "Forgive this question. Is that uncommon? I mean, doesn't pretty much everyone in Sicily have relatives with Mafia ties?"

"No."

"I'm sorry." Stella frowned.

"You're forgiven," Luca chuckled in a low voice, brushing dirt off his hands. "But understand that Americans have a misguided notion about Italians' embrace of organized crime. You romanticize it, make movies about it. When most of us feel threatened and victimized by it. How many movies do you have glorifying the perpetrators of 9/11?"

She closed her eyes. "I get that."

He went on. "There's no easy way to say this. But Roberto and Romina, they were once arrested for human trafficking."

"*What?*"

"I know. I'm having a hard time wrapping my head around it, too. Which is why I wanted to come find you as soon as I read the reports."

"It's . . . it's not possible."

Luca shrugged. "I really thought this whole arrest was part of a government publicity stunt, but I understand now why the informant's information led to Roberto and Romina."

Stella pressed her hand against her eyes. Into the darkness, her mind cascaded, searched, hunted for an explanation.

Luca said, "The good news is, none of those charges stuck."

"The charges didn't stick," Stella chewed on the words. "So, maybe they are innocent!"

"Stella, we have to consider the possibility that they were so entrenched into the organization, so important, the bosses found them worthy of protection."

"Someone bribed the judge," Stella said.

"Or the opposing counsel, or a witness," Luca added. "Obviously, my records fall short there. You might have more luck."

This time Stella didn't even bother pretending she didn't understand. She nodded.

He took a breath. "There's something else. You're not going to like it."

"Thus far I've liked none of it." She closed her eyes. When she opened them, she found Luca watching her. "Tell me."

A hesitation. "Brace yourself."

Stella gestured to the ground. "I'm already sitting. Consider me fully braced."

He studied her for a moment. "Romina. She's stopped eating."

"She what?" The hand at her mouth muffled her words.

"She stopped eating." Luca sighed. "I was afraid you'd take it hard."

"Is the food bad?" Stella whispered.

"I'm sure it's not up to your standards, but I don't think that's the reason."

"Is she sick?"

Luca hesitated. "I don't know. The officer at the holding center happened to mention it to Captain Tribuzio, and I overheard."

"We need to get her out of there. Now."

A pause. "Believe me, Stella. I'm working on it."

"Okay," Stella blinked away tears. She got up and began the walk home, Luca striding beside her.

"She'll be okay, Stella."

"Do you promise?"

"You know I can't—"

"Please!" Stella pleaded, tears filling her eyes.

He put his hands on her arms and studied her face. "I promise."

"Thank you, Luca." After a few minutes' walk, they arrived at her house. She cast a glance at the door. "I need to figure out dinner."

"So early?" Luca checked his phone. "I mean I'm glad you're taking care of yourself—"

"Hardly," Stella laughed, putting her hand on her rumbling stomach. Luca watched the gesture, his jaw tightening. "But guests must be fed."

His hand reached for her cheek before pausing and nudging her shoulder playfully. "Do you ever give yourself a day off?" He turned and jogged down the stairs and down the street, calling a stiff goodbye over his shoulder.

She watched the empty space that once held Luca before turning and entering her quiet house.

Stella knew she should start dinner, especially if she hoped to make the pasta by hand. With a touch of her flushed cheek, she knew she couldn't summon the willpower to knead and roll pasta dough. No matter that grannies up and down the street, in black dresses and sensible heels, would be cracking eggs for pasta right now.

She listened out for Cindy. No sound. But Barbanera came trotting down the steps, so he must have been keeping her company.

The cat sat down and stared at her.

"What?" said Stella.

Flicking the end of his tail, the one-eared cat blinked at her and raised his black chin.

"It's not dinner time yet."

He blinked once more and turned to trot back up the stairs.

"Traitor," mumbled Stella.

"Stella?" Cindy called from upstairs.

"It's me. You okay with Barbanera up there?"

"Oh, yes, he's the sweetest." Cindy came to the top of the stairs. "I talked to James. He said the surgery went well, and he should be able to come home tomorrow, the next day at the latest."

Stella smiled. "Wonderful, I'm sure you'll be happy to continue your vacation together."

Cindy stared at Stella for a moment before saying, "I'm going back to Duolingo now." She turned back to her room, muttering about Duolingo's mistake feature.

Stella watched her go and then went to her room. She peeled off her sweat-soaked clothes and hopped into a cool shower. Letting the water run down her body, she imagined her flooded veins contracting at the drop in temperature. Lathering the cotton-flower scented soap (did cotton flowers have a scent? Stella was not convinced), she breathed in, allowing the floral tones to fill her lungs.

Hurriedly, she dried off and pulled on clean clothes, ignoring the scrape of jeans against her damp skin. She pulled her hair back in a pony-tail so harshly, droplets flew around the bathroom, raining on her shirt.

Stella boiled water for pasta and then pulled the greens and sausage out of the refrigerator. Glopping olive oil into the pan, she remembered she usually cooked the sausage first and used its fat for the greens. Oh, well.

Pasta into the boiling water, greens cooked down with the sausage.

Her phone binged with another text from Giancarlo. Stella covered her phone with a dishtowel.

Shouldn't the pasta be done by now? She pulled out a strand and winced at its sag. She dumped the pasta and water into a sieve set into the sink.

The starchy water burped its way down the drain.

A drop of sauce glistened on the wooden counter. Without thinking, Stella ran her finger over it and popped it in her mouth.

She gagged and ran to the sink to spit it out.

Salty was not a strong enough word. She liked salt, but this was like dipping into the Adriatic's salt pans.

When had she added salt? She didn't remember, she'd been on auto-pilot.

She whipped the pan of sauce off the stove, then tripped over Barbanera. Stella went flying, the pan slopping greens and sausage down the cabinets before pooling on the floor. She gritted her teeth and tried to keep from shrieking. Barbanera dipped his head to lick the sauce and then recoiled as if shocked by an electric fence. "Don't do that!" she ordered him.

The cat shoved her arm with his head, knocking her off balance as she tried to rise. "Stop it!" Stella whisper-screamed through clenched teeth. His single ear flattened and he whisked around before stalking from the kitchen.

In the sudden silence, she heard the clock ticking.

"Barbanera…" she said, her voice regaining its normal pitch. "I didn't mean—"

But the cat had disappeared. She reached for the roll of paper towels and cleaned the mess, the sauce sloshing over her hands. Left with an armful of sodden paper towels, she tossed them into the trash can. Only then did she remember it belonged in the bag for compost. Good thing Matteo wasn't here to give her grief.

Matteo.

Stella's body stilled. Well, nothing to do but pick up more greens. Luckily she had more sausage.

She dashed off a text to Cindy as she rushed down the street. "Didn't want to call up the stairs and wake you if you were resting. I'm ducking out to get a few supplies for dinner, but I'll be home soon."

Stella stepped out of the house. Wet hair be damned.

Her neighbor was hanging laundry and only waved a greeting. Within minutes she arrived at the *alimentari*. She smiled at Cristiana, but Cristiana was deep in conversation with Flavia, who ran the flower shop.

Their conversation ran over Stella like water washing away brine.

"At first I thought the ticket was fake," Flavia complained. "But then Cosimo told me the *autovelox* was back on line."

Autovelox? Oh right, the machine that snapped photos of speeding cars.

Cristiana said, "You hadn't heard? Cosimo told me yesterday. Thank goodness, I've gotten in the habit of speeding down the mountain."

Stella paid for the greens and a package of *amaretti* cookies that somehow wound up in her basket, and walked to Domenica's.

She should go home, of course. She had dinner to make. But she couldn't get the *autovelox* out of her mind. Pushing the door of Domenica's shop open, she strode to the armchair without comment. Stella pulled Ravioli onto her lap. The shower must have cooled her core body temperature, as the cat's heat didn't bother her. Or maybe nothing as mundane as overheating would ever bother her again.

"Stella? Are you quite well, *cara*? Your hair is all—"

Stella held up her hand, thinking. Finally, she said, "You know those police radar boxes? Like the one outside Assisi?"

"The *autovelox*? That one is broken," Domenica said.

"Not anymore. Can you hack into the system and get the photos it takes? When people break the speed limit?"

"Maybe," Domenica hedged. "What are you thinking?"

"Well, if the person who almost hit Leo and then hit the nun came from that direction—which seems likely since there's not much on the other side of the mountain—and if they were speeding, we'd know who was on the road around that time."

Understanding dawned over Domenica's face and she turned to her computer. "Okay, give me a minute."

Stella stared at the *amaretti* in her bag.

Within a few minutes, she heard Domenica mutter, "Got it. Compared to the protections around the DIA database, this is child's play."

Stella sighed. "Great. Check Saturday night."

"Some cameras only capture the license plate, we'll see if this one snaps a photo of the driver," Domenica muttered. "And if not, we can look up the license plates, no problem."

Ravioli purred louder.

Domenica reached for her notepad and then stopped. "That's Luisella."

"What?" Stella said, straightening.

"Isn't it? Look," Domenica said pointing at the screen.

"It's awfully grainy, are you sure?"

"It's definitely the car she drives. Let me check the license plate." In a few moments she nodded. "Yes, that's Luisella. On the road on Saturday night."

"What time?"

"Almost eleven."

"Headed back to Aramezzo?"

"Looks like it."

Stella thought for a moment. "Wait, they found the body Saturday, but if the nun was hit within a couple of hours of Leo, it would actually be Friday night."

"On it," Domenica said, already typing furiously with a rhythmic clacking on her ancient keyboard. Wonderingly, she pointed at the screen, "There she is again."

"Again?" Stella said, eyes narrowing as she leaned forward in the brocaded armchair. "Why is she on the road so late at night? Two nights in a row?"

Domenica didn't answer as her hands flew across the keyboard, her eyes intent on the screen. "Five nights in a row, actually. A day off before that, but then a few more nights. At least. Before that, the box was broken, there are no recordings."

"What time on Friday?"

Domenica studied the screen. "Just after eleven."

Stella closed her eyes.

No skid marks.

No braking.

Luisella, with all those late nights, could have fallen asleep at the wheel.

"Anybody else speed by on Friday night?"

Domenica went back to that page. "No. Not anyone speeding."

Stella sighed. "I need to talk to Luisella."

Domenica said, "Did Sister Serafina ever call?"

"Oh, right." Stella filled Domenica in on her conversation with Serafina. "What do you think valise could be code for? Like an ark or a coffer?"

Domenica cocked her head to the side. "*Cara.* A valise is a bag."

Stella adjusted her scarf. "But in dialect—"

"A literal bag. It sounds like someone was thanking Elena for holding onto a bag."

"A bag," Stella felt her brain defrosting. "Like the bag at the bar?"

Domenica shrugged. "Right."

"Domenica, you are a genius."

"In the literal sense, that's not far wrong, but in this case, it's kind of obvious."

"But I missed it," Stella said. "How did I miss it?"

"Hidden in plain sight, I suppose. Plus, Italian isn't your first language, of course you'd second guess an odd word."

Stella rubbed her temple. "I am off my game."

Stretching out her arms, Domenica said, "The game is vast. It's why we each have a part. Did you tell Luca?"

"Yes, at least I did that right."

"And he didn't catch it either?"

"Oh. I guess not. Maybe I mispronounced it."

Domenica chuckled. "He's such a romantic, he probably thought it was love-related."

Stella shook her head. "Maybe Elena was mixed up with the Mafia? Running drugs for them?"

"I think her convent would have noticed her absence if she kept dropping bags in Aramezzo. Unless she had a key and dropped it off in the dead of night."

The word "key" tugged at Stella. She tapped her knee. "Don Arrigo told me some stories about nuns that made my butter burn."

"Not an expression," Domenica said without thinking. "Maybe she held onto the bag for her boyfriend, but didn't know what was inside."

"Pretty naïve."

Domenica shrugged in response.

Stella went on, "But someone would have to have gotten the bag from the convent to Roberto and Romina's. The question is, who? Who had a relationship with Elena?" Stella imagined Romina, tired and pale, leaning against a rough concrete wall. "Luca told me that before Roberto and Romina took over the bar, they lived in Sicily with Roberto's family. And his family has Mafia ties."

Domenica leaned forward. "But that doesn't mean anything necessarily—"

"They were arrested for human trafficking."

"Roberto's family?"

Stella shook her head slowly. "Roberto and Romina."

Domenica paled.

"The thing of it is," Stella said slowly, "With the heroin found in their house and now this…it's going to be harder to prove Roberto and Romina aren't Aramezzo's drug runners."

Domenica dropped her head into her hands.

Stella's heart lurched. For Domenica, this was akin to a meltdown.

When Domenica lifted her head, Stella said, "Are you willing to look into Roberto and Romina's finances now?"

"Stella, when I first started hacking, I thought it was a game. A magic game where I could learn everyone's secrets and nobody would be the wiser. But then I realized—that way lies ruin."

"We wouldn't tell them—" Ravioli's claws poked through her jeans as she kneaded Stella's lap.

"No. You don't understand. It leads to ruin because with this secret information, I had to mute, to make sure I didn't spill what I knew. Muting became a habit. I had to hold back, from everyone, lest I reveal what I knew." Domenica paused to let this linger in the air. "It divided me from everyone. People came up with theories to explain my quiet. None of them flattering."

Stella thought about it. "Like you were too good for them?"

"That was one of the nicer ones, yes." She paused, her eyes flicking to Attila jumping on the desk.

Stella clapped her hands together in realization. Attila flew to the other side of the room. "This is why you had to leave Terni! I always wondered what made you close up your house there."

"Indeed."

"I figured it out!" crowed Stella.

"Yes, you're an incomparable detective," Domenica said blandly. "Now, if there's nothing you want me to look up—"

"But Domenica, what if peeking into their financial situation would help Roberto and Romina?"

"Stella," said Domenica, "Don't you think Roberto and Romina's lawyers will dig into their financials?"

"Oh," Stella said. "I suppose that's true. That was stupid. Why didn't you tell me this earlier? Instead of letting me fancy myself smarter than professionals?"

"And shatter your emerging confidence?" Domenica said with a smile. "Never."

"I'm not sure about confidence," Stella muttered. "More like throwing myself into one situation after another."

"One book. Two covers," Domenica said fondly.

After a beat, Stella said, "This is why you took me under your wing."

"I'm hardly a chicken, *cara*."

"Let me finish," Stella held up her hand. "I don't hold back. After what happened in Terni, you grew allergic to reticence."

Domenica adjusted her scarves.

They regarded each other and smiled. Finally, Stella said, "So here's what we know. Heroin was found in Roberto and Romina's house, which confirmed for the government that they are Aramezzo's drug runners. Especially with them mortgaging the bar, and their past."

"But we know that the heroin could not have been theirs."

"Agreed," Stella said, firmly. "No matter what their younger selves got caught up in, we know them too well to believe they were drug runners. Which means someone planted it."

Domenica nodded. "The police would have noticed if someone had broken into the bar."

"Unless they jimmied the lock."

Domenica shook her head. "These old doors are hard to force open."

"So someone had a key. Who had a key?" Stella leapt from the chair, Ravioli falling to the floor. "*Adele*! Adele has a key!"

"Adele wouldn't—she and Romina are so close."

"Vincenzo, though. That's another story."

Domenica frowned. "Why does she stay with that man?"

"It certainly isn't for his sparkling personality. Okay, so would you look up *their* financials for sudden cash influxes?"

"Even if I wanted to, I couldn't. You know they don't take credit cards. They ring up bills on that ancient cash register. Vincenzo is so paranoid, I bet they don't even have a bank account."

Stella said softly, "Adele." She straightened. "And the convent! You need to look into *their* records."

"Stella, that is really far-fetched." At Stella's pleading expression, Domenica sighed. "Fine, I'll poke around convent records."

Stella grinned. "Okay, so we're on top of two leads—Vincenzo and the convent. Plus Luisella, I suppose. We also need to keep tabs on the mayor."

"I almost have his bank account number." Domenica said.

Stella's eyes narrowed.

"It's like you say," Domenica grinned. "I'm an enigma."

The door opened and Stella's heart dropped.

"*Ciao*, Stella."

Stella swallowed. "Ciao, Giancarlo."

Stella followed Giancarlo out of the bookshop.

Giancarlo teased, "You don't sound delighted to see me. Has the newness already worn off?"

Stella bit her lip and stared at her feet. "How did you know I was here?" Stop stalling!

Shrugging, he said, "Bar is on lockdown. You weren't home. I took a shot."

"Well," Stella said. "You found me."

"Why haven't you answered my texts?" He smiled at her, corners of his eyes creasing.

"Oh, uh … lots to do. You know." She gestured vaguely, avoiding his gaze.

He moved toward her.

She backed up.

A line appeared on his forehead. "What's going on?"

"With the case?"

"With us."

"Us?"

Giancarlo said nothing.

Into the silence, Stella said, "Why didn't you tell me you have a daughter?"

His eyes widened. "So that's what this is about."

She held her arms close to her body. "We've spent the last few weeks together, how did you not mention it?"

He rolled his eyes. "It's my business how I manage my daughter. I take care of Bierta. Which is more than I can say for my father."

His father? Suddenly, Stella realized he'd never mentioned his father either. What had they been talking about?

"But you lied to me. I asked you if you want kids—"

He put up his hand to cut her off. "I never said I didn't have a child. How did I lie?"

Stella's eyes narrowed. "We were opening up to each other. But you didn't tell me that you have a child. You won't talk about your brother. This is the first I've heard of your father. What else are you holding back?"

"I don't know why you're getting bent out of shape. If it was so important, you could have asked," he said, his body tense.

Stella felt the heat rise in her cheeks. "Oh, right, of course. I know my favorite pick-up line is: 'So how many children have you got?'"

He stared at her for a moment. "You're going to toss this aside over one error?"

"Did you make an error?" Stella countered. "I haven't heard you apologize. You've just told me all the reasons I'm wrong."

"Apologize—and then what? We move on?"

She tucked a loose tendril of hair behind her ear. "Relationships aren't an if-then statement."

"That's not an answer. What do you want, Stella?" He took a step toward her, trying to catch her gaze.

She looked away.

"I thought we had something. Too bad it's not enough for you."

She said nothing.

He went on, "I'm not sure what you're waiting for. What you're looking for. But you're not going to find it here."

"Here? Who says I'm staying here?"

His smile tightened, more leer than grin. He turned away.

"Wait," she said. "You got out of Aramezzo. What's to say I won't get out, too?"

A cat yowled in the distance.

"Stella, you can't possibly tell me that you haven't earned enough by now to pay for a plane ticket."

"I need more than a plane ticket. I need a fresh start."

"The Conti family sold their house. Why can't you do the same? After you put all that work into it? And rehabilitated those olive trees you're so smug about?"

Smug? Stella shook her head angrily. "I looked it up! Property values are worth almost nothing around here."

"You looked at recent property values? You didn't just hit on a decades-old listing and stop there?"

Had she? She didn't know. It was definitely like her to miss a detail like the date of the listing.

"See? If it was important to leave, that would be your goal. You would have a clear idea of what you needed and how to get there. Instead of frittering away all your time."

"You're saying I'm too distractible to ever get myself together to leave?"

"No. I'm saying you're too scared."

A bitter taste rose in her mouth. "You're wrong. I'm leaving. And soon."

He shifted his weight. "You won't. You never will. I'm the one chance you had, your ticket. And you're blowing it because I didn't tell you about Bierta? Who you would have known about if you bothered to read a paper."

Stella set her jaw, clenching her fists lightly. "You don't get it."

"You don't get it. Too bad, Stella. We could have had a good time together."

"Maybe I want more than a good time."

He smirked. "You think real life is like those stories you read? That's cute."

She paused. "Rejection doesn't suit you, Giancarlo."

He laughed harshly. "Oh, I'll get over this before I go to bed tonight. Do you know how full my DMs are?"

"It's nice to know you've kept tabs." She flicked invisible lint from her shirt.

He paused, his eyes darting away. "Good luck with your life in Aramezzo, Stella. Baking the same things. Seeing the same people. Making the same beds. Every day for the rest of your life."

The cicadas went silent.

Stella sagged against the rock wall, the sides of her vision narrowing.

Was he right? Had she not left Aramezzo because she was too scared to go? All those times she'd offered help her guests didn't want, the days of playing detective, the evenings bringing meals no one needed. Maybe it was all to create distraction. To avoid the work of leaving.

After all, she had nothing to show for all her efforts.

She began to suspect she never would.

Stella glanced at Luisella's house before entering her own. Dark. So much the better; she wasn't in the mood to question her. Part of her wanted to tell Luca, but the thought of his eyes narrowing made her hesitate. Would he think it a bridge too far? With a click of the door behind her, Stella decided to talk to Luisella first and take it from there.

She willed her hands to keep from shaking as she fried the sausage. This time, she had to maintain focus. Romina's food strike, her breakup with Giancarlo, and her fight with Matteo—she couldn't let any of it pollute her one place of peace. Her fingers itched to pick up the phone, to check for a message from Matteo. Had Giancarlo talked to him yet?

Remembering years of being the only woman in the kitchen—cooking family meals the male chefs scarfed down without comment before vanishing back to the line—she had never felt so powerless, so shut out, as in this moment.

She tasted the greens and sausage again and again. Her vigilance left no room for connections and ideas, but she would nail this sauce if it killed her.

With the sauce finished, she defied the old adage and watched the pasta water boil. Only then did she call Cindy Copeland to dinner. Cindy arrived and paused at the table set for one. She stared at Stella for a moment. "You aren't joining me?"

Stella shook her head. "I need to get a portion of this across town before it cools. Enjoy!"

Cindy nodded, a little forlorn. She tucked her dress neatly under her as she slid into the seat. With a clink of her cutlery, she leaned over the plate and inhaled. "Mmmm. Smells heavenly. Thank you, Stella."

Stella smoothed the tablecloth so Cindy wouldn't see the tears rising in her eyes.

Barbanera padded silently into the room.

"Want to come to Marta's?" He may act bored at Marta's, but Stella knew he enjoyed bossing their enormous Maremma shepherd around.

He sat and stared, his eyes oddly narrow.

"Oh, right. Your dinner." She waited, hoping for the weight of his head against her knees. He only blinked.

Taking out a Delft blue saucer, Stella heaped it with its usual scoop of food. Casting a glance at the cat, Stella added an extra spoonful. She set it on the tile floor with a clink. Barbanera cast a glance at it, his tail twitching. He looked away.

Stella watched for a moment before pressing her lips together. With forced cheer she told Cindy, "I'll be back in a bit."

"Okay. This is so delicious. I wish you could enjoy it, too."

Stella fought an urge to cradle Cindy's head like a beloved child. "Not too salty?" she couldn't help asking.

Cindy frowned and took a delicate bite off the end of her fork. "Not remotely. Why?"

"No reason," Stella said casually before stepping out into the night air, which was blessedly a few degrees cooler than before. The sun slipping into the dark hills eased the heat more than Stella would have expected.

Within minutes she was on Marta's steps.

"Stella!" Marta said, opening the door. "Ascanio, look, it's Stella!"

The little boy, his hair haloed around his face, careened around the corner, followed by their dog, Orlando, running with the rocking-horse gait he used so as to not overtake Ascanio.

"*Ciao*, Stella! What I smell? Dinner?" He stopped short and looked up at her with a winning smile.

Stella caressed his cheek and remembered Cindy, now eating alone. Maybe she could have waited and made dinner for the both of them after she dropped off food for Marta. "Good sniffing, Ascanio. I made you pasta with greens and sausage."

He cocked his head to the side and said with all seriousness, "I like green." Before bolting off again.

Marta waved Stella in as Stella said, "Every time I see him, it's like he's grown another year older."

Chuckling, Marta said, "He has energy for three boys nowadays."

"You seem to keep up okay."

"I'm glad of Leo's help."

Stella nodded. "He told you I'd be stopping by with dinner?"

"He did," Marta said softly. "I know I shouldn't worry so much, but after the other night—"

"Of course." Stella set the pot on the stove. "But hopefully he's not driving the *porchetta* van to his parents?"

Marta laughed. "That's all I'd need, right? To worry that the van would break down again, leaving him a roadside sitting duck."

"It breaks down a lot."

Marta nodded. "I've told him to find a new mechanic. Rocco might have been great in the race car pit, but I don't think he knows his way around a food truck."

"So Rocco hasn't had this shop long?"

"He opened AutoCura after Leo stopped racing." Marta removed the lid of the pot and inhaled the released steam. "This is the first time I've felt hungry in days. You've got such talent."

Stella kept quiet about the failed earlier version. Instead, she took the seat Marta offered. As they listened to the sound of Ascanio trying to push Orlando on the couch to play runaway train, Marta offered Stella a glass of wine. Stella wondered why her eyes pricked with tears again. "Thank you."

"Don't expect anything fancy. It's from my in-laws' grapes."

"Rough and ready is perfect." Stella admired the almost purple hue of the wine, which made it look like it would be heavy and sweet. Instead, it had a blunt acidic edge, like cassis. Stella closed her eyes and sipped, noticing how the light in the kitchen pushed back the lengthening shadows. "I love it."

Marta set down a bowl of rosemary breadsticks to nibble before taking a seat beside Stella.

Stella tried to remember the conversational thread. "I met Rocco yesterday. Bumped into him when he was bringing gas to the van."

"Oh, you met him! Charming, isn't he?"

At Stella's hesitation, Marta went on, "I mean sure, he can go on and on about the good old racing days, but that man can find the sunshine in any situation."

"He's a good singer," was the best Stella could offer.

Marta laughed and poured herself a glass of water from the pitcher on the table. "Too bad Rocco's mechanical skills aren't as good as his singing. At least not anymore. The way Leo talks about Rocco's proficiency in the pit, I wonder if the man needs adrenaline to keep focused. Without it, his attention to detail suffers."

Stella sipped her wine, thinking. "I remember guys on the line I couldn't stand during prep, the way they'd mouth off or leave skin on the carrots. But once service started, they were all in. By the end of the night, they'd feel like family. Like we got through something together."

Marta nodded. "That makes sense. And helps, actually. As much as I like Rocco, I've been trying to get Leo to take his vehicles elsewhere. How would Rocco know? Leo says he owes Rocco too much."

"I get it," Stella said, sipping her wine and letting the cadence of their conversation wash away the gloom of the day.

Marta picked up a breadstick. "Plus, when he takes the van in, they get to remember good times together."

Stella thought of Giancarlo and Leo, both sidelined from their sport. "He must miss that dopamine rush." *His antidepressant*, Marta had called it.

Marta shrugged. "I thought he would miss it more, except in the end, his heart wasn't in it. He lost races he used to win."

Again, Stella thought of Giancarlo. Maybe he would have been a better match for her if they'd met at the flagging end, like Marta and Leo. "So it was easy for Leo to walk away, then," Stella said.

"I doubt it was easy. Don't we all hang onto hope that things can turn around? But the accident decided for him. His parents say he wasn't the same after that."

Stella smiled. "Until he met you."

"You're sweet." Marta grinned. "Though his parents say the same thing. Or not about me, really, but Ascanio. Being responsible, caring for someone, it's helped him get his feet back underneath him."

Stella thought about it. "And he keeps the memories alive through Rocco."

"Rocco, and the other guys from the shop."

"Do they all have racing backgrounds?"

"No, just Rocco," Marta said before rolling her eyes. "But even without that, they all speak the same language, if you know what I mean. One time I came early to pick Leo up and saw them all in the rear lot, talking around the back of a car. They slammed the trunk closed when I got close and went quiet. I made a stupid joke about leaving my testosterone card back at home, and one of them—I think his name's Stefano?—said something about not dirtying my pretty little hands." She nibbled the breadstick, releasing the scent of rosemary. "They get together, and it's like I don't understand a word."

Stella's mind whirred. Rocco's gloves. Leo's warning. *You don't want to put a target on your back.*

Marta stared out the window. "You know, maybe it's less about speaking car lingo and more about not being used to women. There is a real lack of feminine energy in that shop. What are the odds they'll let me bring in lace curtains and dried lavender?" She chuckled at the image and noticed Stella's still face. "Stella? Are you okay?"

Stella leaned forward and said softly. "You know how Roberto and Romina are accused of working with the Mafia?"

Marta's face tightened and she said softly, "That's so ridiculous. As if they would ever do that."

Nodding, Stella said, "I know. But the story actually gets more bizarre. I'm trusting you not to spread this around, but Roberto and Romina were once arrested for human trafficking."

"What!"

"I know."

"Impossible!"

"I agree. Which is why I don't want this getting around. But it does seem true that back then, they were surrounded by family with ties to the Mafia. So my theory is that they got arrested because of people around them. Maybe they didn't even know those people were doing anything wrong."

Marta tapped the rim of her water glass. "That makes sense."

Slowly, Stella said, "If that can happen to them—two people we know to be good and smart and kind—it makes me think anyone could be vulnerable."

Marta gave a slow nod. Then she froze. Her spine went rigid as she sat upright. "*Aspetta.* Wait. Are you suggesting that Leo got swept up in something? Something like the mob?"

"I'm not suggesting anything, I'm trying to follow every lead and—"

"Stella!" Marta exclaimed, her face paling. "Please tell me you're kidding. Italy isn't like Americans imagine, with Mafia—"

"No, I know. I got the lecture. But today Leo warned me—he said he didn't want me delving into Roberto and Romina's case because he knew Mafia guys back in his racing days, and it could be dangerous for me to get entangled. I'm not suggesting he's involved, but maybe he knows people who could be?"

Marta's mouth fell open. "I thought you gave up this needless crusade against the father of my child."

"Again, I'm not talking about Leo, I'm talking about Rocco or maybe that Stefano guy." Suddenly, Stella realized. "Father of your . . . Marta, Ascanio's father—" Stella's words faded out as Marta touched her stomach.

"Marta, are you . . ." Her fingers tightened on the wineglass.

Marta closed her eyes. "It's early days. I don't want to talk about it."

Stella shook her head. "Forgive me, Marta. You know how I let my imagination run away with me. Of course Leo doesn't know anyone in the Mafia!"

Even as she said it, she pictured Leo diving into the bushes to avoid a collision. Was the driver at the wheel Rocco? Hot-headed maybe, because Leo was threatening to take his vehicle elsewhere? Or was hitting Leo accidental, and Rocco, or one of his men, after the nun?

Marta stared at the clock.

Stella rose. "I really am sorry, Marta; I should know better. Leo has been nothing but lovely. I mean, look at him wanting to make sure you had company tonight and then I went and spoiled it. I'm so sorry."

Marta shook her head. "It's fine, Stella. I'll feel better, I think, when he gets a phone."

"Oh, right, he lost his in the accident."

"Without it, I can't help all the terrible thoughts when he's a few minutes late."

"Well," Stella said, looking around for safer territory. "I'll let you guys have your dinner before it gets cold."

Marta nodded. "Thanks again for bringing it by."

Stella bit her lip, nodded, and turned away.

She walked home, mind awhirl. She couldn't dismiss her theory.

Leo, who admitted to having connections to people in the Mafia.

Leo, who insisted on taking his *porchetta* van to a guy who had erratic hours and did his job poorly.

Leo, who said he owed Rocco.

She stopped in the street.

Maybe he'd overheard something at the auto shop. And maybe that was why someone tried to run him down. Because they were afraid he'd talk.

Passing Luisella's house, Stella noticed the dark windows. She must be gone again, on her nighttime jaunt.

Walking into the house, Stella noticed the dishes stacked clean in the drainboard, still warm from washing in hot water. She also noticed Barbanera's saucer, with one spoonful of food left, crusting around the edges.

MONDAY

Morning again. No texts from Matteo. None from Marta. She'd half expected a text from Giancarlo, apologizing or asking to talk. She wondered how angry he was and realized she was more resigned than angry—hooking up with the wrong man was her signature move. She thought fleetingly of Luca and then forced herself out of bed.

Time to bake the *cornetti*. Stella took a few extra from the bag in the freezer. Maybe today she'd catch Luisella.

Over breakfast, Cindy told Stella that her husband's patient had gone into cardiac arrest overnight. Stable now, but he wouldn't return to Aramezzo until tomorrow. "I decided to see a bit of the countryside today. Take a walk in the olive groves. Did you know that olive trees communicate with each other underground? Kind of like mushrooms. Which reminds me of that time I got lost in the woods looking for fairy rings. You know, those circles of mushrooms?"

Stella smiled at Cindy's zigzagging train of thought as she poured her another cup of coffee. The wafting scent reminded her she'd meant to ask Marta where she got her beans. "My little sister and I used to come up with all sorts of stories about those rings. Once I left her a note in one, from the fairies. She slept with it under her pillow."

Cindy chuckled. "I did something like that for my son once. Put a shark tooth in his sandbox. He convinced himself it was a dinosaur tooth

219

and insisted I attach it to a cord so he could wear it as a trophy."

Stella laughed. She sat down beside Cindy and said, "It's a good idea to walk to the groves now, before it gets too hot." She told Cindy about the demarcation in the soil, the ancient water-line.

Cindy's eyes grew large. "This place is magic. Not ordinary magic, note-in-a-fairy-ring magic."

Stella leaned forward. "I feel that way myself. By the way, when you walk out the town gate and turn right past the bocce courts, look for the old town ovens. There's a trail that leads from the ovens through the groves."

"Town ovens," Cindy sighed. "How romantic. Like the ones outside your door? That you made the focaccia in?"

"Very similar, though the town ones include grills."

"That focaccia was wonderful. The onions."

Stella popped the lid off a jam jar and smiled at the sweet scent, underscored with that spice of Aramezzo plums. "From Cannara, famed for their onions. It's unfortunate you won't be here for the onion festival. It's quite an experience. Especially if you have a hankering for onion doughnuts." How nice to speak in English; "Hankering" had no Italian equivalent that Stella knew.

Cindy pulled a face. "That might be too exotic for me. I'll stick with focaccia."

"Once Mr. Copeland is back, you can drive there for onion pizza. It's not far, and the pizza is delicious."

Cindy reached for her phone but paused, instead stirring the coffee with a clatter before finally dropping her hands into her lap. "James isn't one to travel for pizza."

Before she could stop herself, Stella said, "Sights not sandwiches?"

With a faint flush, Cindy nodded. "He thinks my wanting to travel for food is a little . . . strange."

Stella's shoulders tightened with unsaid choice remarks.

Cindy hurried on, "I know he's right. It's true I can go on and on about a crepe with chestnut cream. He has to remind me that nobody wants to listen to my monologue."

Working to unclench her jaw, Stella said, "Well, I, for one, would be happy for you to catalogue every crepe you've ever had. In chronological, alphabetical, or random order."

Cindy beamed.

Stella went on, "But I can also direct you to the statue of Saint Francis outside Cannara, marking the spot where he fed the birds."

"Really? That happened in Cannara?"

"Among other places. I like to think it's a reminder that there's a kind of holiness to feeding others." When Cindy smiled, Stella went on. "Also, the town is atmospheric, you'd enjoy taking photos there."

Cindy reached for her phone. "I can't imagine it's more atmospheric than Aramezzo. I think I've taken a thousand photos already." She paused. "After my walk, I thought I'd do a little shopping, visit Domenica, and that flower shop she mentioned. I haven't seen the church yet, either."

"Sounds like a packed day."

"Packed with nothing. Perfect," Cindy smiled. "You know, it's that church that brought us here. We were at a dinner party and met friends of friends who take annual biking trips. All over the world! They even bring their own bikes, ship them I guess. Do you think we leave bits of tire everywhere we go?"

Stella paused and inclined her head. "You know, in some way, I think we do."

Cindy took a big bite of croissant, the flakes of pastry falling on her linen slacks. As she chewed, she said, "James said that only I could come up with something that odd. Ha!" The animated expression on her face seemed to crack, leaving her wan.

Stella said, "So . . . the bikers?"

Cindy blinked and then said, "Yes! Their bike tour brought them here and the guide told them some fascinating things about the church…"

As Cindy prattled on, Stella felt torn between trying to keep pace with her guest's branching thoughts and wondering if any of those fascinating facts about the church included buried nuns. She itched to get to Domenica's.

Cindy rose to take her plate to the sink, but Stella took the dishes and said, "Have you seen Barbanera? He's usually down here for breakfast."

Cindy gestured upstairs. "On my bed."

"Is he okay?"

With a shrug, Cindy said, "Seems to be. Though who knows what a cat thinks, right? I mean, I know they're doing studies with electrodes, but until we get a cat scientist, how can we really interpret the results of brain activity?"

Stella gave a small laugh and packed the leftover *cornetti* into a basket for Luisella.

After pointing Cindy toward the town ovens, Stella knocked on Luisella's door. She stepped back and waited. No answer.

Stella touched the door once more before turning and walking to the bookshop. She dropped the basket of *cornetti* onto the desk and flopped into the chair with a noisy sigh. "Sorry I'm late, I was trying to keep up with Cindy."

"Cindy?" Domenica asked, removing the scarves from the computer. "Isn't she a kick in the pants?"

"She was so quiet when she arrived and now she's got so much to say." She shook her head. "Maybe my coffee is too strong."

"Or maybe Aramezzo is her coming-out party."

Stella, who had been reaching to pick up a tuxedo cat she didn't remember seeing before—had Domenica picked up another stray, or had he wandered in?—sat up. "Come again?"

Domenica shrugged. "Maybe this is the true Cindy Copeland, the one she censors around her husband."

Stella stared at her friend. "You never met the man."

Domenica sighed. "Any man brazen enough to tell you that your pasta requires saffron would spare no criticism for his own wife. Even if he told himself it was to make her more palatable to others."

"Like he's protecting her," Stella nodded. She remembered how Cindy's trip to the *alimentari*, on her own, seemed to embolden her. Maybe she fumbled there, brought out her odd angles, and realized the world didn't fall apart. Thoughtfully, Stella said, "I hate to think she's been repressing this version of herself to hide in the shadows. You never know what she's going to say next."

Domenica chuckled. "Sound familiar?"

Stella watched dust motes dance in the sunbeam falling across the floor. "I know what you're getting at, but no, it's not like me. Her thoughts are a wandering path and you don't know where she's going and then you arrive and it's like—*ta-da*! This moment of insight or clarity or observation that's totally her own." Plus, her problem was impulsivity, not fading against the walls. Her mother's face swam up into her field of vision, criticizing Stella for getting distracted during her science fair presentation on ants. She'd segued into how some cultures ate ants, how they tasted like citrus. Stella hadn't bothered entering the fair the following year.

Her voice soft, Domenica said, "Your route goes through the kitchen, but you do have a way of finding your way toward clarity."

"Anyway, her husband has only been gone a day. Seems like a major personality overhaul in such a short time."

"Have it your way," Domenica said. "We'll chalk it up to being over-caffeinated. So, tell me what you've learned."

Should she share her theory about Leo being an unwitting connection between Aramezzo and the Mafia? In the light of morning, it seemed too strange and anyway, they didn't need Leo as a possible connection to the Mafia. Roberto had established connections.

Would she have remembered this if she'd baked last night? Her thoughts seemed so sluggish.

The door opened and Matteo entered. "*Buongiorno*, Domenica. Oh. *Ciao*, Stella," Matteo said, with a frown, and sat with his body angled away from Stella.

"Oh, hello there, Matteo," Stella said firmly not looking at him but instead peering around for the tuxedo cat who seemed to have disappeared.

Domenica looked from one to the other. "Are you two still at it? This one must have been a biggie."

Matteo gestured to Stella to take the floor. "Go ahead, Stella. I'm sure you're just dying to vilify Giancarlo in front of a studio audience."

She rolled her eyes and turned to Domenica. "It seems that Matteo, despite his extensive experience in dating men, somehow missed the memo that a man can sometimes not be worthy of interest."

He went still. "Not just any man. *Giancarlo*."

"Matteo, he kicks a ball around for money. He did not invent the reverse sear."

He shook his hand angrily. "You are being obtuse on purpose. I'm not saying you should like him because he's famous. I'm saying you should give him the benefit of the doubt because he's my best friend."

Domenica cut in. "Can we play soap opera later? Let's just leave it at sometimes the qualities that make someone a good friend aren't the same ones needed for a relationship."

"But—" Stella and Matteo insisted at the same time

"No buts," Domenica insisted. "Fit in a romantic relationship matters far more than in a friendship, and anyone with two eyes could see that the relationship between Stella and Giancarlo wouldn't last. Despite—yes Matteo—his manifold good qualities."

"What!" Stella said indignantly. "I didn't know you thought that. Why didn't you tell me?"

Domenica shrugged. "Just because a relationship is short doesn't mean it's not worth having. Take it from me. Now, can we get on to bigger business?"

The room fell into a sullen quiet that only broke with the peal of Stella's phone. "Saved by the bell," she muttered. Aloud she said, "It's Luca. I'm taking it outside."

Pressing the phone to her ear as she stepped through the door, she said, "*Pronto?*"

"Good, Stella, I'm glad I caught you," Luca said. "The autopsy report is in. The nun was pregnant."

Her legs went wobbly, the stone wall pressed cold through her shirt.

As if she'd spoken, Luca went on, "I know. The whole thing suddenly seems far more tragic."

"But I thought I was wrong! I mean, I realized, totally on my own with no help whatsoever—"

"Of course." She could practically hear Luca nodding.

"That the *valigia* is the bag, the bag from the bar. Not a baby."

Luca gave a low whistle. "How did I miss that?"

Stella brushed stone dust from the wall. "Join the club."

"Hm. Maybe you didn't pick up on the pregnancy from the word *valigia* but instead from the 'I'll take care of you' bit."

"Maybe," Stella wondered. It seemed more like a lucky guess to her. Maybe all her previous mystery-solving success could be chalked up to lucky guesses. "I wonder if the Mother Superior knew."

"That was my thought too. Right after realizing that we now stand a shot of getting DNA evidence on the father."

Stella sagged. "Oh my. I hadn't thought of that."

"It'll take time, especially with the labs backed up." Luca made a sound like he was shifting his phone to his other ear. In the background, Stella heard phones ringing.

"Any word on Romina?" she asked.

"No change, I'm afraid," Luca said grimly.

"I know I'm missing something obvious," Stella said, her thoughts cycling between Adele's husband and the mayor and Veronica and the Reverend Mother. "Something is deeply wrong with me."

"Go easy on yourself. You put too much on your shoulders."

"I have big shoulders."

"Correction: You have tiny shoulders."

She smiled, and wondered if Luca smiled at the other end of the line.

She hung up and turned to find Matteo.

"Oh!" she said, stepping backwards. How much had he heard? "I didn't see you."

He ran his hand down his face and then said, "I see you."

"What? What do you mean?"

"I realized after our 'conversation' yesterday—you assumed I'd take Giancarlo's side. You thought I wouldn't see you. So, I want you to know. I see you."

She nodded slowly. "I figured he'd get you in the divorce." Her voice shook. "I couldn't bear it. I got prickly. I'm sorry for that."

"I do understand that his not telling you about Bierta, especially when you talked about children, would have felt bad or wrong for you."

"I just learned about his father walking out on them."

"Just?"

"Yes. Weirdly when the conversation got tense he started spilling information."

Matteo tried to smile and cast his eyes up to meet hers. "He's always been at his best when there's a man on."

Stella blinked. "What?"

"When the pressure heightens, that's when Giancarlo pushes himself."

Stella nodded before venturing, "Matteo? I'm sorry about the crack about you focusing on my relationship because of your lack of same."

"*Allora*," Matteo breathed. "I'm not sure you're entirely wrong."

She touched her tongue to her lip, wondering if she should say it. "Matteo. Don't you want something for yourself?"

"Sure." He shrugged.

"Then why—"

"I guess I figured it would just happen. Someday."

"But how, Matteo, if you aren't investing in that part of your life?"

"You're one to talk," Matteo smiled.

"*Touchè*," Stella said grimly. "Call me the chef with the burnt pan, criticizing the meat."

He chuckled. "Anyway. It's not like I'm walking away from opportunities. You know Grindr hardly works in a medieval village on the outskirts of the spiritual heartbeat of Italy."

Stella frowned. "Aramezzo isn't close to the Vatican. How could—"

"Assisi, Stella. I meant Assisi. Some Umbrian you are." But he smiled at her.

She picked a cat hair off his shirt. "I need Catholic lessons."

"I'm sure Don Arrigo would be more than happy to oblige."

Stella nodded, distracted by a new thought. "Maybe we need to do more than wait, Matteo. Maybe a real relationship, one with tannins—"

"Tannins?"

"You know, with staying power . . . maybe that takes more than waiting."

Matteo clasped Stella's hand. She smiled at him, and he pulled her in for a hug. From down the street, someone called from the window to a passerby who shouted a greeting back, the words echoing between Aramezzo's walls..

Holding Stella's hand, Matteo led her back into Domenica's.

Domenica smiled as they walked in hand-in-hand. "It's about time. Sit."

"I probably shouldn't. I have a lot to do, but Domenica . . . any luck on the convent?"

"The convent?" Matteo said. "Did you ever hear from the nun?"

"I did," Stella responded. "Turns out Elena was in a relationship. Luca told me the autopsy results show she was pregnant."

Domenica leaned back as Matteo inhaled sharply.

Stella went on, "So we really need more information on the convent. Did you find anything yet?"

Domenica shook her head. "But now that I know this, I have something concrete to look for."

"Mother Maria Teresa knew more than she let on."

Matteo held up his hand. "I have an update."

Stella and Domenica swiveled their heads to stare at him.

"What?" he asked, his wide eyes wider. "You gave me jobs."

Stella shook her head. "But you made this big stink about not wanting to follow the mayor and Veronica."

"And Vincenzo," Matteo added.

"And Vincenzo," Stella nodded.

Matteo grimaced. "I didn't say I wouldn't do it. I just hate following people around with brooms."

Stella blinked. "Matteo, you follow people around with brooms all the time."

"Exactly."

Stella said, "Is this about hating your job? I keep telling you, a job is like a bra—you spend too much time in one to put up with a bad fit."

Domenica and Matteo exchanged glances. Finally, Matteo said, "Bras? I'm pretty sure you've never said that to me before. Like, ever."

Stella waved her hand. "Fine. Bed sheets, toilet paper. You can't expect me to keep track of my metaphors."

Domenica said, "So what did you find, Matteo?" She glared at Stella to keep quiet.

"Well, Stella, do you remember when you saw people you didn't recognize going into Trattoria Cavour?"

Stella nodded.

"I finally saw them myself, and I didn't recognize them either. So I asked Vincenzo about them."

"You did what?" Stella asked, her mouth dropping open.

He looked at Domenica before facing Stella again. "Isn't that what you would have done?"

"Sure. But I'm reckless."

He grinned. "And maybe I'm done playing meek."

"Camouflaged by your service uniform," Stella added with a laugh.

"If you two are quite finished," Domenica said crossly, though her smile belied her words.

"Right, Signora," Matteo said with a little salute. "Anyway, I didn't get anything from Vincenzo. He said it was none of my business and ran to talk to Cosimo."

Stella frowned. "By not saying anything, he said a lot."

"That's what I thought," Matteo nodded. "Once Vincenzo left, Adele told me they were having a family situation. That the people coming in and out are kin."

"Hmmm," said Stella. "How did she seem?"

"Pretty gray. Worn out," Matteo said. "But that's not the update. When I passed Vincenzo and Cosimo, I heard Vincenzo bragging about how much money they made Friday and Saturday, with the bar closed. He said they were going to get a new espresso machine."

"An espresso machine?" Stella's voice scaled up. "Did he say what kind?"

Matteo turned to her. "An Elektra Bella something, I think. Why?"

"Belle Epoque," Stella said softly. "Their commercial espresso machine costs a fortune."

The room fell quiet.

"I could explain away the cups. You lose some, they break. But an expensive espresso machine," Stella said. "It's like they know Roberto and Romina aren't coming back."

Stella loitered outside Luisella's house for fully three minutes before working up the courage to knock.

"*Arrivo!*" Luisella called from within. With a creak of hinges, she opened the door. "Stella?"

Stella held out the basket. "*Cornetti,*" she explained. "I thought you might miss them, with the bar being closed."

Luisella glanced up and down the street, as if suspicious of being punked, before she reached for the basket. As she turned to re-enter her house, Stella said, "Do you have a second? I wanted to ask you a question."

Luisella stepped onto her stone stoop, closing the door behind her and thus blocking Stella's curious eyes. She watched Stella for a moment, her face implacable. "More questions?"

"Well," Stella stalled. Why hadn't she prepared an excuse? Reckless was too kind a word. "I was just, erm ... wondering if everything was okay. With you."

"Why wouldn't it be?" Luisella frowned.

Airily, Stella said, "No real reason, I suppose. But I heard people talking about how you've been leaving Aramezzo. At night. Often." Stella felt her shoulders stiffen, as if bracing for impact.

A storm cloud passed Luisella's face. "People around here do nothing but spin yarns."

"You mean it's not true?"

"I mean it's nobody's business." She turned back to her door.

Stella reached to touch Luisella's arm. Luisella stared at Stella's hand until Stella dropped it, clearing her throat. "You know about the woman killed on the road?"

"Of course. Even without Bar Cappellina, gossip makes its way to me."

Briefly, Stella wondered how. "I wanted to know if you saw anything. On one of your nighttime ... errands."

"I'd hardly call them errands, Stella."

"What would you call them?" Stella tried to keep the urgency out of her voice.

Luisella squinted into the distance. She brought her gaze back to Stella and said firmly, "I didn't see anything."

"On which day?"

"What?"

"Which day are you referring to that you didn't see anything?"

Luisella glared. "Whatever day you're asking about."

Stella clenched her teeth. "I'm talking about Friday night. What time did you get home?"

Narrowing her eyes, Luisella said, "You're a lot like your mother, you know."

Stella took a step backwards, catching herself before tumbling down the steps. From a distance, Stella heard the rising whine of cicadas. "You ... you said you didn't know her. My mother."

"I didn't. But Anna Maria told me. How your mother was always into what she shouldn't be. Making trouble between friends. Showing up where she wasn't invited. Spying on her sister."

"Spying on Anna Maria?"

Luisella shrugged.

Fearing Luisella turning back into the house, Stella blurted, "I heard Anna Maria wasn't close with anyone. It's funny you knew her so well."

After staring at Stella for a moment, Luisella said carefully, "She wasn't a loner, if that's what you think. Sure, she didn't run on and on like some people. And she stayed away from the gossips of Aramezzo."

"Something she and my mother had in common. My mom told me time and again how much she hated Aramezzo."

"Anna Maria loved Aramezzo," Luisella said angrily. "It was the being watched she despised."

In a quiet voice, Stella added, "I'm trying to understand. Really. Why my mother hated it here so much."

"You don't know?"

"No." Stella thought for a moment. "Maybe I'm more like Anna Maria. I love it here. But I get how hard it is to be under a microscope. I don't know if you know I was dating Giancarlo—"

"Obviously."

Stella straightened the scarf knotted around her curls. "Well, dating was challenging. I felt eyes, on me, all the time."

Luisella said, "And you were dating a man."

"Yes. Giancarlo." Stella frowned. On the edge of understanding. "Wait, what do you mean?"

"It's too bad you didn't know Anna Maria. I think you would have gotten along. She was talented. Like you." Luisella said, her eyes peering into Stella's.

"I heard. An accomplished seamstress. As soon as things slow down around here, I'm going to go through the attic and see if I can find any-thing. I'd love to see her work."

Luisella paused. And then looked down at her tailored shell-pink dress. A color that should look youthful and wrong for a woman of Luisella's age, but somehow only underscored her classic femininity.

Stella blinked. "She made your dress?"

"She made them all. Who else?"

"Honestly, I always assumed it was a timeless designer like Chanel."

"Right on the first part, wrong on the second. The timelessness was all Anna Maria."

At the warmth in her voice, Stella wondered if Domenica had been on to something—perhaps Luisella did prefer women. "But…why did she make you clothes?"

"Why do you cook food?" Luisella asked, holding up the basket of *cornetti*.

Stella opened her mouth to protest and then closed it again.

Light flashed in Luisella's eyes as she studied Stella.

Stella said, "I wish I'd known her. My aunt."

"You had a lot in common. From your commitment to your passions to your hating the limelight to your total giddiness when in love."

"Isn't everyone giddy when in love?"

"I'm sure I wouldn't know." Luisella flushed, suppressing a grin.

Stella said, "Luisella? Are you in love?" What she wanted to ask was if she was in love with somebody now, or if she still carried a torch for Anna Maria.

Luisella turned away and said nothing.

Looking at her face in profile, Stella remembered the grainy *autovelox* images. Wait. "That's where you've been going so late."

Luisella turned back.

"But why don't you bring your…friend…here?"

"Didn't we already cover this ground? Too many eyes. Especially on him." Luisella's eyes widened as if she'd said too much and wanted desperately to bring back the words. She straightened her sleeve with a yank.

Him.

Either Luisella's affection for Anna Maria was purely platonic or she'd hopped onto a different track.

"Too many eyes…it's somebody from Aramezzo. Or known to Aramezzo." But how would anyone in Aramezzo know someone in Luisella's life?

Stella had a flash of a striped pasta: Luisella as egg-toned dough, Veronica hued with squid ink, and their shared backstory as the filling.

"Veronica. You're dating someone Veronica knows. From your movie star life."

Luisella froze. Then said, "Don't say anything, Stella. Veronica has always hated it when I got anything she wanted. She will make my life miserable when she finds out about Tazio."

"Tazio. That name sounds familiar."

Luisella pressed her lips together, her eyes gleaming. "It should. Even raised in America, how can you not know the star of *Il Corso della Notte*?" Luisella shook her head. "*Cavolo*. You are like your aunt. I always told her more than I planned."

Stella slowed her breath. "You found him again? Tazio? After all this time?"

Luisella stared at her feet. "He found *me*." She smiled at the ground. "My mother always told me that when we got separated, I should remain in the last place we were together. Who knew how valuable that advice would be?"

"But—" Stella had questions. Did Veronica and Luisella follow Tazio to Aramezzo? And then he left? But what would bring a star like Tazio Vassari to a medieval village?

Luisella held up a hand. "I'll have no more of this forcing information out of me." A smile hinted that she wasn't as cross as her tone suggested.

Stella grinned. "Can you at least tell me what time you rolled into the parking lot Friday night?"

Luisella thought for a moment. "I'm not sure. I know I went to sleep just after midnight, because Tazio texted me good morning."

That didn't help.

"But you saw nothing on the road."

"Honestly, I had plenty on my mind. I wasn't paying attention."

"No people walking? No cars?"

"That I'd remember. No. Nothing like that."

Enjoying this new openness between them, Stella hesitated before asking, "And you didn't fall asleep at the wheel or anything?"

Luisella's eyes narrowed. "Stella, I'm not sure how long it's been for you. But when it's good—when it's really good—you can't slow your heart rate for hours."

Luisella nodded to herself, as if satisfied that she'd gotten through to Stella. Then she turned into her house and closed the door with a snap of the lock.

As Stella stepped down from Luisella's stoop, she saw Luca standing outside her house, facing her, hands in his uniform pockets.

She walked toward him, gathering her thoughts.

"That looked like a cozy conversation," he said, gesturing to Luisella's door.

"Cozy? With Luisella?"

"Interesting, then." He grinned. His flashing dimple distracted her. "Stella?" He moved closer to catch her eye. "You okay?"

"Okay as can be," she said. "As for Luisella. Yes, interesting."

He watched her, waiting.

She continued, "Turns out, she's been leaving Aramezzo every evening. Coming home in the wee hours."

"But . . . why?"

She paused.

"Stella. We agreed to trust each other." He frowned.

"But Luca, when somebody tells me something in confidence, what can I do?"

"Our first priority is helping Roberto and Romina."

"Oh, right. Well, I'm safe as houses then because her being on the road relates to Leo and the nun, not Roberto and Romina. I mean, if you don't think the two crimes are related."

"I didn't think they were related," Luca reminded her, "But the bag may tie them together."

"If that's even what the text meant." Stella sighed. "Frankly it's daunting how little I know."

"Stella. If you'll forgive the presumption . . . you seem overwhelmed."

"Of course I'm overwhelmed! Romina isn't eating, their future is in jeopardy. A nun is dead and Leo injured because there's some crazy person on the road. I'm babysitting a guest while her husband operates on the Mafia raid's collateral damage. Plus," she stopped herself before she mentioned her break-up. "Plus a lot of other stuff." Her voice caught.

"Hey, it's okay, it'll be okay," Luca pulled her in for a hug. Stella stiffened, then relaxed against his body. He held her loosely. Even with his hand running over her hair, it was the most chaste embrace Stella had ever had. Yet she felt her heartbeat slow before galloping forward as if making up for lost time.

She wanted to nestle closer. Had she ever noticed his scent, like a sunny clearing surrounded by thick forest? Forcing herself to pull away, she said, "Sorry about that."

"*Piano, piano*," Luca said, his voice soft. "One step at a time."

"That's hard when everything is tangled and colliding at once."

"Maybe you need to bake something?" He grinned.

"I ruined pasta sauce yesterday." She clapped her hand over her mouth.

The squeak of a laundry line being pulled rang down the street.

"You did not."

She dropped her hand and her smile wavered. "True story."

He shook his head, "You're allowed to fall once in a while, you know."

She stared at the cobblestones, wishing there was some answer written there.

"Tell me what you can about Luisella."

Stella considered for a moment before nodding. "Okay. But there's no more chance of it being related to our crimes than my overcooked pasta."

"Overcooked? How the mighty have fallen."

"If you breathe a word of this to anyone, I'm coming for you." She waggled a finger at him.

"I'd like to see you try," Luca said, both dimples winking.

Stella's breath caught. She shook her head, inhaling the scent of coffee being made in a nearby kitchen. "Luisella has been going to Perugia every night this week. Maybe longer. Friday night, she may have been rounding into the parking lot about eleven."

"Pretty close to Leo's timing. She didn't see anything?"

"Not the *porchetta* van or the nun in the road."

"The nun was wearing dark clothes. Maybe she missed her." Luca's brow furrowed in thought. "But she must have been on the road at the same time as our killer. Depending on how fast she drove. Oh!" He hit his head with his hand.

"What?"

"There's an *autovelox* outside of Assisi. It's been broken for months, but they got it online last week. If she sped by, we can see what time it was, which may help us estimate what time she arrived to the site of the hit-and-run." Luca caught sight of her wide eyes.

"No . . . no!" she stammered. "It seems like a good place to start."

He tapped his finger on his palm. "I can see who else is speeding from that direction. Might be a way to identify the killer."

Stella didn't want to tell Luca it was a dead end. She shifted her weight, glancing at the street. "Can you believe how wrong we were about the valise?"

He held his hand to his forehead for a moment. "How in the world did we miss that?"

"According to Domenica, you read too many historical romances, so you figured it to be some sort of romantic code."

"What's your excuse?" he asked with a grin.

"Language. I'm constantly realizing how little I know, with idioms and dialect. When I hit a strange word in a strange place, I assume I know less than I do."

"At least you knew Italian before arriving. Can you imagine trying to live here with nothing but charades? Though you must miss speaking English."

The blood left Stella's face.

"Stella?" Luca's brow furrowed as he moved closer. "What did I say?"

"Say it again."

"What?"

"Say it again!" Stella demanded. "The thing you just said. I have a thought on the tip of my tongue, and can't reach it."

"Umm," Luca said. "That you must miss speaking English?"

"Before that!" Stella almost stamped her foot in frustration.

"That if your mom hadn't taught you Italian, if you hadn't worked in restaurant kitchens, you would have to do all your sleuthing and guest caretaking through charades? Is that it? I can't remember exactly."

Stella closed her eyes. *Charades*...Domenica had used them in Tunisia. Working with refugees on their way to Sicily.

Yared, age 8.

Roberto and Romina around him, a nun nearby. Something about sardines? Her eyes snapped open. "Do nuns work at refugee camps?"

Luca tilted his head. "Some of them, I'm sure. Why?"

"Refugees....*refugees*. Domenica said Sicily is one of the points of entry for refugees coming from all over, but especially northern Africa."

"You want to tell me where you're headed?"

"In crime novels, refugee charities often turn out to be fronts for trafficking rings. But real life's not always so tidy, is it?" She closed her eyes, thinking. "Lines blur. Good intentions and bad connections can coexist."

Luca said nothing.

Stella opened her eyes. "You said none of the charges stuck. Sure, maybe it's because they had friends in high places. But it's also possible they got scooped up because they were all in the same water."

Luca stared at her. "They're not gnocchi."

"You know what I mean," she insisted.

Luca crossed his arms over his chest. "I'm afraid I don't."

Stella shook her head in frustration. "Maybe Roberto and Romina were working with a Catholic charity to resettle refugees, which would explain the nun in the photograph with Yared."

"Who?"

She waved her hand. "Maybe they were finding housing for those refugees but Roberto's last name raised all the wrong flags. Authorities assumed they were part of a trafficking ring."

Nodding slowly, Luca said, "I think I get it."

"Or!" Stella lifted a finger in the air in excitement. "His family used Roberto's work as a cover for trafficking, piggybacking on their good will. Like using the charity's vehicles or safe houses for their own ends."

"Enough, Stella," Luca said, his hand running across his brow. "I get it. There are innocent reasons they could have gotten mixed up with a human trafficking ring. But I don't know how to find out."

"Maybe see if the human trafficking was in the vicinity of a refugee camp."

"No guarantees, but I'll try," Luca said. After a pause, he said, "See? Look at those connections you made. As if Italian were your only language."

"I learned Italian and English at the same time, so I don't think about it. Only…"

"What?" Luca moved closer to her, his eyes trained on hers.

"Well, you know how they say that your first language is the one you learn about emotion, so it's easier to talk about emotion in that language?"

"That makes sense."

"I heard it on a podcast. Anyway, my mom took care of me when I was small so Italian was my first language. But she never spoke about emotions. Those I got from my father. So sometimes, with Italian, I feel emotions I have no name for."

He nodded slowly. In a soft voice, "That's why it's good you're with Giancarlo. You both speak both languages. Access all the emotions."

Stella said nothing.

"Stella?" At her still face, Luca said, "I overstepped."

"No, it's okay," Stella said. Suddenly finding that it was. "It's just . . . Giancarlo and I, that didn't work out."

"Oh, I'm sorry," he said, moving a step closer, his eyes searching hers.

Stella nodded noncommittally.

"Can I . . . can I ask what happened?" Luca asked.

"No."

"Fair enough." He gave a small smile. "Can I ask if you're okay?"

"You can and I am. According to Domenica, we were never going to make it. Hard to grieve what would never be."

"Domenica," he said, grinning in earnest now. "She pulls no punches."

"It's her speciality. Just wish she'd told me sooner."

He shrugged. "Maybe she knew you wouldn't listen."

"Maybe you're right." She straightened her scarf. "Though I probably would've argued with her just to keep things interesting."

He grinned, both dimples winking. "I'm glad you're okay, though."

"So much for our double dating, right?"

He laughed uncomfortably.

"Luca, I'm joking."

"Right, right." He put his hands in his pockets.

She looked down the street. "I better see if Cindy got to Domenica's yet."

Luca looked distracted as he said, "Sure, that's true. Okay, Stella. Well, I'll be seeing you." He turned, jogged down the steps, and strode away.

Stella wrestled with the lump in her throat. It suddenly occurred to her, the answer to the question she'd been struggling with: how two men could make her feel like she'd stepped off a cliff, all stomach swooshing and weakened knees. That feeling came from a loss of safety. Giancarlo was unsafe, not her match. That loss of safety with Luca came from her defenses crumpling. That was vulnerability.

She lifted her nose as his scent of meadow and forest faded away.

Stella poked her head back in her house to see if Cindy had returned. How long could she stay out in this heat? Stella wished she'd offered her guest a water bottle.

No Cindy.

No Barbanera either.

Stella thought of her shower, of rinsing off the stickiness of the day. With a sigh, she closed the door and walked toward Domenica's.

She paused at the tunnel that led to the town entrance and to the parking lot. Did Leo get home safe last night? She would have heard about it if he hadn't.

Something still nagged at her about Leo and his old friends. He was loyal to them—so loyal he refused to see the connections?

At the foot of the parking lot, she scanned the cars. No *porchetta* truck. She did see Mimmo, walking through the lot toward Aramezzo from his house below town. "*Ciao*, Mimmo," she said. "I haven't seen you for a while."

"It's season," he grunted.

Stella didn't know what he meant and then it occurred to her. "Hunting season?"

His eyes narrowed, like she was being stupid on purpose.

"What brings you into town, then?" Stella tried not to stare at his nose, which still reminded her of an exploded cork. She'd once thought it was a breakout of some kind, but after three seasons in Aramezzo, it couldn't be a temporary condition.

"When are Roberto and Romina coming back?" he asked.

"You miss them," Stella said, wonder in her voice.

"A man needs coffee," Mimmo said. "I have to get it from Marta and deal with that clown."

Stella blinked. "Leo?"

Mimmo huffed and walked away.

"Mimmo! Do you know how to make coffee?"

He kept walking.

She started to follow, but Mimmo, much like the wild animals he hunted, got squirrelly when he thought people were edging too close. She waited for him to get ahead of her.

From the far side of the parking lot, a raised voice carried. She couldn't make out any words, just the sound of the high tone, ringing in the rising afternoon air. Stella moved toward it, ducking behind cars. Looking over her shoulder, she saw Mimmo at the opening of the tunnel, watching her. His eyes trained on her as she tried to ignore him, moving another few cars closer to where she thought the voice had come from. When she looked back over her shoulder, Mimmo had disappeared.

Hopefully he wouldn't tell Marta about her leapfrogging through the parking lot.

The voices were lowered now, but peeking under the cars, Stella spied a woman's legs in pantyhose—in this heat!—and high heels beside a man in slacks and shiny shoes. Stella crept closer, pulling her phone from her pocket to silence it.

"You're the one who wanted it. I told you it was too expensive." A woman's voice Stella almost recognized.

"No, you didn't." A man's voice, pitched so low it sounded like a growl.

A car door opened and Stella heard the click of nails on pavement. She peered under the cars again and saw a second set of russet-colored paws hit the asphalt. She closed her eyes: Marcello. Veronica. The dogs.

The mayor said, "If I'm not mistaken, you said it *looked* too expensive."

"It doesn't matter. We have to sell it. There's no other choice."

A dog head peered under the car, catching sight of Stella, who leapt backwards from her crouched position. Her palms ground against the hot asphalt.

The dog's lip quivered and it began snarling.

"Oh, precious muffin," Veronica said as she scooped the dog into her arms. "You don't like Mummy and Daddy arguing. Well, tell Daddy that if we sell the car now, it'll look suspicious."

The dog growled again.

Stella began scrabbling to the town entrance, hunched down below the level of the cars.

The dog yipped loudly, cutting off Veronica and Marcello's voices.

Stella stopped. If she ran for the entrance now, they'd see her. She ran to the left, searching for Domenica's battered Fiat Panda. Nowhere around. But she spotted Leo's red sports car, standing out from the field of faded Fiats like a traffic signal. Taking a quick peek to make sure Veronica and Marcello were looking toward the town entrance, she rose and gave them a hearty wave, "Hello! Good afternoon!" Afternoon? Had she forgotten to eat lunch again? Did she eat breakfast when she sat with Cindy?

Veronica and Marcello turned to her, their faces stiff. Veronica returned the dog to the ground.

"Hot enough for ya?" Stella said casually. "Oh, I told Leo I'd make sure his alarm is on. You know, after all the mischief going on around here, he got nervous about someone messing with his..." She raked her eyes over the front grill, looking for the make, but only seeing an emblem with a red cross and a green serpent. "Umm...his baby," she finished lamely. She patted the hood of the car with a laugh that grated against the still day. Her eyes caught on the steering wheel. Oh—an Alfa Romeo. Right, Marta had said the car was a company perk. "You don't know anything about this Mafia bust, do you, Marcello?"

He snapped, "How would I know?"

Stella sauntered around the hood of the car, closer to the couple. "No reason. Just, with your connections—"

"Marcello has more important things to do than keep track of your friends, Stella," Veronica said hotly.

Like argue about selling your car. She said, "Of course, of course! Silly me. I assumed he had greater access than the rest of us."

"I have access you can only dream of, little girl," Marcello seethed. Veronica put a hand on his arm. He recoiled, then cleared his throat. "Rest assured, I'm doing all I can."

"That's wonderful to hear," Stella said. She coughed to control the tremor in her words. "Well, I'll tell Leo that his Alfa Romeo is well secured." She turned slowly, walking with purposeful steps to the town entrance.

What was all that about?

Stella pushed open the door to the bookshop and launched into a monologue about the mayor, not noticing Cindy sitting in the faded armchair, a book open across her lap. Stella stopped. "Cindy! How were the groves? Hope you didn't overheat."

Cindy looked up, her eyes unfocused. "What's that? Oh, the groves. The light was too bright. Everything looked washed out. Like when I put bleach in the laundry instead of laundry detergent. James has not let me live that down. Every time I do laundry, he reminds me."

Domenica and Stella exchanged glances, Domenica with a trace of a smile.

Stella scowled. So Domenica did in fact understand far more English than she let on. Maybe she hadn't even been clever, figuring out the source of Cindy's reticence from her behavior. For all Stella knew, Domenica did a spot of hypnosis on her guest.

Cindy held up the book. "Domenica showed me this Italian translation of Shakespeare. I've seen Romeo and Juliet like a thousand times. The Baz Luhrmann version with Leonardo di Caprio. Did you know he wasn't the first choice to play Romeo? The role was supposed to go to

Johnny Depp! Can you imagine, Jack Sparrow climbing Juliet's balcony, drunkenly knocking over flower pots and garbling Romeo's lines? Before getting completely distracted seeing his own image in a nearby window?"

Despite herself, Stella burst out laughing. Cindy flushed, "That was weird, wasn't it? I forgot, I'm supposed to control my mouth."

"Don't you dare," Stella said with a snort of laughter. She remembered Cindy's stiff veneer just two days ago. Who knew it hid such a wellspring of delightfully wacky thoughts? It made Stella wonder what lay beneath other people's reserve or shyness. Her thoughts flickered to Luisella.

Cindy tucked her legs under her as she hunched back over her book, petting Ravioli, perched like a loaf of bread on the arm of the faded pink chair.

Domenica said, "Did your mission to Luisella's pay off?"

Stella nodded. She darted a look at Cindy, blithely turning a page of the illustrated book. "You were right. She has a lover in Perugia."

Domenica grinned. Her hand floated to the desk where Stella noticed an envelope. "Good for her. I know I—"

"One might wonder how you are intuiting all this information. Are you sure you aren't breaking your own rules and investigating everyone around you?"

Domenica's grin collapsed. "Stella. These grapes of yours are awfully sour." She methodically began removing the scarves from around her neck.

Stella hung her head. "I'm sorry. I just don't get how you see so much more than I do. Maybe we should trade places."

After a moment, Domenica said, "Not for the wide world." She paused and said, "Besides, you were on to something. I looked into the convent and there is something funny going on over there."

"Funny how?"

"Well, not haha funny, that's for sure."

Stella stared. Haha funny? Where did Domenica pick up this idiom?

"What?" Domenica asked.

"Nothing," Stella replied. "Go on. Funny how?"

"Well, cross-referencing their lists of nuns, it looks like several nuns disappear every year."

"Disappear from the convent?"

"Disappear altogether. I tried to track what they did after they left the convent, but I found nothing."

Stella sat back, thinking.

"What is it?" Domenica asked, rolling her chair closer to Stella.

Stella closed her eyes and held up one hand. Something was nudging her. She tried loosening her brain the way she did when she baked, allowing new thoughts to enter. Her eyes opened. "Nuns leave so much of their lives behind. Do they take new names? Is it possible that once they leave, they go back to their old name?"

Domenica frowned. "That's definitely possible. Though I should tell you that I hacked the Mother Superior's email—"

"You *what*?"

"Stella, this is hardly the time to develop morals around these things."

Stella arranged her face into one of casual nonchalance. "Pray continue."

"I did a search of the missing nuns' names in her email account. I found that she sought counsel on how to deal with those nuns that didn't value obedience and chastity."

"What was the advice?"

"That's the thing. It seemed in code. As if they knew they needed to be circumspect. And then the correspondence ended with arranging a meeting. Not a call, a meeting."

Stella remembered the nun at the convent hiding from Mother Maria Teresa. Serafina panicked to be caught on the phone. Elena escaping the convent.

Domenica went on, "I'll see if I can figure out the nuns' names before they went into the convent, and what happened to those women after-wards. No promises. But I'll try."

"I hope you find them," Stella said. Living nuns, what a thing to suddenly wish for. "Is that the second thing?"

Domenica shook her head. "No, that was part B of the first thing. The second thing is a little controversial. About our esteemed mayor and his devoted wife."

"You said you'd look into them. That's not so much controversial as an indicator that your rules vary by how much you like someone. P.S., remind me to never get on your bad side."

"Yes, you're very clever, Stella. That's not the controversial bit."

Stella's eyes widened.

"First, their bank account. Yes, I dug into it. Lots—and I mean lots—of ups and downs. Injections of deposits, and then a big outgo."

"Outgo? Where did it go out to?"

"I can't say because it was taken out as a cash withdrawal. So no recipient. What I can tell you is that the withdrawal happens on roughly the same day every month."

"Oh. That's odd. But how is it controversial?"

Domenica blinked. "What?"

"You said what you discovered is controversial."

Pushing her glasses higher on her nose, Domenica said, "Well, there's controversy about whether or not a withdrawal on its own is evidence of misdeeds."

Stella rubbed the crease of her jeans before saying, "I overheard the two of them, Marcello and Veronica, fighting about whether they should sell the car."

"The Mercedes?"

"That's the one."

For a few moments, the only sound was Cindy turning pages.

Finally, Stella said, "Okay, let's think this through. The convent—that looks suspicious in terms of the nun's death. But beyond the bag, can we connect the Mafia to the convent in any way?"

"I'm not sure how." Domenica frowned.

"Are religious orders and the Mafia like oil and water?"

"I suppose it's possible that there are some corrupt religious houses, arm-in-arm with the Mafia." Domenica drummed her fingers on the desk. "Maybe I'm speaking as an Umbrian, but I feel like our local churches are overseen by Saint Francis. Preaching to birds, perhaps, but not steeped in organized crime."

"What if this convent offed some young nuns?"

"Well, you see, I'm not rooting for that one."

"Me either." Stella considered. "And Veronica and Marcello, that relates to the Mafia, right? Not the hit-and-run."

"Maybe. If they were in dire financial circumstances..."

"Remember how easily Marcello was willing to hang Aramezzo out to dry last fall, with the one-euro house scheme," Stella reminded her.

"Because he thought it would better the town, not line his pockets."

Stella stroked Attila who had jumped on the desk. "Maybe he thinks working with the mafia will benefit Aramezzo? I don't think his long-term reasoning is particularly sound."

"Agreed."

Stella tapped the desk. "I need to think on it."

"Baking?" Domenica smiled, brushing Attila's white fur from the desk.

"It's about time." Stella stood.

"What are you making?"

"No idea, I'll go to Cristiana's and follow my nose. In the meantime, a final question for you."

"Final?"

"For these next few minutes at least." Stella stepped around the desk to Domenica and straightened the scarves around her neck. Her voice gentle, she said, "I know I'm leaning hard on your talents."

Domenica pushed her glasses higher on her nose as she regarded Stella. "I want them out. And I need our streets to be safe. As much as you do."

"Right," Stella said softly, patting the scarf into place. "Okay. So, in terms of the Mafia. I'm wondering if Leo has some friends in organized crime."

Domenica sighed. "At this point, I wonder who doesn't have a Mafia connection."

"Honestly, this connection is pretty vague. I'm just putting it together from him warning me to be careful, saying he knew guys like this back in his racing days. And something Marta said about the guys who hang out at the mechanic shop. Any chance you can find out if this guy Rocco is involved with the Mafia?"

Domenica turned to face her computer. "Last name?"

"I don't know."

Domenica whirled back and stared at her.

"I know, I know. But I figure it's easier for you to figure out Rocco's last name than I can with my pea brain."

Domenica turned back and started clattering on the keyboard. "Running yourself down isn't helpful, Stella."

"He works at AutoCura. Or maybe it was AutoCurva? Something like that."

Domenica sighed. Stella listened as Domenica muttered, "AutoCura…Rocco…Rocco…Moretti." She typed for another minute and then swiveled to face Stella. "Rocco Moretti is currently in police custody."

Stella felt all the air escape her body.

Domenica whirled back to the screen, typing madly. "Hang on, there's more, I think. His lawyer's name is familiar. Let me see…"

Stella stayed silent as Domenica typed. She wondered why Domenica didn't seem to mind Cindy knowing her secret. Then again, Cindy seemed completely absorbed by her book.

Domenica pushed back from the desk and pushed her glasses higher onto her nose. "Rocco's lawyer is being paid by Marcello."

"The mayor?"

"The very same."

Rocco Moretti. The mayor.

What thread bound them together?

And what about Vincenzo? How could she find out about his financial situation if he refused to leave a digital footprint?

Stella couldn't remember the last time she hadn't run into Adele in more than a day. The woman was always striding through Aramezzo with an armful of foraged asparagus or leaning across the counter to confide in Romina.

The key, the strangers at the restaurant at odd hours, the investment in a pricy espresso machine. One thing was certain; something smelled like three-day-old fish.

Stella drifted through Cristiana's, oblivious of what items she touched and walked away from and which she placed in her basket.

At the counter, she laid out her items. Perugina chocolate. Eggs. A packet of *amaretti*. Didn't she buy those already?

She tugged out euros and counted them at the register.

Cristiana said, "Making a *crescionda*?"

She nodded, mute.

Crescionda. Yes, that's exactly what she was making.

"Romina's favorite." Cristiana said in a small voice, placing the items into the bag. "Hopefully she'll be home soon for a slice."

Stella's thoughts whirled. Her hand rose, pressing against her damp forehead. Heat be damned. She would bake and she would work her way through this mental maze.

Cindy Copeland met her outside the *alimentari*. "Domenica said I might find you here!"

"Just picking up supplies to make dessert." At Cindy's unyielding stare, Stella added, "Is everything okay?"

"Heavenly," Cindy said, falling in step beside Stella.

Stella glanced at Cindy out of the corner of her eye. A one-word answer didn't seem like Cindy 2.0.

Cindy cleared her throat and in a rush said, "Actually, I wanted to ask you the same question, if everything is okay with you. I'm told my social radar is all off, but, well, you seem tense." Cindy ran on, "I apologize! James would never have let me interfere like this!"

Stella stopped and put a hand on Cindy's arm. "I appreciate your noticing. You're exactly right. Things are crazy."

"Does it have something to do with the bar?"

Stella hitched the bag higher on her shoulder. "How did you know?"

With a shrug, Cindy said, "The way people keep stopping outside the bar to read and reread the sign."

"You don't miss much, do you?" Stella said with a smile.

Cindy flushed.

"The bar owners got arrested in that Mafia bust."

"They're friends of yours?"

Tears pricking her eyes, Stella said, "Friends of everyone."

"Then it can't be true."

"Exactly! So I'm trying to figure out who framed them, and who has been running drugs through Aramezzo."

Cindy shivered and Stella decided not to tell her about the nun in the road.

As they approached the house, Cindy said, "It sounds like a Netflix program."

Grimly, Stella said, "Would that it were."

"Anything I can do to help? Bear in mind, I'm terrible at mysteries.

One time we watched eight episodes of a mystery program before I figured out that the killer and the detective weren't the same person. But really, if you make all the stars hunks with short blond hair and blue eyes, people will confuse them, don't you think?"

Stella let out a half-laugh.

"But if there's anything I can do with my paltry skills, I'd love to."

Stella opened the *casale* door. "Not a thing."

"I can help make the dessert!"

Stella smiled. She couldn't imagine yesterday's Cindy offering to help. Then her stomach clenched. She needed this space, this time, to find her quiet focus. "I'm only making a *crescionda*, it's not terribly complicated. I thought you wanted to edit your photos?"

Cindy clasped her hands to her chest. "I'd love to learn to make a *crescionda*! I can edit the photos anytime. Besides, I hardly took any today. With the light all flat in the groves and I ate my sandwich at the church, but felt funny taking photos there. Which is weird, right? I mean, I have loads of photos from my wedding at a church. I wish for fewer, actually, because my nephew stuck his gum on my veil, as my something blue! James told me to take it off, I looked ridiculous with a blue dot on my face, but it was my mother's veil."

Stella hardly heard a word past sandwich. "I can give you the recipe and you'll have no trouble making it yourself without wasting your vacation time shadowing me in the kitchen."

Cindy laughed, a tinkling sound that made Barbanera pick his head up from his perch on the sofa. "You have no idea how limited my cooking skills are. James jokes that my signature dish is ordering in from Taiwan Garden." Cindy stopped talking. Her face fell and she scratched her chin, blinking rapidly.

Stella put a hand on Cindy's arm. "After we make it together, you can make *crescionda* at home and show James that you have more skills than he knows."

Cindy nodded faintly.

Stella went on, "All right then, can you grab three eggs from the carton there?"

Maybe she could give Cindy tasks that allowed her to work in quiet.

"You don't fridge your eggs? Mine go right into the refrigerator. In fact, I carry them home in a cold case I use for my milk and cheese, too. It's a great bag for shopping, I can get you a link. Though maybe they don't ship to Italy? You'd have to check."

Or maybe not.

Keeping her voice even, Stella said, "Eggs can keep for weeks at room temperature."

"Should I be keeping mine on the counter?"

"Not unless you plan to do a lot of baking."

Cindy laughed again. Barbanera rose to sitting, his single ear twitching. "Not a chance. I guess the eggs James scrambles before work are fine straight from the fridge?"

"Totally fine," Stella said. "Besides, eggs in the States are washed, which removes their protective bloom. Better to keep them refrigerated."

Cindy opened her mouth and Stella quickly said, "So I'll chop the chocolate, and why don't you put these *amaretti* cookies in a bag and gently crush them with this wooden spoon." Not how Stella would have done it, but the old fashioned method would keep Cindy occupied. "You'll want to open the bag and check the texture often."

Placing the chocolate bar on the wooden cutting board, Stella began pushing the blade through the chocolate. Slivers fell from her knife, scattering. She breathed in the centering, comforting aroma.

She thought of Veronica and the mayor, their furtive whispering. Their faces, alternately flushed and pale. Their argument about selling the car. A sliver of chocolate snapped like a small twig. Stella put down her knife. "Blackmail."

"Beg your pardon?" Cindy looked up from her work.

Stella blinked. Had she said that aloud? "Nothing, nothing,"

Cindy put down her spoon and stepped backwards, muttering, "I should have known I couldn't do it. Who else but me would burn a hard-boiled egg?"

She must have assumed critique in the muttered word. Impulsively Stella said, "The mayor of Aramezzo and his wife, I think they are being blackmailed. It would explain why they are suddenly short of cash." With the words out of her mouth, more fell into place. Veronica's stolen jewels? Maybe to get insurance money.

Cindy's eyes grew large. "Could they be connected to the Mafia?"

"Probably just my imagination running away with me," Stella laughed uncomfortably. "Carry on."

Cindy stared at her for a moment before returning to crushing the cookies.

Maybe Marcello and Veronica were so panicked they went tearing down the road. Stella picked up her knife and then put it down again. All the accusations at Luisella's driving, perhaps to deflect the spotlight.

But, wait. That was before the accident.

Still, Stella knew there was a connection between the mayor and Rocco and Leo. Was there a connection between Leo and Vincenzo? She didn't remember Leo's ever eating at Trattoria Cavour, or even mentioning it.

Leo . . . she needed to understand the nature of his relationship with Rocco. Was Rocco at the center of all this?

As the blade pounded a rhythm on the board, Stella realized whether Leo was scared or loyal, he had to know of Rocco's arrest. And he'd stayed quiet.

Images of Leo from the past few days flashed through her mind—at the bar, his worry about Roberto and Romina, at Cosimo's picking up a lamp, asking her to keep Marta company. As she inhaled the earthy undertones of the chocolate, something nudged her memory—

"All done!" Cindy brought over a neat bag of *amaretti* crumbs.

Stella pasted on her brightest smile. "Perfect! Look how even these crumbs are! I feel misled about your skills. I should have given you a harder job." Stella nudged Cindy's side playfully.

"Oh, ha! Really? I did try." Cindy beamed. Stella waited for a non-sequitur that didn't come.

With a nod, Stella said, "Now we'll whisk the eggs and sugar together. Then we'll add in some flour and milk, and dump in the chocolate and the cookies you crushed. How are you with whisking?"

Cindy frowned.

"What is it?"

Shaking her head, Cindy said, "I must be thinking of the wrong dish. I thought this was the dessert from Spoleto that's like a pie, but it's in layers."

"That's this one." Stella explained. "You just aren't privy to cooking magic. In the hot oven, the cookie crumbs absorb moisture, grow heavier, and sink like a crust. The chocolate floats, leaving a custard layer between." Something tugged Stella.

Cindy nodded. "I get it. Wow, it is like magic."

Stella smiled. "Much of cooking is."

"Though with my luck when I get home and try to make it, the ingredients will crash against each other."

Stella laughed. "Like an earthquake in a pan."

Cindy laughed too. "Exactly."

At a low rumble like a truck passing by, Barbanera jumped to the ground and jogged to the glass door, staring into the dark.

Suddenly, Stella stilled.

"What is it?" Cindy said, a crease forming between her eyebrows.

Stella could only shake her head and turn away, trying to hold the thought in her head before it evaporated.

The *amaretti* crumbs, shifting downward. Like an earthquake dislodging stones and mortar.

The chocolate.

She closed her eyes.

Something like chocolate.

Coffee!

With a quick intake of breath, Stella remembered.

Leo, coming out from Cosimo's side room, a room she hadn't known existed. She remembered the scent of coffee. Not the homemade kind in a moka, with its bitter tang, but rounded and sweet and chocolatey—the smell of Bar Cappellina.

She remembered Roberto's saying they needed to repair the crumbling stone wall. Could the stone wall connect the bar's cantina with Cosimo's? Their shops didn't abut, but with years of renovations and divided buildings, it was possible. Cosimo said his shop was built on a former worship site; was it a stretch to imagine that worship site once connected to the church that became Bar Cappellina?

Which means someone could have sneaked the heroin into Roberto and Romina's house from Cosimo's shop. Without needing a key.

She pressed her hands on the counter.

Who knew about that hole in the wall?

Cosimo must.

The mayor? He was so incensed about Roberto fixing the wall in the cantina.

Did Leo know? Did he make up the story of needing a lamp to access the hole? After all, the smell of coffee hung about him, not the shop.

She remembered the panic in his face when he ran into Bar Cappellina on Friday. His drop, it was *his* drop the government officials intercepted. Had he dragged Roberto and Romina into this by accident? If the Mafia was closing in, maybe the nun hadn't even been the target. Maybe the target was Leo.

She turned back to Cindy. "Sorry, a piece of chocolate in my eye." She wiped at her eye before stumbling to the crumb-strewn counter.

Thunder boomed in the distance.

Cindy's fist was at her mouth. "Oh, is that … you scared me."

"So now we pour the batter into the pan and bake it."

With shaking hands, Stella opened the oven, the heat blasting toward her. She steadied her breath, her mind on Leo. Where was he now? She needed to find him, to tell him of the danger. Later she'd tell him off for framing Roberto and Romina.

"Cindy, I have an … an errand to do. At Cristiana's. Maybe you could take the *crescionda* out when it's ready?"

"You're leaving me alone with something in the oven?" Cindy's voice rose.

"I can tell you how to test for doneness."

"Stella," Cindy laughed awkwardly. "I can't even tell when toast is done."

"Of course," she said, distracted. Should she tell Cindy why she needed to leave? No, it meant explaining the nun and she didn't want Cindy as worried as Marta.

A crack in the sky alerted her to the storm, heaving over them. How long had it been raining?

As the *crescionda* baked and Cindy went upstairs to keep her Duolingo streak, Stella tried to track down Leo.

Domenica didn't pick up.

Stella considered calling Marta, but remembering Marta's reaction when Stella wondered if Leo was mixed up with the Mafia, she knew she wouldn't be able to sound casual, that Marta would accuse her of blaming her boyfriend again.

Rain lashed at the windows.

She called Luca, fingers tapping on the counter. "Have you seen Leo?"

"This morning, on his way out."

Her shoulders loosened as she checked the *crescionda*. Still not done.

His voice laced with concern, Luca asked, "Why?"

She paced in her oven mitts. "I need to talk to him. Do you know if he was heading to a market today?"

"Not a market, the medieval *festa* in Bevagna. He should be on his way back. What's going on?"

She spun the timer on the counter then picked it up and stared at it. "Probably nothing, but—"

"Oh, Stella, can I call you back? I'm getting a call from the captain." He ended the call.

Stella opened the oven door and squinted into the heat. When would this *crescionda* be ready?

She called Matteo, who told her Domenica had gone to pick up cat food. "I need to talk to Leo," Stella said, her voice taut.

"I have his number—"

"He lost his phone in the accident," Stella reminded him.

"Oh, right." She could imagine Matteo's frown, narrowing his large eyes. "Call Marta, he's probably there."

Stella shook her head. "No. Luca said he was selling *porchetta* in Bevagna. I'll catch him in the parking lot."

The timer dinged.

As soon as she closed the door, the rain soaked her as if she'd stepped in the shower fully clothed. The memory of her umbrella left on the couch while she grabbed her phone briefly crossed her mind, but Stella was already running toward the parking lot.

Once she had the idea of Leo as the Mafia link, more fell into place.

His injury. He told her the accident took him out of racing at the height of his career, but didn't Marta say his career had started flagging before then?

Stella stopped in the street. Exactly what had Marta said? That he'd started losing races he'd once easily won.

Why had he started losing?

Was he no longer getting the right support from the guys in the pit?

Or maybe Rocco and the rest of the guys had exerted some pressure on him. To make him lose.

On purpose.

Fixing races.

That sounded like something the Mafia might have a hand in.

Stella felt out of her element as the rain increased in intensity, battering her face. For a moment she considered dashing back for her umbrella, but she needed to catch Leo before he got to Marta's. She ducked into the tunnel, racing for Aramezzo's entrance.

His injury…was it his attempt to get out of racing with his head held high?

At the bottom of the tunnel, Stella cleared the rain from her brow.

His attempt to get out.

Could it be that this was his attempt to get out of the *Mafia?*

Shielding her face as the rain shot like BBs into her skin, Stella ran into the parking lot.

There. The *porchetta* truck.

By the time she knocked at the door of the truck, her hair streamed rain down her back like a water slide.

No answer.

Leaning against the side of the truck, Stella watched the raindrops become heavier, the sky darkening like midnight. She wanted to ask somebody in the parking lot if they had seen him, but nobody in Aramezzo ever went anywhere in the rain. Domenica herself probably waited out the storm in the pet shop.

What now?

She breathed in the calming scent of *porchetta*—roasting meat, the green brush of herbs. She remembered the first time she met Leo, the *porchetta* smell clinging to him. It had made her like him instantly.

Funny, though, that the last time she saw the *porchetta* van, the smell had been absent. It must dissipate quickly. Because she hadn't smelled the caramelizing pork skin or the lilt of fennel pollen. No, she'd smelled...cleaning fluid.

And something else...what had it been? Something told her if she could just remember, everything would snap into place.

Rain pelting her face, she closed her eyes, trying to imagine being back on the side of that scorching road. Inhaling. And smelling...

Asphalt. Yes, from the hot road.

Motor oil. No surprise, it was a smell she associated with mechanic shops. And cars. She smelled it here, surrounded by vehicles, even in the rain.

Cleaning fluid, bleach. Yes, those made sense, though it seemed odd that those smells clung to the van when the *porchetta* scent faded after a stay at Rocco's.

Another scent hovered at the edge of her memory.

Gas.

She ran her hands over her arms at the sudden chill.

At the time she hadn't thought anything about it, maybe because the car had just come from the mechanic. But why would she have smelled gas if the van was *out of gas?*

She inhaled.

The gas smell was gone. As was the other smell, the sharp, industrial cleanser.

The rain howled now, attacking her face with a ferocity she couldn't associate with water.

Hail.

Stella ran her hand over her face, thinking.

Making her way to the front of the van, she rested her hand on the front—still warm.

She could go to Marta's and make up an excuse for why she needed to talk to him alone. She wouldn't let on how angry she was that he allowed Roberto and Romina to go to prison for his crime. Not until he understood that he was in danger, that he needed to be careful. Then, she'd tear into him. She'd have to turn him in, of course, for drug-running. But she didn't need to think of that now. Right now, she needed to warn him.

Yet, she didn't move. Even under the sky's assault, she stood stock still. Deliberating for a moment, she put her hand on the door handle. She stopped and knocked again. Though even if someone were in the van, how could they hear over the sound of the hail pounding the roof of the van?

Taking a breath, she tugged at the handle.

"Hi, Stella! Can you believe this hail?"

"Cindy? What are you doing here?" Stella whipped her hand away from the handle as if burned.

"I saw your umbrella on the couch. So I figured I'd bring it to you." Cindy's brow furrowed. But she didn't hand over the umbrella in her hand or the one lofted over her head. "But you weren't at Cristiana's. So I decided to try out this new shutter speed feature for my phone. It's supposed to capture rain in this mysterious way, especially with the street-lights in the parking lot. I didn't know the rain would turn to hail!" Her gaze lingered on the van door. "Is this your van?"

"Umm. No, it belongs to a friend of mine. He, uh, thought he dropped his keys outside the van. Since I was close by I said I'd check."

Cindy squinted against the dark and rain. "How did he know you were close?"

"Oh," Stella laughed nervously. "Happenstance, you know. I was, er, out walking, like I said. He called and—"

"Walking? You said you were going to Cristiana's." Cindy frowned. Her face lit up. "Wait! Is this about the case? It is, isn't it? You're hot on some trail!"

With an uncomfortable laugh, Stella said, "You got me. I needed to ask Leo, who owns this van, a question."

"About the mayor?"

Stella pushed wet hair off her forehead. "And some other things. But he's not here."

Cindy blinked. "It couldn't wait till morning?"

"Oh, I'm just impatient, you know," Stella affected a laugh.

Cindy studied Stella and then the van and then Stella again.

Where were her usual words? Or her usual blank stare? Instead of blankness, Cindy's eyes radiated doubt, distrust.

She needed to get Cindy gone. She also needed to check the *porchetta* van for clues.

Maybe Stella could convince Cindy that she was indeed out for a walk. They could go down the road to where the *porchetta* van had run out of gas. There was something she needed to know for sure.

When was the last rain?

"Stella? Should we head back?"

"You go on ahead, Cindy. I'll wait for Leo."

Even in the darkening air, Cindy looked uncertain. "Stella, if you'll forgive me, something seems off."

"I know," Stella adopted a note of cheer. "Odd to prolong being out here. But really, it's fine. I've always loved storms."

"It must be an awfully important question."

Stella nodded. "It is."

Cindy nodded once and trudged back toward the town entrance, casting a glance at Stella over her shoulder.

Thank the Madonna.

Creeping around the van, Stella trailed a hand along its surface. She stopped back at the darkened headlights. The hood felt cooler now.

There it was again—that tang of disinfectant. But it didn't smell quite like disinfectant anymore. It still had an ammonia base, but not the same as before. She ran her fingers over the bumper and noticed a faint ridge. Suggestive of paint. Paint covering part of the bumper.

Suddenly it hit her.

A split second before something hit her.

Stella jerked sideways, crumpling to the pavement.

The world went dark.

Was she floating through space? What was needling her body?

Her eyes opened, instantly filling with rain.

Panting, she touched her head. Rain, yes—but also sticky warmth.

Blood.

She froze, her heartbeat loud in her ears. Scrambling, she tried to stand, turn around, and squint through the hail.

"Surprised to see me?" Leo asked with a grin.

"Not really, no," Stella said, stumbling to her feet. Then she saw the tire iron in Leo's hand.

Catching her gaze, he spun the iron like a baton. "Oh, come on, Stella. Give a guy a break."

"You want me to stroke your ego by telling you how shocked I am that you framed Roberto and Romina? That you killed Elena?"

His iron dropped to Leo's side. "You know her name?"

She recognized she had given too much away. "I mean, it's a theory, right?"

He swung the iron in another circle, thinking. "The paint gave it away?"

"The paint," she said, holding her breath while backing up a few inches, her eyes locked on the spinning iron.

"A risk, it's true. But I knew you'd be sniffing around and didn't want you coming with a black light."

"An ammonia-based paint won't block a UV light from illuminating blood," Stella said. *Shut up!* Was Cindy rubbing off on her?

"Is that a fact?" Leo said, moving closer. "Well, then I'll have to freshen my paint job."

A flash of movement.

Cindy appeared from behind Leo. What was she doing back here? Stella caught sight of the umbrella outstretched in her hand.

Carefully, Stella shook her head slowly, a slight gesture she hoped Cindy would catch and Leo would miss. She should have told Cindy everything.

Cindy stalled, confused, her eyes going from Leo's swinging tire iron to Stella's wide eyes. Her mouth dropped open. She looked behind her as if to dart backwards but then her knees seemed to give out and she leaned against the side of the van. *Move, move, move*, Stella screamed at her internally. But Cindy only put her hand to her heart as if struggling to find breath.

Leo noticed Stella's eyes fixed on the side of the *porchetta* van and he started to follow her gaze. Stella shouted, "Don't you want to know how I figured it out?"

"Elena? Not really," Leo said, though his eyes flashed with interest. "Why should I care how you snooped your way into my business?"

"Oh, come on. Don't villains stall with talk?" Stella said, noticing Cindy quietly drawing out her phone.

"That only happens in movies," Leo clucked in mock disappointment. "When are you going to understand, Stella? I'm the victim here. Not the villain."

"I get it, the Mafia got its claws into you. You didn't know how to get out."

The tire iron stopped spinning.

Her words tumbled out in a rush as she tried to keep his attention.

"You caused the accident on the track. The one that injured your wrist. So you'd have an excuse to get out."

"It should have worked. It did work. I dropped off their radar the moment I went in the hospital."

"Until?" Stella realized. "The photo. In the paper. From the Americans' ball. Salvatore Mancini saw it."

Leo's eyebrows raised. "That photo gave Lupo the idea. He connected with Rocco, who was forced out with my accident but had been wanting back in." His face contorted. "Don't you see how the race conspired against me?"

"You framed Roberto and Romina, who showed you nothing but kindness."

He shrugged. "Survival of the fittest, right? I didn't plan on that one, but when I was late and the agents came and made the mistake, well, who was I to argue with Lady Luck? It's about time she was on my side," he added with a grumble. The frown flipped to a sudden grin. "Well, that and Matteo coming by ten minutes ago, saying you were looking for me in the parking lot."

"You killed a *nun*," Stella said loudly, more to create noise than to remind him.

He shook his head. "I didn't want to. Such a nice young thing. So trusting. It felt like slaughtering an innocent—"

"So she wasn't involved with the Mafia? That was the one part I couldn't figure out." Stella's gaze slipped past Leo to Cindy, swiping at her wet phone in frustration. Either no emergency number or she couldn't make the touch screen comply with raindrops on the screen.

"It's the one thing I'll miss about the *porchetta* van, all the people you meet."

"Seduce, you mean."

"Oh, Stella. That's your problem. You don't have a romantic bone in your body. You should have seen it, like the meet-cutes you see in movies—the way I asked her out at the Assisi market. How she blushed! She blushed the second time, too. And the third. It drove me wild. There's nothing more attractive than a blushing woman. You should try it sometime."

"I'll make a note of it," Stella said coldly as blood dripped into her eye. She wiped it from her forehead. "So you used Elena to hold your bag."

"Once I got wind of the tracking, what choice did I have?" he said irritably. Stella could tell she was losing him. How could she get out of this before he brought that tire iron on her head a final time? He shrugged, "But then she grew tiresome."

"You broke it off."

He shrugged again.

"And she didn't take it well. Came looking for you." Her eyes slid past him to Cindy, desperately wiping her phone on her saturated dress.

Leo followed her gaze. He spun around and spied Cindy.

Stella's body locked.

With a squeal of his shoes on wet pavement, Leo lunged for Cindy. He grabbed her around the neck, pulling her tight against his chest. Her phone clattered to the ground, the sound barely discernible with the hail pounding on the van's roof. His teeth practically biting Cindy's cheek, Leo leered, "Why, hello there."

As Cindy clawed frantically at her neck, Leo glared at Stella. "Bringing your guests on missions? That certainly won't help your reviews."

He swung the iron in a circle, his eyes going from Stella to Cindy, flailing against his torso. Stella could see that he was calculating his odds.

Finally, he said, "Sleep well, Stella. By morning I'll have figured out how to make you pay."

"You're leaving? With all you have here, Marta? Ascanio?"

"Doesn't look like I have a choice, does it? Open road for me. Kind of poetic if you think about it. The road started it. The road will finish it."

"A winner doesn't take off, Leo."

"What do you know about winning?" He snorted. "With your sneaking around and whining about how everything is so hard for you, so unfair."

She bit her lip.

"But me, I was the best," Leo raised his chin. "They forgot I was the best. This will remind them. It will remind them all who I am."

Cindy's silent eyes begged Stella. Stella blurted, "The toll roads will slow you down. The cops will catch you."

He chuckled, yanking Cindy tighter against himself. "Luckily, I know more about our backroads than you ever will." He looked excited, his eyes flashing at the race ahead. "The only question is, which direction . . . .which direction . . . until I disappear beyond the border."

Stella opened her mouth to say something, anything, but the words never formed. Leo brought the iron down on Cindy's head with a sickening thud.

Before Stella could react, Leo yanked open the door of the *porchetta* truck, shoving an unconscious Cindy in. He leapt behind the wheel.

"She needs medical attention!"

"You never know when you'll need a spare."

Tears mingled with rain as Stella watched Leo speeding away. Her eyes narrowed. Well, not exactly speeding. A *porchetta* van was not designed for speed. Stella felt her heart rate slowing. She could practically jog to catch the thing, and even with Leo's head start it would be no problem for the police to catch up and—

Her phone.

On the ground.

Shattered.

But Cindy's phone! Stella scanned the ground where she heard it fall. In the darkness, she couldn't see anything. Then, in the reflection of the brake lights from the van, Stella saw something glinting.

Her fingers scrabbled across the wet ground until they closed around the phone. She stared at the screen, the numbers glowing. Where was the button that allowed her to override the password and call the police? Stella couldn't find it in the maze of camera icons.

Stella glanced up as the *porchetta* van gained momentum. The *porchetta* van with her guest inside it.

Could she guess the code? No chance. There wasn't even a spot to input the password.

Only a rotating circle, trying to recognize her face.

Stella heard brakes squealing. Glancing up, she saw the *porchetta* van slowing. Out of gas again? No, the van had never been out of gas. After killing Elena, Leo had dumped it to sell his story.

Stella remembered her plan from what could have been five minutes or five hours or five days ago . . . to check the grass next to where the van had been parked, to see if it was burned from the gasoline he'd dumped.

She wiped her face of mingled rain and blood. And ran. Faster, *faster*. Full out, faster than she knew she could. Her feet slid on the wet asphalt. She could catch him now, and at least yank Cindy out of the van. Faster.

The *porchetta* van's brake lights flashed and then held. Stella watched Leo leap from the driver's side of the van. A second later she heard the rev of a smaller, lighter, sleeker vehicle. New brake lights, round ones, shone through the rain's onslaught.

Leo's Alfa Romeo.

Faster!

What was she doing? She couldn't outrun a sports car.

She squinted through the rain, holding her hand against the gash on her forehead. Did he dump Cindy so he wouldn't add kidnapping to his charges if caught?

No, Leo didn't plan for failure. Contingency plans only slowed a body down.

The Alfa Romeo skidded around the corner before speeding out of the parking lot.

At the van, Stella threw open the driver's side door. *Cindy*. Slumped against the passenger side.

Stella groaned. Should she run to a house, ask to use a phone? She glanced up at the nearby houses. Dark. She couldn't leave Cindy while she wasted time searching for a phone. Not when she could be getting Cindy to a hospital.

She caught sight of Leo's vanishing taillights.

Without thinking, she jumped into the van. She hunted for the key before realizing he hadn't killed the engine.

Stella pressed her foot against the accelerator, wiping her eyes clear and flicking hail off the back of her neck.

Thanking the heavens she knew her way around a food truck, she navigated the van through the parking lot, following the Alfa Romeo's round taillights. At least she knew he hadn't gone right, toward the east side of Monte Subasio.

Which meant his path to freedom and her path to the hospital were the same. What were the odds that she could overtake him on the road?

She shook her head. Ridiculous. At his speed, he could make it out of Italy in as little as four hours. Well, she might as well stay as close on his tail as possible. Maybe they'd pass a police officer she could flag down to chase him while she continued to the hospital.

Stella yanked the wheel to follow a turn and Cindy slumped against her. Stella's hand felt for her neck. Relief nearly broke her when she felt a faint heartbeat under her fingers. Stella stopped the van to buckle Cindy in.

Pressing the accelerator against the floor, Stella waited, and waited. And waited. Was it even accelerating?

Finally, the van gathered momentum and chugged down the road.

This was hopeless. There was no way she could catch him. But if she didn't, he'd be out of range of capture by the time she could summon the cops.

Stella hunched over the wheel and trained her eyes on the road ahead. She used the lack of curves on the sudden uphill section to figure out how to maneuver this behemoth.

Behind her, a box slid and banged. Suddenly the cab filled with wind. The back doors must have flung open when a box slid down the galley, banging into the door handle. It must have been a heavy box. Salt? Whatever it was, it lay in the road now.

Stella shook her head.

Never mind! She ordered herself. She had to focus on those taillights.

Taillights that grew fainter with every breath. How in the world could she catch up to Leo? A literal race car driver in a literal sports car. Meanwhile, she chugged along in a *porchetta* van. She yanked the wheel to round a bend and from the corner of her awareness, she saw a *prosciutto* leg swing alarmingly.

Stella remembered the section of road ahead, full of curves. She could gain ground here. He'd have to slow down to take—

But he didn't slow down. Not remotely. The wheels of his car hugged the road, a hand sliding over a lover's hip.

A pit growing in her stomach, Stella realized how much farther the lights were ahead of her. In a handful of minutes, he'd hit Assisi with its bevy of choices—the *autostrada*, the backroads.

She took her foot off the accelerator.

I know more about our backroads than you ever will.

Backroads. The road with Luca. The shortcut.

She could barely see it through the rain.

She yanked the wheel into the turnout and leapt out to open the gate. Throwing herself back into the cab, she floored the *porchetta* van again, cursing its gentle acceleration.

The gate remained behind her, a gently swinging admonishment.

Stella hoped no cows escaped. Or wild horses wandering down Monte Subasio. She couldn't worry about that now.

Like cold honey oozing from a jar, the van finally hit maximum speed. The engine shuddered and Stella prayed that all Leo's complaints about Rocco had been excuses to hand off money to him, not actual mechanical issues.

She hit a pothole, wincing at the sudden jolt. Hands tight on the wheel, she jumped at the sudden bang and clatter. A drawer must have slid out, sending what sounded like knives skittering around the back of the van. An image loomed in her mind—her braking suddenly and the knives flying at her. As if the van had the ability to defend itself, martial arts style.

She had to do something.

"Cindy! Cindy wake up!" Stella shouted.

In answer, Cindy's body slumped to the left, almost onto Stella's lap. *Please don't be dead.* Stella reached over again and felt for her pulse.

Nothing.

Nothing?

No, Cindy had shifted. Stella had been searching for a pulse on Cindy's cheek.

A sudden turn and Stella gripped the wheel.

"Cindy!" she shouted again.

Please don't be dead.

Cindy moaned.

Hospital, she needed to get to a hospital. Leo would get away, but she couldn't think about that now.

Cindy moaned again. Was that good? Or was it bad? Was it bad? Stella shook her head.

"Cindy!" Stella shouted above the wind whipping through the van. "Wake up! I need you to call the police! I can't do this alone, Cindy! It's too much!"

Stella's voice caught and she realized she was on the verge of crying.

Her temple pounded and she pressed a hand against the gash, wincing at the lashing pain.

She couldn't fall apart. Not now. Later. Later, she could fall apart.

Using her sleeve, Stella rubbed a clear spot in the clouded windshield.

Was there a payphone somewhere?

Assisi maybe.

If he beat her to Assisi, perhaps she'd at least be able to call the police. But how to explain? How to convince them of the necessity of a manhunt? No, she needed to talk to Luca and Luca alone.

Her shattered phone, illuminated with Luca's name. No photo associated with his contact, as there was with Matteo (the selfie he'd sent her before the Americans' ball) and Domenica (a photo Domenica hated that Stella had taken in the bookstore, with its low light, where Domenica had her head thrown back in peals of laughter that she said made her look deranged).

Luca would believe her.

The road curved again and Stella hunched tighter over the wheel. A metallic scraping and clattering sounded as knives slid across the floor, followed by an enormous thud as something—maybe a leg of *prosciutto*, maybe the leftover *porchetta*—swung to the metal floor.

That spot where the shortcut met the main road—how would she know if she arrived there before or after Leo?

Stella's stomach clenched and she knew it was the thought of giving up the chase, more than the pothole she just hit, sending a fresh supply of boxes to the floor of the van with a crash.

The lights in the van blinked to life. Had the impact tripped a switch?

She cast another furtive glance at Cindy. *Stay with me*, Stella prayed, her eyes on Cindy's still face.

Keeping the accelerator pressed firmly on the floor and ignoring the grating sound coming from under the van, Stella dug into her pocket.

She aimed Cindy's phone over Cindy's face. She kept waving it, begging it to recognize its owner. Praying to a Madonna she suddenly needed to believe in.

She cast a glance at the screen.

Unlocked.

She swiped, but then stalled. Luca's number. With a quick intake of breath, she slammed on the brakes and jumped as the loose *prosciutto* tumbled down the galley, slamming into her seat. The number, she did know it, she'd seen it on his card. Fingers shaking she dialed 333 312 22 22.

Ring.

Pick up pick up pick up. Stella hit the gas, willing the van to move faster, faster.

Ring.

Pick up pick up pick up!

Maybe he wouldn't pick up, not recognizing the number.

Ring!

"*Pronto*," Luca said, his strong voice laced with uncertainty.

"Luca!"

"Stella? What's that sound? Why are you—"

"No time! It's Leo! Leo was working with the Mafia! Leo hit the nun!"

"Are you sure?"

"The gash he gave me and Cindy's unconscious body are pretty convincing, yes."

"*Madonna mia*, are you okay?"

"There's no time. Leo took off, headed to Assisi, to the autostrada. I'm on the road you showed me. I'll meet up with the road he's on in a minute or two. I can't be sure, nothing looks familiar and I can't even tell how much time has passed."

She tensed, waiting for the inevitable questions.

None came. "I'm on it. Get off the road."

Between clenched teeth, she said, "I can't. I have to get Cindy to the hospital."

Luca's words grated, like he was speaking through gritted teeth. "Stella. *Get off the road.* Now. I'll send an ambulance to you."

Stella thought of how long it would take the ambulance to find her. "Okay, sure." Stella hung up and tossed the phone to the dashboard.

The van strained up a hill. Stella heard a *thump thump thump.* The back door of the van slammed back open. The *prosciutto.* Or *porchetta.* It must have rolled right out of the back.

Stella heard clinking and rattling. Knives must be scattering, following the prosciutto.

Fairytale stories with breadcrumbs filled her brain before she clapped her hand to her head to focus. She shouted at the sudden pain.

Clenching her teeth, her hands gripped the wheel until her knuckles whitened. She had to make it. She had to make it.

The gate appeared before her.

She set her jaw and slammed through the gate, throwing her arm across Cindy, who groaned, "What's happening?"

Stella's heart leapt and for a moment she forgot all about Leo, gliding along the road toward his escape. "Cindy! You're alive!"

"I'm not sure that's true. This reminds me of the . . . oh, oh . . . . I think I'm going to be sick."

Stella practically skidded as she turned hard on the main road, headlights pointed down the road, toward the hospital, toward the autostrada. "Cindy, hang on! We're not far from the hospital."

"I don't want to go to the hospital. I want to get out of here! Stella, let me out of here, I'm going to be sick!"

Stella pulled the van onto the grassy shoulder and slammed on the brakes. Cindy moaned again. In the quiet, Stella heard an engine's sharp growl. Her hands tensed on the wheel.

"That's Leo, isn't it?" Cindy whispered.

"I thought you needed to be sick?"

Cindy waved her hand. "I'm better now that we're not rocking."

"How is your head?"

"Stella, answer me. Is that Leo I hear coming?"

Stella pressed her lips together. "I believe so, yes."

"He's escaping?"

"It would seem so. Yes."

Cindy stared at Stella unblinkingly. "You're going to let him get away?"

Stella wiped at the tears in her eyes. "What can I do? I can't stop him. And we need to get you to the hospital."

"Stella! You know you can't let him get away! After what he did to you! After what he did to me!"

"But you—"

"Look at me!" Cindy's voice wobbled and then strengthened. "I'm sitting. I'm breathing. I know today is Monday and I'm far from home. I'm not dying. If you take me to the hospital now and that man gets away, you'll regret it in a way medicine can't fix."

"I don't even know how to stop him." The engine roar grew louder.

"Stella," Cindy said with a sigh, leaning her head back against the seat. "Yes, you can. Of course you can."

Stella drummed her fingers on the steering wheel. Should she block the road with the van? No, she couldn't move Cindy out of it.

Leaping out the van, she briefly considered standing in the road to stop him. But he didn't stop for his lover, why would he stop for her?

She glanced at Cindy who caught her eye and said, "Don't mind me. I like it here. Good view. Nice breeze. No pressure to be normal." Her grin wavered, but her eyes were clear.

Cindy, who had more within her than Stella ever imagined.

The Alfa Romeo's visceral whine grew louder.

Think! Stella yelled at herself. *Think!*

Her eye caught on the back of the van, the doors swinging open.

With a yelp, Stella ran to the open back, snatching up anything that gleamed. Cleavers, utility knives, carving forks. Stumbling over a raised patch of grass, the knives nicked her arm and hands. She ran up the road from the *porchetta* van. Holding her breath, she felt a utensil tumble away from her, but she didn't stop for it.

Cindy's cheers urged her footsteps as she ran. Stella threw the knives and forks across the road with a wild clatter, the blades flashing. With a quick glance over the scene, she noticed the knives lay flush with the road.

The roar of the car drew closer.

She ran back and lodged a cleaver and a chef's knife against tongs to angle upwards.

Would it work?

It had to work.

She ran up to the van, just as the Alfa Romeo careened from around the bend. Cindy met her at the back of the open van, and they flung themselves into it, grabbing each other's hands as they held their breath, waiting.

More a flash of color than a car, the Alfa Romeo sped toward them. She caught a glimpse of Leo in the driver's seat, his eye wide as he spotted his van on the shoulder ahead. A split second before he hit the patch of knives.

Did Stella imagine the explosion? Her hands went to her ears and she closed her eyes, hunkering down.

She forced herself to open her eyes, to see.

The car slid sideways, fishtailed.

A crunching sound as it smashed into a tree. One wheel still turning. The smell of burned rubber.

Stella and Cindy stared at each other for a moment. "Stay here," Stella said. She ran to the car, flinging open the door. Please let him be okay. Okay enough to stand trial.

He gazed up at her, dazed.

From below, she heard the sounds of sirens.

"Leo? Leo, can you hear me?"

He stared at her, his voice airy with confusion. "What . . . what did you do?"

She stared down the road, willing the sirens to come faster, faster.

Leo turned his body, lifting his legs until his feet hit the grass.

No seatbelt. No airbags. It was a wonder he hadn't been thrown clear.

He braced his hands on the car and rose to his feet. "I'll kill you for this, Stella." He staggered.

Stella backed up, wishing she'd kept one knife. She could run from him, he wasn't moving quickly, but Cindy couldn't run and no way would she leave Cindy within Leo's reach. Could she grab a knife from the road? Her eyes scanned the asphalt, hoping to catch on any glare.

Leo took a step toward her. He stopped, pressing a hand to his head. Swaying for a moment, he muttered, "No way she beat me to Assisi. No way."

Stella took another step backwards. "I did, though, Leo."

He looked at the van. "It can't be."

He stared from the van to Stella, his eyes wide with wonder as the blood drained from his face. "You beat me?"

"I beat you."

The sirens closed in. Stella heard doors opening and slamming, footfalls racing toward them.

Police surrounded them. Stella felt herself crumpling.

It was over. The nightmare was finally over.

Arms caught her, held her.

She breathed in . . . the scent of sun-warmed trees. "Luca?" she said turning her face up, her knees so weak she wasn't sure they would support her. "How did you—"

Was there yet another shortcut?

"I was in Assisi," he said by way of explanation.

"You're here," she said wonderingly.

"I'm here." He smiled.

THURSDAY

Stella hesitated outside Bar Cappellina.

The light within—it seemed a hallucination, a dream.

The doctor had ordered her to stay indoors with the lights low for at least three days.

But if she didn't get out, she'd go crazy.

She shifted her weight and glanced down at Barbanera. *Am I ready?*

The cat sat at her heels, gazing steadily at her. He blinked. It seemed an answer. Maybe he, too, had grown tired of lying in bed. He hadn't left her side since the moment she stumbled through the door, bandage across her forehead, supported by Luca and Matteo.

Stella pushed open the door and the conversation stopped.

Roberto and Romina hurried out from behind the bar, enfolding her in their arms, creating a barrier between her and the storm of curiosity. She felt Barbanera press against her knee.

Romina pulled back, smiling at Stella. "Stella. Thank you."

Stella waved away her thanks. "Luca was on it."

"Behind enough that Leo would have gotten away."

Romina's eyes caught on the snowy Bandaid across Stella's forehead. "He hurt you."

Stella shrugged. "He hurt us all."

Roberto stroked her hair as she leaned into him. "Do you want coffee? Or maybe something to eat?"

"Yes." Stella smiled, her heart warming.

"Which?" Roberto grinned back.

"Yes," Stella said, her smile broader.

Roberto squeezed Stella's hand before walking behind the black-veined marble counter as Romina said, "You know you're going to have to describe that chase."

"Luca didn't tell you?"

"Briefly. I need the whole thing, from first grind to last sip." Romina smiled, patting Stella's arm before joining her husband behind the bar.

As the two walked away, Stella noticed Luisella at her usual table, dressed in a tailored suit of moss green with a forest-hued silk lining peeking out from the neckline. The women watched each other, Luisella's small smile echoed in Stella's. Her eyes held a kind of satisfaction Stella had once seen in Barbanera's when he accidentally-on-purpose knocked over the cream.

Luisella said archly, "Nice outfit."

"You think?" Stella looked down at her boat-necked, terra-cotta shell, edged with ivory piping. "It's cooler than anything I've been wearing."

Luisella reached out to finger the fabric. "Linen and silk. Nice."

"Also, more tailored than I'm used to."

"Bespoke apparel usually is."

"But this wasn't made for me."

"Wasn't it?" Luisella smiled once more before leaning down to scratch Barbanera between his ear and his non-ear.

"Stella!" Stella turned at Matteo's greeting. "Look at you, out of your nightgown. I'd begun to consider it your uniform."

"Two days, Matteo. That's all I was laid up."

Matteo chuckled but then stopped. "New threads?"

Stella looked down at the top. "You don't like it?"

"It's not what you usually wear." He frowned briefly. Then he nodded. "But weirdly, it seems like something you should have been wearing all along."

Luisella smiled to herself.

Stella turned back to her. "I figured it out, you know. About Anna Maria and Romina's sister, Lavinia. Why Lavinia left Anna Maria the bar." Wait—was that common knowledge or a secret? Everything seemed so foggy.

Luisella adopted her air of perpetual mystery. "I hadn't realized there was anything to figure out."

"They were a couple."

"They were?" Matteo said his mouth hanging open.

"Sorry about him," Stella said to Luisella. "His gaydar needs tuning."

"You said gaydar is reductive," Matteo protested. "Besides, I never really talked to either of them."

"Is that right," Stella said. "We're talking about the same Lavinia who snuck chocolate powder on your milk?"

"Oh. Right."

Luisella's lift of her cup didn't hide her smile.

Matteo protested under his breath, "But I was young, I didn't even know *I* was gay."

Veronica entered the bar, without her dogs and without her husband. At the sight of Luisella, Veronica stopped, the door ajar. With a furtive thrust of her hand into her purse, she pulled out her phone and started speaking emphatically before turning back to the piazza.

Stella glanced at Luisella, who refused to make eye contact. Had Veronica figured out that Luisella was back with Tazio? Stella could hardly prod her with Matteo standing there. Instead, Stella said, "No wonder Anna Maria was so private." She tugged at the hem of her shirt.

Luisella seemed done speaking. She straightened the angle of her purse on the table and took a noisy sip of what Stella had to assume was air, since the cup held only collapsing bubbles of milk foam.

Matteo took Stella by the elbow, pulling her through Flavia the florist and Orietta the pharmacist and Luca who seemed a two-headed blur. "Good to have you back, Stella," they patted her arm as she passed and then returned to their conversation about Adele and Vincenzo. She heard Orietta say, "They're finally in consensus and selling Vincenzo's mother's estate. Her dementia has gotten too bad, she's almost burned the place down twice now."

Flavia clucked, "She won't go easily, though, will she? I mean, one thing I've learned, some blooms last longer than you'd imagine, right? If—"

Orietta interrupted, "She won't have a choice. Adele told me it took a bit to convince Vincenzo's brother. But now they agree. It's time."

Stella turned her head to follow the conversation as Matteo led her to the bar. Once the sound closed around Flavia and Orietta, she blinked. Wondering if she'd imagined the conversation, though she seemed to remember Matteo had told her something much like this yesterday. Or the day before.

Roberto set a cappuccino in front of Stella. She leaned over it and breathed in the fragrant steam. With a clink, he put a fork and plate on the counter. "Not as good as your *crostata*, I'm afraid. But the shortcrust is filled with Sagrantino grape jam."

Stella wedged her fork through the crust and popped a piece into her mouth. "Profound and wonderful, *grazie*." Roberto held her eyes for a moment before smiling and moving to talk to Orietta.

Matteo waited for Stella to have a sip of coffee before he said, "So you did go through your aunt's boxes."

"I told you I was going to."

"You also said you'd rest."

"How much work is it to open a few boxes?"

He harrumphed. Then leaned forward to ask, "Did you find anything else? That medallion you and Cosimo hunted for before?"

"No," Stella said, her voice fading. Should she mention the dress she'd found in the first box, the one with splotches of brown across the inside?

The memory of that dress still filled her with a faint horror. She'd shoved it back in the box and pulled another box closer to her to open, trying to forget.

"What is it, Stella?" Matteo said, his eyebrows contracting.

"Oh, nothing," Stella said. "Did you hear what Leo said when he was led away? About it being Cosimo's fault?"

"*What?*"

"I know, he was grasping. Desperate. Plus, I know the ways of a head wound."

"Why didn't you tell me earlier?"

"I just remembered."

Matteo shook his head. "Wow, that guy will blame anyone. I heard he told his parents that Marta had gotten him mixed up with the Mafia."

She put a hand to her bandage. "I hadn't heard that." What would happen to Marta now? She closed her eyes.

"Marcello told me." Marcello. And Veronica. Were they really being blackmailed? She found she didn't care. She wanted the hum of her friend's voice and another forkful of *crostata*, with its bold depth from local grapes.

She tried to tune into Matteo's words, but he had stopped speaking to watch her grip her head. She let her hand float back down and tried to look natural.

She said, "When Luca came yesterday—"

"He did, did he?" Matteo grinned.

"Haven't you had enough of matchmaking for a bit?" she said with a beleaguered smile.

"Okay, okay," Matteo agreed.

"Anyway, there is still a little thing called the stunning Lilliana." She tried to shut out the instant image of Lilliana, all effortless grace, who probably never said a thing without running it through some sort of inner autocorrect that Stella had no access to.

"Oh, well, I think 'stunning' is a bit of a stretch." He tucked an errant curl behind Stella's green scarf, and then paused, remembering. "So what did Luca say?"

"Right," Stella said, closing her eyes. "Maybe I pushed it coming here. I can't think straight."

"I'll walk you home."

"No, let me finish my coffee and this delightful *crostata*." She closed her eyes and inhaled. "*Madonna mia*, I have needed this. Anyway, Luca said that Leo confided in Cosimo about his money trouble and started bringing items by for Cosimo to appraise. Cosimo bought some of it and told him he had to take care of his family at all costs." Stella's thoughts hitched, remembering Leo coming out from Cosimo's side room.

"And Leo interpreted that as 'Go kill a nun?'" Matteo shook his head, before snagging a passing Roberto, "*Macchiato* when you have a chance." He turned back to Stella.

She said, "You know what I can't stop thinking about? In the United States, you can tell something is a front for a money laundering operation when it's so bad, the business has to be relying on black market money to stay afloat. But here . . . well, that was some seriously good *porchetta*. What a loss for Aramezzo."

"About that," Matteo began. "I'm having a kind of crazy thought. *Ciao*, Domenica."

Stella hadn't even noticed her friend's arrival. Details blurred and sagged. She hoped the part of her brain responsible for cooking hadn't been crumpled by the tire iron. Her thoughts drifted to the failed sauce.

At least Barbanera had forgiven her. Where was he? *Ah*—sitting on a chair, the newspaper spread across the table before him, like he was reading about the drug busts.

Domenica hugged Stella from the side before dragging a stool and settling in. "You haven't told her yet?"

Matteo shook his head. "Remember, we were supposed to keep

her calm."

Stella looked from Matteo to Domenica. "You've been keeping me out of a loop?"

"Just this one thing," Matteo said. He paused. "Okay, maybe two things. Giancarlo left. Yesterday. He told me to tell you goodbye."

Stella ran her finger over the rim of the cup.

Domenica leaned closer. "Stella? You all right, cara?"

Shrugging, Stella said, "So what's the other thing?"

Matteo brightened and shot a look of mingled triumph and anxiety at Domenica before saying, "I'm buying Leo's *porchetta* van."

"You're what?" Stella's voice hit an octave that sent Barbanera leaping from his perch. All eyes turned to her. She cleared her throat. "Sorry. Spasm."

Everyone returned to their conversations. Stella could hear Orietta and Flavia debating whether or not Marta had had any idea.

"As I was saying," Stella began, her voice a murmur, "You're *what*?"

"I'm buying the *porchetta* van," Matteo jammed his hands in his pockets and rocked onto the balls of his feet. "I worked it out with Leo's parents. They gave me a great deal. Of course, I have to wait for the police to clear it of evidence. But then, it's mine."

Brushing crumbs off the counter into her palm, she said, "I can't believe you're doing this."

"Why? You know I need a change. I complain about my job all the time." Matteo reminded her.

"But every time you complain about it, I tell you to find something else and you get all snappy with me, saying I'm too American, not everyone needs to identify themselves through their work."

Matteo shrugged. "*Boh*."

"And you think you'll enjoy running a *porchetta* van?"

He shrugged. "Why not? I like talking to people. I like going to other towns."

"Plus," prompted Domenica. "Don't leave off the last part. She needs to hear it."

He rolled his eyes. "Okay, and I guess you've rubbed off on me. I like thinking about food."

This brought a genuine smile to Stella's face. "That's great, Matteo. Really. You'll rock it."

"It does mean I won't be available for garbage rummaging anymore. You'll need to bring another sanitation worker into the group."

"Oh," Stella said airily. "No worries on that score. I'm hanging up my Sherlock Holmes cap."

They stared at her. Finally Domenica said, "You can't be serious."

"Oh, but I am. I definitely am. I've had nothing but quiet to think, and it's obvious that it's time for me to bow out."

As they continued staring, Stella looked down, pressing crumbs onto the plate. "I nearly got Cindy killed."

"She's going to be fine," Matteo reminded her.

"She's in the *hospital*," Stella reminded him.

"Where they *love* her," Matteo countered. "When we saw her yesterday, she had the family of the woman in the next bed in stitches acting out the chase. Mr. Copeland hung on her every word."

"For someone unconscious during much of it, she sure tells it well," Domenica said fondly.

Stella said softly. "If I hadn't gotten mixed up in this mess, she wouldn't have either. It's one thing to sacrifice my well-being. Quite another to sacrifice someone else's."

Domenica touched Stella's hand. "Cindy is very clear that she's the one who wandered into danger."

Matteo frowned. "Enlighten me, how is this your fault exactly?"

"Look, we just finished saying that Leo needed to take responsibility, rather than blaming Marta or Cosimo. Can we leave it at maybe I need to do the same? I'm heedless, reckless, impulsive and I've seen the error of my ways and from now on, will be safe and methodical. Prudent, even."

"Dear Lord, I hope not," Domenica muttered.

"You solved the case," Matteo said emphatically. "Why do you keep missing that?"

"Luck," Stella said. "That's what Luca would say." She noticed Lilliana touching Luca's cheek as he stared at the bar. When had Lilliana gotten to town? Wait, had Luca been here since she arrived to the bar? She pressed the heels of her hand over her eyes, her fingertips trembling.

Matteo frowned, leaning closer. "Luca wouldn't say that. He told Captain Tribuzio—"

Domenica stopped him. "Until she's ready to hear it, until she can believe it, anyone else's assessments will ring false."

"You got me there, Domenica," Stella said before pushing the crumb-filled plate away.

"Sleep on it, *cara*." Domenica said.

"I'm done sleeping," Stella said, watching as Luca made his way toward her. They regarded each other for a moment before their eyes dropped. Stella felt her cheeks flush at the sudden awkwardness. Had her night-gown been full of holes when he'd come by yesterday with a pot of his mother's *tortellini in brodo*?

His eyes ran over her vintage shirt. Stella went still. His hand reached toward her bandage before he stopped himself, his hand dropping to the counter. "I wish I'd gotten there sooner."

She smiled wanly.

"I still can't believe you were driving the *porchetta* van. When you called, I had no idea."

"I'm glad you were in Assisi." Stella thought for a moment. "What were you doing in Assisi?"

"Picking up Lilliana from the train station."

"Ah," Stella said, throwing a smile to Lilliana. Was it her imagination or did the woman scowl in response? She certainly had a knack for scowling. How did she manage to look even more charming? Her twisted mouth seemed ironic rather than displeased. "Well, my apologies for interrupting the reunion."

Luca's dimple flashed before he regarded her seriously. "That's a strange thing to say."

Stella sighed, hoping to project world weariness. Suddenly, she felt world weary. "Blame the blunt force trauma."

"One thing I still don't understand," Matteo mused. She'd forgotten he was there. "How did Leo plant the drugs."

Luca cleared his throat and dragged his attention to Matteo. "With his back and forth attempts to pawn anything of value, he discovered the crumbling wall between the cantinas. The earthquake."

Domenica nodded. "I'd forgotten about Cosimo's room that leads down to his cantina."

"You knew about it?" Stella turned her gaze.

"It's where he keeps the old books. We spent a very pleasant after-noon in that room, sipping sherry and paging through vintage texts." She beamed.

Luca, his eyes still on Stella, said, "It's good to see you up and around."

"That's me," Stella said, trying for brightness and fearing she landed closer to manic. "Up and around."

He looked at her for a minute longer and drifted back to Lilliana.

Stella watched him leave.

The espresso machine let out a low hiss.

Matteo said, "They're cute together."

Domenica put her hand on his. "Read the room."

Stella clasped her shaking hands on the counter. "It's okay, Domenica. This is as good a time as any to tell you. I've decided to stay celibate forever."

"Like the nuns?" Matteo frowned.

"They don't seem to have too bad a time of it."

"Except for getting run down in the road," Matteo muttered, stalling at a glare from Domenica. He cast his eye down. "Too soon."

Stella sighed. "But she did that to follow love. I'm done with love. I'm gonna put my head down and focus on work. It's clear my time here is done."

His eyebrows flying upward, Matteo said, "Here? What do you mean? Like with investigations? Or Aramezzo? You don't mean Aramezzo?"

Stella crossed her arms across her chest.

"I know it feels hopeless, *cara*," Domenica said gently, "but take it from someone who has seen enough good times and bad to know—we need both to make music. What's down will be up again." She smiled a secret smile.

"Oh, it'll be up again. I'm making sure. Because I'm focusing solely on the bed-and-breakfast. No romance." Her eyes flicked to Luca, laughing with Lilliana at the end of the bar. Stella blew an errant curl off her face. "And definitely no detecting. Work, and work alone."

"And us," Matteo announced.

Stella smiled wanly. "As long as you're helping. How are you with polishing silver?"

"Not as good as tasting *panna cotta*."

She tried to smile but swooned a bit, Matteo catching her. Roberto rushed around the bar, arriving at her side as her eyes fluttered closed. Matteo said, "We'll get her home."

Stella blinked. "My purse—"

Roberto shook his head. "Your money is no good here."

She nodded.

Tired.

So tired.

Barbanera waited for her at the door.

Matteo and Domenica had her by each arm. She tried to shake them off. "I'm okay. Barbanera will walk with me."

Domenica chuckled and Matteo said, "Stella. He's a cat."

"Tell *him* that."

As they walked through town, Domenica and Matteo kept chattering, first about Matteo finding out from his mother that the reason Roberto and Romina mortgaged the bar was because their son-in-law's mother had a psychotic episode on a safari in Namibia, and the couple emptied their bank account to hire a jet to fly her home. Domenica said that didn't surprise her, she'd dug into human trafficking accusations and discovered the charges didn't stick because Roberto and Romina were shown to have been working with a refugee resettlement organization.

Stella noticed Domenica's flicker of a gaze toward her, but she was too busy making sure her feet moved one after the other to respond.

Matteo wondered if any evidence of the Mafia remained in the *porchetta* van. Maybe secret compartments? What if he got the van and discovered money in a hidey-hole the cops hadn't known existed? Perhaps Stella faded out because suddenly he was talking about where he could roast the *porchetta*, if he should do it in a drum like Leo, or roast it old-school, on a spit, outside.

Stella thought the conversation made her imagine the scent of smoke.

Until she saw Alvaro stoking his wall oven. He waved, "Stella, can I bring you some pizza tonight?"

"I'd love that, thank you," she said. To her friends she said, "Another meal I don't have to worry about." She paused. "Maybe along with never dating, never detecting, I can add never cooking again. How long can I play the sympathy card?"

Her voice serious, Domenica said, "This is your life, Stella. Open the doors you choose. Make the most of what you find behind them. Thus is your life well lived."

Quietly, Stella said, "I don't think I can open any more doors."

Stella could feel Domenica and Matteo exchanging glances over her head. Avoiding their gaze, her eyes caught on a patch of green sprouting from the rock wall. She said, "Don't vines make rock walls crumble? Why are these allowed to grow all over the town walls? They'll destroy them."

Gently Domenica said, "Stella, those aren't vines. They're caper plants."

"*Caper plants?*"

"Caper plants. You must know."

Stella stopped walking. She ran her hands over the abundance of leaves. Her fingers nudged caper berries, oblong and glowing greenly from the shade of their leaves.

"How do they grow from walls? Where is their soil?" Stella asked, still touching the shiny capers in wonder.

Domenica and Matteo said nothing.

Finally, Stella's arm fell to her side, and she turned to her friends. "You can just pick the capers? And then what?"

Matteo took her arm and smiled.

Domenica took her other arm. "You cure them."

"But I don't know how to do that," Stella said crossly.

"You'll figure it out, *cara*," Domenica said. "All in good time."

I HOPE YOU ENJOYED YOUR VISIT TO UMBRIA, THE GREEN HEART OF ITALY!

More mystery is already brewing in Aramezzo; look for book five in the *Murder in an Italian Village* series coming soon!

Don't want to miss a clue? Sign up for my monthly newsletter, the Grapevine (*michelledamiani.com/thegrapevine*), and you'll be the first to know when the next book is available.

As a welcome to the Grapevine, you'll receive *Santa Lucia*, my best-selling novel set in Santa Lucia—where Stella has a great aunt who is married to the mayor. The books will eventually cross, so now is the time to discover Santa Lucia!

Along with top-secret book news and deals, and your free copy of *Santa Lucia*, every month you'll receive expert travel tips, delicious recipes, and wanderlust stories.

Hope to welcome you soon!

Ciao for now,

—Michelle
michelledamiani.com

CRESCIONDA SPOLETINA

INGREDIENTS

75 g high quality dark chocolate (~2.6 oz)

150 g high quality amaretti cookies (~5.3 oz)

425 ml whole milk (~1¾ cups)

38 grams sugar (~3 tablespoons)

55 grams flour (~3 tablespoons)

3 large eggs (room temperature)

---

1) Preheat oven to 325°F (160°C).

2) Butter an 8 inch pie pan and line with buttered parchment paper (optional for easier removal).

3) In a food processor or by hand, grind/chop the chocolate.

4) Add the amaretti cookies and pulse/chop until resembles coarse breadcrumbs with some larger pieces.

5) In a large bowl, whisk eggs with sugar.

6) Add the flour and whisk until smooth.

7) Gradually add milk while whisking.

8) Stir in the amaretti-chocolate mixture gently without overmixing

9) Pour into the prepared pan, let sit for a few minutes so the amaretti settle to the bottom, and bake on lower middle rack for 20–25 minutes. It should still wobble slightly in the center and show cracks on top when done.

10) Cool before slicing. Best served at room temp or chilled.

Buon appetito!

ALSO BY MICHELLE DAMIANI

Il Bel Centro: A Year in the Beautiful Center

*The Road Taken: How to Dream, Plan, and
Live Your Family Adventure Abroad*

MURDER IN AN ITALIAN VILLAGE SERIES

Death in Aramezzo

Bread and Murder in Aramezzo

Unmasked in Aramezzo

SANTA LUCIA SERIES

Santa Lucia

The Silent Madonna

The Stillness of Swallows

Into the Groves

Find out more at michelledamiani.com